KINGS AND DAEMONS

KINGS AND DAEMONS

MARCUS LEE

BOOK 1
THE GIFTED AND THE CURSED

ISBN: 9798646561931

For more information visit: www.marcusleebooks.com

First paperback edition May 2020
First eBook edition May 2020

Book design by Jacqueline Abromeit

M&M

BY THE SAME AUTHOR

THE GIFTED AND THE CURSED TRILOGY

***

KINGS AND DAEMONS

TRISTAN'S FOLLY

THE END OF DREAMS

Prologue

The moon shone fiercely, brushing aside any attempt by the clouds to diminish its radiance. Usually, the glow would have brought comfort, a respite from the night's black embrace, but not this night.

Instead, it brought everything into stark contrast, creating shadows in which evil spirits might lurk waiting to snatch the unwary who were foolish enough to walk the streets at this hour.

Except, there was nobody left to walk these particular streets.

Doors hung askew on rotting hinges, thatched roofs sagged or had already collapsed, windows stared vacantly like empty eye sockets. Weeds grew but were sparse; their lifespan numbered in days.

Rats scurried about, seeking something palatable to eat. The bodies of the village's inhabitants had long been picked clean, insects were few, and the malnourished rodents eyed each other hungrily. Soon they'd turn on each other, and only the strongest would survive, but only for a short while.

Next to the settlement had stood a vibrant forest, providing the building materials for the once-thriving community. Now the trees were rotting. Many lay fallen like slain giants, a stinking bog beneath slowly sucking them down to a watery grave.

Astren sighed, the bleakness overwhelming him. One day the whole world might look like this place.

He'd spied a dozen or so similar settlements, but hundreds of others still clung on. Those furthest from the capital, Kingshold, continued to eke out an existence, the land still providing, albeit barely. Within those communities, the blacksmiths' forges still spewed out weapons of destruction, and farmers laboured over crops that scarcely had the strength to push from the soil. Good people still lived within those places, but they were the minority, for so many were darkened by the blight that afflicted this land.

He remembered travelling the length and breadth of this kingdom as an emissary in his younger years, a frightening yet exciting time. Back then, the landscape had been mostly green and verdant, and he'd thought that the localised disease he'd witnessed was temporary. But no, it had spread like a cancer.

The sound of approaching wagons caught his attention, and he turned to see them rattling toward him. Grim-faced soldiers rode aboard, guarding the bounty within. Food was piled high, along with weapons and armour, newly crafted, crude but serviceable. They were heading to the capital to ensure the army was well fed and supplied. If he waited here another hour, more would pass this way like a vein bringing sustenance to a rotting heart.

The lead wagon was almost upon him, and he closed his eyes. He felt nothing as it passed straight through him, the soldiers oblivious to his presence, for he was in spirit form, unseen, intangible. Nonetheless, he waited for the wagons to pass before opening his eyes again.

He wasn't a brave man, although some might consider his actions so, for he was scouting near the heart of the neighbouring kingdom. Yet he did so under duress, the consequences of not following orders as dire as if he were caught.

A crow flew down to sit upon a wooden railing, beady-eyed and foreboding. Even if it couldn't see him, Astren felt a chill run down his spine. A premonition of approaching danger, perhaps? He looked around quickly, suddenly vigilant. The spirit-paths were travelled by many who would kill him without hesitation should he be discovered. It was time to return home.

He willed his spirit form into the sky, heading east, alert for danger. Leagues away, his king would be waiting impatiently, wanting to hear everything. Yet the news was full of ill omen and, in truth, was nothing new.

The invasion was imminent. War and death were coming.

Chapter I

Maya was special, so her father said from the moment she was born.

Of recent years it was far less common that a mother survived childbirth. Upon delivering, the bleeding so often wouldn't stop, and where one life was given, another was too often taken away.

Being with a child was now more a curse than a blessing, and what should have always been a joyous event for any couple, husband or wife, soon started to become a sentence of death. A husband knew that to gain a son or daughter was to often lose the mother, or if she survived, for her to be a pale shadow of her former self.

When Maya was born, her mother, like so many others, had started to bleed terribly, more than most, and the midwife solemnly declared there was no hope. So she pushed Maya into her mother's dying arms to feed from her breast in her last hours and left. Tears fell from both the eyes of Mika, her mother, and Jalan, her father, and they were not of joy but parting sorrow.

Yet as Maya suckled, her mother's bleeding slowed, and instead of passing from this life, she held on. Jalan fed Mika a little broth each day, thinking it would be her last, but instead, she grew stronger; Maya never far from her breast and arms. In fact, her family seemed blessed by her birth, for not only did Mika fully recover, but Jalan, who'd been plagued with a terrible cough that all the mine workers suffered from, began to cough less and less.

1

Instead of revelling openly about this miracle, Mika and Jalan kept quiet, knowing that such things were met with distrust. They also feared the overseer would take an interest in Maya, for if it was discovered she was special, to have a gift, then she'd be taken from them both. A large reward was given to those who identified a gifted one.

So, Jalan feigned his cough, and Mika rubbed dirt under her eyes to give them a hollow appearance, and when in public, shuffled like an old lady. Thus the circumstances surrounding Maya's birth were kept hidden.

Over the years, as Maya grew, so did her gift, and out of necessity, so did the deceit which surrounded her.

A bird with a broken wing would recover to fly again if she cared for it. The vegetables that grew in the dusty back yard grew healthier than usual near where she played, hidden behind a tall wooden fence.

Beauty was almost unknown now in this land, and while still only a young child, her obvious health amongst the weaker, paler children would have made her stand out. Her lustrous, black hair she had to cover in dirt and dust, cut short and jagged on purpose. Her fingernails strong and firm, she broke by pushing her fingers constantly into the hard soil. She rubbed dirt on the clear skin of her face and under the eyes and wore threadbare and plain clothing.

To keep her out of sight even more, her parents sold almost everything of value to bribe the town's cleric to appoint her as a forager and hunter as she turned seven. Girls were not strong enough to work in the mines or the furnaces, and this was the one job, albeit dangerous, that constantly took a girl outside of the settlement. Thus she spent her days absent, from early sunrise to just before sunset, always out of sight, keeping to the shadows, learning the land and how to harvest its frugal bounty.

At the age of ten, her mother passed away.

Maya came home from foraging one day to find her father inconsolable. Her mother's body was already upon a pyre, and her father refused to tell her what had happened. She knew from the look of hatred on his face when he looked at the overseer and the town soldiers that something untoward had transpired. When she had recovered enough from her grief, she approached the neighbours to see if they would tell her, but they closed their doors in her face. They didn't like her, and people didn't fare well if they fell afoul of the overseer.

As the years passed and the death of her mother faded, she grew into a beautiful, young woman, with large, dark brown eyes, slender and tall, so unlike any of the other townsfolk. Every morning she would wrap bandages around her breasts to flatten them against her body, sprinkle dust into her eyes to make them appear red and bloodshot, and wrap one knee to give her an odd stiff-legged hobble before going out.

'Keep to yourself, keep quiet, keep hidden, keep dirty, keep stooped, keep shuffling.' Always her father would repeat these and similar mantras. 'Don't draw attention to yourself and keep out of sight,' and then he would hobble off to the mines for the day.

The problem was, Maya was lonely. Lonely and bored. Forbidden by her father to mix, she'd never made friends and was now actively shunned by everyone. She'd never been kissed, although she'd watched many of the settlement's men and women pair, and some even marry, and dreamed of it happening to her, though it never would.

Thus from an early age, to help her deal with boredom, she started to do the very thing her parents had never wanted her to do, explore the possibilities of her gift.

'You mustn't keep practising it,' her father often scolded, when at the end of a long day, Maya told him of what she'd done as they sat eating dinner in their hut. Yet he couldn't keep stern for long, for she was the sunshine of his life when all around was darkness. He saw in Maya's dark looks a reflection of her mother, especially the eyes. So

3

the frown would soon give way to a smile as she tossed her hair or pouted, and all would be forgiven.

Today had begun like every other day.

Having said goodbye to her father, Maya had left the settlement a moment before sunrise and finished collecting her daily quota of provisions before the sun had fully risen above the horizon. The bushes she visited were always full of berries, and her traps were so artfully laid that she never failed to bring back meat, whereas others often failed.

As ever, having finished early, she had climbed quickly to the rim of the valley, to her secret place. The high ridges between which the valley nestled held many smoking craters, but the fires in this one had long ago gone cold.

When she'd first explored it, sheltered in the depth of the crater had been the thickest nest of brambles, thorns, and twisted, stunted trees that she'd ever seen. Even in this land of ugliness, it stood out, and the pain it seemed to exude had almost made her cry. A pool of foul-smelling brackish water had completed the unpleasant picture.

Now, it was anything but.

Maya lay on her stomach and gazed north over the edge of the crater toward the distant smoke that marked the settlement of Angora, a full day's fast ride north. Between here and there, all her eyes could see was a blighted land. Swathes of blackened grass and withered trees, growing but barely clinging to life. Even in her own valley, things were only slightly better. The crops had failed this year, and even the orchard fruit, while sustaining, was bitterly unpleasant. Everything that grew seemed tainted unless touched by her hand.

Then she rolled to her back and looked down between her feet into the crater, at her secret place, where she spent every moment she could, for it was now a paradise in this broken land.

4

Thick green grass, colourful flowers, and a fresh, clear spring that fed a small pond. There were also healthy, strong trees, one of which was starting to bear apples, and the rose bush; the rose bush where this transformation had started many moons ago.

When she'd first climbed into the crater when she and her gift were still young, amongst the thorns and bracken that made this place so uninviting, a blackened, twisted rose flowered. It had caught her eye, and she'd gone to investigate. The thorns of the bush had been wickedly sharp, the bloom's scent the soft sweet smell of decay, cloying and overwhelming, yet Maya had imagined that it was the red told of in the old stories, to be given as a gift to the one you loved.

So every day, she came to pour a little tepid water from the brackish pool onto the roots beneath the soil, carefully straightened the twisted leaves, and smoothed the warped petals. While doing so, she would softly hum a nameless tune and dream of a handsome suitor bearing a red rose.

Then after months of tending and nurturing the rose, the bloom had fallen, dead to the ground. Maya had felt disheartened, yet continued to tend the bush. She removed the flies that plagued it, cleaned the dust off that coated it, and then a change had slowly begun to take place.

The blackened stems had visibly started to turn a shade of green, dark at first, but then as the days passed by, lighter.

Excited beyond imagining at what was happening, to enable her to spend more time here, she'd pushed herself to finish her foraging earlier every day, and this became easier as the bushes she visited also became healthier.

Then, beyond her expectations, a rosebud had appeared, followed by others, deep red, a shade that touched her heart. Every day she sat and watched, caressed the plant softly, and willed it to grow. Then, between one day and the next, several of the buds had opened, and the roses that awaited her arrival were more beautiful than she could have imagined, their scent a heady perfume that filled the air.

Inspired, she'd turned her attention to the water and thrust her arms in elbow deep, believing that now, if she willed it enough, she could help more than just a rose bush grow. A slight glow had emanated from her hands, and she'd tried all the harder.

Sure enough, within days, the water began to run clear and free of taint, refreshing to drink.

But that wasn't all. After she'd run her hands over the branches of the blighted trees, the bark had stopped peeling, the wounds that dripped sap had disappeared, and they grew firm and healthy. Amongst the blackened grass surrounding the bush, sprouts of bright green had begun to appear, here, there, and everywhere. They pushed their way through the soil to rise above their withered counterparts, and over time became a lush carpet that extended to the rim of the crater.

Now, Maya could take her boots off and wiggle her toes in the softness.

She rolled onto her stomach again and turned her attention back to Angora. Was it the same, dark, dull, and boring as her settlement? Occasionally the soldiers on horseback could be heard talking about it, but none of the townsfolk were allowed far from the settlement where they were born, and where they would likely die.

As Maya lay with her head on her hands, the green grass soft beneath her, her tired body relaxed, the weak sun warmed her body, her heart slowed happily, her mind drifted ... asleep.

Taran looked at the sky, rubbing his jaw ruefully, aware of a loose tooth. He would easily have known that punch was coming had he not been showing off a little in front of a small crowd of baying townsfolk, who'd taken a wager that he wouldn't last three rounds against the towering town champion.

Taran wasn't exactly small either. Years spent in his father's smithy during his youth, where he'd worked the bellows, swung the heavy

6

hammers, and chopped wood for the furnace, had given him strength beyond most of his peers. Yet he concealed his muscled frame in loose clothing and constantly feigned a slight stoop.

Every settlement in the kingdom had a justice turf. It was a square area where bouts like these could be held. However, it was also where the local overseer handed out any punishment required by the law, including executions by the Witch-King's soldiers for often trivial infractions.

Now, as he lay in the dust, he thought that perhaps he should have listened to his father's advice about never giving an opponent a chance.

For a moment, as he gathered his senses, other memories of his father came to mind. Such as when he'd misbehaved or tried to skip his duties, how his father would discipline him with his fists.

Taran had developed lightning reflexes as he grew to deal with such punishment, ducking or sliding out of the way with ease. His father had often grown so angry at this that Taran sometimes let the blows land when he knew they wouldn't hurt too much, just to calm his father down. It was either that or those fists would find release on his mother instead. Perhaps it was because of this that Taran had practised fighting from his youth and excelled at it.

Of course, his gift had helped. People's thoughts and intentions seemed plain for him to see as if written down before him. He could tell someone's name as easily as where the next punch or kick was coming from before they even threw it.

It was a secret he'd kept from everyone, including his parents. The revelation of such things would have led to the overseer sending him off to the Witch-King, a dubious honour he'd happily avoided.

Then one day after Taran returned to the smithy late in the day, after dallying for too long with one of the girls from his settlement, he'd discovered that his father's fists had found their mark one time too many.

His mother lay lifeless and bloodied in his sobbing father's arms.

The rage that welled up inside had almost overwhelmed him, and he'd nearly killed his father before letting some townsfolk pull him off.

His father was too valuable as the settlement blacksmith to be executed, so he was whipped instead for the crime. Taran, however, was banished. Branded with a hot iron on his forearm to warn other settlements from taking him on, he was thrown out to a lonely life, and possible death, as a wanderer on the kingdom's roads.

Taran had hastened north that day with tears in his eyes and anger in his heart, wondering whether joining the army was his best bet, but he'd swiftly discarded the idea. He'd always disliked the soldiers in his settlement and found it hard to accept authority or routine.

He had nothing but his clothes, a few belongings in a pack, and two silver coins to his name. After two day's travel, he'd made it to the neighbouring settlement just before the second horn blew. In the morning, he was told to leave. With no settlement keen to give a home to a stranger, let alone a branded one, he'd been wandering since. So he took odd jobs here and there but mainly scratched out a living, having fun doing what he knew best. Fighting.

Bringing his mind back to the present, he groaned. If that tooth came out, it would spoil what he thought were roguish good looks, but were in fact, only slightly better than average. Irrespective of his visage, he liked to think of himself as a good sport. When he'd knocked down this towering oaf a short while ago, he'd stood back to let the man rise in his own time, and it had taken time, for his punches had been true and square on his opponent's rather big jaw.

'Pretty good punch,' he said to his assailant, who was moving in carefully. 'I don't suppose you'll let me get up?' he asked, raising an eyebrow.

In reply, Urg, who was aptly named, moved swiftly in to deliver a vicious kick to Taran's ribs to finish the fight and possibly put him in the healers for a week or two.

Taran read the move early and twisted, hooking his foot behind Urg's ankle to sweep his feet from under him, a move that sent Urg crashing to the floor. Taran rolled to his feet smoothly.

'Let's call it a draw,' he suggested, smiling broadly. He knew it wasn't allowed but wanted to seem dashing in front of the local girls, even if they didn't look that attractive.

Urg surged to his feet to swing the biggest punch Taran had ever seen. Even without his gift, Taran would have seen it coming, so he ducked and stepped in to plant two deep punches into Urg's gut. As Urg doubled over, Taran kindly, or so he thought, stepped around and kicked him in the back of the knees to send Urg face down into the black dust, then followed it up with a sharp punch to the side of the head, finishing the fight for good.

Taran raised his arms in triumph to the hushed crowd, only to realise they weren't quite as happy about his victory as he was. Likely they'd bet a lot of their meagre savings on the home champion and now felt the loss keener than did Urg. An angry murmur started.

He moved to the winner's table then swept the tarnished coins into his hand before putting them into the pouch at his waist. The mood was hostile, and he considered leaving the settlement immediately, but it was way past noon. It wasn't always safe outside on the roads after dark, for groups of bandits, whilst rare, still roamed, and sleeping under the stars whilst seeming romantic, was cold, unpleasant, and shared only with biting insects instead of a warm woman.

So, instead, he kept his head down, and quickly pushed his way through the thinnest part of the converging crowd, then half-walked, half-ran to the ugly tavern he'd intended to stay in.

Taverns didn't see many visitors and were often frequented by the king's soldiers. Taran didn't like the idea of sharing the place with such an unpleasant crew as were currently in town. They were answerable only to the Witch-King and to themselves and perhaps the town overseer. This made them insufferable at best and downright dangerous at worse, as they could kill with almost impunity. As he pushed in through the tavern door, Taran held his breath, hoping to go straight to his room, bar the door, and remain inconspicuous until dawn when he would make a very swift and early departure.

His luck was about to change.

As Taran walked into the main room, it was not empty. As feared, many of the king's soldiers were standing at the bar drinking and laughing noisily, with more sat around taking up nearly every seat. He closed the door of the tavern behind him and quiet settled over the room. A sense of menace gripped his stomach, and the hairs on the back of his neck stood up.

Taran lowered his head, and as he walked toward the back stairs, one of the seated men, a corporal by the look of the single matching scars on his cheeks, thrust his leg out in an attempt to trip him.

Taran sensed this was coming and simply hopped over the foot, smiled in apology as if it had been his fault, then continued on as if nothing had happened.

However, three men suddenly stepped from the bar to block his way. One was the captain of the squad, three matching scars on his cheeks showed his rank, and a host of horrendous open sores kept them company.

There was no way around the trio and Taran stopped, thinking quickly of a way to head off the danger. He might be a good fighter, but against swords, daggers, and so many men, there was no way he could hope to fight his way out of this situation. He would die if this were their intent, and from the way these three looked at him and the sound of scraping chairs as others got to their feet, it seemed this was the likely outcome.

He reached out with his gift and swiftly looked into the captain's thoughts ... words and images formed in Taran's mind.

'Rakan!' he cried, thrusting out his hand in greeting to the captain. 'Rakan, is that you? It is, isn't it? Tell me it is!'

'By all the gods,' cried Taran, 'I can't believe it's you!'

Maya awoke with a chill, not just from the setting sun but from the terrible realisation that too much time had passed. She was late for her return to the settlement and likely in serious trouble.

She leapt to her feet, pulled on her boots and grabbing her belongings, then scrambled over the crest of the crater and ran. Tree branches whipped past, and sharp thorns sought to score her face, yet her nimble feet and graceful stride kept her from their grasp. Surefooted, she pushed herself as fast as she dared, sweat making her threadbare clothing stick damply to her skin.

Darkness loomed, for she'd left her return to the settlement too late. The foraging bag on her shoulder bounced against her back, and her bow seemed determined to snag on the undergrowth as she ran. She wanted to be released of their burden to run unhindered, but this was food for many tables, and the bow was a gift from her late mother. Without the food and bow, people would go hungry, and she'd have to face too many awkward questions from the town cleric or worse, the overseer, so she struggled on.

The settlement's horn sounded mournfully through the fog that seemed to spring from nowhere, to warn of the impending sunset and the closure of the gates. Not that she needed reminding, now that the gloom of the day's end was so obvious, shadows stretched long on the ground, twisted and evil looking.

As Maya ran, she thought that no one other than soldiers had ventured outside of the gates after dark in all the years she could remember. It was against the settlement's strict rules, punishable by flogging, or for a repeat offender, death. This knowledge spurred her on, fleet of foot even in the reduced light.

She knew these woods close to the settlement like the back of her hand, every rocky mound or cave, the dangers, and rare wonders … yet all of a sudden, she couldn't recognise her surroundings. Calm down, she thought, and slowed a little, trying to orientate. Yet it was no use as everything seemed unfamiliar.

The fog was heavier now, and when the horn sounded twice to warn it was mere moments from the closure of the gates, Maya realised her fleet steps had taken her no closer. She'd become disorientated in her haste, and there'd be no sanctuary in the settlement this night.

Resigned to her fate, knowing that a severe punishment awaited her return on the morrow, Maya stopped and considered where to build a shelter and a fire. However, as she came to a decision, a long soul-chilling howl sounded on the night air.

There would be no making a shelter now.

Maya ran again, away from the sound. She pushed herself fast, lungs straining as her heart beat hard within her chest.

The howl sounded again, joined by others, seeming closer, but they didn't have her scent yet. She had to find somewhere to hide, to shelter, somewhere safe, but where?

Thoughts brought on by near panic flashed through her mind. She wanted to see her father again, the settlement, even the seamstress who repaired her worn old clothes …

Hold it together! she scolded herself. She'd been a hunter her whole life but would soon be the prey of the wolves if she didn't make the right decisions. She had to think differently now. What did animals always do when hunted? Of course they ran, but some would also go to ground. From her time as a hunter, she knew her scent was the big betrayer. She could hide from sight, but scent could give away her position like the brightest fire even in the darkness.

She came across a game trail and hastened along until it bisected another bigger one, the undergrowth flattened by a large animal. Usually, she would have avoided going anywhere near this. It was a trail made by one of the very few mountain bears, and they were the only predator in the forest that a wolf would be wary of.

As Maya followed the new trail, eyes straining in the darkness, she came upon a large mound of fresh bear spoor. She knelt and reached down to scoop up a handful, then started to cover her clothes. Next, she rubbed it into her face and had to fight hard to keep her stomach contents down, but the howls kept her at work.

There were many caves near the valley's edge, and she started following the terrain upslope, not knowing where in the dark, but knowing that up was good enough. This meant the howls, which had increased in sound, were now at her back.

12

Suddenly the howling reached a frenzied level, and fear gripped her stomach. They'd found her scent! In the distance, she heard the sound of the wolves crashing through the undergrowth. Forgetting her woodcraft, she threw every ounce of her strength into running uphill, pulling herself past trees, the rush of panicked blood in her veins giving her extra strength. In time she came to a scree slope, at the top of which a dark opening loomed forbiddingly, and she dropped handfuls of the bear spoor she'd brought with her as she scrambled up to the entrance.

If a bear inhabited the cave, her death would be just as horrific as if the wolves had caught her, but she had no choice. So she drew her short dagger, determined to put up a fight, and moved into the darkness.

The cave wasn't deep, and she breathed a sigh of relief, for it was too shallow to offer enough shelter for a bear should it rain as it often did. She moved to the back and huddled into a corner, then tried to quieten her breathing, which seemed so loud, not to mention her heart's thudding.

The pack seemed to be right outside the cave, the wolves and the scrape of their claws on the scree slope sounded so close. Tears fell from her eyes, the fear almost overwhelming, then thoughts of her mother came to mind, and she calmed a little. Slowly the noise became quieter as the pack was put off by the smell of bear, and she allowed herself to let out a soft sigh of relief, only for it to be answered by the loud sniff of a wolf close by, as it scented the air.

She strained to see in the darkness, and there framed in the entrance of the cave, it moved. It was a large beast, and it held its muzzle close to the ground as It smelled the spoor. It was wary, but it was also strong, very hungry, and feared so very little.

Maya held her breath as she looked at the wolf, its yellow eyes peered back into the dark, and she felt them pierce her even in the depth of the cave. Its tongue lolled from its mouth, and saliva dripped to the floor as it turned side to side, slowly edging into the gloom. Yet it couldn't see anything but its prey, so it grew bolder.

Maya abstractly noted that the jaws of a trap remained around one of its legs, all twisted and bent, no doubt driving the creature mad with pain.

Having made up its mind, the wolf moved toward her. Its muzzle drew back, exposing its fangs ... a few more steps, and that would be it.

Maya's hands trembled so much that she dropped the knife.

Then the beast came for her, all sharp teeth, foul breath, and those yellow eyes.

'No!' she cried, and thrust her hands out in a pointless defense.

.

Chapter II

Rakan's head spun as he carefully placed his tankard back on the bar.

Ordinarily, he'd have taken the soldiers back to the training ground many hours ago, but he'd been enjoying himself too much to make that decision. He couldn't remember the last time he hadn't trained hard throughout the day, and his men had made the most of this unusual respite from the harsh regime that was typically imposed upon them.

Now it was way too late to do much else apart from maybe eat. The sky was dark, and even if it was still a little too early for sleep, the amount of ale he'd drunk made him think that perhaps it wouldn't be such a bad idea.

It had been the strangest of evenings.

He'd been on the verge of gutting the lad straight away before his obvious recognition had given Rakan pause for thought, and for once, he was strangely relieved he hadn't killed someone.

Rakan was a long term soldier, reliable and cruel, and dealing death came as easily to him as breathing. His men usually followed him out of fear ... fear of what would happen to them if they didn't follow his orders, certainly not because they liked him.

He'd killed more men and women than he had scars and sores on his body, and there were plenty of those. Most of his victims had been warriors from the Eyre, a morass of stinking swampland that served as a convenient proving ground for the Witch-King's soldiers. Of late, more had been townsfolk who'd not met their quotas or turned to banditry, and some had even been fellow soldiers. He regretted none and enjoyed reliving the memory of killing them all.

He longed for fighting and bloodshed, to best another warrior in combat. The chaos of battle was far more satisfying than killing a weeping civilian, but he got what pleasure he could whenever he could find it. Thankfully it wouldn't be long before the king's forces were gathered together to spill across the border into the neighbouring Freestates, and then the real fun would start again.

Sadly, in the interim, he'd been put in charge of this relatively new group of soldiers who didn't know him, his history, and they'd annoyed him immensely with their complaining. He'd planned to kill one of them before this Taran had walked in, so they could understand what kind of man he was and what he expected of them.

Strangely, violence was no longer required to get this point across.

Throughout the evening, Taran had called the other soldiers to the bar and had bought everyone's drinks.

As Rakan listened, a new goblet of ale was pushed into his hand. Taran began to tell yet another outrageous tale about Rakan that involved an Eyre captive, a dozen throwing knives, a keg of ale, and a blindfold.

The soldiers laughed in appreciation, and after a little pause, Taran launched into his next story. Rakan shook his head with a wry smile as other exploits he'd forgotten were brought back to life, and he felt the last remnants of his desire to spill blood dissipate as he revelled in the looks of admiration the men sent his way.

It seemed the lesson he'd intended to make was coming from the mouth of another - the lesson of how anyone who crossed him ended up dead.

The wolf moved forward.

Maya cried out in fear and raised her hands, and suddenly they were enveloped by a blinding light that made the wolf jump back. As a creature of the night, its eyes were not accustomed to the brightness, so it growled and snapped its jaws, spraying saliva.

Maya was amazed, her gift had never manifested itself so visually and with such strength, but then she'd never experienced such peril. As it moved forward again, she desperately sought to channel the flow of energy toward the wolf. Having only ever healed, whether it was the land, her family, or occasionally small animals, it was the only way she knew how to use the gift.

So when the wolf leapt to try and break through the light, Maya grabbed its head and willed her gift to soothe the wolf, to still its anger, and ease its pain.

Its terrible weight bore her to the ground, and it stood, paws either side of her shoulders, breath hot on her face. It opened its terrible jaws, and she thought these were her last moments. Yet the gaping jaws didn't close. Instead, they opened wider and wider in a yawn, then the wolf collapsed on top of her, asleep.

Maya could barely breathe, the weight of the wolf was so heavy, and she struggled to wriggle from underneath, fearful of waking it. Eventually, having pulled herself free, she looked around in the darkness as the blinding light from her hands had disappeared and saw the glint of her knife on the cave floor.

Swiftly she picked it up, and turned back to the wolf, then put the blade to its throat. A quick, clean death while it slept, she thought.

The wolf whined softly in its sleep, and Maya simply couldn't. She'd killed many animals over the years as a hunter, none of which had just tried to kill her. But there was something different about this beast, that had just whimpered like a baby, that stilled her hand.

Maya felt exhausted and needed to sleep. The run for her life and the subsequent strength-sapping fear of facing death had left her barely able to keep her eyes open. Yet she needed to do something about the wolf.

Quickly she took some bracken from around the cave and started a fire using her flints, which allowed her to better view the surroundings. She stepped outside the entrance of the cave, gathered sticks and some larger pieces of wood and brought them in, and built up the fire so that it filled the cave with its reassuring glow and warmth.

Now able to see clearly, Maya swiftly took some leather bindings and rope typically used for traps and the spare string for her bow. She swiftly fashioned a leash, then tied it around the beast's neck and from there to a large rocky outcrop. Next, she bound the wolf's legs, giving it a small amount of looseness so as not to kill circulation.

It was surprising to see how sick it looked close up. Its leg was weeping and bleeding around the warped jaws of the broken trap. Its fur was patchy, leaving bare skin, and its paws had thorns bedded deep.

Maya took a final binding and wrapped it around the wolf's jaws, then turned her attention to the broken trap. It was heavy and twisted, so she took her knife, carefully worked it under the metal, and then twisted the blade until it opened, making a loud clang as it fell to the floor. It took much of her remaining strength to lift the wolf's leg and slide the device from under it, and she felt a little sickened by the contraption.

She almost fell backwards with shock when she saw the wolf's eyes were open and fixed on her as it let out a deep throaty growl. 'Be still,' she scolded, a little more confidently than she felt, and the beast seemed to settle under her commanding tone.

Next, she turned her attention to its paws, and the wicked thorns buried deep in the padded flesh. Its every step must have been agony. So she took her knife and a needle and started worrying them loose. The wolf whined piteously, but apart from flinching in pain, it made no further attempt to move.

It took no inconsiderable time to remove them all, and her eyes were nearly closed as she finished, yet she didn't stop there.

With her fading strength, she lay her hands on the beast's huge head and let her gift flow, willing it to heal. The beast opened its eyes again, and in the flickering firelight, they seemed almost a warm gold. The healing power flowed from her hands into the wolf, and it fell into slumber once more, its wounds closed.

Tiredness was about to overwhelm her, so having checked her handiwork on restraining the beast, Maya wondered briefly how she'd free it without dying should it awake, but decided to worry about that in the morning.

She staggered to the opposite side of the fire to the slumbering wolf, strung her bow, and nocked an arrow just in case. She then took a handful of berries from her foraging pouch and fell asleep the moment after swallowing the first mouthful.

Maya slept fitfully at first despite her exhaustion; unbidden images flashed through her dreams. Her father worrying about her lying injured or dead somewhere. The overseer laughing at the harsh punishment he would hand out when it was apparent there were no broken limbs to blame for her late return. People shouting, angry at their children going hungry because she hadn't returned in time. Then the hungry wolf, slavering jaws tearing at her flesh.

She awoke with a gasp, heart racing, angry at herself and the predicament she was in. Having managed to stay clear of the overseer all these years, her foolishness would now bring her right under his piercing gaze.

The fire crackled, burning low, and the beast whimpered softly in its sleep. It sounded strangely comforting, so Maya drowsily tossed some more branches onto the fire, and this time her sleep was deep and her dreams completely different.

She stood and looked down at her sleeping body in the cave. There were dark circles under the eyes and not just from the dirt rubbed around her face.

The wolf was thankfully still fast asleep, breathing deeply, and she marvelled how in slumber it looked nothing like the ferocious beast that had almost taken her life.

Maya walked from the cave, or rather floated, for her feet didn't seem to need to move and looked up into the cloudy night sky. She wished she could see the stars, and suddenly found herself lifting higher and higher. She felt free, like never before, with no fear of falling, and after looking around a while, she began to fly over the valley toward home.

Below, the settlement drew closer, and she sought out her hut on its southern outskirts. Approaching it, she willed her dream-self inside to find her father asleep. His cheeks were tear-streaked amongst the grime on his face, and he clutched Maya's favourite doll that her mother had made just days before she'd died. Maya had stopped playing with the toy many years ago but could never put aside something crafted by her mother's hands.

Reaching out, she tried to wake her father, but her hands simply passed through his form. 'Rest easy, father,' she whispered, and her dream tears fell upon his face before she moved away, 'I will be home on the morrow.'

Back outside, she willed her spirit aloft and begun to fly northward. Why not? Once beyond the valley, the landscape became unfamiliar. Maya looked down as she travelled to see the sickness that ailed her valley extend to every horizon. She flew further and noted with interest that every road headed this way, toward the capital, like veins toward the heart, but it was more than that. It was as if something intangible was flowing in the same direction, rippling, almost like water.

Despite her speed, there was no wind whipping the hair from her face. How could a dream feel so real?

Over large towns she passed, and then a city appeared that surrounded a foreboding fortress with lofty towers and high walls. This had to be the capital of the land, Kingshold.

Maya moved above the streets, which even at night thronged with people and soldiers. Curiosity led her to the castle and past the guards at the main gate who chatted away about the sickening land and an impending war.

She drifted through the entrance, along corridors, and brushed past sentries, maids, and minor lords. The flow of people drew her in their wake, and she found herself floating before a large open doorway with guards on either side.

Maya entered the room, and at its head, a large, powerful man with a golden circlet adorning his brow sat upon a large throne. His face was pale in contrast to his dark armour, yet there was no denying his strength. Despite the noise, he closed his eyes as if to sleep.

Another man dressed in black leather leaned forward over a table covered in maps to make notes on parchment. Intermittently, retainers hurried in, gave him scrolls, whispered in his ear, or moved small carved wooden soldiers on a large map spread out on the table.

She floated closer, not fearful, for this was her dream. There on the map, the boundaries of the kingdom and the neighbouring Freestates were marked, arrows drawn connecting the carved soldiers. It seemed these were plans of a military nature, a preparation for war perhaps.

Suddenly, the spirit of the Witch-King, for who else could he be, stood from the throne, leaving his physical self still seated. 'Have I caught you spying, girl?' he snarled, and he lunged, eyes fierce, his fingers firmly grasping her wrist.

'No!' she screamed, and let her gift shine, knowing instinctively that in this darkness, light was the only answer. The Witch-King shouted in shock and snatched his hand away as if burnt.

Panic took her, and she swiftly flew out of his reach, higher, up through the castle's roof into the sky above. His laughter followed, and then suddenly, she was not alone, for there floated a man dressed in blood-red robes beside her.

'You need to awaken,' he said, and tapped her once on the forehead with his fingertips.

A short while later, she opened her eyes back in the cave and screamed again.

Taran, his head spinning, barely made it to his room, but at least he was alive even if almost all of his money was now gone. His head hurt not just from the ale that he'd drunk, but from pulling memories out of Rakan's confused, befuddled mind throughout the whole night.

Rakan's thoughts were full of pride at his evil doings, and Taran had initially recoiled from the pictures that spilled into his head, but he knew his life depended on it and so had carried on reading them. Using the knowledge he garnered, he'd spun a tale of once being a young apprentice blacksmith attached to the army where he'd known Rakan as a sergeant. He'd embellished the story and told everyone of Rakan's creative cruelty and unmatched skill with a blade whilst they'd both been based at Kajhold, from which the lands of the Eyre were raided.

At the start, he'd felt that Rakan was unsure about him, but having pulled so many distant events from Rakan's mind had dispelled those doubts quickly. So by the end of the evening, Rakan's arm had been around Taran's shoulder, as if Taran were a younger brother. Rakan even offered him a place in the squad so they could revel further in the stories of the good old days.

Taran had artfully refused again and again, and to help ease any suspicions of the other soldiers, he'd paid for drinks all night, and occasionally dipped into their thoughts as well to make them feel like they knew him.

It was only a short while to daylight, and Taran wanted to be up and out before any of the soldiers. Sober, they might see things more clearly, and his tale might no longer hold. So before retiring to his room, he'd told the tavern owner to rouse him shortly before sunrise.

Even if he only had a few coins left to his name, he still had his life, and as Taran slipped beneath the coarse sheets, he congratulated himself on still being alive, and apart from his painful head, unscathed.

He closed his eyes, and sleep quickly overwhelmed him.

Maya awoke in the cave, mind racing about the dream that had seemed so real. She sat up and opened her eyes to the warm glow of the campfire still filling the cave, only to find a man sat next to her.

22

She cried out in shock and rolled away, then drew her dagger to point it threateningly toward the figure who just sat there.

'There's no need for that,' said the man. He stood up, and Maya seeing the blood-red robes, recognised him from her dreams.

'Who are you? How did you get here, and how did you get in my dreams?' she demanded, still holding the dagger.

The man sighed. 'So many questions, and we have so little time. But they are well asked, so I will answer them quickly. Afterwards, let me talk, for my time here is short, and your time in this life will be short as well if you're not careful.'

'Firstly, my name is Astren, and I am often called a seer. I'm not actually here. Rather this is a projection of my physical self, for I managed to follow your spirit here as it fled to your body, and this area is familiar to me.'

Maya snorted in derision. 'Really?'

Seeing her sceptical gaze, Astren reached out and put his hands into the glowing embers of the fire. 'Do you believe me now?'

Maya gasped in astonishment, yet still not satisfied, she picked up a stone and tossed it at Astren, who made no attempt to move. It passed right through him to clatter on the floor.

'Unless you want further proof?' Astren asked, raising an eyebrow. 'So, how did I get in your dreams? Well, this night, you travelled the spirit paths. Years ago, those who enjoyed the gift of spirit talking discovered them and found ways for a select few not just to talk, but to visit one another across great distances during the night hours. Last night our travels fortuitously brought us together.

'Now, you tell me. What made you visit Kingshold? Were you taken there when younger?'

Maya looked surprised. 'I've never been anywhere outside of my valley.' Then she picked up on something Astren had said. 'A gift of spirit travel, is that what I have?'

'Yes, exactly,' replied Astren enthusiastically. 'You have the ability to travel the spirit world. Whilst others dream, you can do what others only dream of.'

'I have another gift as well,' Maya hesitantly offered. 'I can heal.'

'This is the first time I've heard of anyone possessing that gift,' mused Astren. 'I am very interested in finding out more, especially in such dark times.' He was silent for a moment before continuing. 'There are other dangerous travellers who share the spirit paths. Daleth, who you know as the Witch-King, has many such in his service. As you likely already know, gifted ones, when identified, are sent to the capital. Those who show they have the gift of spirit talk often become Daleth's eyes and ears, whereas any who show darker or other useful gifts are taken into his army. But someone such as you. I think it unlikely you would have been allowed to live as a child. Now you've reached adulthood, your fate, if discovered, will almost certainly be dire.'

Astren's image started to fade. 'I cannot stay any longer. I'll need to sleep for a day after this,' he said. 'Continue to keep your gift hidden, and you'll remain safe. I'll try to reach you again so we can talk some more.'

With Astren's image and voice fading, Maya raised her voice. 'The Witch-King, what gift does he have? Answer me this before you go.'

Astren's image, almost invisible now, turned to her, his words barely a whisper.

'He enjoys youth eternal. I believe he is a drainer of life, of the people, of the land.' And then he was gone.

Taran awoke to the noise of pounding, and he wasn't sure if it was his head or the tavernkeeper's fist on the door that pounded the loudest.

'Alright, alright,' he growled, and looked at the meagre light coming through the window. It was approaching sunrise, and he needed to hurry if he wanted to get out of here before the townsfolk and soldiers roused themselves.

He pushed his face into the water bowl on the room's only table to wake himself up, then pulled on his clothes, grabbed his belongings, and unbarred the door before stepping quietly out onto the landing with a view to making his exit. As Taran walked to the top of the stairs, angry voices were coming from below. Discord at this time of the morning was never a good sign, so he moved swiftly down the stairs, intending to be on his way.

When he got to the bottom, to his dismay, the common room was packed, full of shouting people, a few soldiers, and the town overseer. The townsfolk were loudly demanding justice for a killing, and Taran certainly didn't want to be here to see the execution when it happened. The soldiers seemed to be arguing some point, but Taran wasn't interested. He just wanted to leave, so he approached the tavernkeeper, pouch in hand.

While counting out some coins from his dwindling supply, he glanced up briefly and met the tortured gaze of a townswoman whose face was puffy and red-eyed. Tears had run filthy tracks down her dirty cheeks. 'There he is!' she screamed, then raised a shaking finger to point straight at Taran. 'That's the man who killed my husband!'

Taran's head spun, and the floor seemed to shift under his feet. 'Just wait a moment,' he said, lifting his hands. 'There must be a misunderstanding. I was in here drinking all last night, ask the tavernkeeper or these soldiers,' and he gestured at them both.

The woman spat at him. 'Drinking while my poor Urg died in my arms,' she hissed, and Taran's stomach sunk, and it felt as if his whole world turned upside down.

Urg was dead! He'd never killed someone before. Suddenly Taran felt like being sick, while his trembling legs barely supported him. He took a step back, unaware as the tavern keeper raised, then brought a cudgel down on his head, which knocked him barely conscious to the floor. The next moment he was being punched and kicked, and his gift was useless even if he could have concentrated. It was such a crowded space with too many people.

On the overseer's orders, he was restrained by two soldiers he'd been drinking with the previous night. They shrugged in a kind of mute apology as they held him, but not so apologetic that they didn't bind the ropes incredibly tight around his wrists. He was pulled to his feet and had to be supported on either side.

The overseer stepped forward, a look of barely concealed glee in his eyes as he sneered at Taran. Bringing his face close, he rasped. 'You've been accused of killing Urg the joiner, and I find you guilty. Your fight was witnessed by many here, all of whom saw you strike the murderous blow when the fight was already over.'

Taran thought to protest. It had been a fair fight, one of so many, but he realised the townsfolk wanted revenge for losing their money, and the overseer had lost some too. Only the wife was perhaps justified in her need for vengeance. It was unfair, but nothing Taran could say would change this outcome. He wasn't a valued part of this community or any for that matter, he was a banished one, and his life meant nothing to anyone here, in fact, anywhere at all.

'Fetch the captain wherever he is!' ordered the overseer, and one of the soldiers in the crowd ran to find him.

Taran was half-dragged, half-carried to the justice turf where only yesterday he'd fought his bout. The crowd followed, and other townsfolk drawn by the noise and the chance of a spectacle filled the ranks of onlookers. He was tied upright to one of the corner posts, a scarred ugly old piece of wood stained and weathered but still hard and unyielding. Taran tested the strength of the ropes. If only he could break free ... but they were too tight, and he knew even if he did free himself, the crowd would tear him to pieces.

The people's mood grew uglier as they waited for the captain, and the sun had fully risen over the horizon before he appeared, flanked by a dozen soldiers, a menacing and hard look on his scarred face.

As Rakan approached, Taran met his stare, and whilst his legs shook, and the injustice of it all made him want to cry, he tried not to look away. He wanted to face his end with something approaching dignity. He'd seen far too many executions and always hated it when people begged and cried before the end. Face the gods with pride ... that's what he'd always thought. Now it was time to see if his courage would hold, or flee, to leave him snivelling before the inevitable happened.

The overseer raised his hands as he stood next to Taran, and the crowd hushed.

This was absolute silence, Taran thought. Not even a gust of wind or a distant birdsong. It seemed like the world was holding its breath, waiting for him to die.

'The sentence for killing someone is to face death yourself. Do you have anything to say before sentence is passed?' the overseer crowed in a raised voice.

The crowd hushed, waiting for the begging, the crying, the screaming.

Taran cleared his throat. 'Yes!' he shouted, his voice finding strength at the last. The crowd waited, and he let them for a moment. 'Your breath smells like the pig's arse you were bedded with last night.'

What little colour was in the overseer's face fled in an instant as laughter rippled through the crowd, and Taran felt some satisfaction. Still, the brief feeling vanished in an instant as Rakan moved onto the justice turf with some soldiers behind him.

'You want to see blood?' shouted Rakan, then drew his dagger as he walked closer. The crowd screamed in a frenzy once more, and the overseer's face contorted in glee.

Rakan stood and looked into Taran's eyes for what seemed like an eternity, 'This is going to hurt, but not for long,' Rakan said simply.

In that moment, Taran saw his mother hold him in her arms when he'd broken his wrist, felt her hands smooth his ruffled hair when his father had beat him. He remembered her fingers softly trace the cuts on his face after a fight, and saw the look of deepest love and deeper sorrow in her eyes every day of her life before his father had ended it.

Rakan stepped forward, and his dagger flashed up.

Taran saw blood spray in front of his eyes. Mother, I'm coming, be waiting for me, he thought, and then everything went black.

Moments later, Rakan cut the bonds that held Taran's limp body to the post and lowered him to the ground, and all the while, the crowd screamed in hatred.

Chapter III

Kalas lay on the ground weeping. He wanted to die, and soon he would, but it wouldn't be soon enough.

He'd wanted to die almost fifty years ago after all his friends around him had perished, but he didn't have the courage then. But now, now he didn't need courage; he just needed to wait a little longer.

He didn't weep for himself, but for his poor wife Syan, who lay dead in the dust just beyond his reach. She hadn't deserved this, poor sweet Syan. She'd taken him into her home, him a bloodied beaten stranger, cared for him, helped him through his nightmares, giving him a reason to live, and now she was dead. He stretched for her hand, but a soldier trod on his fingers, and he sobbed.

He'd been in the dusty fields when he'd heard her screams. Over seventy years old and still he worked them, finding comfort in the simple manual labour. He'd run for home then, or rather shambled, but even so, he was faster than expected for his age.

Yet however fast he'd crossed the fields of withered wheat, pushed through the slow-flowing waters of the brackish stream, and then made his way down the dusty path to the farm, it was never going to be fast enough.

The screams had stopped long before he'd entered the yard and seen her lifeless body, clothes all torn and bloodied sprawled in the dirt. Her son, Jay, hung from the porch by his neck, swaying in the breeze. He'd never been close to Kalas, who wasn't his father, but he'd been a good man irrespective, and now he was dead too. No doubt killed while trying to protect his mother.

The Witch-King's soldiers had been sat around, eating the food they'd stolen when he'd arrived. They'd turned to look as he lurched into view, breathing loudly, and had laughed as he ran toward his wife's body, calling her name, but they hadn't yet had enough fun. So they'd stood around and had pushed him between them until he tripped and fell to his knees, and then a spear shaft had struck him between the shoulders.

Now here he was face down, awaiting the killing blow which would put an end to his misery. A long-overdue death that should have come fifty years earlier.

'Kill me.' he croaked. 'Kill me now. I need to die before it's too late.'

The soldiers, eight of them in this squad, bellowed with laughter. One of them, a hatchet-faced corporal with pockmarked skin, called Meech, pulled him to his feet. 'Soon,' he laughed, 'but not yet.' Having said this, he drew his fist back and started to pound Kalas' face.

Blow after blow, Meech struck, and the world started to grow dim to Kalas.

'I'm coming, Syan,' Kalas muttered.

As Meech continued, he gashed one of his knuckles badly on Kalas' teeth. Despite it bleeding freely, he unleashed another punch, and his blood splashed into Kalas' mouth.

Suddenly Kalas' eyes opened wide. 'Kill me,' he pleaded. 'Kill me!' but his final desperate plea fell on deaf ears.

'Finish the old sod off,' shouted one of the other soldiers, and bored now with the beating, they turned back to their food.

Kalas fell to the ground, and Meech knelt either side of his shoulders.

Meech was about to draw his dagger when he saw Kalas was trying to tell him something with his last breaths, beckoning with his hands.

'What is it, you old fool?' asked Meech. 'Have you got any coins hidden you want to tell me about? If so, I'll bury your wife instead of leaving her to the crows,' he lied.

Meech leaned down and put his ear next to Kalas' broken mouth to hear his whispered response. In an instant, the old man's hands were on the back of his head, and Meech couldn't pull free.

'I told you to kill me,' said Kalas. His voice that moments ago had been broken and pleading was now deep and menacing. 'Now … now it's too late, for us, for everyone!'

With that, he opened his mouth and bit deep into Meech's neck. Meech tried desperately to pull away but couldn't and felt his blood being drained from his body. He wanted to scream, to cry to his friends for help, to beg for mercy, but it was as if his body was locked, frozen, unable to move. In the last moments before his life left him, he saw Kalas' eyes glow red.

The other soldiers who sat around the well eating their food, noticed the absence of sound and turned their attention back to Meech. He knelt on top of the old man, twitching in a strange puppet-like fashion.

The horses were whinnying and skittish where they were tied to an old wooden fence, their eyes wide and rolling with fear, and the soldiers looked around.

'Meech, what in the gods' names are you doing to that old man?' laughed Antoc, the squad leader, suggestively. The others roared with laughter and started jeering, but it soon died away as something obviously wasn't right. The horses had sensed it, and now they did too.

As they looked, Meech seemed to be shrinking, shrivelling before their eyes. Then like a bag of bones, he was cast to one side, his arms and legs mere sticks covered in taut skin wrapped in scale armour.

The old man sat up then, but he didn't look as old as before, and when he got to his feet, it was with a smoothness of one much younger.

A silence settled across the yard, and slowly Kalas looked up. His face, which had been old like wrinkled leather, was now firm, the skin taut. Blood ran down his chin and neck, but it was his eyes … they glowed a fierce red as if a fire raged behind them.

'In the name of the gods!' cried Antoc, surging to his feet. His sword blade whispered from its scabbard as a cold chill ran through his bones.

He moved to a fighting position, and all around him, the other men followed suit, all bravado, all the laughter gone. Swords and shields at the ready, they quickly surrounded Kalas in a ring of bared steel.

'Kill that thing!' Antoc ordered, then lunged forward with his blade for Kalas' unprotected chest as the others also started to move. But then those fiery red eyes fixed on him, and it was as if everything slowed, except the red-eyed fiend.

Kalas twisted and spun, dodging the blow, then his hand snapped up, palm open, to break Antoc's nose. As Antoc's head rocked back, Kalas turned the man's wrist sharply, taking the sword away, and then before Antoc's had time to recover, smashed the flat of the blade into the side of his neck and jaw.

As Antoc fell stunned to the ground, blood pouring, he saw Kalas flicker like a flame amongst his men, and they fell in his wake like wheat under a scythe. It was over in a few heartbeats, everyone dead and him wounded. He couldn't stand, let alone fight, but maybe he could still get out of this alive. 'I'm sorry, I'm sorry. Let me live, don't kill me,' he begged, holding a rag frantically to his bleeding neck while also trying to stem the blood flow from his nose.

As Antoc watched, Kalas knelt over him, and the glare of the red eyes faded a little to be replaced by the dark green they'd been before, full of sorrow. He felt his hopes rise.

'You should have killed me when you had the chance,' said Kalas softly, 'but I promise I won't kill you.'

Antoc felt relief wash over him then, and he sobbed a little, feeling the warmth of the sun replace the death chill that had been seeping through his bones. A chance at life again, he thought, things would be so different from hereon, maybe he could run away from the army, find a girl, have children.

'I am sorry though,' said Kalas, interrupting Antoc's thoughts.

'Sorry?' asked Antoc, through the pain. 'You have nothing to be sorry for,' and tears ran down his cheeks. 'I am the one who is sorry for all of this,' and his eyes swept around the courtyard, encompassing everything from the dead soldiers, to Syan, to Jay. 'What do you have to be sorry for?' asked Antoc. He could feel the blood flow from his wounds slowing, and his heartbeat steadied. Yes, he would try and live a better life after this.

'Well,' said Kalas, 'I am sorry. I promised not to kill you, and I won't, but you see, he's hungry after so long and still needs to feed.' With that, his eyes flamed red, Antoc screamed, and Kalas began to drink.

Rakan sighed. He'd never been close to anyone.

As a child, he was beaten by his father, his older brother, and his cousins because he had skin rot. It was a malady that caused his flesh to be covered in sores that rarely healed, and that made him disgusting in their eyes, something to be despised.

They couldn't kill him, as death was answerable with death, but they'd certainly hoped he would kill himself. His mother offered no warmth either, she had barely touched him, and from an early age, he'd felt the hatred of everyone around him.

The constant beatings would have broken most people, but Rakan, after a while, had stopped feeling the pain, came to accept it, came to enjoy it. He'd toiled harder than any to chop the trees in the woods, becoming stronger, and he revelled in the physical work and resulting pain from his exhausted muscles.

When he'd reached fourteen summers and was old enough to join the army, the local sergeant at arms had recruited and sent him to the nearest garrison fort to take the oath and amulet. His ability to ignore pain while inflicting it was noticed during training, and he was transferred to the Nightstalkers, an elite unit.

He had to wait for two years before he was given his first leave; two years of punishing training, putting down an occasional insurrection, fighting the green folk of the Eyre, and stepping over the bodies of his fallen comrades.

After two weeks of riding hard, even at night, revelling in the risk but knowing he was the equal of any dark things that were abroad, he'd arrived back at his old village just after sunrise. He'd ridden in, nodded to the local garrison soldiers, and enjoyed the look of distrust they gave him in his black uniform. He was only a young corporal then, but the black uniform showed him as being in the Nightstalkers, and he was something to be feared.

One hour later, he'd ridden back out again. He'd killed everyone; his father and mother, his brother, his cousins, and when anyone else tried to stop him, he'd butchered them too.

Two guards ran to investigate the screams and had come upon Rakan covered in blood up to his elbows, sword covered in gore. However, they'd dared not intervene, for he outranked them, and he'd only killed townspeople, and a member of the army didn't have to answer for that.

The town overseer also came in time to witness the slaughter, and he had the authority to stop the carnage. But when he saw who it was, Rakan returned, he'd scurried from sight, praying to all the gods who would listen that Rakan didn't come for him too, and when Rakan left town, he'd sobbed in relief.

Years had gone by since then, and Rakan was surprised to find himself thinking back that far, but what now surprised him most was that he felt almost liked for the first time in his life.

That young lad Taran had not only idolised him, but with his tales, the rest of the squad had started to look at him differently. They'd applauded his exploits, showed respect for his rank, and the nods they gave him when they met his eye had made his heart swell.

Normally his scarred visage, his cruel look, the marks of rank on his cheek, and the open sores from the skin rot meant people rarely ever held his gaze for long, yet last night the men even sought to be next to him.

Rakan had hardly been able to believe the accusation and sentence when they'd been told to him by one of his men. He'd even considered recruiting Urg because of his size, and found it hard to believe Taran had killed him. But everyone had heard about the fight, and it seemed

Urg had died during the night. The law was clear; if a civilian killed another civilian, their life was forfeit.

It might be unfair as it had happened from an agreed bout on the justice turf, but it seemed the townspeople and the overseer had lost money, so this was a way of exacting petty revenge.

As he'd walked through the village, he'd heard the sound of the shouting rabble, demanding Taran's blood, and it had sickened him. These peasants, these land grubbers who'd never held a sword... Yet he'd carried out executions more times than he could count, some on comrades he'd known years, and they'd never caused him pause. So he'd shrugged off his concerns and strode faster, thinking to get this over and done with and to be on his way before Taran's dead body cooled.

Yet when he'd approached the justice turf and seen Taran tied to the post, had felt the lad's steady gaze meet his own, then heard him deride the overseer who was so keen to end his life, Rakan thought of a solution.

Now, as he looked down at Taran's body and the blood being soaked up greedily by the dust, he felt satisfaction.

His blade hadn't delivered a killing blow. As it swept up toward Taran's throat, instead of cutting it slowly, he'd slashed the dagger across Taran's cheeks to carve the marks of a corporal on his face.

Rakan didn't judge Taran harshly for blacking out, the pain would have been quite excruciating, but it would have been the expectation of a death blow that would have caused his body to shut down in self-protection. So, for the moment, while the silence continued, Rakan cut the bonds on Taran's wrists.

The crowd, realising that the sentence they'd expected hadn't been passed out, began to scream in hatred and confusion, then surged forward in a rare act of bravery onto the justice turf.

'Swords!' called Rakan, and the troop of soldiers who were with him drew their blades in smooth unison and faced outward. The throng, shocked by the strength of Rakan's voice and the glittering steel waiting to shed their blood, came to a hushed standstill.

Only the overseer found the outraged strength to speak.

Spluttering, he started screaming. 'He is sentenced to death; you cannot pardon him! Do your duty and carry out the execution. It's the law, and you are held by this law, captain. If you don't carry it out, it will be carried out on you!'

Rakan raised his voice so everyone could hear and nodded down at Taran, who was starting to stir. 'That man,' he stated loudly, 'was conscripted to the army of the Witch-King last night before Urg died, and therefore the law states.' He raised his voice even louder. 'That as a member of our king's army, he is not answerable for the death of a stinking civilian!'

Taran was aware of the sound of screaming. 'It seems I'm damned,' his mind quailed, and he was scared to open his eyes for fear of seeing the nine hells he'd apparently been consigned to. Yet open his eyes he did, and saw Rakan's scarred, ugly face looking down at him.

'Welcome to the army, corporal,' said Rakan with a wolfish grin, and reached down to grip Taran's hand then pulled him to his feet. 'No rest when you're on duty, lad.' He slapped Taran on the back hard enough to rattle his teeth.

Taran's hand reached up to his painful face only to have Rakan knock it away. 'Touch those cuts with those filthy hands before they're stitched, and you'll likely end up dead of rot,' he warned.

As Taran's head began to clear, he searched Rakan's mind and understood what had just happened.

Rakan and his men, blades still drawn, pushed their way through the crowd with Taran between them, the townsfolk muttering curses as they realised their chance of vengeance was gone.

As Taran walked, blood splashed down his shirt, and he pulled a cloth from his belt pouch to try and staunch the flow.

'If you think it hurts now,' laughed Rakan, 'wait till I start stitching you up!' and with that, some of the men laughed half in sympathy, half in malicious jealousy at his sudden elevation to a corporal's rank.

Taran, though, was just happy to be alive irrespective of the pain and began to think about how to get out of this new mess he found himself in.

Maya had managed to fall back to sleep, but the glimmer of dawn's early light and the rumble of her empty stomach grumbling in protest awoke her with a start.

She reached for her scavenging bag, only to see it in shreds and the remains of its contents strewn around the floor of the cave.

Then memories of yesterday flooded back like a wave, and her eyes flew to where she'd tied the wolf, only to see the leather tethers in shreds and the wolf no longer there. A chill ran down Maya's neck as she picked up her bow, then nocked an arrow before moving quietly to the entrance of the cave, ready to draw and loose should the wolf still be there. Yet of the great beast, there was no sign.

Relief washed over her. She wasn't sure one of her arrows could bring it down and was glad she wouldn't have to find out. Returning to the cave, she threw the last of the branches onto the fire and enjoyed the heat as it banished the cold of the fresh morning air.

Next, she carefully gathered the few unspoiled berries that had rolled around the floor during the wolf's midnight feast and bemoaned the fact that the two rabbits she'd caught had been eaten without a trace. Better them than me, she consoled herself, and was glad those small snacks had been enough for the wolf, and she hadn't woken to its jaws upon her throat.

She sat back against the cave wall and chewed on the berries while trying to make sense of the night before. She needed to choose a plan of action.

Astren, her dream, and the punishment she faced gave her pause, but it was thinking of her father that made up her mind. He would have spent a terrible night worrying about her, wondering whether she was alive or dead, injured or otherwise, and she couldn't let him suffer any longer.

The best course, she decided, was to return to the settlement as soon as possible to face the overseer. Get this over with, put whatever punishment that was inflicted behind her, and get back to living her life. The dream was just a dream, and she shouldn't sit here dwelling on it any further.

She paused and looked at the berries before dropping them. Likely they were off or somehow different from what she usually picked and had made her hallucinate. She knew mushrooms could make people see things that weren't there. Now that was far more plausible than Astren being real.

So mind made up, she kicked dust over the dying fire to extinguish it, grabbed her bow, quiver, and knife, and gathered the bits of leather twine that were still long enough to be useable.

Before leaving the cave, she dipped her fingers in the cooler ash to the side of the fire and rubbed it onto her face, strapped her knee as she always did before returning to give herself a limp, and left the cave to head off toward the smoke of the settlement she could see in the distance.

As Maya descended, she wondered how on earth she'd ended up on the east side of the valley in unfamiliar terrain.

Each of the settlement's four foragers was given a sector. The valley was quite vast, and if a forager got to know the land they worked more intimately, they could better gather, hunt the animals, be aware of the dangers, and so on. It made sense.

Now, as Maya hastened through the unfamiliar forest, she needed to keep glancing up at the rising sun through the canopy of the trees to orientate herself, and because of that, she failed to see the trap at her feet. Suddenly her legs were swept from under her as she triggered a snare, and the sapling to which it was tied, sprang upright. She landed with a heavy thud on her back, the wind knocked out of her.

Despite being stunned, Maya pulled her knife to sever the bindings around her ankles. While sawing through the leather, there was a sound of something crashing through the undergrowth.

'It came from over here,' a woman called.

Maya's heart sank. The voice belonged to Seren, one of the other foragers, and there was no love lost between the two. In fact, all the other foragers hated Maya due to her constant luck, always bringing back more than anyone else.

She'd been assigned to the west of the valley once, and it had been the other foragers' bribes that had seen her moved to the barren north. Nonetheless, she'd soon started to bring in more than the others again. There was no beating her, and they were insanely jealous.

Seren came crashing through the bushes like a wild animal. My god, no wonder she never catches anything, except for me, thought Maya.

'By the gods,' cried Seren as she came to a halt.

Maya, finally loose of the bonds, rose to her feet, brushing mulch from her clothing.

More crashing, and onto the pathway came Krispen, one of the other foragers. 'What did you catch?' he asked, before any further words died in his throat as he spied Maya.

'Maya,' hissed Seren, 'look what you've done to my trap!' Her face was screwed up angrily. 'How am I supposed to catch any meat today now?' she demanded, her eyebrows lifting.

Maya looked over Seren's shoulder at Krispen. 'It seems to me that you've already caught some rotten meat today,' she said, then started to turn away.

Seren grabbed her arm hard. 'Not so fast!' she said, and Krispen grabbed the other as Maya twisted to free herself. 'Everyone in the settlement is so, so worried about you,' Seren continued sarcastically, 'especially your father *and* the overseer. I think bringing you back will make up for any lost foraging today.'

'Oh yes,' agreed Krispen, smiling but without any warmth in his eyes. His fingers dug hard into Maya's arm.

'I *am* going back to the settlement already. Now let me go!' Maya demanded, but neither relaxed their grip; however hard she struggled, and they just laughed nastily at her.

'What *is* that smell?' asked Seren, wrinkling her nose at Maya. 'You stink like bear crap,' and Krispen laughed.

Maya couldn't help herself. 'At least I don't smell like I've rutted with a pig,' she said, looking at Krispen. This comment earned her a nasty punch to the stomach, but it was worth it. She made a final effort to twist free, but they wouldn't let her go and as they marched her between them back to the settlement, the merciless jibing continued.

Antoc lay frozen in fear and shock as Kalas knelt alongside him.

Turning his head to the side, Kalas retched before spewing blood. The horrid saltiness of it filled his mouth, and he needed to drink to take the foulness away. His eyes that had glowed red up until mere moments ago now returned to their deep green.

Antoc just lay there and looked up at the sky, amazed that he still lived. His heart pounded, and his eyesight was blurred and dim from loss of blood.

'I'm sorry,' said Kalas softly, 'but at the very least, you still live, which is more than everyone else here.' He stood up and moved toward the well, stepping over the bodies, causing the flies that had already begun to gorge to rise up in angry, complaining clouds before returning to their feast.

They were so fat and heavy these flies, but there was always so much for them to eat. Spoiled vegetables in the fields, dead or dying fish in the rivers, the whole land was teetering on a knife-edge. He lived almost as far south as he could, the sea just over the horizon. A long way to the east, supposedly the Freestates lands thrived, and they were behind the sickness that destroyed this land, or so the tithe collectors said.

After he pulled the bucket up from the well, he looked into the water. The face that looked back at him was now the one of his youth, fair hair, taut skin, green eyes albeit somewhat bloodshot, and a solid chin. Certainly not handsome but as strong as the sword he'd used to wield.

The wind blew softly across the yard, a faint saltiness from the sea carried upon it, and Kalas closed his eyes and let his mind think back to when he last looked like this …

The land into which Kalas had been born was golden, at least to him way back then.

It was called the Ember Kingdom and had been ruled by a lineage that stretched back over four hundred years. The land was blessed, full of precious natural resources with good soil for farming to keep its people fed. Most importantly, the iron ingots produced by the central and northern regions, sought after by the Freestates and the nations beyond, helped the kingdom thrive.

The north, west, and south of the realm abutted the endless sea, and only to the east did the kingdom share a border. Toward the northeast, the mountains ended abruptly to be replaced by a thickly forested swamp, an unforgiving land within which lay the Kingdom of Eyre, an insular people who loved their trees more than any outsider.

Further to the south was the Freestates, a land of trade linking east to west. The Freestates sat on the other side of the Forelom Mountains, towering peaks with but one pass allowing travel between the two neighbours.

Born of minor nobility in the southern outreach of the kingdom and only a second son, he'd but two options. To bend the knee before his father and brother while helping at the docks like a commoner or, to leave his family, travel to the capital and join the royal guard.

He chose the guard, and his father and brother disowned him on the day he left. Their curses heavy on his ears, shoulders, and heart.

They stripped him of everything, including whatever love they might have once felt, and his regret was such that the pain never once faded.

There was no standing army, for the kingdom itself had been united for longer than anyone remembered. So Kalas had thought it was a posting that would allow him access to the capital's delights amongst educated peers and to look dashing in a royal guard's uniform without ever having to put his life at risk.

How wrong he was, he soon came to find out.

Despite there being no wars to fight, there were bandits to hunt down, peasants who rebelled at the work that was naturally required of them, and a surprising amount of disillusioned noble houses who needed reminding of who their king was. The Eyre would often raid, and then to the far north, brigands would often come down from their mountain caves to kill farmers and steal livestock. All of these needed to be repulsed and were the responsibility of the king to deal with.

Thus the royal guard trained and trained. Kalas had erroneously thought no one left the royal guard because it was such a soft job, but lots of people did actually leave, but only if they'd stopped breathing.

So, with but two choices, to train hard or die, Kalas had chosen to train, finding to his surprise that he had a gift for the sword and shield, the lance and spear, the dagger and the bow.

He frequently tried to repair the rift with his family, but his letters were returned. The notes attached advised that there was no longer anyone in the family of his name. One day his father and brother came to the royal court on business, and as he'd approached them, his brother had turned away. He stood in front of his father then, heart in hands.

'Will you forgive me now, father, after all these years?' he'd implored beseechingly, eyes wet with emotion.

His father had looked steadily at him, with no emotion of his own, then replied. 'If I were truly your father and you were my son, you would never have left your brother and I all those years ago. I have no son by your name and never will.' With that, his father had turned away and left the very same day.

Despite this never healing wound, this one regret, life was good, and it had been easy to turn a blind eye to the poverty that he saw when surrounded by such friends amongst the opulence of the capital. The Ember Kingdom, he felt, was just, ruled harshly but fairly, and surely if its people suffered a little hardship, it made them so much stronger. Everyone knew their place.

Kalas had risen through the ranks to be the weapon master in the king's guard, one below the captain, his best friend Alano. Alano was the only one to almost equal Kalas in the fighting pits, and the bond they had shared was unbreakable.

But the good life had come to an end. One day a great fleet of longships landed on the southern and northwestern shores of the coast. Where they came from, no one had known, but the men that spilled from them were hardened and cruel, hungry not just for food but for blood and conquest.

Spirit talkers had informed the king of their arrival, who in response, sent emissaries on the fastest horses both north and south, one after another to offer peace, gold, even land, yet none returned.

The foreign armies swept across the lands. The northern army, led by a warrior who called himself Daleth the Witch-King, brushed aside local resistance from the noble houses and their small personal armies. Thousands were slain, and hundreds just disappeared, and the reports were that the Witch-King was a giant amongst men, a near-immortal warrior.

Local peasants in their settlements and towns were mostly spared in a shrewd move, and only the castles and fortresses of the kingdom's royal houses were brought down, the nobles executed, their knights slaughtered. Being mostly left alone, the peasantry just shrugged their shoulders and carried on doing what they did, having exchanged one taskmaster for another meant very little.

The malaise that slowly fell over the land more symbolic of the war than anything malignant.

The Ember Kingdom's few gifted, the mages who wandered the lands or who were in the nobles' employ simply disappeared, and the news of the invading armies stopped coming in.

The high mages that remained in the capital, by order of a desperate King Anders, had turned to the rarest tomes of elder magic in a final bid to defeat the invading forces. Yet the only spell they'd found offering any hope had been the darkest of them all. With no other choice, the mages sacrificed themselves in the casting of this long forbidden incantation, so that the king and his legion of elite royal guard were possessed by minor daemons in a final throw of the dice.

Kalas sighed and shuddered at the horror of the memory. Men, friends he'd spent years training with, doused themselves in blood. No one knew where it had come from, but worse was to come, for they had to drink it too. As the magi spoke the words in a harsh forgotten tongue, a portal opened to the nine hells, and daemons were summoned through to possess the king and his men.

The agony of being possessed was nothing that Kalas or any man could have prepared themselves for. The sense of defilement had almost overwhelmed them.

The magi had believed they would gain the strength of the hell-born, the speed, the inexhaustible stamina, and they were right, but they hadn't known that they would share their minds, their thoughts and that the daemons would try to twist them to their wills and ways.

In the first hour after being possessed, those weakest of will turned against their brothers, the daemon's thirst for blood too strong for them to resist. The king, Alano, Kalas, and the strongest willed of the guard were forced to slay their friends in self-defense. The lower halls of the palace flowed with blood, and the howls of the despairing survivors at what they'd been forced to do echoed from the vaulted ceilings.

Gone was the easy laughter thereafter, every moment a fight to tame the beast inside, that whispered to kill, to feast on the life of innocents. Kalas remembered the worse thing about that first desperate fight, wasn't just that he'd killed his sword brothers, men he'd known for years, but it was that he'd licked their blood from his hands and blade and revelled in the taste of a slain friend's life.

Once they'd won their individual battles with the will of the daemons inside, they'd all made a pact there and then. They had, each and every one of them, unintentionally become far worse than the very evil they'd set out to fight. So they swore an oath to kill the Witch-King or die in the attempt. Should they succeed, they would not allow themselves to live beyond the day of battle. The risk was too great.

Two weeks later, more men had succumbed, having lost their wills. The combined armies of the Witch-King had stood before the gates of the capital, ready to do battle. Had they arrived much later, it was doubtful that there would have been any royal guard left to face them, for over two thousand of the guard now lay dead and buried by the hands of their brothers.

By this time, all the population of the city had left. They'd not only run from the invaders but the demonic goings-on within the fortress. Only the king's son and a few retainers had stayed against their lord's wishes, and they'd watched from atop the battlements as all that remained of the guard followed their king out to battle, riding horses who whinnied in barely controlled terror at those who sat astride them.

Barely nine hundred men against an army of a hundred thousand. White cloaks billowed in the wind, and burnished armour shone in the morning sun. They'd drawn their swords and ridden toward the enemy.

Kalas remembered looking at his best friend Alano on his left, the king astride his charger on his right, and the rest of the men as they rode out. He should have felt pride or perhaps sadness at impending doom, maybe sorrow at his family having been erased as had all the other royal houses, but he'd felt none of this.

Instead, the daemon inside his head had howled its glee, urged him to give in, to let go of his last vestiges of restraint. Kalas had looked around and seen everyone's faces were twisted, sick apparitions of what they used to be, eyes glowed red, and then as they had closed on the enemy, he'd let the daemon take partial control.

The approaching army had stopped its advance for a moment. Laughter had rippled through its vast ranks, led by the bass sound of the Witch-King, no doubt with amusement at this last pathetic resistance to his invasion.

Even as King Anders and the royal guard charged into the foremost ranks of the Witch-King's army, the laughter continued, as had the jeering from the other enemy troops who had yet to join the fight. They watched in amusement as horses were cut down by long spears, and men fell to the ground, but the laughter died as the screams continued to grow in force.

Despite being pierced by sword and spear, King Anders and his men had continued to fight with unbelievable speed of blade. Along with his king, Kalas had his horse cut from under him in the first few moments and was thrown heavily, but his mind hadn't registered the pain. Instead, he'd just rolled with the fall and come to his feet as quick as lightning, swords in hand.

Despite the impossible odds, they'd cut through the ranks of the enemy horde. Their manic laughter and howls of glee, the shining red eyes as they'd slaughtered, had sent shivers of fear down the spines of the men of the attacking army, who had fought in countless battles and stood undefeated.

The centre of the enemy line had disappeared like sand through an hourglass, and those who had yet to enter the fray had started to push back frantically as panic had taken hold.

Thousands of arrows had blotted out the sun and fallen indiscriminately on everyone as the Witch-King, in desperation, had sought to turn the tide of battle whatever the cost. Kalas had fallen, pierced half a dozen times, yet he'd wrenched the shafts free and turned to bite the neck from a mortally wounded soldier next to him. Renewed strength had surged through his veins, and he'd leapt to his feet and fought on as had many around him, and still the arrows had fallen like rain.

They'd pushed behind King Anders toward the rise where the Witch-King had stood, victory impossibly getting closer. Yet, the enemy emboldened by their dwindling numbers had fought on anew, and with every step more of Kalas' brothers had fallen, but the cost on the enemy ranks was hideous.

Kalas was almost on his knees when the enemy cavalry had started their charge, pierced through again by arrow and sword, an inconceivable number of enemy bodies behind him. The Witch-King had ordered his cavalry to ride everyone down irrespective of side to finish the battle.

The daemon knew Kalas' demise would end its existence and was scared. It had left his mind free at the very end, having scurried to hide in the farthest reaches of his subconscious.

He saw King Anders, a great warrior in his own right, finally go down, his head crushed by a mace. There had been perhaps a hundred of his brothers left, and the toll they had taken on the horsemen was horrific, the sounds of the wounded beasts louder even than the screaming men. Yet despite their prowess, his brothers had fallen one by one, their advance slowed, and their hopes died.

His friend Alano had stood firm until the end. He had fought with his sword in one hand and long dagger in another. As the cavalry had ridden by, Alano had rolled and twisted to cut the legs from under them. Despite his wounds, Kalas had fought on in similar fashion and surpassed everyone in dealing death.

Yet one of the falling horses had cannoned into him, crushed him into the ground. The weight nearly suffocated him, and as more bodies fell on top, he'd struggled to breathe. The last sound he'd heard before his eyes had closed was the screaming as Alano had continued with his own personal slaughter...

Kalas opened his eyes, the images so fresh, and looked around the yard as he sat on the edge of the well.

He should have died that day, he thought, died with his friends, died with the king. However, the flowing blood from the dying horse and men that had buried him from sight nourished the daemon even as it cowered, kept him alive. Until at last many days later, he dragged himself from under the bloated corpses that had been left to rot in the sun.

He'd lost his mind then for a while, and the daemon, unable to pierce his complete madness with its will, had itself withdrawn again to his subconscious, and there it had remained.

The Ember Kingdom had died that day, to be replaced by the kingdom of the Witch-King. King Anders' son, he later heard, had been impaled and the last of the retainers butchered. All written records, all the banners, all the royal houses, wiped from the land in the following months.

Kalas had long ago realised that the Ember Kingdom and King Anders were not the utopian dream he'd naively thought back when he was younger, but the reign of the Witch-King was far, far worse. Kalas was over seventy summers old, whereas most only lived into their thirties or forties in this harsh land, so few remembered the green fields, tall trees, fresh water, and bountiful harvests.

Instead, almost everyone had been born into this miserable land of decay and thought the old tales were just poor man's dreams as opposed to what had actually been.

Now, after all this time, the Witch-King had built an army to fulfil his dreams of conquest that had been shattered by Kalas and his brothers those decades ago.

Kalas turned his attention to Antoc, who struggled to sit up, and deliberated killing him after all before casting the notion aside. He'd already been punished enough beyond what he realised, and perhaps he could still serve a use.

He'd made an oath over fifty years ago to kill the Witch-King or to die in the trying, and he'd lived with the shame of failure ever since. Now that his daemon kin was awakened once more by blood, it was time to fulfil the oath if he could.

He strode over to Antoc, whose eyes widened in fright at his approach. 'I need you to ride to your garrison, tell them of what happened here.' As he said this, he lifted Antoc to his feet and stripped him of his armour, then, with little effort, lifted him onto the back of one of the horses whose wide fearful eyes mirrored those of Antoc's himself.

Antoc nodded, a worried look on his face. 'It will be the death of you,' he replied, scared of telling the truth, yet feeling compelled to. He also wanted Kalas to feel fear as he felt it. He felt so weak and just wanted to be gone, get this over with, and sleep for years.

Kalas nodded. 'In time we all die,' he said, 'it's always just a matter of time. One more thing, go to your garrison's overseer, try and get him to send a message to the Witch-King.'

'What message would that be?' asked Antoc, keen to be on his way. It was a long ride to the garrison, but he would warn them, have them send men to kill this thing.

'Tell him,' said Kalas, breaking into Antoc's thoughts of revenge. 'The message he must deliver is ... Kalas is coming!'

Maya was furious. Several hours of being pushed roughly around by Seren and Krispen, as well as their constant unpleasantness on the way back to the settlement, had darkened her mood. Finally, however, its wooden walls were in sight; guards dimly visible patrolled the gates.

She knew a harsh punishment awaited, but at least she would be reunited with her father soon. Once recovered from her flogging, things would go back to normal as she was too good to be replaced despite her unpopularity.

As they neared the gates, Seren called out a warning to the guards. One peered at them closely as they entered the clear ground around the walls.

Maya saw him turn and call over his shoulder that she'd been found, and felt some small relief that at least they'd been worried about her, even if only because some people had gone hungry. Perhaps this would make them value her more after this, and maybe, just maybe, be more civil.

Seren and Krispen finally let go of her arms as they walked through the wooden gates' shadow and into the main square just beyond. It was midday, and it was busy, full of people going about their business.

Maya kept her head stooped as was her custom and limped to keep up her appearance of being slightly crippled without even thinking about it. She looked from under the cowl of her hood to see people point at her, looks of distaste on their faces. Some also started to catcall and voiced their displeasure over having gone without adequate food because she hadn't bothered to come back the last night.

Seren laughed. 'Look how much you've been missed,' she said, barely hidden glee in her voice.

'Oh, and guess who's coming to greet her personally,' added Krispen.

Maya turned to see the overseer, with a small retinue of town guard close behind, walk toward her.

Whereas her limp was fake, his was genuine. He was a twisted man and looked like the land itself, all sharp and jagged, darkness around and in his eyes. Maya shuddered. If she was disliked by most, the overseer was feared by all, for he was the law.

She'd pondered how best to approach this meeting and had decided that open contrition was the best option, so she knelt as he approached and lowered her head.

'I am so sorry,' she cried, and the fear in her voice was real. 'I was chased by a wolf and must have dropped my pouch before I found sanctuary in a cave.' Then she continued into the silence that had fallen. 'I couldn't leave, and I fell asleep. When I awoke, the first thing I wanted to do was come back. I will work twice as hard to make sure I bring in more food for everyone, and I will go without so others might have more.'

The words tumbled from her mouth, and then she fell silent. She kept her head down and watched as his sandaled feet moved closer. He dragged his left foot, which was turned badly inward, and the soldiers slowed their march behind him.

'Welcome home, Maya, we hoped you would return,' rattled the overseer, and the sound of his voice was like bones being shaken in a bag.

She took no comfort from the words, for they held no kindness whatsoever.

'Bring her!' he commanded the soldiers. Two stepped forward and lifted her to her feet. As the overseer turned away, they followed after, the other soldiers close around her.

As they walked, a crowd started to follow, and Maya knew they were going toward the justice turf. Her legs felt weak, for without doubt, she would be flogged, and all these people who normally wouldn't even look at her were coming to revel in her pain. She wanted to cry but wouldn't let them see her weakness, even though she felt anything but strong.

It seemed to take forever thanks to the overseer's slow gait, and thus, the agony of expectation was drawn out even longer. As they reached the edge of the justice turf, the crowd stopped, not daring to tread further as she was escorted to one of the many thick posts, although she wasn't bound to one, not yet.

Maya noticed the overseer look around, and then his eyes seemed to settle on something. As she followed his gaze, a ripple went through the crowd as someone pushed through.

'Maya, Maya!' called a voice.

'Father!' she called, and suddenly there he was, all stained black from the mines, but she'd never been happier to see him. He paused for a moment at the edge of the justice turf but then ran forward to take her in his arms, weeping openly.

'Maya, you're alive,' he sobbed. 'I was so worried, what happened, where have you been, are you hurt? We need to get you home.'

The overseer nodded then, and two burly guards stepped forward to pull her father away.

Raising his voice, the overseer spoke loudly. 'We are here today to see a just punishment carried out. The law is written, and we must all abide by it or face justice when it is broken.'

Maya held her father's desperate gaze. 'I'll be ok, father,' she reassured him, seeing tears swell in his eyes. She'd known this was coming, had seen many times the agony a flogging could inflict, and also knew she wouldn't be able to endure it long. I hope I pass out quickly, she thought. Her father would have to endure in his own way as well, her screams, her bloodied body, and then cleaning her wounds, looking after her for weeks to come.

Her father, worried beyond reason, struggled with the guards, trying to wrestle from their powerful grip to no avail. 'Don't father,' she implored, fearing for him as she saw the overseer approach closer.

'I accept the law, I accept the punishment!' she called, bringing the overseer's attention back to her.

The overseer raised his voice once more as everyone stilled to hear his words. 'The law states the punishment for staying out beyond dark is a flogging,' he said, a twisted grin spread across his pale face.

If the guards hadn't gripped her so firmly, her legs wouldn't be holding her up by now. Maya felt faint, but was relieved to see her father calm down and the guards relax their grip. She turned to the overseer to see him uncoil a long whip, the dark leather of which was stained with previous victims' blood. He cracked it maliciously, smiling as he did so.

'This was the very same whip that took your mother's life,' he said, just loud enough for Maya and her father to hear. 'Who'd have known she'd be so pathetically weak as to die from a few lashes?'

Maya couldn't believe her ears. Her father had never spoken of that day, and then even as she was processing what the overseer had said, her father, whose arms had been released, sprang forward to grab the whip from the overseer's hand. It was a desperate attempt to stop the same punishment, and possibly the same fate being brought upon his beloved daughter, but as he did so, the overseer fell hard to the floor.

If the crowd had been hushed before, now the silence was absolute, and Maya felt her stomach turn over at what her father had done.

The guards recovered quickly and held him tight once again in their grasp.

The overseer slowly got to his feet, eyes burning with hatred, yet with a satisfied smile across his face.

'However, the punishment for striking an overseer is death!' he screamed, and whilst those fateful words were still registering in Maya's brain, he turned to her father, and drawing a dagger, plunged it again and again into his unprotected chest.

The crowd's scream's almost drowned out Maya's as the overseer stepped back and pulled the blade free a final time.

She stared in shocked disbelief as the blood pumped from the terrible wounds, then her father's wide, panicked eyes met hers for an instant before they glazed over. The guards on either side of him let go of his arms, and he fell lifeless to the floor.

'Father, Father!' screamed Maya, tears spilling down her face. She struggled with the guards, pleading with them to let her go, while the crowd yelled its approval. They'd come to see a flogging of someone so disliked as Maya, only to be rewarded by a killing instead.

Surprisingly, the overseer nodded to her guards, who released their grip, letting her run to her father's body. The roar of the crowd receded in her ears as she knelt by her father's side. 'No, no, no,' she sobbed, 'you can't leave me.' She felt something hard strike her head and glanced up, expecting to see it was a guard who'd struck her, but instead realised someone from the crowd had thrown a stone, as more were getting ready to hurl them.

Their dislike of her gave them courage, but the guards drew their blades, and the crowd settled, content to revel in her misery.

Maya ignored them and turned back to her father, 'I won't let you leave me,' she whispered, and put her hands on his chest then reached for her gift.

It was a dark day, and everyone watching saw it happen. One moment Maya was on her knees, the lifeless body of her father catching her falling tears on his dead face, and then a glow surrounded her, spreading, moving down to cover his body.

Maya called upon her gift to flow like never before, and her father's wounds healed, the gaping holes on his chest closed, yet despite this, he didn't breathe. So she called upon it even more, and the light shone brighter and brighter, causing everyone to take a step backwards and shield their eyes.

She was unaware of anything around her, oblivious to the ground shaking, the guards and the overseer stumbling away. She was blind to the bright green grass pushing up from the dusty ground all over the justice turf, of flowers blooming in the brightest colours. She was unaware of the hard wooden posts that had held countless victims, shooting skyward, growing branches and leaves until the whole justice turf was a green oasis of life in a blighted blackened place.

Maya willed for her father's heart to beat again for him to awaken, but his eyes stayed closed despite her efforts. He remained lifeless. Barely able to keep her eyes open, exhausted, Maya felt something hard strike her again. This time it was the haft of a guard's spear, and she collapsed on top of her father's body, breathing, but otherwise as still as he was.

The overseer, shocked beyond all belief, finally found his voice. 'Take her and lock her up. She is tainted with darkness, and there is the proof,' he shouted, and gestured all around. 'By the orders of the Witch-King, she'll be taken to Kingshold as do all those who exhibit a gift, where her fate will be decided.'

Maya's body was lifted by the guards and taken away to the settlement gaol, and still, the crowd remained. They whispered, pointed, and looked in wonder at what they now beheld in the midst of their filthy settlement. This girl that they all despised had done *this*. She had healed her father's wounds, not brought him back to life maybe, but healed his wounds and healed the land.

How could someone who did this be tainted with darkness? It was beyond their comprehension. Finally, people were chivvied by the equally shocked guards, and they started returning to their work, their stalls, the mines, but as they did, they kept glancing back.

For there was now a wondrous garden where once had been the justice turf. A place of suffering was replaced with one of unimaginable beauty … and as they returned, the word spread of what they'd seen and of what Maya had done.

Chapter IV

Later that evening, almost a thousand leagues to the north, the Witch-King sat upon his throne, eyes closed as he breathed steadily in a light sleep.

At the bottom of the steps leading to the dais sat his general, a drawn sword across his lap. As he waited, the man ran his callused thumb over the blade, watching as it paired the hard skin without any resistance. This sword had taken so many lives, so many. How easy it should be for him to stand, walk up the five steps to the throne, slit the Witch-King's throat, or even plunge it into his chest, to watch and revel in the king's dying moments.

He stood fluidly, and with every ounce of his will, he tried to take those steps. Sweat broke out across his brow, his muscles bulged with the effort, and he tried, oh how he tried, but he couldn't take them. He'd been trying for so many years, so why should today be any different, but one day, if not today, then maybe tomorrow. He sat down again, crossed his legs, allowed his breathing to settle, and started thinking again … how easy it would be to stand and walk the five steps.

As he did, the Witch-King's eyes opened. Those white eyes, devoid of any emotion, pale as a corpse, all-seeing, all-knowing.

Daleth, the Witch-King, smiled and slowly shook his head.

The general sheathed his blade. 'How may I serve you, my king?' he asked.

'You would have thought,' said Daleth in gentle mockery, 'that you would be grateful for your life and for the lives I give you, for the power you have because of me. Maybe one day I will free you and let you choose your fate, but not yet. We are close to launching our attack on the Freestates, and despite your internal conflicts, you have proven invaluable, and I know you are looking forward to the campaign even if you pretend otherwise.' He sighed, seeing the lack of effect his words were having.

'Anyway,' said Daleth, 'I have just been conversing with the repulsive overseer of Angkorian. He advised me of a gifted young woman who is now languishing in the settlement gaol due to a rather interesting infraction of the law. It transpires that she's the one I discovered spying on us just the other night.

'It seems that on top of keeping her gift of spirit travelling hidden until now, she has also concealed a far more remarkable one. She tried to heal her recently deceased father and, in doing so, healed the very land that had already given me much sustenance. What advice would you give your king?'

The general looked up, considering. 'You should have her killed, my king,' he said. 'You are a drainer of life, and she is apparently a gifted healer, the direct counterpoint to your power and thus possibly dangerous. We are about to launch an invasion, and we do not need distractions when everything you desire is on the other side of the border. Better to have her killed now, don't take any risks, however small.' The general fell silent.

'Is there another option you would care to share?' asked Daleth again.

His general pondered further. 'Another option would be to let her live, have her brought here to restore life to the land, and then see if you can drain it again. If so, this would provide you with a renewable source of life, at least until her mortal body perishes. However, you need to consider that if she heals the land, the peasants who farm it will be happier, and thus you will feed less from their misery and pain. You will gain with one hand but lose with the other.'

'Good advice and very insightful,' mused Daleth. 'We are so close to invading the Freestates, and our lands and its people are drained, with the life they give diminishing as do they. Oh, to feel the surge of new strength run through my veins again.'

The Witch-King leaned back in his throne, eyes closed, contemplating for a while before they snapped open, his mind made up. 'I have decided to have the girl brought to me, as her gift may be invaluable in years to come.'

He picked at some fruit as he sat there, then smiled. 'Where are my manners?' he asked in amusement. 'Here I am eating, and you haven't eaten properly, for what, weeks? Loyalty and service should always be rewarded, even if it isn't always entirely freely given.'

He clapped his hands, and shortly the doors to the throne room opened. The guards outside ushered a serving girl through the doors, and they closed behind her. She walked a little nervously toward them, the two most powerful men in the kingdom who had reputations that could scarce be believed.

Moments later, she stood before the throne. 'What can I get you, my king?' she asked, head lowered in deference.

'My general here is hungry,' said the Witch-King, smiling without a hint of kindness. 'I want you to feed him.'

The serving girl turned. 'What would you like, my lord?' she asked, then stepped closer for the general's head was down, and he seemed to be saying something she couldn't quite hear.

Suddenly his hand shot out to pull her roughly to him. He opened his mouth as his eyes shone a terrible red. Before the girl had a chance to scream, his teeth closed on her neck, biting deep, and as her struggles grew weaker, he began to drink noisily.

'Why do you still endeavour to kill me after all of these years?' asked the Witch-King, as he watched the feast. 'Didn't I show you mercy those many years ago when all around you had died?'

But his general didn't answer, nor could he, for the insatiable hunger of what lay within consumed him.

Daleth yawned, then rose to his feet, turning toward his chambers; it was time for him to sleep. He looked over his shoulder as he walked away. 'Good night, Alano,' he said.

Taran sighed as he lay on his bunk, looking up at the ceiling. He was resigned to never getting out of this mess, for now it seemed inevitable he was destined to live and die in the army.

He'd hoped Rakan would discreetly let him go his own way once the furore over him still breathing had died down, but it seemed Rakan had decided that full-time army life was the only way to save him.

'Listen to me, lad,' he'd said, that first night while stitching Taran's face. 'That brand of banishment on your arm means you'll never be safe, never have a home or respect, and next time you hit someone too hard, it's unlikely anyone will be there to pull your sorry self out of the fire. Take the uniform, swear the oath, wear the amulet of the Witch-King, and your worries are mostly over. After that, your only concerns are not being killed during training or getting stabbed in the back by one of the other men. Oh, and not forgetting the war we'll be fighting with the Freestates now the army is ready.'

Taran hadn't found the arguments that persuasive. There seemed to be many ways to end up dead, and he'd no wish to be involved in any killing either. Still, he'd nodded his sincere thanks to Rakan, pretended to be grateful for his corporal's rank, and promised he would make him proud.

He'd felt sorry for lying, as he intended to escape this predicament as soon as possible, but it dawned on him that with the scars on his face, there'd be no hiding the fact he was in the army. No one left at his age once conscripted unless from loss of limb, so he'd be identified as a deserter, and his life would end very quickly.

So thanks to his immediate promotion, he would be stuck where he least wanted to be, amongst these degenerates, murderers, and general bullying scum who made up the Witch-King's army. What else could he do unless he lived the rest of his life on his own in the depths of a forest somewhere, or managed to escape across the border to either the Eyre or the Freestates?

His thoughts were interrupted as Rakan stomped through the barracks, talking to each of the men briefly before making his way to Taran.

'In three days, we go to the garrison town of Pilla, and there we will do the formalities. I'll pull in a few favours and keep you posted with the lads and me. You'll fit right in.' advised Rakan.

Taran didn't feel exactly complimented by that statement, but he had to make the best of this terrible situation.

'Over the next few days,' continued Rakan, 'unless new orders come in, we are going to be training and training hard. You and these lads need to get your weapon skills honed. War is coming, and we need to be ready.'

Rakan's eyes looked misty, 'I can't wait,' he said, 'I just can't wait. The slaughter, the blood, the pleas for mercy, it makes you feel so alive!'

Taran was reminded then of just how twisted Rakan was and smiled in pretend appreciation. 'Just show me how it's done,' he said, 'and I'll follow you into the nine hells.'

The next day Taran rose at dawn to a horrible breakfast of foul porridge and bread. Still, he thought, as he wolfed it down, it was plentiful, and he didn't have to pay for it, so perhaps it wasn't so bad after all.

The small settlement barracks had a training yard behind it, straw dummies for bow, spear, throwing knife practice, and an open area for duelling with the extra heavy wooden practice swords and shields that weighed much more than the real blades.

'Get used to swinging something this heavy,' Rakan had said, 'and when it comes to fighting with the real thing, it'll feel far lighter in your hand!' Taran couldn't disagree with that logic.

As the soldiers walked out into the cold morning air, Taran wished he could be somewhere else, but perhaps this would be better than going from settlement to settlement, fighting for coins before being moved on.

The sun moved slowly across the sky as they went to work on their archery skills. Taran had never used a bow before. How difficult could it be? But he soon found out. The other soldiers had all practised at length before, and whereas they could hit the target dummies all of the time, Taran missed frequently.

They were merciless in their derision, and Rakan came over to Taran. 'You are making yourself and me look bad,' he said. 'I made you a corporal, and if they don't respect you, they won't follow your command.'

Taran redoubled his efforts, but whilst he improved a little, he mostly failed and felt miserable for it. Men who had only a couple of nights before looked favourably on him soon started to mutter under their breaths, all in the short space of the morning. Why had he been given a corporal's rank while for the most they were still privates, and he so inept?

When they stopped for lunch, and he took his platter of grey food to the tables, the other men moved slightly away from him in a visible display of contempt. The break was short, and Taran groaned at the thought of more bow practice, but to his relief, Rakan was giving out heavy wooden practice swords.

Rakan said nothing until Taran came at the last. 'Don't make me cut those corporal's marks off your face,' he said, 'otherwise you won't have a face left!'

Taran laughed, but when Rakan didn't respond, he realised it had been no joke.

As the men moved into the yard, they spread out and pulled off their shirts in the weak sunlight to limber up, swinging the heavy blunted wooden weapons back and forth in practised swings. He noticed they'd all taken the oath already because all of them wore the dark amulet of the king around their necks, hanging heavy against their chests.

Taran thought it best to emulate and pulled off his loose upper clothing and saw some of the men turn to watch, ready to find something further to laugh at. He'd always hidden his frame under baggy clothes, walked slightly stooped so that people would underestimate him on the justice turf, but now he saw in their eyes the first signs of grudging respect.

All those years spent in the blacksmith as his father's apprentice had left their mark. The thousands of times he'd lifted the weighty hammer, again and again, worked the bellows throughout the day, and felled trees had made Taran's upper body as strong and solid as it could be. His chest was deep, his arms long and powerfully muscled, and his shoulders broad.

Rakan walked past. 'Short warmup,' he shouted, then slapped Taran hard on the stomach. 'Need to lose a little bit down there,' he said.

Taran grimaced at the stinging blow as well as the truth of the comment. He did like his ale rather too much.

Swords were not unfamiliar to Taran, as both he and his father had made them more than any scythe, hoe, pot, or pan, as the growing army needed to be armed. So Taran, at an early age, had forged them, tried them on the hard wooden post outside the smithy, to ensure the blades were true, so he and his father's life wouldn't be forfeit for providing a poorly made weapon.

He'd also watched the soldiers train and emulated them whenever he tested the blades, so whilst his moves were clumsy in comparison, still, he knew some basics. However heavy, this wooden sword was nowhere near the weight of the smith's hammer that he'd swung day after day, and it felt light in his hand.

'Right. Time to work. Pair up!' shouted Rakan.

Taran found himself opposite Lexis, a tall and lithe soldier who had been making the majority of the biting comments that very morning.

Lexis smiled cruelly. 'I've been watching you,' he sneered. 'You seem likely to have as much idea about swordplay as you do about bow craft.'

'Three turns of the glass sparring!' shouted Rakan, and Taran turned his attention back to Lexis.

'I'm going to have those corporal's scars,' Lexis said, 'and you ... you will have no face left.' He laughed at his own joke, having overheard Rakan's comment to Taran earlier.

Taran knew Lexis would be the better swordsman, and it was obviously his intent to showcase his skill at Taran's expense. This was the first time he'd faced something other than a wooden post with a sword in his hand, but he also had his gift, and that would give him the advantage.

'I can smell your fear!' said Lexis, lunging forward in the same moment, arm extended, sword tip flashing for Taran's bare chest.

Even though these wooden swords were blunt, a blow like that would likely crack ribs. This wasn't a sparring blow; this was meant to hurt, to put him down, firmly in his place, and likely in the hands of the settlement's disgusting excuse for a healer.

However, Taran had used his gift to read the move and stepped past the thrust. He closed the distance before Lexis could recover, firmed his grip on the hilt of his sword, and punched Lexis full on the nose with the crossguard.

Lexis hit the ground hard, his eyes glazed. Blood splashed down his face as he looked up in incomprehension at Taran, standing casually over him.

'I'm not sure you can smell my fear now,' said Taran, with a mocking grin. 'In fact, I think you might find it hard to smell anything for a while with that broken nose of yours.'

Quietness descended on the courtyard as the rest of the soldiers stopped sparring and stared at Lexis as he lay moaning on the ground.

'I ordered sparring, not a bloody execution. Now get back to work!' commanded Rakan furiously, and as he said this, he pulled off his shirt. 'Lexis,' he shouted, 'get yourself to the healers, and the rest of you, it seems like you are now short a practice partner, so I'll be joining in today.'

Mutters of dismay answered this announcement, and as Taran sparred against other opponents, he wondered what would happen when he faced Rakan, for he didn't seem to be at all happy with what had happened to Lexis.

The next bouts would have been fun if he hadn't worried about what Rakan had in mind. He wanted to read him, but there was so much going on, and he had to focus on his direct opponent, so never had a chance.

One after another, he faced his more experienced squadmates, and each time he used his gift without conscious thought to block and sidestep, to parry and trip.

Unexpectedly, Rakan called a halt, and Taran, with relief, thought that would be that, but instead, Rakan asked for the men to form a circle and called Taran forward.

Gone were the mocking looks, the sarcastic comments, the envy in their eyes. As Taran stepped forward, they clapped him on the back to encourage him. In turn, he'd defeated each of them, but now he was going to be schooled by Rakan, and they were all behind him as one of them, even if he was going to lose.

For the first time that day, Taran felt some warmth for the other soldiers, well, maybe not Lexis, but he felt a strange sense of belonging.

As Rakan stepped forward, Taran reached out with his gift and straight away could tell Rakan was there to give him a lesson, and a hard one.

Taran had a choice, to let it happen or to give a lesson himself. He smiled, time to teach Rakan a lesson. Not a harsh one, not even make him look bad in front of the others, just tire the older man out.

He looked at Rakan properly for the first time, meeting his steely gaze, and confidently met it with his own. Rakan's body was strongly muscled but also hideous, a quilt of scars covered his skin, and where there weren't scars, there were sores from skin rot. Taran was just glad this wasn't wrestling, or he would have surrendered straight away before getting into any sort of clinch.

There was no talk. Rakan, his face serious and frightening to behold, raised his wooden sword in salute, and Taran did the same, the soldiers chanting in the background as they faced off.

Rakan attacked with an overhand slash, but Taran was already raising his shield to deflect while stepping forward in an attempt to land a blow of his own. Back and forth they exchanged cut and thrust, slash and parry.

After several exchanges with neither gaining an advantage, Rakan stepped back a little, his eyes wide open in surprise. 'You are very talented,' he said, 'but it's time to finish this now.'

Taran smiled to himself, time to finish it indeed, then Rakan swapped his sword from left to right hand, settled his shield back on to the left. Taran raised his eyebrow in a question.

'I'm better with my right hand,' Rakan answered with a grin.

Several moments later, Taran opened his eyes to find himself looking up at the grey sky with a ringing in his ears and the taste of blood in his mouth. 'What happened?' he asked groggily.

Rakan leant over him, pulling him to his feet. 'I'm always picking your damn lifeless body up off the ground, that's what happened. Stop fainting all the time!' The men laughed, and Taran couldn't help but laugh with them as they filed back into the barracks for a break.

As Taran went inside to help himself to some food, some other soldiers sat at a table, made room, and beckoned him over. Before he could oblige, Rakan pulled him briefly to one side. Here comes the lecture, thought Taran.

Instead, Rakan gave a rare genuine smile. 'I'm impressed with you, lad. After this morning's debacle with the bow, I thought I'd made a big, big mistake giving you a corporal's rank. But, the way you put Lexis down so damn hard, so quickly, and then took it a little easier on the others just earned you their respect. Well done.

'As for your sword fighting skills, your footwork is good, your defense is impressive, but your attack is awful, and your technique is raw. Saying all of that, your reflexes are like nothing I've ever seen. I didn't think you'd last a few heartbeats against me, and instead, you made me use my best hand!'

Taran grimaced at this. He hadn't lost a fight before, but then again, he'd never fought with swords before either. He didn't like losing.

Rakan laughed at the look on his face. 'From now on,' he said, 'I'll be working closely with you. You've got real talent, lad, and it won't be long before you're able to use a sword properly, as opposed to swinging it like a smith's hammer. Now, go sit with the boys; you earned a short break.

'Three turns of the glass, and it's spear practice!' Rakan yelled as Taran walked away, and everyone groaned.

Antoc felt exhausted. He could barely hold on to the horse's reins, even stay awake, but he knew he had to. Fortunately, the horse knew the way to the garrison, and devoid of any meaningful instruction, it followed its training to return home, where food and water awaited it.

That damned creature, breaking his face, killing his men, and then drinking his blood. He felt physically sick at the memory of the hideous sound Kalas had made while drinking from his wound.

'Just wait,' he muttered under his breath, trying to rouse himself to anger. 'Just wait, you filthy creature. Once I warn the garrison, they'll hunt you down whatever you are.' He just hoped there was no need to be there when it happened, for he couldn't shake the bone-deep fear which he still shook from.

Finally, the walls of the garrison fort came into sight. Antoc dug his heels into the flanks of the mare, and she obediently broke into a trot, almost dislodging him from the saddle, but he held on. As the horse approached the gates, they opened, and a group of soldiers waited inside.

He wanted to cry with relief but bit his lip hard to stop himself. He'd made it, but now he had to keep a brave face. The army didn't take kindly to cowards; they had a way of finding themselves a target for archery practice.

As the gates closed behind him, Razad, one of the other sergeants, stepped forward. Antoc smiled in relief, he wasn't a friend, but as a fellow sergeant, he would surely help. 'Razad,' he said, his voice sounding weak and strange, 'help me, will you?'

Razad, his eyes cold, sneered up at him. 'Who the hell are you?' he asked, 'and why are you in uniform and riding one of our horses?'

Hands pulled him roughly from the saddle, and he couldn't help but cry out in pain at the treatment. 'Watch how you handle me,' he said to one of the privates who pushed him to the ground. 'I'll have your bloody guts for this!' Yet his voice was weak and lacked the bite of command it usually had. The group of soldiers laughed.

Razad stepped forward and planted his boot in the small of Antoc's back, and pushed him face down into a muddy puddle. Everyone laughed even louder.

'Razad. It's me, Antoc!' he implored, scared now, water dripping from his face. 'Why are you doing this? They're dead, all dead, every one of them, only I survived. I need to report to Captain Hess, and the overseer needs to be there too.'

Antoc pushed himself to his knees and the muddy water of the puddle slowly stilled beneath him.

'There's something strange going on here,' he heard Razad say to one of the men. 'Fetch the captain, and while you're at it, the overseer too. We've got nine men overdue, and if this wretch knows anything, we're going to find out exactly what it is.'

'Wretch?' thought Antoc. 'What's wrong with everyone?' He leaned forward to look into the puddle and saw his reflection for the first time and understood now why they didn't recognise him. He understood why his vision was so blurred, his voice so weak.

He started to cry then, wracking sobs that shook his body, and as his tears fell, they shattered his reflection in the puddle into a thousand more, all mocking him as they rippled away. All mocking this old man on his knees, who was older than anyone had the right to be and still be alive.

Kalas watched the gates close behind Antoc, who rode unsteadily into the garrison town and then settled himself down, his back against an old tree. His fingers idly picked at the soft bark. It was full of beetle holes and smelled of rot.

It had been hard to concentrate as he followed Antoc, him on foot and Antoc astride a horse.

The daemon had frequently broken into his thoughts, awakened from fifty years of dormancy in his subconscious, where it had retreated to, first when his death approached, but then to escape his madness. It had slept in the depths, barely a whisper in his dreams.

Now, however, the blood from Meech's broken skin, the essence of life that it held, had awoken the daemon, rested and ravenously hungry from its hibernation, and it was relentless in its assault.

As he'd followed Antoc, he'd seen people working the fields in the distance, and the urge to go over and open their throats, to kill, to drink their life, had been hard to resist. One moment he would be thinking of whether Antoc would even make it, and the next instant, he would find his sword in hand, his footsteps taking him to end lives.

He needed the daemon, needed the youth it could give him, the strength, the speed, the ability to fight on with wounds that would incapacitate a normal man. How else would he be able to have a chance of killing the Witch-King? He sighed then, for he knew in his heart, there was little if no chance. Even when there were nigh on nine hundred of his brothers by his side, they couldn't do it, and now there was just him left.

He was skilled with weapons beyond anyone, yet the Witch-King had been building his army again for decades. Once again, they numbered a hundred thousand by all accounts, ready for the invasion of the Freestates.

Yet what choice did he have? He'd made the vow those fifty years ago and now wanted to take it up again, to kill the Witch-King or die in the attempt. He had to die whatever the outcome, ridding the world of two monsters. And Antoc, poor old Antoc was probably delivering his message inside the very gates at this moment as he sat watching. If he didn't fulfil his vow to kill himself this time, and the newly awakened daemon ever took full control … how many would die at his hand, hundreds even thousands perhaps? Would he grow in strength, conquer the kingdom, march on to enslave the Freestates, become godlike with the world at his feet, all-powerful …

'Quiet!' he commanded the daemon in his head and pushed it to one side. It infected his thoughts, promising glory, preying on subconscious desire, trying to lure him into relinquishing control, consciously or otherwise.

The daemon screamed in frustration thirsting for blood. It urged Kalas to draw his sword, kill everyone in the fort, hack and cut, carve, and dismember. 'Hush,' he told it, 'soon you will have what you want.' He needed to be able to decide on a course of action, and the daemon stilled and quietened, a little like a child being promised something sweet.

He thought about joining the Witch-King's army. To rise through the ranks and get close by joining Daleth's personal guard, but that might take years, and the daemon's thirst for blood would betray Kalas far too soon. Nor was he a skilled assassin, able to travel the length of the kingdom to climb invisible into the fortress at Kingshold to slay the Witch-King in his sleep. He might be a master of weapons but knew going unseen for so long would never happen. He'd die surrounded by a hundred corpses perhaps, but it was unlikely he'd get close.

A final option came to mind. To face and defeat the Witch-King, he could position himself alongside those who needed his help the most, the Freestates. That way, in due course, the Witch-King would come to him, riding with the invading army. Then maybe, just maybe on the field of battle, he could get close enough to kill Daleth or fulfil his vow to perish while trying.

The Freestates must know an invasion was imminent and would surely recruit every mercenary unit and able-bodied man east of the border. Somehow he had to cross either by force or stealth and enlist.

His mind made up, he rose smoothly to his feet, unconsciously brushing the mulch from his ragged clothing. He looked down at himself and snorted at his pointless action. He hardly looked a figure to be feared. Threadbare peasant rags, torn and filthy, open-toed boots. The mulch was probably an excellent addition to his attire.

He should have looted the armour from the dead soldiers back at the farm. He was far from invulnerable, as a blade, spear, or arrow to the heart, even a severe blow to the head would finish him, despite his daemon kin. But the daemon had been so distracting when it first awakened, that he'd barely had enough clarity to carry the sword he'd taken from Antoc in the opening moments of the fight. He could hardly walk up to the gates with it bare in his hand, so he took some of the twining that held up his trousers and fashioned a lanyard. He crossed it over his shoulders, so the sword hung down his back under his shirt. The pommel banged annoyingly against the back of his head when he took a step, but he just shrugged because it wouldn't stay there for long.

As he stepped out from the cover of the dying tree, the daemon started to bay for blood. The sun must be setting, he thought, as it cast its red light across the land. But then he realised he was looking through eyes that were glowing instead.

'Not yet,' he admonished. 'Be patient, my brother, soon, soon,' and he soothed it again. 'You will know when it is time, and then you can drink your fill. But for now, lend me your strength.'

He walked toward the open gates of the garrison, head down, a peasant coming to beg for scraps, and he laughed to himself.

He was definitely coming for something to eat.

Taran sat uncomfortably astride a horse as they rode through Pilla's gates, the local garrison town. It was huge compared to the settlements he'd visited, with everyone in uniform moving around with a sense of urgency and purpose.

There was a steady flow of wagons arriving. They were filled with supplies and came from the region's settlements to keep the army well fed and stocked. Indeed, as Taran looked around, he realised that if the land suffered and people starved, it was also because so much of the harvest was sent here to keep the soldiers fit and strong.

Rakan, who rode next to him at the front of their troop, saw his face and laughed. Some of the other men followed suit. 'Close your mouth, lad, before you swallow a fly, and try not to look like such a country peasant. You might wear the uniform, but if you look like a boy who just saw a girl's bare bottom for the first time, you'll attract the wrong type of attention.'

Taran nodded, closed his mouth, and looked bored instead as if he'd been here many times before.

'That's it,' said Rakan, 'now pay attention.' He started pointing out various soldiers who had different markings on their uniforms and armour. Taran could soon distinguish between standard infantry, healers, engineers, cavalry, and more.

'Who are those with the black?' asked Taran.

Rakan's eyes took on a faraway look. 'Those are the Nightstalkers, elite shock troops, and when I finish being a bloody recruiter, I'll hopefully be donning my black once again.'

Taran looked down at his uniform and at the others the troop were wearing. 'We're infantry,' he stated, then looked at his horse. 'I think I prefer being in the cavalry, even if I can barely ride; it sure beats walking.'

Rakan laughed. 'It sure does, but once the war starts, we'll be walking everywhere, so don't get used to it. Now, it's time for you to join the other conscripts and take the amulet, then you'll truly be one of us.'

Taran felt his stomach flip. In the back of his mind, he'd hoped at some point he would find a way to wiggle out of this unwanted destiny, but here he was, and there was no escape. 'Right, let's go,' he said.

Rakan led the troops to the stables, and as they dismounted, handlers came out to lead the horses away. 'Right, lads,' he said, gesturing at Taran. 'Let's go see this one signed up, then find out what our orders are and where we're headed next. Hopefully, it won't be for a few days, and we can get some rest.'

The men cheered.

'Did I say rest? I meant training!' Curses and dark mutters met this announcement, and Rakan smiled. 'They might hate me for it now,' he said quietly to Taran, 'but they'll stay alive longer when the fighting starts, and maybe they'll thank me then.'

With that, they walked across the town. It was full of shouting, bustling men, everyone crossing paths, everyone cursing. Taran was utterly lost, but Rakan navigated the streets with ease, stepping nimbly from sidewalk to road, over muddy puddles at a fast pace with everyone straggling behind trying to keep up.

Finally, they turned a corner. 'Here it is,' stated Rakan, as he came to a halt, and the men groaned. There was a long queue of men stretching halfway down the street waiting to take the oath at the enrolment office. 'Dammit,' muttered Rakan, and the men cursed as well, for it would be hours before Taran was seen.

Taran's hopes rose a little. 'Do we have to do this?' he asked. Rakan turned and frowned at him. 'I only meant,' Taran added, 'that we could do this tomorrow instead?'

Rakan shook his head. 'No, it's now.'

'Meet us at the Angry Pig Tavern,' Rakan told the other men, then gestured for Taran to follow and strode across the road. Not toward the back of the queue, but instead toward the front.

'I don't mind waiting,' Taran muttered, as men who'd been waiting for hours started to complain, as did the soldiers who escorted them.

'Hush, don't worry,' said Rakan, tapping his Captain's scars. 'They might not like it, but it seems I outrank everyone here, so they can shout all they like.'

With that, they pushed to the door, angry shouts loud in their ears. 'See,' said Rakan, 'that wasn't so difficult, was it?' But as the words left his lips, quiet descended on the mob. They both turned to see an enormous man bending down to fit through the doorway before straightening up before them both. He had Captain's scars across both his cheeks too, and he looked at Rakan and Taran with contempt.

'Damn,' breathed Rakan with a strange smile under his breath. The man lifted a muscled arm and pointed the largest finger Taran had seen to the back of the line.

'Go,' he rumbled, so deeply that it sounded as if his voice came from below ground.

'Come on, Snark,' said Rakan. 'We've been on the road for days. Let's get this lad signed up, and we'll be on our way.'

'Go,' repeated Snark, and poked his finger hard into Rakan's chest, pushing him backwards.

'That's fine,' said Taran. 'We'll go to the back.' The nearest men laughed mockingly, and Rakan turned with fury on his face.

'No,' said Rakan. 'We are next!' and his fingers closed around the hilt of his sword, and Taran took a step away.

A wide grin spread across the huge face. 'Rakan,' Snark growled, 'as we both very well know, if you draw that blade, you'll have your head swiftly separated from your shoulders as is the law. No blades to be drawn in town, but if you want to draw, go ahead. At least you'll probably look better with maggots coming from your dead eye sockets. Now go!' This time he shoved Rakan hard, making him take two steps backwards.

The long line of men was silent now, waiting for what would happen next. Taran feared Rakan would try to kill this man, yet his face was strangely calm, and he smiled as if in satisfaction, opening his arms wide.

'You're right,' he said, 'no blades, but that's because you wouldn't last a few heartbeats, so you hide behind the law. But how about fists? I reckon these years have made you soft sitting behind a desk.'

Taran couldn't believe his ears! This giant might well be bested with weapons in a duel, but in a hand to hand fight, he had everything on

Rakan, his reach, strength, and size. He wondered if Rakan's heaviest blow would even make him blink.

'Rakan, Rakan, Rakan,' Snark laughed, 'you haven't forgotten how I helped that face of yours get so ugly, have you? You haven't grown stronger in these last years. In fact, you've just got older. I beat you easily before, and this time won't be any different other than I'll make sure you're dead.'

'You fought this beast before?' asked Taran under his breath. 'By all the gods, how long did you last?'

Rakan turned and grimaced. 'About as long as it took him to catch me, to be honest. He thought he'd killed me, so he left me in the dirt, the bastard. I spent twenty days in the healers, broken ribs, arm, nose as well as other things I'd rather not remember.'

Taran shook his head in disbelief as Rakan turned back to Snark.

'Ah, so it's real blood you want,' said Rakan. 'But I do think you've gone soft. I tell you what, you beat my new recruit here, and if you do, I'll fight you to the end. I'll see you at the justice turf at noon tomorrow if you have the stones for it!' and he said this loud enough so that everyone close enough heard. 'But only if you stop wasting my time and sign this lad up first!'

'What! Are you serious?' exclaimed Taran, as Rakan dragged him into the recruiting office behind Snark, who was laughing out loud.

'Oh, Rakan,' Snark said. 'Tomorrow will be the best day of my life, one I'll never forget.'

He opened a dark leather-bound tome and thrust a quill into Taran's hand. 'Put your name here,' he said gruffly. As Taran signed, Snark reached into a heavy metal chest, pulled out a dark amulet that Taran had seen on all the other men, and dropped it over Taran's head. The heavy metal felt strangely cold against his skin as he tucked it under his shirt, and he shivered.

'I'd tell you about how to collect your pay, your weapons, and so on, but there isn't much point,' said Snark, then ushered them out of the door.

'Why isn't there much point?' asked Taran, as he and Rakan exited the building.

'Let's meet the men,' said Rakan ignoring the question.

Taran persisted. 'Why not?'

Rakan stopped and turned to face Taran. 'There's no point,' he said quietly, 'because if you lose, which is what Snark believes will happen, he will kill you, then he will look to kill me after. However, if it comes to that, I'll gut him with my blade and face the executioner's axe knowing I sent him to the nine hells before me.'

'Why?' asked Taran. 'Why? We could have just gone to the back. Now we'll die because of what, a lost fight how many years ago?'

Rakan's pushed his face close to Taran's. 'A lost fight? It's not just the lost fight or the broken bones. It's the fact that I was thrown out of my regiment after he beat me so badly, a regiment I loved, the Nightstalkers. Ever since, I've been recruiting boys like you, turning them into soldiers, and seeing his smirking face each time I bring them in to take the amulet. Worst of all, he's made a point of staying in town ever since I promised to gut him, so I haven't been able to get my revenge until now.'

'Why by all the gods do you think I can beat him?' asked Taran. 'Sure, I've fought with my hands for a living, but he's bigger than even Urg by at least a head. He's an absolute monster!'

Rakan took Taran by the shoulders. 'You can do it. I've been watching you closely. I've seen you train, seen you fight. You have a gift for it.'

Taran snorted. 'Sure, I have some talent because I've fought all my life, and I am way better with my hands than with weapons, but ...'

'No,' said Rakan interrupting him. 'It's not just talent or those big shoulders of yours. You have a gift, a proper gift, a gift which had it been discovered, would have seen you taken away while you were young to the Witch-King's castle.'

'I couldn't understand for a while how you knew me so well at the beginning, or how you fought with a sword for the first time and beat men who'd been training for months, but then, the more I studied you, the more I saw you were different. You have a gift.'

Taran's heart almost stopped, and his legs felt like they would give way; Rakan knew!

Rakan watched Taran's face turn white. 'Now lad, don't worry, I won't turn you in, or I would have done so by now and got a fair bounty for you, maybe even got back into my old unit, but that wouldn't have helped me get revenge, would it? So in return for that favour, you now need to do one for me.'

Taran, not seeing any other option, sighed in resignation. 'It seems I have no choice. I'll beat Snark for you if I can.'

'No,' said Rakan, leading him toward the tavern. 'You won't just beat him for me; that's not nearly enough. You will utterly destroy him!'

Maya sat crossed-legged on the dirt floor of a wooden cage.

It offered scant shelter, and she wondered if she would first die of a broken heart over the death of her father, from exposure if it rained heavily, or from being eaten alive by the countless insects that had decided she was their evening meal.

She'd managed to hold back her tears since the first day, and now it was the fourth. Why she was still here had been answered by two guards as they walked by. They'd been talking about how soldiers from out of town were being sent to take her on the long journey to the capital.

What fate awaited her at the Witch-King's castle? She had no idea. But from rumours and her dream, she had a feeling that it would be better to die before reaching her final destination. Would she have the strength to take her own life? She doubted it, at least not yet. Maybe as her despair deepened it would be easier to take that way out.

She'd tried each time she fell asleep to recapture the freeing of her spirit, to fly or to reach out to Astren, yet she couldn't. Maybe it was her grief or the shackles that bound her ankles, or perhaps it was because that had all been a dream, and it was a figment of her imagination.

However, what should have been an unbearable tenure took the strangest turn on the second day. A small group of women and children had gathered near the cage, whispering, quiet, obviously in disagreement, and Maya had wondered how long it would take them to pick up either the chunks of mud or the stones strewn on the ground to throw at her.

The cage bars offered little protection, and Maya had been close to sobbing in anticipation when one of the children ran to the cage bars. The boy looked around to make sure no one was paying attention, then quickly pushed a small leaf bound package through and then ran back to the group.

Maya had lifted her eyes to see them all looking at her, nodding and smiling. She'd then reached out to take the package and peeled back the leaves to find a small piece of cooked meat inside and some edible roots and had looked up in astonishment to see the group watching her expectantly.

Her stomach had growled. Had the food been poisoned? She hadn't been fed for two days and thought that if she died from eating it, then it would solve all her problems about how to kill herself, or if not, her stomach would feel a lot better. So without further hesitation, she'd tucked into the food.

As she'd eaten, Maya had looked up to see the whole group subtly bow their heads in her direction before moving away. She'd sat there chewing, pondering. For the first time, at this darkest of moments, people who'd shunned her their whole lives had shown her kindness.

She'd felt her gift like a voice in the back of her mind demanding to be heard, and for whatever reason, couldn't hold back the tears, and they'd flowed down her cheeks and fallen to the ground. Maya had let herself grieve then, memories of her father and the love he'd bestowed somehow taking away some of the pain.

As the tears flowed, so had her gift. The packed soil floor of the cage burst into colour as grasses and flowers thrust through to create a lush carpet beneath her. She'd leaned against the old wooden bars and focussed. The bars had sprouted leaves, vines erupted at their bases and twisted upward to create a fragrant roof of blooms above her head.

As more moments passed, her tears had slowed and stopped, as wonder at what she'd done pushed aside other emotions.

Maya had looked up to see dozens of people staring while more ran in her direction. Soon a crowd had gathered, and everyone looked on in wonder. The guards had reappeared with the overseer, and his face had grown so red that she'd thought his head would burst.

He'd approached the bars and knelt, a look of malice on his face. 'You have a choice,' he'd hissed like a snake. 'If you decide to carry on with your tainted ways, you'll still get sent to the Witch-King, but I'll make sure it's less your fingers and your tongue as well. Your choice!'

With that, he'd stood and barked an order at the guards to start dispersing the crowd. But as they'd left, almost all of them had bowed subtly in her direction.

Now, two days later, as she sat waiting for whoever was being sent to escort her, gifts kept arriving - a little food here, a small carved figurine there, a blanket to keep her warm. Even the guards looked at her differently, slightly less hostile perhaps, maybe even with a hint of awe, and they turned a blind eye to the children who turned up whenever they could with their little offerings.

As darkness started to fall, Maya wrapped herself in the blanket and lay on the soft grass. Maybe death wasn't inevitable. So she tried to stay awake to think of different ways to escape, but tiredness overtook her, and she fell asleep.

Chapter V

Taran was furious.

Rakan had used him, manipulated him into a situation where he had to kill a man whom he had nothing against or be killed. And for what? Because Rakan had lost a fight years ago, been thrown out of his unit, and wanted to take revenge.

All through his life, he'd always had choices and made them as he saw fit. Even after his mother's death, when his fury knew no limits, he'd stopped himself from killing his father, despite wanting to. The countless times he'd stepped onto a justice turf to fight for money had again been his decision, and he'd always, always fought in such a fashion that even if he had an unfair advantage with his gift, he'd never set out to really hurt anyone.

Now, over the last week or so, everything had turned upside down. It had started with Urg dying, then being forced into joining the army, and now he was in a situation whereby he had to kill someone or die trying.

His life, which was hardly gifted by the gods, was now certainly cursed. Taran wanted to scream in frustration at the injustice of his situation, and yet he was the only one who seemed to feel this way.

Rakan had led him in a daze to the Angry Pig tavern, where the rest of the squad were in the process of getting rowdily drunk. On arrival, Rakan had immediately told everyone in great detail how his devious plan for revenge had come to fruition, whilst of course, omitting to mention Taran's gift.

After a moments pause as they considered the prospect of a fight to the death between Taran and Snark, the men began to laugh at the situation and placed bets amongst themselves as to how long Taran would last and how exactly Snark would kill him.

Now the tavern had filled with other men who'd heard the story of the impending fight. It had torn through the garrison town like wildfire, and they hardly took a glance at Taran before they also burst into laughter, often shouting some cruel insult about his impending doom.

Taran turned to Rakan. 'Why aren't you saying something? It's not just me they're laughing at, it's you as well, even if they aren't mentioning it.'

Rakan tapped his nose, a crafty look on his face. 'The more confident people get about you and me losing, the easier they'll be parted from their money.'

Taran realised Rakan was going to use this as an opportunity to bet on the fight as well.

'I need to sleep,' Taran said, and turning toward the tavern keeper, paid the man for a room rather than go back with the squad to the barracks.

Rakan leaned in close before he headed upstairs. 'I will come and get you just before noon tomorrow. If you're thinking of running, the tavern keeper here, and his boys, will keep an eye on your room and the windows, just in case. So don't even consider attempting to escape. Now, you better get your rest, because tomorrow is your big day, or maybe I should say our big day, and Snark's last!' He laughed at this, and Taran wondered how he'd ever started to think Rakan was not as bad as he looked.

As Taran climbed tiredly up the stairs to his room, leaving behind the hoots of laughter and jibes, he pushed any thoughts of running from his mind and considered his options. Of course, he had to fight and win, but even with his gift, that was unlikely. Snark was enormous. His height, his long arms, his sheer strength would be overwhelming. How could he beat someone that big?

If he went on the attack, he would need to be within the giant's reach for far too long to be safe, and should even just one or two of Snark's heavy blows land in a toe-to-toe exchange; it would probably end the fight immediately.

The other choice was to be defensive. Let Snark attack. Counterpunch and move away to keep his distance while Snark hopefully tired. He might win eventually, but more likely, once Snark recognised the tactic, he would invite Taran to strike first, and if Taran didn't, he would be judged a coward, and cowards were executed in the army.

Taran shook his head. He was thinking about this all wrong, because this wasn't a fight whereby he had to beat Snark, it was a fight where he had to kill him. The only rule was no weapons. There was no need to fight fair or play to the crowd. To win, he had to fight dirty and destroy Snark before the giant realised there was something different about him.

As Taran focussed on the ways he might kill Snark, he began to feel better. A warmth filled his chest until he became almost giddy with excitement, and a feeling of euphoria settled over him.

Taran lay back on the bed and looked at the ceiling, his mind was made up, and he fell into a deep contented sleep straight away.

He dreamed of blood and death - such sweet, sweet dreams.

Taran awoke to a banging on the door. He laughed as he leapt from atop the bed, still in his clothes from the night before, feeling like he'd never slept so well. His dreams, full of killing and bloodshed, he would once have considered nightmares, had shown him his destiny in all its blood-drenched glory.

He opened the door and pushed past the tavern keeper, who, instead of seeing a man walking to his death, saw Taran breeze past with a determined smile on his face. As he descended the stairs into the common room, he saw some faces turn away from him, no longer interested in meeting the eye of a dead man walking.

Taran called over a barkeep, ordered a hearty breakfast of ham, bread, and milk, and tucked in with a hunger he hadn't felt for food in a long time.

Shortly after, Rakan walked in with the squad in tow, and he raised his hand in greeting to Taran.

Taran felt his calmness slip a little. Rakan had betrayed him, manipulated him. He would find the right time, but when that time came, Rakan would die beneath his fists or a blade.

Taran felt better again at the thought and greeted them. The men looked a little sombre except for Lexis, who seemed to find it hard to keep his grin in check. Taran smiled back, looking at the swollen nose and blackened eyes that he'd given him a few days before, and felt even better.

'It's time,' said Rakan.

Taran rose to his feet, feeling like a king. For a moment, he wondered why, but pushed the thought aside and stepped out of the tavern into the street. He stopped in astonishment. Throngs of soldiers packed the sidewalks, cheering and jostling to get a view of him and Rakan as they strode through the town toward the justice turf. As they walked, men closed in behind and pushed them forward like a wave.

Rakan leaned in close. 'Listen up. There are no rules to this other than no weapons. You'll enter the turf while I stand outside, and you beat that bastard, because if ...'

Taran held up his hand, stopping Rakan mid-sentence. and Rakan spluttered to a halt. 'I know,' said Taran, and walked on quickly, leaving Rakan to catch up, his face red with anger.

As they approached the turf, Taran saw Snark already there, bare-chested to show he had no concealed weapons. His chest was massive, his arms like tree trunks, rippling muscle, not an ounce of fat, and certainly not soft from sitting behind a desk.

People cheered him on from the sides, but none dared step foot inside the turf as it was a hallowed place set aside for punishments, fights, and executions, and this, Taran thought, would be all three.

The crowd, which had roared so loudly as he approached, quietened down. Taran felt their eyes on him, assessing, then dismissing him, and he ignored them all, walking confidently. As he did, he stripped off his shirt and tossed it at Rakan to annoy him, then stepped onto the turf at the far side of the square to Snark.

As he entered, he reached out with his gift and looked into his opponent's face. Snark was going to taunt before the fight just as Taran had expected because he wanted to make a spectacle. He would enjoy his moment with Taran and then finish Rakan off, making a bloody mess of them both. Taran could see Snark didn't consider him a threat, a new recruit, untried and unworthy.

He slowed his walk toward Snark, became hesitant, a look of worry on his face.

Snark laughed, opening his arms, flexing his muscles, turning around to his audience, showing them his strength, and then fixed his eyes on Rakan. 'You're next, little pig!' he said, pointing his finger at Rakan, and the crowd roared. They couldn't wait.

Snark turned back to find Taran right in front of him and barely had time to register Taran's right hand as it flashed forward, fingers rigid before they crashed into his throat. Snark tried to breathe but couldn't, and his hands went to his neck as he staggered back, gasping for the air that he struggled to suck down his crushed windpipe.

Taran followed up and moved in quickly, this time landing swift blows, not so heavy, but with thumbs slightly extended to smash into Snark's eyes one after the other, causing them to rupture in a bloody mess.

Snark managed to scream into the shocked silence that had fallen upon the crowd and stumbled, crashing to his knees. Even so, his head was almost level with Taran's, which was perfect, for now Taran unleashed a torrent of heavy punches like he'd never thrown before.

Snark fell as if poleaxed onto his back, and for a heartbeat, Taran thought to stop, but he was enjoying this too much. He stepped around Snark's writhing body, raised his booted foot, and brought it crashing down on Snark's head, again and again, feeling the skull shatter, but still not stopping, not until there was almost nothing left to stamp on.

Taran roared in triumph and raised his arms, enjoying the look of complete shock on everyone's face except for Rakan, who was smiling from ear to ear as he ran forward to throw his arms around Taran's shoulders in celebration. The crowd started chanting Taran's name, and as he exited the turf, his squadmates surrounded him, laughing, as hundreds of soldiers followed them back to the Tavern.

As the sun crossed the sky, Taran lost count of the amount of ales that were pressed into his hands, the number of times people clapped him on the back and laughed as they recounted Snark's demise, and Taran revelled in every second of it.

The whole day seemed to fly past, and as twilight started to fall, Taran finally felt exhaustion settle upon his shoulders like a heavy weight. The crowd of soldiers who had filled the tavern the whole day started to thin, and then there was just him, Rakan, and a few other random soldiers passed out at various tables around the room.

Rakan stepped close. He'd disappeared for some of the evening, Taran had noticed, and his smile stretched his scarred cheeks so that they shone white in the torchlight. 'Taran, my lad,' he said, 'I've let you enjoy your day in the sun, and you deserved it. I had my doubts, I must admit. I wasn't sure if you could beat Snark, but you did everything I hoped for and more.

'The damage to my honour has been answered with blood, and Snark is now burning in the fires of the nine hells. May he scream for all eternity.' He looked around to see if anyone was paying attention, and seeing that at last they were finally alone, Rakan beckoned to the barkeep who brought over something long, wrapped in a bundle of rags.

Rakan reached out and took it from the barkeep, and Taran could have sworn there was almost a look of shyness on his face as he passed it to Taran. 'I bet my every last coin that we would win,' he said, 'and the odds as you can imagine favoured us hugely. There's almost nothing that money can buy when you are in the army. You can't buy land, titles, or even early retirement, but money can buy one thing, a good weapon.'

As Taran unwrapped the rags, therein lay a sword alongside its scabbard. He'd yet to officially receive any armour or weapons, thanks to Snark, but now before him was a sword of such craftsmanship that it shone in the torchlight. Taran himself had helped forge swords for the army; they were reliable, with a decent cutting blade and a good point. But whereas they were functional and dull, this had seen an artist's hand.

'It's a commander's blade,' volunteered Rakan, as he saw Taran's face looking on in wonder. 'It cost a pretty penny, but it was worth every single one.'

Taran carefully lifted the sword and looked at the runes etched into the flat of the blade, the crafted hilt which fit so perfectly into his hands, the filigree cross guard, and the razored edge. Even the scabbard was a polished dark wood, lacquered and with a supple leather belt.

Taran shook his head at the expense of the gift. 'I don't know what to say,' he said in hushed disbelief, 'how can I thank you?'

'Well,' said Rakan. 'Firstly, it's a sword fit for a giant slayer. They said Snark had giant blood in him, and I wouldn't have doubted it. But how to thank me, well, how about not stabbing me in the back with it when you feel you have the chance!' and as he said this, he looked Taran straight in the eye.

Taran felt cold, his elation draining away. 'Don't worry,' said Rakan, 'I might not have your gift, but I can still read a man pretty well. I reckon this makes us even. Yes, I used you, but don't forget I saved your life, so it was mine to use in some regards. Now though, now we start afresh.'

Taran looked at Rakan, this time with warmth. How on earth could he want to kill Rakan one moment and then see him like a father the next?

'Afresh,' agreed Taran, and they reached out to grasp the other's forearm in a warrior's grip.

'Now,' said Rakan, 'the holiday is over, as tomorrow some of us have a hard ride south. We've been assigned an errand, and to be honest, we need to get out of town fast. Many people lost a lot of money when you put Snark in the ground, and they also know I must have made even more. Better we disappear for a while in case someone takes a silly risk to try to get some back.'

With that, they bade one another goodnight, and as Taran went up to his room, he ordered hot water from the barkeep to be brought up.

As the evening had worn on, his hands had started to hurt horribly from the punches he'd landed on Snark's granite head; also, he was covered in bits of Snark. Blood and other flesh and bone pieces were all over Taran's clothes, and as he looked in the mirror, he noticed it was on his face and in his hair.

He laughed then, and as the barkeep brought in some steaming bowls of water with the help of two assistants, they looked at him with an admiration that filled him with pride. They put them on the table in front of the mirror, and he started to strip off. He tossed his blood-soaked boots, trousers, and shirt at the barkeep, ordered them to be cleaned and left outside his door for the morning, and then sank his hands into the hot water.

His knuckles were all horribly swollen, he noticed, but he felt little but satisfaction as he thought about Snark's demise. He ducked his head down into the bowl, washing his hair, and as he did, his amulet kept snagging on the handle on one of the table's drawers. Irritated, he swung it around onto his back, but the heavy metal kept slipping around.

Frustrated, Taran stood up and tossed his wet hair back. It was still filthy, and the water was pink with blood.

He started to lift the amulet over his neck, but as he tried, a feeling of unease fell upon him, so he let it drop and bent his head again. This time the amulet caught solidly under one of the drawer handles, and Taran straightened up forcefully. 'This damn amulet,' he thought, and as he did so, one of the links broke, and it fell from his neck to the floor.

Taran staggered backwards, his body, his hands, his heart all suddenly gripped with a terrible pain. But worst of all, his mind cleared, and he seemed to see for the first time what he'd done.

He fell back onto the bed as tears streamed down his face, and sobs wracked his body. He hadn't just killed Snark; he'd done something so dark and evil. He'd felt sick when he'd accidentally been the cause of Urg's death, and here he was just days later killing, laughing, and celebrating. How could he have changed so quickly?

Taran leant over the side of the bed and retched, and his attention was caught by the dark metal amulet glinting in the fading light. He knelt next to it and took a closer look. There was a small grey stone on the back that would have laid against his chest. It was strange, for even as he looked at it, something seemed to move below the surface of the polished exterior. He cautiously reached out, closed his hands around the amulet, and instantly felt better. Feelings of guilt started to recede, and he had to force himself to let it go, such was the relief.

As soon as it left his grasp, the guilt and pain returned, and he knew without question that this was the reason. He sat back on his bed, thinking. This amulet had some kind of power to influence his thoughts and feelings. It definitely made him more bloodthirsty and gave satisfaction and joy from killing.

No wonder men in the army were always so unpleasant, he realised. He'd witnessed bullying behaviour, unwarranted beatings, and even killings by the soldiers throughout his life and had put it down to the army just recruiting the scum of the land. Now he realised there was something a lot more sinister to it.

He took his knife, and using a towel, held the amulet carefully, working the point of the blade behind the stone until it fell free. It rolled onto the floor, and Taran brought his foot down, crushing it.

Laying the towel aside, he gingerly picked up the amulet, and this time felt no change to his emotions. He repaired the link by twisting the metal, then lifted it cautiously above his head and paused. Would he be able to remove it again if its power remained? But he couldn't feel anything now, so he lowered it to his chest, and the amulet settled near his heart.

Never had he felt so relieved to feel the grief and pain that still coursed through him. Now he just had to keep up the appearance of being under the amulet's influence until… yes, until he found a way to escape from the army.

His decision made him feel better, so he finished cleaning and then fell gratefully on to the bed. It seemed they would be on the road early tomorrow, away from this place, and Taran couldn't wait because hopefully, an opportunity to disappear would present itself. Maybe living in the wilderness would be no bad thing after all, or perhaps he could find a way to cross over into the Freestates ahead of the invasion.

This time when his dreams came, full of Snark's grisly demise, he awoke with tears coursing down his cheeks. This was how it should be, he thought. No one should take a life without feeling remorse.

Fortunately, when he fell asleep again, it was without dreams.

Astren opened his eyes to find the sun just rising and shadows still long across the stone floor of his study. This room was his favourite, as being on the highest level of his villa, it had an amazing view over Freemantle, the capital of the Freestates, home to the ruler, King Tristan.

His home had been a gift from the king to buy his continued loyalty. The people of the Freestates believed everything could be bought and sold; hence they were the trading hub of all the surrounding lands. A kingdom of merchant states who had historically come together hundreds of years ago to dominate and monopolise the trade routes over the Forelorn mountains with the Ember Kingdom, now also known as the Kingdom of the Witch-King.

Astren stood from the couch that he'd been lying on and stretched his arms above his head. He then rang a small bell that stood on a table, and waited patiently while ordering his thoughts.

He had a splitting headache and was famished, for he'd been spirit travelling most of the night across the border to spy on the Witch-King's gathering forces, and what he'd seen was sobering. They were mobilising, and within the next couple of months, would try and force through the pass in the Forelorn mountains. Astren only hoped they could be stopped.

He'd also decided to try and locate Maya briefly but had been unsuccessful and didn't really have much time to indulge in such whims. A servant entered in response to his summons with bread, cheese, and water. He moved to his desk to eat while he looked through the parchments that lay upon the desk, making notes of the forces he'd seen, and marked a map with their whereabouts while still fresh in his mind.

Astren had warned King Tristan over ten years ago that he believed this was Daleth's immediate intent, having returned from a long posting as a trade emissary that had seen him travel the length of the Witch-King's lands. Initially, his warnings were met with horror and action. The great fortress that had been built over half a century before to bar the pass when Daleth first invaded the Ember Kingdom had been restocked, its walls strengthened, and siege weapons repaired.

Soldiers had been hurriedly trained and hired from far afield, many stationed just a day's march from the border pass in anticipation of an invasion. The member states, in a panic, had sent units of their city garrisons as reinforcements. The men and machines of war waited.

The cost of this had been vast, a breath-taking half a million gold pieces from the Freestates treasury, and all on Astren's word.

Yet, the only thing to approach the border in the following months was the continual supply of iron ore and precious stones. So when it became apparent no invasion was forthcoming, and the horrendous cost of this exercise was deemed to be for nothing, Astren was cast from the court in shame, and the forces disbanded or sent home.

Thereafter, the fortress was referred to as Tristan's Folly for the money wasted, and it almost cost the king his crown.

Astren was lucky to have escaped with his life, and he'd wondered at the time which of the gods had decided to spare him. His fall from grace was widely applauded as he was from common stock and likely lied about his ability to travel the spirit paths. Those who couldn't, often thought of them as merely a fantasy, and Astren had met enough real charlatans claiming mystic skills that he hardly blamed the king for his final decision to expel him.

Yet now, after all this time, Astren's fortunes had been restored.

A half year ago, one of the Freestates emissaries to the Witch-King's court had a lucky escape. His peers had been executed, yet fortune had smiled, and he'd managed to flee across the border to the Eyre, then bribed his way back to the Freestates. His tale to Tristan was chilling.

All of Daleth's forces were being mobilised, and great siege weapons were built to help breach the fortress walls guarding the pass. The sickness that plagued his lands reached to every corner of the realm. It had gotten so bad that starvation would soon destroy Daleth's people and army, thus reaffirming that an attack would be coming before too long.

Having received this report, King Tristan ordered the Witch-King's emissaries to be executed, border trade stopped, and preparations for war to begin again. Realising that all along Astren had been right, even if his timings were wrong, he'd sent out scouts to find him wherever he may be to have him reinstated.

They'd tracked him down to a small trading post near the border with Eyre. He'd been making a living as a scribe to a cross-border merchant, managing the man's finances as well as using his skills to procure information on his competitors.

The summons back to the capital was met with mixed feelings, his fall from grace still so bitter in his mind despite the many years passed. But when he returned, before being presented to the king, he'd been taken to this opulent villa near the palace. Here he'd been met by a court official who graciously showed him around before handing him the deeds with the royal seal, which showed him as the owner, with servants, a salary, and pension to befit his rank and return to favour.

Being a man born and bred in the Freestates, he'd appreciated the value of the gift, and his loyalty had once again been reaffirmed. Upon seeing the king, he'd been met open-armed as if a long lost brother.

So, once again, he served Tristan, gathering intelligence, acting as the eyes and ears of the Freestates, their greatest spy.

Anthain, the king's bodyguard and general, had been placed in charge of the Freestates forces, and specifically the defense of Tristan's Folly. He was directly responsible for readying it for war, training men, and hiring skilled warriors from the Eyre in the north and the desert lands to the southeast to defend its walls and was supremely confident in their ability to withstand the invasion.

Astren wished he felt so sure, yet there was no denying the amount of gold that had been spent in ensuring the fortress was brought back to readiness. It was a mighty fortress, but the question was, did they have enough men to hold it and repulse the invasion? Daleth had an army of over a hundred thousand warriors, and whilst the small pass through the mountains would minimise the direct number the enemy brought to bear, should the worse happen and they get through, there would be nothing to stop them.

Astren had considered gathering his wealth, to then quietly slip away to distant lands, for if the Witch-King's armies prevailed, all those connected to the palace would be slaughtered, be they noble or otherwise, and he'd rather that not happen to him.

Yet even though he'd prepared for it, he decided to stay. They still had maybe a couple of months, and a lot could happen in that time. Anthain, already confident, was hiring even more men, and it was also possible starvation might hit the Witch-King's army.

Or maybe, just maybe, a girl with a gift of healing might have a part to play.

Antoc sat on a chair in a dark room. Was it dark, he wondered, really dark, or was it just that his old eyes could barely see the light anymore? He sobbed a little then. If only that monster had killed him. This was a fate worse than death.

He looked up to see Razad staring back in disgust, seeing nothing but a feeble old man instead of the young fellow sergeant he'd known and occasionally drank alongside in this last year at the garrison.

Captain Hess sat behind his desk, and his gaze shamed Antoc into silence as they waited on the overseer.

'Kalas is coming,' mused the overseer. 'A daemon in human form. Hardly a message I can bring to the Witch-King even if your story were partly true. At least you are who you say you are. Razad here believes there is little doubt, as does the captain. But your men either deserted or are dead having killed one another in a quarrel over dice, and you, well you would have done better not to come back at all with whatever disgusting illness you have fallen prey to.'

The overseer, his mind made up, turned to the captain. 'The sickness that infects our lands comes from the evil doings of the Freestates as we all well know.'

The captain nodded in assent. It was common knowledge that the kingdom suffered while the Freestates flourished. Why else would this be the case unless they weren't behind it?

'Whatever inflicts this wretch,' the overseer continued, 'is just another heinous justification for the coming campaign against them, to stop their evil sorcery that brings suffering to us all. Your report, Captain, will be that Antoc and his men died from the sickness that claims so many of this kingdom's lives, and the blame lays fully at the door of the Freestates. I would suggest this type of report would be better for your career than anything this old fool said about a daemon who drank his blood and youth away.'

Hess nodded in relief. Thank the gods, they would soon rid the world of the Freestates who brought such evil upon them. 'What about him?' he raised an eyebrow and turned his head to indicate Antoc.

The overseer smiled cruelly. 'I believe your report was to be that they all succumbed.'

Antoc, who'd been finding it hard to concentrate on the conversation, suddenly realised the enormity of what had been said and started to rise in protest.

Razad pushed him back down in the chair, hand heavy on his shoulder. He bent close to Antoc's ear. 'Sorry old friend,' he said with a smirk, and Antoc's world, which had been so dark already, went darker still then turned black.

Razad was about to pull his dagger from Antoc's chest where it had skewered his heart but decided to leave it where it was. He would get another because it was definitely not worth the risk of catching something from Antoc's blood.

'Right,' said the overseer rising. 'Time to get rid of that disgusting body and ...'

The door crashed open, and a soldier pushed in.

'What the hell is this about?' growled the captain.

The soldier's gaze flicked around the room between the dead man in the chair, the captain, the sergeant, and the overseer.

'Out with it, man!' snapped the Captain. 'You better have good reason to barge in, or that old man will soon have company!'

'C-c-captain,' stammered the man. 'You and the overseer are needed at the gate right away.'

'Why?' demanded Captain Hess.

'Because,' said the soldier, finding his poise, 'a man is holding a gate guard hostage. He says he'll kill the guard unless the overseer comes immediately.'

'What? Who the hell is this fool who thinks he can come into my garrison and threaten my men?' demanded Hess, rising to buckle on his sword belt. He beckoned to Razad and the overseer, then strode quickly out of the door.

The soldier, thinking this was a direct question but finding himself alone, muttered the answer. 'He said his name is Kalas.'

Captain Hess strode through the small garrison toward the north gate, swearing under his breath with Razad right next to him and the overseer shuffling behind. He was incandescent with rage, first losing nine men when they were soon to march out to meet with the gathering army, and now this.

'Let's find out what the hell is going on!' he said to Razad, 'and then, I don't care who this man is, we'll gut him and the stupid guard for letting himself get taken.'

As they turned into the yard by the gateway, Hess slowed to take in the scene and chuckled to himself despite his anger. This wouldn't end well for the fool because despite holding the guard hostage, there was no leverage, and he would soon be fed to the crows. Almost thirty of the garrison soldiers stood around the yard, most with weapons bare, having been drawn to this unusual event, and were waiting for his orders to cut the man down. Still, he thought, let's find out what he wants first.

As he strode forward, the guard who was on his knees, hands tied behind his back, looked up with hope in his eyes, but Hess didn't meet his gaze. Instead, he looked at the stinking peasant who held a sword to the man's throat. From its look, the sword was army issue, and as the guard's weapon was still in its sheath, Hess could only assume the peasant had stumbled across it somewhere.

'Well,' said Hess, moving to stand on the porch outside the guardhouse that overlooked the gateway. 'What do we have here?' He leaned against a wooden support and pulled out his dagger. Razad joined him, and looking behind, he saw the overseer come into view.

'As you can see,' Hess said, sarcasm heavy in his voice, 'we have done as you ordered. The overseer is on his way. Now, what demands do we need to meet to secure the release of our fellow soldier? Food, some good clothing perhaps?' Some of the men standing around laughed in appreciation at his joke. 'No?' said Hess. 'You want gold, a king's ransom for this man's release? Tell us, what do you want?'

The peasant slowly pushed the cowl of his robe back, revealing a strong-looking face. There was no fear in his eyes. In fact, the sun seemed to be playing some tricks, Hess thought, for they reflected the light in a strange way.

'We are a little hungry,' said the man with a smile. His voice, strong and loud, carried across the courtyard with ease. 'But that will come later. First, I wanted to ensure my message was passed on.'

Hess stepped down off the porch and moved toward the man, slightly intrigued, and as he did so, he felt a small chill settle on the back of his neck, and a feeling of unease nagged at him.

'What message is this?' asked Hess, then drew his sword, having decided that this conversation had gone on too long and would shortly have a satisfying and very bloody ending.

The other men, following his lead, started moving forward.

'Well. I wanted just one of you to deliver a message,' and the man nodded at the overseer. 'The rest of you ...' he said, sweeping his gaze around, 'as I said, we are a little hungry.'

Hess, angry now, growled through his teeth. 'So what's your message? Say it now, for it will be the last words you utter.'

The man smiled again, and Hess realised now why he felt something was wrong. There was no sun, and this man's eyes had started to glow on their own, red, as a daemon's eyes might.

'Oh,' said the man. 'The message is simple. It's for the Witch-King, tell him,' and as he uttered the words, Hess found himself saying them as well.

'Kalas is coming!'

As the words hung in the air, Razad almost flew past Hess, sword in his hand, swinging to cleave Kalas in two, but suddenly Kalas was no longer there. Instead, as the sword chopped down, Kalas was gliding past, his blade slicing across Razad's body. The next moment, Razad fell, screaming alongside the restrained guard he'd just killed by accident with his final blow.

From there, chaos reigned. But inside the chaos, as men ran forward, swords clashed, blood flew, and screams shattered the afternoon air, there danced the daemon, moving fluidly, every blow deadly, men falling behind him like leaves from a tree.

Hess, a swordsman of some considerable skill, saw his own death approaching and tried desperately to make something meaningful come of it. He threw himself forward, both sword and dagger flashing, but as the daemon passed by, his legs gave way, and he knew that he'd caused it little more pause than any of his other men.

He fell facedown, warm blood pooling stickily around his face from the deep cut in his neck. He watched the last of the men in the courtyard fall, and wondered how this thing could survive with his dagger deep in its chest, and someone else's in its leg.

But then even the warm blood couldn't stop the cold that surged through him before darkness pulled him under.

On the far side of the courtyard, Kalas finally stopped. The dagger in his chest had pierced his lung, and the one in his leg had possibly nicked an artery. He didn't have much time.

He turned to the overseer, who just cowered in open-mouthed shock at what he'd witnessed. Kalas had to act fast. He grabbed the overseer by the chin, and the man whimpered in fear. 'Deliver my message, and you will live,' said Kalas.

The overseer looked up, a blank look in his eye.

Kalas shook him until he focussed. 'Deliver this message to the Witch-King. Tell him everyone is dead; tell him Kalas is coming. Do this now, immediately, and you live. Tell him anything else, and I will know.'

The man nodded frantically and closed his eyes, only to open them a few moments later. 'I delivered the message as you asked,' he whimpered. 'I said exactly what you told me and nothing else. He wanted to know more, but I cut the conversation.'

Kalas searched the man's eyes and felt sure he told the truth. He was too frightened for his life not to have done so.

He pulled the dagger from his leg, followed by the one in his chest. Blood frothed out full of bubbles. The pain was sickening, and he sank to his knees, then pushed the overseer to his back.

'You said you wouldn't kill me!' screamed the overseer, as Kalas leaned closer.

Kalas looked on dispassionately, his eyes beginning to glow a fearsome red again. 'Once, when I was just a man, I would rather have died than break my word. Now I fear the daemon inside makes a liar of me.'

Kalas, the daemon, began to feast.

Chapter VI

The Witch-King they called him, and it was a name he relished, for it conjured an image of eldritch power. Only his general Alano called him by his birth name to his face. Daleth. A name given to him in a different time, in a different land, before he crossed the seas.

He'd been born nearly a hundred years ago, in a small village on one of the many Islands of the Sea Kingdom as they were known, far away across what people called the Endless Sea.

When he'd been born, it had been a cause for celebration for his village. A boy was always a blessing, a strong arm to help till the fields, or maybe to pull the oars as he grew older. If the gods should smile, as a man, he might even one-day bear arms for his fief lord, manning the longships which raided the coastal towns of the land-born to the west.

Yet the celebrations didn't last long for into a land of the strong he'd been born, and from his earliest days, he was a sickly child.

Before he turned nine, there was not much to remember, too many years had passed, but what early memories he had were of his father cursing the gods for his cursed son and his sickly mother. Yet despite this, she nursed him constantly, for he was often plagued with cough or fever.

The whole village barely accepted him, as he did little to contribute, but his father was the village chief, having been an oarsman and reaver on the fief lord's longship in his younger years and thus commanded respect. So instead of Daleth being cast over a cliff and into the sea to drown, he was tolerated.

Some of his father's wealth was in books that detailed the history of the Sea Kingdom, a parting gift from his grateful fief lord when he'd taken up the role of village chief after a land-born spear had left him with a crippled leg that ended his days of reaving. So, instead of working long days digging the hard rocky soil planting crops, or spending days on the village's fishing boats out on the rough waters, Daleth had spent his hours inside poring over dusty parchment and tomes.

Years of illness, and reading in the dim light, instead of working the land or sea, had left him skinny, pale, stooped of shoulder, and weak of chest. However, he was learned beyond all his peers, understanding the strategies employed of old, of battles on land and sea, of the patterns of swordplay, the thrusts and counters. Despite this, no one would listen to such a pathetic boy even had he been invited to the tale-telling around the hearth fires at night in the village's great hall.

However, he still lived the dream of might and conquest through the parchments he pored over, determined to become a famous warrior, a reaver. His father could barely look him in the eye whenever there was the need to speak to him, but one day, one day, he would be proud.

On his tenth birthday, he remembered his mother leading him into the sunlight from their lodge's shelter. For that was the day of his passage from child to man. Daleth had looked around, yet his father was nowhere to be seen. On that day, his father should have been there to strap a dagger to his waist, lay a cloak around his shoulders, and to look into his son's eyes full of pride at what the future might hold, especially if he found favour in the eyes of the gods. Yet his father hadn't even given him this, and Daleth had felt the cold of rejection like a knife to his heart.

His mother had knelt, took him in her arms, eyes moist with tears, for now he had to make the journey to the lord's manor to offer his services as an oarsman. It was she who gave him his dagger and cloak, and he'd felt ashamed in front of the villagers who stood and watched.

Her kiss was warm on his cheek, and his own eyes were shiny with tears that he'd barely held back.

Yet Daleth had known that when he arrived, he would surely be turned away, for if his father saw no use in him, neither would the lord, and he would be sent home to till the fields, a farmer. Yet even this would be too much for his feeble body, and he would forever be a burden upon his village until such day the gods decided to take his cursed life away.

Another boy had also set out to make the journey, his cousin Gilbar. Gilbar was a typical island-born, strong even at such an early age, eyes as hard as his young body. It was obvious from the look in his eyes he hadn't wanted to make the journey with Daleth, yet he couldn't refuse the village chief who had made him swear an oath that he would at least accompany Daleth to the fief lord's hall.

So that morning, he'd set out with a small pack of provisions on his back, his fragile heart beating fast as he tried to keep up with his cousin, who had slowed just enough so he could at least walk in his shadow.

As the village slowly receded then vanished behind them, Gilbar had turned to him with a look of abject despise on his face. 'I should do you the favour right now of slitting your throat and leaving you to the gulls!' he'd said, pulling his dagger for emphasis. 'But I have a feeling there will be no need to sully my blade, for I doubt you'll even last the week's journey. I suggest you turn back now being the pathetic creature you are or better yet cast yourself from the cliffs into the sea, so your parents and our village never have to shoulder the disgrace of keeping you alive any longer.'

With that, Gilbar had sheathed his blade and strode off at a pace, leaving Daleth blinking back tears.

Daleth had stood there for a moment, and tears had flowed, burning hot rivers of shame down his face. He'd so wanted to be stronger and had desired above all else to be someone his father could be proud of, or the villagers looked up to. His success should have been assured, with his father being the village chief. Yet, Gilbar was likely right. He would die on the journey, and even if by a stroke of luck, he didn't, what kind of life would he have, hated and despised by all.

He'd looked to the cliffs and the crashing waves below. A few steps, a moment of freedom, and then the sea could take him. He'd taken a faltering step toward them. Yes, better to give himself to the gods and end this torment. Yet as he'd neared the edge, the gulls screaming their encouragement at his decision, he'd heard above their calls a different cry, and this had stopped him a mere step from a watery grave.

He'd cocked his head to one side, and sure enough, the cries had been real; his name was being called.

His legs had trembled as he'd backed away from the edge. Death had been so close, and the realism hit him like a blow, yet he steeled his small heart and pushed himself back to the path and followed the sound of cries, followed the sound of his name.

The paths around the islands mostly followed the coastal routes and were often steep and dangerous. Throughout any given year, deaths from falling were not too uncommon. As Daleth drew closer, he'd recognised his cousin's voice and the pain it held. What must it have cost him to call for help?

As he'd rounded a rocky outcrop, there lay Gilbar. His eyes were red from crying, and one of his legs was pinned beneath a large rock that had fallen somehow during his passing.

'Help me, Daleth!' his cousin had screamed as Daleth stepped unsteadily forward, yet as he did, he'd found himself slowing, for inside, something strange was happening.

His cousin's screams sounded like music in his ears, and he'd sat down a few steps short, letting the sound wash over him.

'What in the hells is wrong with you?' Gilbar had cried. 'Either help me or get some help but don't just sit there!'

But sit there he did, and far from feeling wrong, things had never felt more right. With every piteous scream, he'd felt himself grow slightly stronger. His heart, instead of fluttering like a small bird, now beat with the power of a storm, and he revelled in the feeling.

'Please, see if you can help shift the rock?' Gilbar had begged.

Daleth had slowly risen to his feet, his legs steady, his cousin's misery feeding him, nourishing him, and he walked with purpose to where his cousin lay. The rock that had pinned him was big, likely weighing more than a full-grown man.

'You're lucky,' Daleth had said, seeing that Gilbar's leg was trapped but not crushed, and noted that his voice sounded different, deeper, more resonant.

'Lucky!' Gilbar had screamed. 'Why are you smiling, you runt? Get some help!' and he'd started sobbing again. Daleth couldn't help but smile; the feeling had been too exquisite.

So Daleth had knelt, wrapped his arms around the boulder, and before his cousin's wide eyes, stood, lifting it with him and placed it back on the ledge above the path from where it had fallen.

Gilbar had stopped sobbing, his wide eyes full of both disbelief and relief, the absence of panic and pain making his face break into a smile, and he'd started laughing, his misery disappearing like a puddle on a hot day.

And as this had happened, so Daleth's feeling of wellbeing also started to disappear. He'd still felt strong, but not as much as before, nor as at peace.

So as his cousin still lay on the ground, he'd turned and lifted the rock from its resting place and dropped it back on to his cousin's legs where he lay. This time however, instead of one leg being trapped, the rock crushed both of them, shattered the shins, and blood spurted.

If Gilbar's screams had nourished him before, then it was as if his veins flowed with the very essence of life.

His cousin had taken two days to die. Whether it was from blood loss or his heart giving out to the relentless pain, it didn't matter. He'd felt as if he were eating a banquet, but when the screams finally stopped, he'd started to feel faint hunger pangs grow.

The shepherd he'd come across the next day, he'd killed with his dagger but had felt no surge of life or strength, so from that point on, he'd started experimenting.

As he grew stronger over the years, he'd tortured men, women, and animals as well, and with their suffering, he'd grown, but with their death, the nourishment ceased. It was their misery, their torment, their pain, whether emotional or physical, that fed him, and feed he did with relish.

The fief lord's men starting hunting for this evil one in their midst who preyed on the people of the land, yet by the time they'd found him, he was too strong, and it was they, not him, who'd succumbed that day.

Soon he was the Fief Lord himself, and his rule upon the islands was more oppressive than any that had gone before. The people suffered under his rule, and he grew stronger. No one who spoke out against him lived.

The island's few mages, for theirs was a people of might over magic, to save their position of influence and ingratiate themselves, created what they called soul stones from a rock that had fallen from the skies to bestow upon the soldiers of his army. These stones deadened the soul, enhancing base emotions such as hatred and cruelty while suppressing others such as kindness or remorse, making whosoever wore them ruthless and cold.

Daleth had been ecstatic with the transformational effect the stones had on his soldiers but had the mages killed anyway, not wanting others with powers that might threaten his own.

He'd continued to surround himself with men of war, and his army grew in strength and depravity. He went with the army across the sea to the west and dominated the land-born, conquered their kingdoms, and enslaved their people. He'd felt like a god.

Forty years had passed under his iron rule, and his empire came to lay at death's door. His power had grown to such an extent that he drew life from the very land itself, and he kept this a secret even from those closest in case they turned upon him. This terrible famine was blamed on the capricious gods who were jealous of his greatness.

Sleep always found him dreaming of finding new lands, new life. Then one night, his spirit seemed to separate from his body, and he'd soared high above his castle, able to fly like a bird. Over the following months, he'd explored this new ability and travelled across his lands, recognising the slow death of not only his people but also himself if he stayed, and his thoughts in his darkest hour turned back to his childhood.

He remembered reading of a land of legend, far to the east beyond the endless sea that a reaver captain had claimed to have seen when driven there by a storm. Of course, the captain and his men were never taken seriously, yet the account had still been written down, and the words shone in Daleth's mind as a beacon of hope.

He'd sold that hope, that legend to his people, his army, and drove them to make a fleet like never before seen.

Two years later, he'd left behind his people, taken only his army, and sailed east. Two hundred thousand men, half of them never to see land again.

Those who survived had landed on distant shores to find the Ember Kingdom a swollen fruit, ripe for the picking. Despite the unexpected final battle, he'd conquered the lands and had been feasting ever since … until now.

Now, he gained almost no sustenance at all because these lands had near nothing left to give. His hunger increased daily, even as his strength and youth diminished.

So, after decades of preparation and patience, he was ready to invade the Freestates to the east. To expand, to conquer, to grow strong once again.

Over recent years, he'd considered invading through the lands of the Eyre to bypass Tristan's Folly entirely. Yet the pathways were treacherous with deep swamps on either side that could swallow up whole units, and that was before you added thousands of angry Eyre archers into the mix who would be in their element. Despite its allure, he'd regretfully discarded the idea.

They'd be dealt with in good time. He'd attack them from the east once he'd conquered the Freestates.

His thoughts were interrupted by a whisper in his mind, a spirit voice.

He sighed and closed his eyes. The image of an overseer filled his mind, and the man's face and thoughts were full of fear, but he recognised straight away it wasn't the fear of talking to his king; instead, it was something else. 'Speak,' commanded Daleth.

'My king,' said the man. 'They're dead, he killed them all, he is coming for you lord, Kalas is coming!'

'Who ...' Daleth started to ask, but the man's image faded. He tried to reach the overseer but couldn't detect his presence.

What should he do? The logistics of launching an invasion would have to come before investigating this strange message, but it certainly deserved looking into.

This was likely nothing more than a raid by some emboldened group of bandits. Of late, several settlements had been destroyed by his soldiers in response to local uprisings and lawlessness, as some peasants on the verge of starvation found strength in desperation.

He'd look into it shortly, but whether they died at the swords of his men or to starvation, the perpetrators would find death visiting them soon.

The day's planning now demanded his attention, and as he entered the throne room, the dreams of conquest pushed everything else to one side. What matter the death of a few dozen, when he had a hundred thousand ready to unleash, and it was almost time.

Maya's spirits were faltering.

Two days ago, she'd awoken in her cage, surrounded by flowers and gifts on a soft bed of grass, wondering what to do, when suddenly the wild hope of escaping her confinement, the townspeople mounting a rescue, or even the guards turning against the overseer, vanished. For that morning, soldiers had arrived and thrown her into the back of a wagon for a journey to the capital.

Eleven soldiers just for her. She'd noted that five of them, the ones dressed in darkest black, kept themselves away from the others who wore dark grey, looked at them with utter disdain, a look they seemed to bestow upon everything they gazed upon. They'd moved with an arrogance that repelled her, showed next to no emotion, and their eyes were all black like bottomless pits. Just having one of them look at her made her insides turn cold.

Not that the other six were much better.

She'd picked up the name of one, the captain, Rakan. He always seemed to be looking everywhere at once, his face crossed with the scars of his rank, and his skin, wherever it was bare, showed signs of skin rot. He seemed to resent the other five soldiers who ordered him and his men around without any kind of respect.

The other five soldiers were younger, all cruel-looking, and one had new wounds on his face, indicating a promotion in rank to corporal. She'd wondered what foul deeds he'd done to deserve that.

The first night they'd stopped, the men had made two fires. The men in black camped around one, the others in dark grey slightly further apart around the other, slightly closer to the wagon where she was confined. They'd sat down around the fire, their cruel laughter wafting across as they drank and ate their evening meal.

The young corporal had asked the captain if he should bring her food and water, but the question was met with an emphatic shake of the head. The captain's explanation that; the less she consumed, the weaker she would become, and the less trouble they would have with her seemed to be enough for the corporal, who just sat down to eat his food.

Maya had no idea how long it would take to get to the capital, to the Witch-King, but it would be several weeks, maybe her last ones alive. So despite her spirits often turning toward despair, she'd taken that first night to look to the stars, to the moon, to appreciate their splendour, and to try and lift her spirits while she could still do so.

Now, as Maya rode in the back of the wagon under the weak midday sun, she considered that while two days ago, her situation had been bad, things were now even worse. The iron cage that now confined her might have been tall enough to stand in, but she quickly found out that it was nearly impossible to do so as they bounced over every rock on the way to the capital with a bone-shaking crunch that left her body complaining in pain.

Her stomach growled. She was famished and thirsty. Occasionally a soldier would give her a quick sip of tepid water but barely enough to wet her lips.

The wagon crunched over a large rock, and the driver swore. Maya almost joined in as she got tossed to the rough floor of the wagon from the small seat she'd wedged herself into.

The soldiers riding nearby laughed.

It was strange, she thought, whether it was the soldiers based at the settlement, those who had sometimes visited, or now these taking her to whatever fate awaited, the only time they seemed to laugh or smile was at someone else's misfortune or something unpleasant.

As she rose from the floor, the cruel laughter loud in her ears, she looked up and noticed the young corporal riding by, looking at her. He wasn't laughing, but then nor was he smiling. His face looked puffy and swollen from the wounds of his recent promotion, and seemed so hard and devoid of emotion that she turned away, not wanting to see such dispassion.

Yet as she did so, she did a double-take. Had he winked at her?

The corporal just dug his heels into the horse's side and moved on.

Yet she was sure of it. He had winked at her!

She wondered whether this was a good or bad thing, but at least there was some humanity in him, and if so, maybe in the others as well.

The thought cheered her slightly as she settled back onto the rough bench and tried to make herself as comfortable as she could as the wagon rattled onwards on its journey, toward whatever her fate held.

Taran berated himself as he urged his horse forward. He shouldn't have winked at that girl, and needed to be careful, for he didn't know what behaviour might spark unwanted curiosity. Everyone who wore the amulet only seemed to see the funny side of darkness. He needed to go along with everything, be cruel, make unpleasant jokes, and laugh when something nasty happened to the girl. Not wink at her!

Still, he'd felt pity when seeing her fall and had wanted to show her something even if it wasn't compassion.

When Taran, Rakan, and the men had ridden out early those few mornings ago after his fight with Snark, they'd been accompanied by these five black-clad soldiers. Rakan was furious, but surprisingly he'd held his anger in check when told, just accepting their addition to the mission of escorting a prisoner with a gift to the capital.

She was, it seemed, an unusual case, having been discovered as gifted at such a late age. Thus it turned out the men in black were five Rangers personally dispatched by the king, or as Rakan said when he'd asked, they were five of the most ruthless, soulless killers in the army. Merciless takers of lives.

For the first time since Taran had met Rakan, he'd seen concern in his eyes, and when he'd briefly read his thoughts, he found fear. Taran was shocked. He'd thought Rakan was afraid of nothing, but here he was, afraid to be in the company of those he saw as his betters, and because Rakan was a little scared, so was Taran.

But, not just at the fact that they had five ruthless killers escorting the girl with them, but also because they were heading to the capital and the Witch-King. The last place where someone with an undiscovered gift wanted to be, and his first mission in the army was taking him right there.

He'd searched Rakan's mind deeply that first night, not liking the depravity he found there, but there was no hint of a plan to betray him, to hand him over. Somewhat surprisingly, if there was anything he'd found at all, it was that Rakan had started to care for him, even though he was struggling with the concept.

It was hard to delve so deep and not pleasant either. He'd glimpsed Rakan's slaughter of his family, almost his entire village, in his thoughts. It seemed so fresh, and he'd shuddered at the images.

He'd then tried to read the Rangers' minds, but strangely he couldn't read them at all. Maybe that was a good thing, he thought.

Kalas had finished his feasting a little while earlier. His wounds were gone, although the memory of the pain remained. His daemon kin was quiet, sated by the bloodshed and feeding, purring like a cat in the recess of his mind. To feel its satisfaction was almost nauseating.

He took this opportunity to consider his next move. He needed money, transport, provisions, armour, and weapons, and they were all here.

The garrison town was quite small, and immediately after the slaughter, he'd searched every corner, coming across almost a dozen soldiers in ones and twos who'd been unaware of what had transpired at the gate. His hideous visage, completely splattered head to toe in gore, was a foretelling of their fates, as they quickly joined their fellows wheresoever death took them.

Now safe in the knowledge he was alone, he found the captain's quarters. They were not sumptuous, there was little room for luxury in this army, but it did have a bath full of nearly cold water. He looked at himself in the silvered mirror on an otherwise bare wall and decided it would be no bad thing to clean himself up.

Before doing so, he opened the chests in the room that had served as the captain's bed quarters and found spare clothing and boots. It looked as though when he changed from his peasant's rags, he would acquire the rank of captain, and he laughed to himself. Now all he needed were some hideous scars on his face, and he could travel unseen.

Kalas barred the door. While he was sure there was no one else in the town apart from the lost souls of those just killed, there was no point taking chances. He undressed and climbed into the bath, spent as short a time as possible cleaning, and left the water a filthy red by the time he stepped out. There was no towel, so instead, he used a sheet from the bed to dry himself before he threw it on to his pile of clothes.

Now truly clean for the first time in so many years, Kalas could smell the stink on his old belongings and wrinkled his nose in distaste. How far had he fallen in the depths of his despair all those years ago?

The captain's clothes were a touch too big, but they were of good quality, his boots fit well, and that was the most important thing. He smiled in amusement. There was a whole town full of dead, and it wasn't as though he didn't have plenty of choices if they hadn't fit.

He rifled through drawers and wardrobes for a while and found the captain's pouch of coins, spare sword belt, and dagger. He was glad this dagger would go in the belt and not into his chest. That captain's blow had come perilously close to his heart, and this reminded him of his mortality. He needed armour, not just clothes.

Again there was plenty to choose from, but as he looked at the captain's mail vest and other items, he decided what he had to do.

He knew it was mostly vanity making the decision, but there was a practical aspect to what his mind had settled on. He would reclaim his old armour and weapons if he were able to find them.

As a member of the royal guard all those years ago, his enchanted armour had been handmade, crafted to fit perfectly, while his weapons were forged from silvered steel, subtly inlaid with gold. They never rusted, and given time, any damage would repair itself.

Each suit was worth a small fortune and was linked to its wearer's heart and soul by the kingdom's mages. Should the owner die in battle, the armour and weapons would lose their enchantment, so Kalas felt sure his would still be intact, assuming time or distance hadn't broken the charm.

When he'd wandered crazed and half-mad from the battlefield all those years past, he'd spent weeks travelling south with little purpose other than to get as far from the slaughter as possible. He'd felt like a coward skulking under cover of night, but the Witch-King's soldiers had been busy hunting down any survivors of the royal families. Kalas had known his armour and weapons would mean his death if captured, so a week's travel northeast from where he stood, he'd buried his armour and weapons by a small waterfall, between the roots of a tree.

He'd spent a few days there, soothed by the sound of the water and nourished by the fish he'd managed to catch. Then he'd left the last of his old life behind and travelled further south only to fall into the simple life of a farmer and the arms of his now-dead wife.

Now it was time to return to a life he'd long ago left behind.

Kalas spent the remainder of the day getting ready for his trip. Travelling on foot wasn't plausible, so even though horses didn't like him due to his daemon kin, he'd gone to the stables. The horses shied away when he first approached, but he'd brought along some fruit and sugar and eventually bribed by so many gifts the horses decided he could be trusted, and thus he had one to carry provisions and a gelding to ride.

He let the other horses free so they wouldn't die of starvation, and then rode out with the sun setting behind him.

Yes, time to reclaim his armour. If he ever had the chance to face the Witch-King in battle again, he wanted him to see that despite the years that had gone by, the Ember Kingdom still had a champion that lived and sought his head.

Chapter VII

The journey north to Kingshold would take about a cycle of the moon, Rakan had advised, and soon after leaving the settlement with the girl, a routine had been established, and everyone knew their places.

Every sunrise, Rakan made Taran and the four other men in the troop rise to practice swordplay before they broke fast. Then, once they set out, the black-clad Rangers scouted in the distance, whereas Taran, Rakan, and the others rode a little closer with one on wagon duty.

It was their ninth morning, and they were coming to the end of their morning routine. While the others complained under their breath as Rakan pushed them through the last drill, Taran loved it. He revelled in every moment of whatever punishing exercise was demanded of him and found himself disappointed whenever Rakan finally called time.

Taran knew he was improving quickly, and only yesterday, as they'd returned from their session, Rakan had slapped him on the back and said. 'You amaze me. Give it another few sessions, and you'll be my equal. You almost had me today with that counter. Now your stroke play is improving, combined with your reading, you'll soon be feared.'

He'd warmed to Rakan then for a moment, but only until he remembered how Rakan had put his life on the line for petty revenge, let alone all the other murderous deeds he'd committed. But he'd smiled and nodded his head, accepting the compliment.

Whilst Rakan was still his better, that wouldn't be the case for much longer. Taran's shoulders, already strong from years of work in a blacksmith, found the sword and shield as light as a feather in his hands.

'Right, practice is over,' Rakan shouted, and the men were too out of breath to rouse even a small cheer as they started to gather up their equipment.

A slow clap broke the silence, and there was Darkon, a look of disdain on his face as he stood beneath a tree, another Ranger at his side.

'When I look at how badly your men wield a sword, I have to wonder if it's them or you that's the problem,' he said pointedly, looking at Rakan.

Rakan's face went red with anger. 'I can assure you it's not me, and your comments aren't helping the men's morale,' Rakan retorted.

'Really?' sneered Darkon. 'Well, maybe you're right. So, to prove it's not you, we should show them some real skill. How about you and I have a brief duel to first blood? That way, we can show them how skilled you really are!'

Taran looked at Rakan, expecting to see him gleefully accept, but his face, which had been red a mere moment ago, turned white as the blood drained from it.

Rakan bowed his head. 'Thank you for the offer, but I'll respectfully decline,' he said very formally, unexpectedly conceding defeat.

Darkon laughed. 'Of course, you'd say that. Anytime you change your mind, just let me know,' and he walked off.

Taran moved over to Rakan, shocked by this unexpected turn of events.

'I hate those bastards,' Rakan hissed as they started back to camp. 'I would happily gut every one of them and leave the crows to feast on their disgusting eyes.' But he said it quietly so as not to be overheard.

Taran noticed the fear in Rakan's voice even without reading his mind. 'Come on, Rakan, I've seen you fight. Are they really that good?'

Rakan turned to stare at Taran. 'The problem is they are. Most are selected from the gifted sent to the capital, and they are taught to kill from the moment training begins. I have no idea what else they're put through, but supposedly the final test involves giving up their actual soul, hence the empty black eyes. They're a hurricane. Maybe I could take one, just maybe, but I would die in the attempt. That much is certain.'

They returned to camp and started to eat a quick breakfast.

Whilst the food wasn't great, eating it made Taran think about the girl. She barely moved in the back of the wagon from weakness, and sometimes when he rode close, she looked no more than a bundle of filthy rags thrown onto the seat. Her eyes, which he'd looked into after she fell, were becoming lifeless and dull.

As they moved around the fire, Rakan turned to Taran. 'Your turn on the wagon today,' he said, 'you've avoided it for long enough.' The other men laughed. Riding on the wagon was a bone-jarring job, and no one wanted to do it.

Taran just nodded, knowing that if he made a fuss, it would only invite more unpleasant jokes, and carried on eating, putting some extra food into his pocket for the journey.

Taran climbed up onto the seat and settled down, then looked over his shoulder. The girl's eyes were closed, and she was still sleeping. Not for much longer, he thought, the moving cart would be enough to awaken the dead.

He wondered for a moment if she would last the journey and a part of him realised that if she reached the capital alive, it wasn't necessarily going to be the best thing for her, or indeed him. If she died on the way, she would avoid whatever unpleasant fate likely awaited her, they would then turn back, and he would be free of the risk of being discovered. They'd both be better off.

By the gods, what an awful thought. He was trying to justify her death to protect his own life. Just being around these soldiers had a negative effect on him.

The Rangers moved out but ensured they kept the wagon just in sight; Rakan's troop spread out as well, but for a moment, Rakan remained close.

'Why, if we're in kingdom lands, are these Rangers even needed, and why are they always so on guard?' asked Taran.

Rakan smiled and leaned in close. 'Two reasons. First, it would seem this girl is of great value to our king. Of late, there's been an increase in lawlessness, and they're here for extra protection. It's quite rare to see them.'

'What's the other reason?' prompted Taran.

Rakan looked bitter. 'It's because they don't entirely trust us.' He nodded at Taran's shocked look and chuckled. 'I feel the same. They're making sure we complete the menial task of getting the girl to Kingshold without messing things up. Not forgetting they're ensuring we behave ourselves just in case one of us isn't who he seems.' He winked as he said this, then laughed sarcastically. 'Don't fret, your secret's safe with me,' and with that, he rode off.

Taran cursed under his breath. He'd hoped that when everyone relaxed a little with the monotony of the journey, he could simply ride into some woodland and never be seen again. But if they were being watched all the time with suspicion, then he wouldn't get far, and no excuse would save him when they found him.

He cracked the whip, and the cart horse obediently trotted forward. The girl stirred as expected, moaning in protest as she moved to sit on the bench, her back close to Taran's. She had heavy manacles on her wrists and her feet. The skin was raw and in some places bleeding as they chafed at her flesh.

She smelled terrible. Not that he blamed her. She wasn't allowed out of the wagon to bathe or wash, and if she had to pass, it was through a small hole in the floor. It was a grim way to travel.

Taran glanced over his shoulder and saw she was studying him from beneath unkempt hair that lay matted against her forehead. He looked around quickly to see if anyone was paying attention, but there were far more interesting things around, he guessed.

He was about to say something then stopped, thinking. No one had issued an order not to talk to the prisoner. Maybe it was an unspoken order, yet none had actually been given. What would he say anyway? All his usual approaches to girls hadn't been when they were tied up, well, not unless they asked for it. So saying 'You look beautiful this evening,' or, 'are those stars in your eyes?' in these circumstances, would definitely be the wrong way to start a conversation.

Just say the first thing that comes into your head, he told himself. He'd always had a way with words, especially with the girls. 'Hey,' he started. 'Why do you smell like a bear took a crap on you?' Horrified at what he'd just said, Taran shut his mouth.

The girl let out a small surprised laugh. 'Now of all the things you could have said, I never saw that coming,' she murmured, just loud enough for him to hear.

He smiled with relief. 'My name's Taran, and yours?'

'Maya.'

'Well, Maya, I have to ask. When we came to collect you, all those flowers and plants, the bright colours, it was the most amazing thing I have ever seen. I was told it was the Witch-King's doing, but others said it was yours. What gift do you have, and exactly what does it do?'

A look of fear and distrust appeared on her face. 'I see,' she said. 'Trying to find out what you can about my gift, what, so you can report to the Witch-King all you learn and earn a reward. You are all despicable men!' and with that, she turned away, arms folded, and refused to respond to any of Taran's attempts to get her to talk again.

Taran gave up trying as he couldn't exactly blame her. He was one of her captors, and this day he was the one driving her closer to her fate, most likely death. The crazy thing was, he was also driving himself toward a potentially unpleasant fate if other people somehow learned he was gifted too.

They rode in silence after that while the sun rose. The dry summer heat and dust just added to the misery of the rattling and jarring of the wagon as it rumbled along the kingdom's minor roads and plains.

Come midday, they stopped as they usually did, and the wagon became the focal point for a short while as it carried not only the prisoner but also the water barrels along its side with the provisions and equipment further in the back.

The men as always threw jibes at Maya, and she curled further into a corner, head down, knees pulled up to her chest, and Taran pitied her. How sad to be so tormented in her last weeks. There was nothing he could do to stop it without jeopardising himself, but at least he might be able to make her journey less torturous.

Whoever drove the wagon was responsible for giving the prisoner a few sips of water, so Taran waited for the men to move away, start eating their midday meal, and then took the metal water cup. Instead of the few drops he'd been told to give her, he filled it near to the top.

He walked around to where she lay huddled. 'Here,' he said. 'You need to drink.'

Maya thought to refuse, but her thirst was overwhelming, and even a few drops relieved the torment a little, so she reached out, ready to take the cup from Taran.

'Careful,' he said, his voice quiet. 'It's almost full, don't spill any, and don't let anyone see how much you have. Drink it while staying as low as you can.'

How cruel, Maya thought. Making her believe there was enough water to quench her thirst, let alone wet her parched lips. But sure enough, as she took the cup, the water was near the top. Her hands trembled at the treasure she held, and she carefully bent forward and let her hair fall around the cup before she drank deeply. It was warm, but for the first time in days, her thirst dissipated a little.

'More?' she asked, pushing the cup back between the bars.

Taran shook his head. 'If anyone saw me give you more, I don't know what would happen, but it wouldn't be good.' He looked about carefully, and reached into his pocket, pulled out the food he'd saved from breakfast, then hastily passed it through to Maya. 'Here, only start eating when we're on the move.'

Taran then moved away to sit with the other soldiers.

Maya would have cried then. This simple act of kindness and she was on the verge of breaking. What if this was their plan? To raise her spirits and hopes only to crush them later in a sick game. That must be what this was about, but if only it wasn't.

As she watched Taran sit with the men, one of them made a joke, and everyone laughed in appreciation. It was obviously about her and not for the first time. As they looked over, she hated them all for their cruelty, but what hurt the most this time was that Taran laughed with them despite his recent act of kindness.

Taran had tried to talk to Maya when they'd set out again after lunch, but she'd refused to engage, and for some reason, that upset him. He'd shown kindness, and now she didn't respond to any of his attempts to talk with her.

He had to be careful and not look as if he were attempting to converse, so concentrated on keeping the wagon on the dusty track, as he couldn't exactly force the issue. He tried to read her thoughts a little but found that they were hidden. All these years of being able to read everyone easily, and now he couldn't perceive the Rangers' or Maya's thoughts at all, it was so frustrating.

What he could see, however, didn't require his gift. Sadness, desperation, anxiety, and hopelessness were written upon her features as if on a page. He decided to respect her silence and let her start a conversation in her own time, as and when she was ready.

The afternoon thus went slowly, and by the end of it, Taran's whole body felt shaken to bits. How must she feel, having endured this day after day? At least he and the other soldiers took it in turns on the wagon.

Taran heard his name called and looked up to see Rakan gesture to a small clearing. Taran knew it was time to stop for the day and steered the wagon as directed carefully, trying not to shake himself or his cargo any more than possible.

The other men had started to gather wood for the evening fire as Taran dismounted. Every bone seemed to ache, and he moved to the back of the wagon to help himself to a ration of water. As he did, he looked about and saw everyone was busy, so discreetly offered some to Maya, who took the cup and drained its contents quickly.

She looked up then and gave him a small nod of thanks.

Taran suddenly felt his mood lift, so responded with a smile which made his cheeks hurt, but she didn't smile back. As he returned the cup and sealed the keg of water, he thought himself a fool. Why should she warm to him, a soldier taking her toward death? Giving her water if only to keep her alive until she met her fate.

Still, irrespective of what she thought of him, this was about how he felt about himself. He couldn't let her suffer unduly; orders be damned. He would try and make her last week's bearable, even if not comfortable.

As he sat amongst the men, the fire roaring before them as they unpacked the night's food, the men all started jibing, asking how he felt after a day on the boneshaker. He was about to admit that he wouldn't be able to sit comfortably for a week, when he quickly changed his mind. 'Hah,' he laughed. 'It's not all that bad. To be honest, I'm so awful at riding a horse. I rather prefer the wagon.'

Lexis hooted. 'If that's the case,' he said, with a sly grin and wink at the others. 'Why don't you take our turns for the rest of the journey.'

Despite his whole body screaming for him to say no, Taran smiled back, and without a hint of sarcasm, said. 'Sure, I appreciate it. Really I do, thanks.'

There were howls of glee from everyone then, and Taran saw Rakan shake his head slightly out of the corner of his eye, but he kept his head down as everyone tucked into their food. Taran ate his but put some aside to keep in his pocket.

The conversation turned as usual toward women and stories of fighting. Kazad, one of the privates, raised his voice and told everyone that however good their stories were, none of them had ever beaten a giant as had Taran. He stood, raised his voice, and retold Taran's tale in all its bloody detail, at times acting along with the words. As the story finished, he raised his voice. 'Taran, the giant Snark killer!' he saluted and lifted his mug.

The others joined in, but as they raised their mugs and voices in salutation, into their circle of firelight stepped Darkon, and everyone fell into an uncomfortable silence.

'So, here is the mighty slayer of giants,' he sneered, looking down at Taran. 'He doesn't look like much to me, strong yes, maybe even fast, but Snark was twice your size and as strong as five men. So tell me, *corporal*,' and he said the word as if it were an insult. 'Tell me your secret, the secret of your victory.'

Taran felt a brief urge to tell Darkon the truth, about his gift, to tell him everything, to unburden himself. It was as if Darkon's words were not a question but a command, and at that moment, he realised that the reason he couldn't read Maya, the Rangers, or even the overseers was that they had gifts too. It seemed Darkon's gift was to command the truth, yet just like he couldn't read them, neither could Darkon coerce him.

He stared back up at Darkon as a complete and uncomfortable silence fell upon the circle of men, and without pause, he answered back. 'The secret,' he said in a steady tone, not loud, but clear. 'Is that arrogant people often look down upon their betters without knowing them, and thus underestimate them.'

Roars of laughter erupted, and Taran shook his head. 'I'm sorry,' he apologised, 'I didn't mean to say it like that.'

Darkon's face was white with rage, and his hand went to his sword hilt to answer this perceived insult with blood, but Rakan stepped smoothly in between Taran and Darkon.

'Surely it's not his fault that he answered truthfully, is it?' he asked, 'It would be annoying to lose our wagon driver so soon into our journey.'

Darkon held Rakan's gaze and then looked at Taran, who had turned away to unroll his blanket. 'The truth,' he said, 'is not always what it seems, and in his case,' and he nodded at Taran, 'there is possibly far more to this one than meets the eye.'

'What about you, Rakan? Tell me, are you loyal to the Witch-King? Is there anything you desire more than to serve, and can you be trusted?' asked Darkon menacingly.

A frown crossed Rakan's brow as he felt coerced into answering, yet he wasn't afraid of what he would say, just more annoyed that he had no choice in the matter. 'I am loyal,' said Rakan. 'The only thing I desire is to serve in my old unit, the Nightstalkers, and I'd do anything to make that happen.'

Darkon smirked. 'Anything, really? Maybe we shall soon put that to the test!' and with that, he turned away and walked back to his campfire.

Rakan waited a moment and then called Taran over, a smile playing around the corners of his mouth. 'I'm not sure if you realise how close you came to being killed there, but that was as funny as hell, and since you're still alive, that was definitely worth it to see him made to look a little foolish like that. I'd heard that some Rangers can always get the truth from their victims, but I had assumed it was through torture. Now I know better. He has the gift of truth-saying, it seems. I had no choice but to answer. However, it seems you did, and I'm glad more than you know. But now you need to be even more careful. He's got his eye on you, and that means they all do, and the last thing you want is their attention.'

Rakan raised his voice, looking around at the other men. 'You better all get some rest, as we'll be training extra hard in the morning,' and everyone moaned in concert. 'Another day in the army, isn't it glorious!' he said with a malicious smile.

Maya had watched the soldiers from the darkness in the back of the wagon, hearing most of what was said.

They were all so loud, and their stories were so horrible and unpleasant. The tale one of the men had told about Taran killing a man by crushing his skull in a fight made her feel physically ill. She had thought he was kinder than the rest, but apparently there was a terrible darkness in him too.

Why were they all like this?

She closed her eyes to try set her spirit free, but failed. It really must have been a dream before, but it had seemed so real. In the distance, a wolf howled, long and mournfully, reflecting her feelings.

Maya leaned back to look at the sky. Broken clouds gave a glimpse of the heavens, and she wished she were back in her hidden garden, or with her father, watching him cook over the hearth fire.

Her father had said stars were the eyes of the gods as they looked down upon mortals in judgement of their deeds. They would then decide on a person's fate, and Maya wondered what she'd done to deserve their enmity.

She sat there huddled under a threadbare blanket staring into the darkness, enjoying the tranquillity as the soldiers finally settled down for the night. Suddenly, she noticed yellow eyes peering at her from the darkness beyond the campfires glow, steady and unblinking.

Initially, she felt a chill rush through her veins, but as she returned the gaze, there was nothing hostile in the look, just a recognition. As the moon came from behind a cloud, there bathed in its light was the wolf. That it was the one she'd saved, there was no doubt. It tilted its head to one side as if thinking, then turned and disappeared silently back into the cover of the trees.

She waited for a while, but it didn't return - a final goodbye from an animal she'd saved.

On the one hand, it made her feel better, but from another worse, as she realised there would be no more goodbyes from anyone.

Maya fell asleep exhausted but was comforted in her dreams by soft yellow eyes that watched over her while she slept.

The next day after sword practice and breakfast, they got underway again. As Taran climbed aboard the wagon, the mocking cheers of his fellow soldiers rang in his ears, and Taran was jealous, for they would all be in a soft leather saddle.

As the men fanned out, creating a perimeter, Taran cracked the whip, and the cart horse moved into action to begin a day of bone-shattering bumps that caused Taran to wince from the very first.

He heard Maya moan in the back as the movement awoke her and turned back to see her eyes open and meet his own. He flashed a quick smile. 'Good morning,' he said, just loud enough to be heard. 'Here, this is for you!' and he slipped a small package between the metal bars of the cage.

Maya reached out to accept it and smiled quickly in thanks. She opened the leaf wrap to see dried meat, bread, and some fruit and quite a lot of it too. Her hunger, which had dissipated during the night, came back in a wave. Saliva filled her mouth as she hunkered down in the bottom of the wagon to stay out of sight, then tore into the food. She ate the bread and meat first, it was dry, and had to be chewed many times before swallowing. Last, she took the fruit and ate it slowly, savouring the juice even if it was a little sour as it ran down her throat, helping to quench her thirst a little. Having finished, she felt better than she had in days.

Taran briefly looked over his shoulder. 'I'll give you some water when we stop for the midday rest,' he said, then turned back to look at the track, guiding the horse and wagon around the largest of the rocks.

Maya studied him as he drove. His young face was horribly marked, the fresh wounds all swollen, red, and weeping as they tried to heal in a land where everything was corrupted. Here he was again, the man who had revelled in crushing someone's skull, showing her a kindness.

Concerns about him working her, trying to gain her trust for some evil purpose didn't seem to fit. That there was a conflict between who he could be from one moment to the next was obvious, but in these last weeks, she would take whatever kindness and solace she could.

'Taran. Why are you doing this for me?' she asked, registering the surprise on his face as she used his name.

He didn't reply, and she wondered why, but from the look on his face, he was thinking hard. Perhaps thinking of a lie.

After a while, Taran looked over his shoulder and smiled as if in apology. 'I'm sorry. It's so hard to know who to trust nowadays, to know what you can or can't say.' He carried on guiding the wagon around the rocks, and when he started talking again, Maya had to strain to hear him.

With a sigh, Taran spoke. 'I'm doing this because while I don't have a choice around being in the army or taking you to the Witch-King, at least not if I want to live, I do have a choice over who I want to be whilst I'm alive. I want to be the kind of person that can look at their reflection without feeling the need to look away in shame.'

Maya couldn't help but say. 'So how do you look in the mirror when I hear you have killed and mutilated men with your bare hands and revelled in it? How can you like what you see when your very face is marked with the rank of cruelty? How can you ally yourself with killers all around and find peace in who you are?'

After the angry words had passed her lips, Maya regretted saying them. They were hard words meant to hurt, and whilst he and his ilk deserved them, still, she'd never been the type of person to speak so harshly to anyone whether they had it coming or not.

Taran was quiet then for some time, and Maya thought that perhaps she'd said too much, but then he nodded.

'You are not wrong,' he continued softly. 'The story you have heard is true, and yes, I find myself keeping the company of very unpleasant men, most of whom are killers. However, at the same time, the truth isn't always what you first see.'

'So, what is the truth?' Maya asked sarcastically. 'That you're some knight in shining armour who'll save me?' Even as she said it, there was a small spark of hope inside of her that this might be the case.

Taran shook his head, and the spark died before it had a chance to grow.

123

'I'm sorry, I'm not a knight, and I'm in no position to rescue you.' Yet even as he said it, Taran found himself wishing he could not only escape the shackles of the army, but release Maya as well.

Rakan cantered over on his horse, and his face was dark as he pulled up alongside. He secured the reins to the side of the wagon then leapt onto the seat beside Taran. He put his arm around Taran's shoulders, yet it was not a friendly gesture with such a cold smile upon his lips. 'Taran, my lad,' he said. 'What in the hells do you think you are doing? If I can see you talking to this girl, then don't you think the Rangers will see it too. Do you really want their attention on you? I somehow doubt you do!'

Rakan's squeezed his fingers hard into Taran's shoulder for emphasis, yet as he did so, Rakan felt a gentle touch on his forearm. He ignored it, but then the girl spoke.

'It's not his fault,' she said.

As Rakan turned around, he noticed it was the girl's hand on his arm that she'd slipped between the bars. He pulled his arm away from her hand as if burnt. 'Don't touch me!' he hissed, and in his eyes there was such anger that Maya fell back fearful.

'You keep your distance from me, and from him,' Rakan said, jerking his thumb at Taran. 'Don't let me catch you talking anymore. You think your journey's bad at the moment? Well, cross me, and I'll show you how much worse it can be!'

With that, he looked hard into Taran's eyes a final time before he vaulted onto his horse, then rode away without looking back.

'I'm sorry,' said Maya, keeping her head down low, but Taran didn't respond, and she wondered if he ever would again, such was the power of Rakan's command.

Having had this small companionship denied her made her feel more alone than ever before. So she huddled in the back of the wagon and watched the grey landscape move by as tears welled in her eyes.

Rakan scanned the surrounding grassland from the saddle. He could see a couple of the Rangers scouting ahead but couldn't spot the others, and he cursed them for the hundredth time since they'd been assigned to oversee what had initially seemed to be a pointless escort mission.

That the girl had a gift was not in doubt. He'd struggled to keep his face neutral when they'd first collected her from the village. The new growth and colours that infused the usual dismal and dreary setting had started to make him feel something unusual inside, at least for a few moments before it faded.

The overseer and the Rangers had told them that it was the Witch-King's blessing that had brought this respite to an otherwise dying land, but he wasn't stupid. He'd heard the villagers' whispers and saw the way they looked at the girl, something akin to worship in their eyes.

Had he any doubts before that she was special, there could be none now, not since she'd placed her hand upon his arm. He looked around to see if anyone was watching, then pulled up the sleeve of his shirt a little. He still couldn't believe his eyes.

His whole life, he'd suffered from skin rot. A horrible affliction that blighted many and even killed some. It had been the cause of untold torment when he was young and the cause of countless fights as he grew older. He knew he looked as ugly as sin with every inch of his body covered with either scars or these stinking weeping sores.

No girl would ever lay with him looking like this, at least not out of love or lust. It cost him ten times the going rate at the garrison brothels, and for what; a few moments of pleasure that died the second he saw the look of relief on a woman's face that it was over.

He looked down at his arm, his fingers idly scratching at the perfect skin where her hand had gently touched him that morning. There was no itching, no redness, no sores, just the skin of a normal man for as wide as her handsbreadth. It was a shame she might die, for that was her likely fate at this age. He would have paid everything he had to see if she could cure him, or at least get rid of some of the sores on his face so that people didn't always have to try and hide their revulsion.

Yes, definitely everything, so that he could look in the mirror and see what he might have looked like without this curse.

Only Taran had looked at him without disgust when first they'd met, and for that and other reasons, Rakan had felt himself warm to the young man even before Taran had helped him get even with the now-dead Snark.

He looked back at the wagon where Taran sat rigidly as it bumped along the track and sighed again. He'd been hard on the boy and frightened the girl, but the Rangers would have gone harder, and Rakan wanted Taran to stay alive.

It was a strange thought, he realised. Soldiers he'd known for years had died horribly, and not once had he been bothered by their passing. Yet here he was worried that Taran, who he'd only known for less than a cycle of the moon, might get killed by the Rangers. Strange indeed.

He looked at his arm a final time before rolling the sleeve down. That damn girl, why'd she have to go and do that. She was likely going to die and for what, having a gift of healing. Maybe, just maybe, the Witch-King would use her to heal the land and his people. Yes, that must be it. A feeling of relief swept over him. The faster they got her to the capital, the better for everyone.

With that, he dug his heels into the horse's side and continued scouting, a smile on his face.

The day had passed slowly without a further conversation with Taran, slower than Maya had thought possible.

That monster Rakan had frightened her so much, and Taran had not looked back once since, nor met her eye as he passed the water cup at the midday rest. Now the long day was over, and the men were busy as they set up camp, clearing the ground to sleep on and gathering wood to keep the fires burning.

As she watched, Taran moved away from the group and came to give her the evening ration of water, and she moved to the back of the cage to the bars.

His back was to the other men as he passed her the cup. She looked down and noted that once again, he'd filled it, even after Rakan's threat. She tried to seek his attention, but he was still avoiding her. 'Look at me,' she said softly, and reluctantly Taran's gaze lifted until their eyes locked.

She felt her heart jump a little as his eyes finally met hers. Until this point, she'd only seen the harshness of his face above a soldier's uniform, the wicked sword at his waist, or the weeping wounds on his cheeks. However, in the dying light, the lines of his face seemed softer, more youthful and innocent, his eyes kinder.

They seemed to hold each other's gaze for what seemed forever. Maya knew it was just for a few heartbeats, but she was sure her heart had never beat so hard and loud in her life.

Taran reached out with his other hand, and for a moment, she held her breath, wondering if he would try and hold hers. Instead, he pushed a small leaf-wrapped package of food through the bars.

'Thank you,' she said, her voice barely a whisper so as not to be overheard, and as she saw a smile dawn upon his lips, to reach the corner of his eyes, she realised that she was smiling too.

He seemed about to say something, but harsh laughter from the campfire shattered the moment, and as he turned away, she saw the smile fall from his face and the hardness return.

Which was the real him? She settled into the shadows to discreetly eat the food he'd given her. Despite her captivity, the food, water, and perhaps most of all, his small acts of kindness left her feeling stronger, not just of limb, but of mind. She began to wonder once again if escape might be possible as opposed to going to her fate like a lamb to the slaughter.

As she chewed, she thought of her father and his needless death, and whilst there was still sorrow, there was also now anger, and the beginnings of a fire started to burn inside her. She wanted to end this injustice, not just for him but for the suffering all of the people endured.

By the Witch-King's order, she was imprisoned when she could be free healing others and the land, but instead, she was likely going to her death. If she ever found freedom, whatever time she had would be used for the good of the land and its people, no longer in the shadows hiding her gift. She would leave something behind before she died that would live way beyond her meagre years.

She stared fiercely into the darkness now surrounding the camp, and there staring back at her again were the golden eyes of the wolf, soft and comforting. It turned its head, and she followed its gaze, seeing it look first at the soldiers around one campfire where Taran sat next to Rakan, and then back to the other where three of the Rangers sat. She knew the other two would be in the darkness keeping watch as was their routine, but she was unsure where.

Finally, the wolf stared at the other side of the wagon, and its lips pulled back from its fangs. Despite being behind bars, Maya felt a shiver run down her spine as she realised that despite her perceived kinship, this was still a wild, ferocious and dangerous beast, and it seemed that it was here to hunt.

A low growl that Maya could feel in the pit of her stomach emerged from its throat, and she glanced over her shoulder to see the horses tethered for the night. The wolf crept forward, keeping low. She held her breath, waiting to see what would happen next, and suddenly the wolf was all flashing jaws as it leapt, teeth snapping, into the midst of the horses who whinnied in terror at this predator amongst them.

The horses reared in panic as the wolf's teeth drew blood. The Rangers and soldiers all surged to their feet, swords drawn, shouting, but this just added to the mayhem.

The mounts, desperate to escape, broke the picket line before any men could intervene and galloped off with the wolf behind as it drove them into the darkness. The two hidden Rangers appeared from the shadows, bows drawn with arrows nocked and let loose at the disappearing wolf. Both missed, and Maya realised she was still holding her breath and let it out in a sigh of relief.

The whole camp remained in an uproar, with recriminations being shouted back and forth between the Rangers and the soldiers. Finally, they organised themselves and made torches, then several disappeared into the night to try to find any of the mounts that might have escaped from the wolf.

Despite her tiredness, Maya waited for the men to return, and all of them did, but not a single mount between them. Exhausted, they fell around the dying campfires, and Maya couldn't help but smile to herself as she closed her eyes.

It seemed the journey to the capital had just grown a lot longer.

Chapter VIII

Daleth's spirit finally separated from his body.

Spirit travel was not always easy for him, yet he spent as many nights aloft as his skill and strength allowed. Whenever he did, he journeyed far and wide to keep a wary eye upon his kingdom.

The message he'd received from the garrison town's overseer had deserved far more immediate investigation and had plagued his thoughts for days. However, spirit travel took a harsh toll and left a person as tired as if they hadn't slept at all. He couldn't afford to have his attention dulled by exhaustion with invasion preparations at such a crucial stage, however impatient he felt to investigate. Of course, he could have sent someone else, but his weakness was control; he took on everything he could, for he trusted no one more than himself.

Now, however, with everything as ready as it could be, he flew swiftly south from the capital over mountains, hills, and valleys, the greyness of the landscape below him. He knew it was not the moonlight that made it so dull … this land was close to giving up all of its life to him.

As he passed above the might of his army gathered at the different staging posts, he felt reassured with the knowledge that he would shortly crush the Freestates beneath his mailed fist. He put the thoughts of conquest to one side and focussed on the task at hand.

He'd recognised the overseer, a wretch called Varsav, and he flew unerringly to the small garrison town that oversaw some of the far southern reaches of his kingdom.

As Daleth approached, the gates stood open, creaking loudly in the wind. He drifted down to see movement inside the yard beyond the gates and walked forward, under the gatehouse, not a grain of sand disturbed by his ethereal feet. What the movement was, soon became apparent.

Dozens of carrion birds tore away at the bloated corpses of the soldiers strewn about like ragdolls. This couldn't be the work of just one man, he thought, yet as he studied the footprints that remained in the sand that had yet to be disturbed by the scavengers, he read the signs of just one set of boots linking death after death. He placed his feet into those very marks and soon found himself twisting and turning in a parody of a dance as he moved between the corpses.

Finally, the dance led him to the porch where the body of the overseer lay mostly undisturbed. His death was different from the rest. There was no sign of an injury from a weapon, yet his throat was torn out and not by birds. The marks looked like those of human teeth, but more interestingly, his body was an aged husk.

He knew of only one man who could create such carnage on his own, who fed upon the blood of man or woman, leaving them in such a drained state. Yet where he stood was several weeks' journey from the capital, and Alano was rarely ever gone for more than a few days on duties and this last week, not at all.

He felt a presence back in the chamber where his body sat at rest and knew it would be Alano. Alano, with a sword in hand, trying to plunge the blade into his unprotected body, yet the blood oath he'd made with his daemon was too strong for him to overcome.

For a moment, his mind briefly wandered back to when the oath was made.

It had been a day of total victory yet utter disaster for him that day, nigh on fifty years ago.

He'd watched the battle against King Anders and the royal guard come to its conclusion with many mixed emotions. Relief at his victory, when for a brief moment, it seemed defeat might be a possibility. Anger that his plans for future conquest had been destroyed along with his army. But also awe at the enemy warriors who'd fought with incredible skill, and one in particular. In silver armour and white cloak, on a mound of corpses the size of which beggared belief, sword and dagger still in hand, knelt the man he came to know as Alano.

Daleth had never seen a man pierced by so many weapons still breathing, and the voice that issued from his mouth had sent shivers down his back. It was the daemon inside who begged to live and slaughter in Daleth's name if only it were allowed to continue its immortal life in this mortal's body. It would serve and never betray.

Seventy thousand men and his plan to invade the Freestates had died that day, but he'd gained a daemon that had bound Alano by blood and oath, and true to its word, had served him well.

His reverie over with, he flew back to his body and opened his eyes in the chamber. His head pounded from the sleep weed he'd taken to assist in his travel. There as expected, stood Alano, not disappointing him, sword in hand, yet the daemon's will held him easily at bay.

'My king,' said Alano. 'You sent for me. How can I serve?'

Daleth nodded. 'I received a message. I wonder if it will make sense to you more than it does me. It seems one of our garrisons was recently attacked and to a man completely slaughtered.'

Alano's eyes widened. 'I have not heard of this. The Freestates can have no military presence in our lands, and I cannot believe the people of the Eyre would ever dare to incur your wrath directly.'

Daleth smiled. 'I know Alano, I know, don't fret, it was one man who did this. He sent a message, and I wonder if it wasn't, in fact, somehow meant for us both.'

Alano raised an eyebrow, waiting, but he didn't have to for long.

Daleth held his gaze with his cold white eyes. 'The message he sent was; 'Kalas is coming.'

Alano stared steadily back into his king's face. 'Kalas,' he mused, 'I've never heard of him.'

132

Maya had barely fallen asleep it seemed, when she awoke to Rakan's voice calling his men to practice, and she saw them move to an open patch of land to train.

She usually looked anywhere but at them. Men and swords meant death, and they were everything she was beginning to despise about this land, but this time she watched.

Taran squared off against Rakan with a heavy wooden sword in one hand and a short wooden dagger in the other. The other four soldiers paired off as well, but she found herself studying Taran as he moved. He was broad of shoulder and strong of arm, but not overly bulky, and when he pulled off his shirt in the morning sun, she smiled when she saw he had a bit of a tummy. He obviously enjoyed his drink a little too much, it seemed.

In turn, Rakan started to strip off his shirt but paused and left it on before raising a sword in mock salute, and then they began.

Despite her loathing of soldiers and their swordplay, she soon found herself appreciating the rhythm and fluidity of the moves. As Taran and Rakan circled one another, their blades, although unwieldy, whirled in patterns, rarely still, and she marvelled at how they could maintain such a tempo whilst the other soldiers seemed so broken in their movements by comparison.

Suddenly, the movement ceased, and there stood Rakan, his sword resting lightly against the side of Taran's neck. Rakan smiled in victory, and Taran responded with a smile of his own, bowing his head in respect. However, Taran also tapped his sword against the inside of Rakan's thigh where it rested, and she felt herself smile as well.

'Enough of your pathetic child's play!' Darkon shouted as he strode forward. 'Time to ditch those toys.'

Rakan bridled under the stinging insult and started to raise his voice in protest.

However, Darkon would have none of it. 'Quiet!' he barked. 'If you haven't noticed, we are without horses, and in their absence, unless you fancy hitching all of your men to the wagon, we'll all be walking until we reach the next garrison town. From here on, we're on foot, and that includes that damn girl. So Rakan,' and he spat the word as if it were something horrible from his mouth, 'you and your men will carry as many provisions as you can without slowing our progress.' With that, Darkon turned away and walked back to his own men.

Rakan angrily barked orders, and the wagon was quickly stripped of everything, which was then split into essentials for the road and non-essentials to be left behind, such as the practice weapons.

Every time one of the soldiers came to take something from the back of the wagon, Maya felt their gaze on her, and from the barbed comments that kept coming her way, it seemed they were blaming her for their ill luck. Curses fell upon her ears, and she felt herself tremble at the hatred.

Only Taran occasionally slipped a smile her way when no one was looking, and now strangely, Rakan seemed to view her differently.

'Right lads,' called Rakan, gathering his men together. 'The girl needs a guard for the rest of the journey.'

They all raised their voices immediately and started complaining, saying it was beneath them to look after the girl.

One of the men called Lexis, who seemed to dislike Taran, suggested that as Taran had volunteered to ride the wagon, he should be the one who continued to guard the girl. Taran protested loudly, and Maya felt surprised by the hurt she felt that he didn't want to demean himself by guarding her anymore.

Rakan let the argument grow for a while before he raised his voice and bellowed. 'SILENCE!' Looking at Taran, he said. 'Lexis has it right. You volunteered to guard this girl before, and just because the circumstances have changed and not to your liking doesn't mean you can drop those duties just because you want to.'

The rest of the men laughed in relief, and Taran swore, which only served to increase the men's merriment, Lexis more than any.

Taran bowed his head in defeat, his hair falling across his face, and as he turned briefly toward Maya, he flashed a quick smile, and she realised that he had played a ruse and her spirits lifted. To want something was the best way not to get it in the company of men who seemed to thrive on the misery of others.

Rakan came over and unlocked the gate at the back of the cage. He reached in and grabbed the chain connecting the manacles on Maya's wrists and pulled her unceremoniously to the rear of the wagon. He looked at the chains around her ankles then and swore.

'Darkon!' he shouted, and the captain of the Rangers came over.

'What is it?' barked Darkon.

Rakan nodded at the manacles on her hands and feet. 'We'll make slow progress if she can't walk properly on her own,' he said. 'The boys can't carry her even if they take turns. The manacles need to come off.'

Darkon stood and looked at Maya with those dead black eyes for a while, and she felt her blood turn to ice in her veins. She was sure he was contemplating killing her there and then, but the order had been to bring her to the capital, and until that changed, she would stay alive.

Suddenly, Darkon moved forward, a wicked blade in his hand, and pushed her head back against the cage, the sharp tip of the dagger so close to her eye she didn't dare blink, let alone breathe. He lowered his voice, and it sounded like a serpent's hiss. 'My orders are to bring you to the capital, but just try to escape, and you'll lose this eye. Try again, and you'll lose the other, along with some other very nasty things you could only likely think of in your worst nightmares.'

The blade slowly withdrew and the silence that had settled over the camp lifted.

As Maya's heart started to beat normally again, Darkon reached into his pocket and pulled forth a heavy key to unlock the manacles. As they fell away, Maya felt as if something more than just the chains had been removed. She couldn't tell what, but she felt like she could breathe freely.

Darkon turned to the surrounding soldiers. 'I will say this just once. If she escapes even for a moment, whoever is guarding her will also feel the punishment of my blades, and trust me, you'll lose more, much more than just an eye!'

He moved away, and Lexis raised his voice to Taran. 'You better keep her close, because otherwise, it'll be your head that leaves your shoulders.'

Taran knew he spoke the truth.

Rakan came forward with some heavy rope and thrust it into Taran's hands. 'She's your responsibility now. You tie her as you will. You lead her. If she manages to escape, however briefly, there will be no saving you. You understand this, don't you?'

Taran just nodded and felt cold at the thought. He turned to Maya and asked her to hold out her hands. 'I need to bind you,' he said apologetically.

Maya looked him in the eye. 'You know, if it means your life, I promise not to try and escape. Just bind the rope around my waist.' She then held up her arms.

Taran saw the terrible open sores the manacles had left from the constant rubbing and wondered how much pain she must be in. He sighed and stepped forward, then looped the rope around her waist, idly noting how slim it was under the loose garments as he drew it tighter.

'If I'm ordered to, I might have to bind you properly at night,' he said, 'because if I don't, someone else will, and they won't care how much it hurts.'

Maya couldn't believe his choice of words. *Won't care how much it hurts*. Did that mean that he cared?

She smiled to herself because she was sure there could be no other answer.

Kalas had been travelling for several days, and they had not been easy.

The decision to travel at night, staying out of sight, was a good plan, but it was not to the liking of his newly awakened daemon who constantly distracted him with its demands for blood and life.

It was so insidious now it was newly awakened, its strength like when it had first possessed him after the ritual all those years ago. Only spilling blood and draining life brought a respite, and it reminded him why they'd all made the vow to take their own lives had they killed the Witch-King.

Kalas knew that the chance of the daemon taking overall control was a risk, and the more he resisted it, perhaps the more chance that would happen. To keep his mind clear, he had to slake its thirst; kill, and commit heinous deeds.

Was the end worthy of the means? It only took him moments to come to a conclusion ... it was. Whether it was his conclusion or the daemons, he couldn't tell yet, but once it was quiet, once it was asleep, he would ask himself the question again.

'Silence!' he shouted in his mind. 'Today we feast,' and the daemon reluctantly retreated a little. 'Today we fight together, dine together.'

The daemon started purring, and the world turned a hazy red through his eyes.

It was still light, and he mounted his horse, leading the other pack animal, and rode out onto the plains searching for one of the many military roads that crossed the kingdom to allow for speed of movement.

It took him a while as he'd purposely distanced himself from them earlier, but as the horses moved on to the road, their pace picked up, and the daemon started to gibber excitedly in his head. Images of him standing bloody and victorious over mounds of dead bodies filled his thoughts. He shook his head, trying to clear his mind, and succeeded just enough to deduce from the disturbed dirt and tracks that many soldiers had passed this way not long before.

'Soon, soon,' he said to the daemon. It receded a little again, sensing the truth, a dark shadow in the back of his mind, watching, waiting, calculating.

The sun started to set, and as darkness fell, there on the horizon, a glow of campfires gave away the troops' position.

Kalas urged his horse forward, even though he didn't mean to. The daemon had made him spur it to a canter, subconsciously influencing his decision with its hunger. The clatter of the hooves was loud, and Kalas knew the sentries would soon be aware of his approach as he drew closer. From the number of campfires, this was a smallish contingent. Eight fires meant eight tents, ten men a tent, eighty men give or take a few. Eighty men and him riding in alone, this was crazy.

'No,' said the daemon. 'You're not alone. You're never alone, my brother,' and despite himself, Kalas felt energy rush through his veins. Fighting against impossible odds, as a warrior, if he were to die, this is how it should be.

The road curved, and around the corner, Kalas knew the camp would be set, the sentries waiting, arrows nocked to bows. There were no enemy soldiers within the kingdom, but it was standard procedure, so they would be waiting.

He spurred the horse faster and then leapt from the saddle, rolling effortlessly as he hit the ground. He came to his feet smoothly, then ran into the darkness beneath the trees abutting the road, trees that had provided the camp with firewood. Now they would give him the cover he needed to approach. They had gained light but at the expense of darkness leading up to their door, and yet he could see perfectly well now - the benefit of having a denizen of the nine hells as a personal companion. As he came to the edge of the woods, he couldn't help but snort in surprise at how close the camp had been set. This would cost them dearly.

He noted his horses being brought into the firelight. A sentry was crossing the camp to fetch the captain, likely so the man had first pickings of any valuables strapped to the beasts. Other than two sentries at either end of the camp where it sat astride the road, there were no others. Being on kingdom soil, it seemed that vigilance was lax. The men around the fires had divested themselves of armour, and while there were some weapons racked close by, most of the soldier's weapons seemed likely to be in their tents.

Kalas, his plan of action set in his mind, simply strode from the woods, hands down, fumbling with his trousers as though he'd just been into the trees to relieve himself. Some of the men around the nearest campfire looked up, but all they saw was a man in the armour of the Witch-King's army and didn't even think to question that he wasn't one of their own.

First, he wanted to identify where the overseer's tent was. Maybe he was staying with the captain. Yes, it was time to send another message.

The daemon inside his head urged him to let it have control. 'Just a little,' he said to it. 'Just a little,' but suddenly, his sword was in one hand, and his dagger in the other, the bloodlust overtook him, and the screams of the men pierced what little there was left of his soul.

He slew the first twenty before any even had time to lift a weapon; it was butchery. Even after that, with almost none of them wearing armour, they had no chance. His eyes shone red in the night, and the men's courage left them. Those who paused; died. Those who stood against him; died. Soon everyone left in the camp was a corpse. Many toward the end had run screaming into the darkness, and he'd let them go, but not the overseer, for he'd foolishly stayed hiding in his tent.

As Kalas stepped inside, the overseer fell to the floor and grabbed his ankles, crying, pleading for his life, as the blood of the slain soldiers rained upon him, dripping from Kalas' armour and weapons.

'Deliver this message to the Witch-King,' Kalas commanded, and the man nodded, eyes wide, looking at this creature above him. 'Let him know that Kalas is coming. Do you understand? Kalas is coming! Now do it!' and the overseer closed his eyes for a moment before hurriedly opening them again.

'I, d-d-delivered the message,' he stammered.

Kalas knew he told the truth.

The daemon inside his head, while sated with the amount of slaughter, still demanded to feast.

'No,' said Kalas as he looked over himself. Not a scratch to be healed this time. 'There is no need to feed.' The daemon screamed in rage, then whined piteously in his head, cajoling, pleading, demanding, then begging, going from one extreme to another. Finally, it quietened down, and he looked at the overseer trembling at his feet.

'Who are you speaking to?' asked the overseer nervously, and Kalas realised he must have been talking aloud.

He sighed. 'Should a man keep his promises, strive to keep his word?'

The overseer, confused but relieved at this sudden conversational turn, nodded. 'Yes, Lord,' he said ingratiatingly. 'A man, yes, a lord most definitely. What may I ask, did you promise?'

'Ahhh, I promised to eat, to dine with my brother.' The daemon inside of him screeched in pleasure, purred, rolled around in ecstasy in his mind, and Kalas drew his blade across the overseer's neck then dropped to his knees to drink.

The Rangers had decided that staying on the track, while quicker, would leave them in the open and without horses too visible and vulnerable. The memory of the wolf was still fresh in their minds.

Taran took a while to get his head around that, for he doubted there was anything that made the Rangers feel vulnerable. But they were consummate in their attention to detail and wanted to ensure that Maya was delivered to her fate.

Therefore, they moved toward the trees. Forests covered much of the land, yet as they passed into the shade of the leafy canopy, the smell of rotting wood was in the air.

The Rangers stayed nearer now, but still far enough away to scout out any possible danger before it got too close. Rakan and his men were closer still. Rakan and Lexis marched ahead of Taran by about thirty strides, and the other three followed a similar distance behind. This left Taran and Maya quietly walking along in silence as he led her by the rope.

The silence was strangely comfortable to Taran, despite the circumstances. The wagon had been a horrible way to travel, but in the woods with soft mulch beneath his feet, it somehow felt as if their destination was now so much further away.

Maya spoke. 'Talk to me?' she asked quietly.

Taran was about to stop in surprise, but didn't want to draw attention, so he kept his head down and feet moving. 'About what?' he replied quietly.

'I don't know,' said Maya. 'I've never been beyond my village and valley before this. Just talk to me about whatever you wish.'

Taran was silent for a while, and Maya waited patiently, wondering if Rakan's warning to not talk would hold sway over Taran, but all of a sudden, he started.

What better way to start a story than at the beginning, and Taran started at his. He talked of his childhood, his mother's love, and his father's uncontrollable rage. He spoke of his time working as an apprentice in his father's smithy, making everything the village needed, but more importantly, what the army wanted. He told of growing up using his fists and how his father used to beat him and his mother. He blinked back tears as he told Maya of his mother's death at his father's hands, how this led to an unusual life on the road, then Urg's death, which led to him joining the army.

He told her about everything, everything but the one thing he had to keep secret, his gift.

By the time the midday rest was called, Taran had talked since first light and had told Maya things he'd shared with no one else. She hadn't made a sound the whole time, and Taran wondered if she'd listened to a word he'd said.

Why he'd chosen to talk to her about such close and personal things, he had no idea. Maybe it was because she was not long for this world, or that there was something different about her to the other girls he'd dallied with over the years. Whatever the reason, he felt better for it, even if she hadn't said a thing.

There was no need for the soldiers to come together now that each of them carried their own provisions, so they sank to the ground at the midday break wherever they stood, and made themselves comfortable.

Rakan strolled back down the track looking around, always watching, and Taran noticed he was rubbing his arm but didn't care to ask why.

Rakan nodded at Taran, giving the rope a passing glance to ensure it was in his hand, and carried on toward the men further down the track, to check they were vigilant despite the rest.

Taran could have read his mind, but there was so much darkness in his head, and strangely he didn't want to intrude on Rakan's thoughts unless he had to. He wasn't shy about using his gift, yet he didn't use it that often either. Sometimes reading people's minds wasn't as pleasant as he thought it might be, and Rakan, well, he hated to admit it, but there was something about Rakan that he almost liked on occasion.

He looked down to the sword at his waist, the gift Rakan had given him after he'd killed Snark, and sighed at the memory of how Rakan had used him and how often he hated him too.

He leaned back against a tree and closed his eyes. It would be foolish to talk to Maya when everyone was settled, even if they weren't too close, and he was glad she'd perceived this even without being told. That or she was bored out of her senses by his ramblings.

Maya sat, observing Taran through the veil of her hair. It was thick, dark, and unkempt, and after so long without washing, she knew it looked like a bird's nest, all frizzy and likely full of twigs.

She laughed to herself, realising how ridiculous it was to think about looks in such circumstances, but then realised to her surprise it was because she didn't want to look so dishevelled in front of Taran. Her hair was but one of many worries. The clothes she wore were also filthy, and Maya could smell her own odour, and it wasn't pleasant. Then again, everyone on this journey had been without bathing for quite some time now, so she was in similar company.

Taran opened his eyes, and she lowered hers, finding herself unable to meet his gaze square on. He passed over his water skin, and she took it, drinking, enjoying the water despite its tepid warmth.

He also took out some leaf-wrapped food from his pack and slid some across to her.

As he did so, Darkon stepped from the underbrush a dozen steps down the path and moved toward them. 'What are you doing?' he snarled at Taran, indicating the food parcel.

Maya felt a chill run through her veins.

Taran got to his feet and saluted. 'Sir, I thought it best to feed the prisoner so that she didn't slow us down on our mission. It pains me to give good food to the likes of her. Should I have not done so?'

Maya held her breath as she looked at her feet, not daring to look up.

Darkon searched Taran's face and nodded, although not in a friendly way, then stalked down the path shouting Rakan's name angrily.

Taran sat down again, and Maya felt her heartbeat slow a little as Darkon's figure receded.

She reached out, took the food and started eating. The bread was stale, and the meat was tough, but her stomach appreciated it nonetheless.

As she chewed, she thought back over the morning and Taran's tale.

Initially, she'd expected him to talk about his army life, his fights, his victories, a chance to boast. But instead, his tale had surprised her, for it was a story about what had made him who he was: no excuses, no apologies, almost a tragedy yet one which he faced with stoicism.

More surprisingly, was how quickly she'd become enthralled by the story. The emotion with which it was told had her hanging on every word, and she'd heard many times in his voice the pain he'd endured over the years. Yet, there was more to his voice than just emotion. It was a voice that was smooth and easy to listen to, a storyteller's voice from the mouth of one of the Witch-King's soldiers. That he'd missed something out of his story was obvious, yet it didn't feel like he'd lied, and this omission only served to deepen the intrigue.

Maya was still hungry after their small lunch, and she heard Taran's stomach growl at the same time as did hers. She was leaning against a tree, and next to it was a small blood berry bush. Like everything here, it was covered in grey dust, the green of its leaves dark and sickly, and the berries it bore were withered and spotted.

Taran saw her looking at it. 'Don't bother,' he said softly. 'They'll only make us sick. They're not fit to eat.'

Maya looked around and spied Darkon and Rakan in a heated discussion with the other soldiers in the distance and reached a decision.

She reached out her hand and gently wrapped it around the base of the bush, closed her eyes, and summoned her gift. It came so quickly, almost as if it had waited impatiently to be called forth after being dormant for so long, and within moments the tiny bush was heavy with ripe succulent berries.

She opened her eyes to see Taran open-mouthed, staring in disbelief, and couldn't help herself. Quickly she plucked a berry and flicked it toward his open mouth. Sadly, her aim was off, and it hit him on the forehead where it burst to leave a bright red mark like blood, hence the bushes name.

Maya giggled, and Taran slowly reached up, removed the offending piece of fruit from his forehead, and flicked it back at her, missing entirely. It disappeared into the undergrowth behind her.

Maya gathered all the berries, and they ate quickly, well aware that discovery would lead to dire consequences. For Taran, it had been forever since he'd tasted anything quite so sweet and tasty, and he wondered again at this girl.

Voices came closer as Darkon, with Rakan stomping behind him, came walking down the path.

Maya closed her eyes and leaned back against the tree, feigning sleep so as not to draw attention.

However, Taran quickly realised that despite the bush being bare of berries, its leaves had turned a bright green and stood starkly out in this grey world. Swiftly he stood up, took his cloak from his shoulders, draped it over the bush, and then started stretching.

Darkon paused, and his eyes narrowed as they moved up to Taran's forehead, where the juice from the berry was still fresh on his face. 'I don't care if you get sick and die from an infected scratch,' he said. 'But know this. If you slow us down, you'll end up dead before any infection kills you,' and with a scowl, he walked on.

Rakan nodded. 'Best clean it.'

Taran breathed a sigh of relief. The blood berry was well named, but it showed how close again danger had come, and he resolved not to allow himself to be at such risk again.

Rakan's shouted commands were rousing the men, so Taran shook the rope. Maya opened her eyes and smiled up at him, but he didn't respond. People might be watching, he thought, so he collected his cloak and pack then settled them upon his shoulders.

'Time to move,' he said, and ushered Maya in front of him. His thoughts were conflicted, and he needed time to find a way to balance this crazy situation he'd made for himself. Getting closer to this girl was not the right thing to do. He had so much to lose, and for what? Making himself feel better over the next couple of weeks while he led her to her death?

He sighed, and when Maya pulled on the rope as she moved ahead, his heart and feet felt so heavy that it was almost as if she were leading him to his death instead.

Kalas was alive!

For the hundredth time, Alano repeated it to himself, and his mind reeled. How was it possible? It couldn't be possible!

145

As he sat in his chamber with a goblet of wine in his hand, he briefly recalled the last moments of their final battle together…

The mocking cries of the enemy turning to terror as they fell in their thousands, the glee of the daemon, as he gave it free rein to wreak havoc. He remembered each of his comrades being cut down as they hacked a swathe through the Witch-King's ranks toward him on the hill. Mighty Suresh, his head hacked from his neck whilst eight of the enemy pinned him to the floor, or Linden the joker, a lance through his eye piercing his brain, that would kill even the possessed straight away. King Anders, who he'd fought near and was supposed to protect, had gone down, his skull crushed by a heavy mace even as Alano had disembowelled the attacker.

Then there was Kalas.

Kalas, his brother, his closest friend. He could still remember seeing him pierced a dozen times, dancing through the enemy ranks, his movements slowing as so many wounds finally took their toll. Then as the cavalry charged, he'd had to focus again on the slaughter to hand.

Alano realised he hadn't actually seen Kalas die. For one heartbeat, he was there, and the next, he was gone.

'Kalas is coming.'

Every time Kalas had trained in the duelling pits over those many years long past, the weapon master had uttered those words as he entered. Kalas was the only one Alano knew who could kill so many men at once other than himself, and the only one who would say those words.

Kalas was indeed alive!

When the Witch-King had confronted him with those words in the throne room, he knew there was no choice but to answer honestly, for the daemon bound him and made sure he served without question. Yet, for the first time in fifty years, it had not only allowed him to lie but had even encouraged him to do so.

'Why?' demanded Alano of his daemon kin. 'Why now? Why let me lie about this and force me into obedience over everything else.'

'SSSSSSsssssssh,' hissed the daemon. 'Our brother is alive, and the bond of blood and hell's kinship is strong. Whilst the oath that binds our obedience to Daleth still holds us, blood must protect blood.'

'Kalas isn't my blood brother, though,' said Alano. 'He is my sword brother.'

'Foolish man, still you do not see. It is not Kalas I am talking about. It is his daemon to which I am kin, and our daemon blood and soul binds us and always will. We cannot betray the Witch-King, yet if we can prevent harm falling upon our last remaining brother in this world, then we shall do so. Now it is time to consider this news.'

Alano couldn't remember the last time the daemon's presence in his mind had moved completely away, receding, unseen and unfelt. Yet the daemon was right. It was time to consider how Kalas' return might affect the course of things, for indeed, if Kalas was coming, he might find himself forced to face him, sword in hand.

Now that was something he would ask the daemon about when it was talkative again.

Alano lay back on his bed; no terrible thoughts of blood or hunger disturbed him. Instead, he thought back to happier times when he was young, and the Ember Kingdom was bright, and with his whole life ahead of him, anything had been possible. He, the captain of the royal guard, and Kalas, his brother, his closest friend. At the time, he'd thought those days would never end.

With such bright thoughts, he fell to sleep without drinking himself into oblivion and wasn't even aware when the maid cautiously came in to tidy his room.

Chapter IX

Maya enjoyed the feeling of stretching her legs as she walked, and even if every step brought her closer to Kingshold, she felt a transient sense of freedom without any bars around her.

Rakan and Lexis were about fifty strides ahead, not that she needed to see them, for the trail they left through the woods as they passed was easy enough to follow. On the other hand, the Rangers seemed to have considerable skill in concealment, which caught her interest.

A key skill of any successful hunter was the ability to spot an animal before it spotted you, so Maya began to look for them as if they were her prey, not the other way around.

Their armour and clothing were black, so they used the shadows in the woods to their advantage, staying within the darkness. But even darkness has its shades, and Maya could often make them out whether they moved or stood still as they surveyed the land around them. That two of them carried bows was another giveaway. The soft sheen of the polished wood caught even the subtlest light. So it wasn't long before Maya was satisfied that she could find them all without much difficulty.

Now, how to take advantage of this knowledge.

Maya had surprised herself by promising Taran not to attempt an escape if it meant him losing his life, yet neither did she want to arrive at her destination. She would need to convince him to swap his guard duty with another of the soldiers before slipping her bonds and using her woodcraft to evade the Rangers and escape.

She was feeling fairly strong thanks to the extra food Taran had provided, and her legs were used to carrying her all day, sometimes with a small deer over her shoulders if a hunt had been fruitful. Yet the question was whether she could get away from the Rangers once the chase was on.

Rakan, Taran, and any of the other soldiers wouldn't prove a problem. However, the Rangers gave her pause, for even if they weren't as skilled at moving through the woods as she was, they no doubt excelled as hunters of men.

Maybe if she managed to take one of the bows, not only would it help to provide food following her escape, but as an expert with the weapon, maybe she would be able to kill the Rangers if they ever got close. Maya sighed. To kill a highly trained armoured man was a little different from killing a deer when it was unaware of her loosing an arrow at it.

Finally, of course, was the one overriding question. Even if the soldiers were malicious or the Rangers evil, could she actually kill them if necessary? The answer was obvious. In her heart of hearts, she knew she wasn't like a wolf to slay without mercy. But then again, nor was she a lamb either.

Her heart felt heavy, and she wanted to change her mood. So, she thought of her secret place back in the valley, but found that it wasn't enough, and once happy memories of her father now saddened her. Then she thought of Taran's story, so tragic at times, yet also full of humour despite his pain, and she smiled and felt better.

How strange, she thought, and wondered what he was thinking.

Taran was in a bad mood.

He had of late suffered a great deal of darkness, and he wanted to be the type of person who enjoyed life as a carefree spirit. Over the last few years, he'd tried to do this while living life on the road, and even if it was somewhat lonely, he'd mostly succeeded.

Then over the last few weeks, it was as if the gods had cursed him. Responsible for the deaths of two men, in an army he despised, that was shortly to fight a war that he could only imagine would be full of horror and a grisly death for him. Then there was Maya, and he would soon be jointly responsible for her death when she seemed deserving of anything but.

He lifted his head. Until now, he'd just been following the rope and Maya's feet in front of him, too engrossed in his thoughts to try and talk or even to see how she was coping.

Then suddenly, all the darkness in his mind started to drift away like smoke on a breeze.

Despite her filthy, baggy, hunter's clothing, and the twigs in her hair that made her look like a walking bush, she moved with ... Taran searched for the right word, yes, she moved with a grace he'd never seen before.

He'd fought men who were fast and agile, strong or supple. He'd enjoyed the company of women both tall and short, dark or fair, skilled and otherwise, but as he watched, Taran realised he'd never seen anyone move like her.

As a fighter, studying the way people moved was a must. His talent helped him win, but relying on that alone wasn't enough, and as he watched her, he became captivated. She moved amongst the woods like a creature of nature, a tread so delicate and light that she left almost no mark of her passage. She seemed to place her feet without thought, and yet nothing was stirred by her passing. Branches and limbs that hung across the path she simply flowed under, bending with a suppleness and balance that defied belief.

He also recognised that while everything around her made noise, whether him with his boots, the other men crashing through the forest like it was a battle, or even the wildlife in the trees and undergrowth, she made no noise whatsoever. As he studied her, he wondered what she would look like once the dirt was washed away, her face and hair cleaned, wearing fresh clothes or maybe not wearing ...

Stop! He berated himself. Here he was taking Maya to her doom, and he was starting to allow himself to want to know her better in too many different ways. He needed a distraction.

'Talk to me,' he asked Maya softly, repeating her words from that very morning, but as she continued her stride unchecked, Taran wondered whether she'd heard him.

Yet Maya had heard Taran's request, and maybe because he'd opened up earlier, or perhaps because she wanted to tell her story, so that when she was gone, someone might remember her, Maya talked.

She told the stories of her birth, how her father had known she was special, how she had saved her mother from death. Then tales of growing up, and how she was kept apart from everyone to help disguise her differences, from becoming a hunter to not seeing any of the men in the village, how this kept her distant and hidden so that nobody ever really saw her.

She spoke of her father and her mother, different yet so close, and how when her mother had died, her father had filled the void. She told of her love of nature, how she never tired of walking the woods around her village, finding joy in everything around her.

Maya talked and talked, and the story jumped from here to there and back again, disjointed at times but intriguing, captivating, full of passion, laughter, sadness, and pain.

Lastly, she talked about her special hidden place beyond the settlement walls, how a night out beyond curfew had led to her father's death, the exposure of her gift, and her incarceration.

Taran felt drawn in with every word and wished he could see her lips and expressions as she talked, to read her emotions as well as to hear them. Nonetheless, he still garnered so much, for her hands constantly moved, expressive, almost crafting an enchantment as they formed and weaved pictures along with her words.

Why, oh why, did she have to be his prisoner? He'd done many things in his life, especially of late, that he didn't want to do, but this, this was so wrong. There was no escaping the fact she was a prisoner whose fate would be anything but pleasant, and he was the one taking her to it.

He allowed his mind to dwell briefly on thoughts of escape from this situation, the army, but this time not alone. Perhaps having someone along who could turn rotten, sour berries into sweet ones, and who could tell stories that gripped his soul, would be a good companion on the road.

He laughed cynically to himself then. Dreams never came true, and he knew any attempt to escape would lead to his death. There were the Rangers, and even Rakan was scared of them, and of course, there was Rakan himself.

However much Rakan seemed to like Taran, he was a career army man and would never stand aside, and Taran couldn't best Rakan completely at swordplay, let alone the Rangers. These dreams would end up with his cooling corpse left for the scavengers.

Damn, he thought, there must be a way out of this. Now think!

Rakan stalked along through the woods, his brow furrowed. He'd been in a bad mood ever since they'd been assigned to this task. There hadn't even been the time to celebrate Snark's demise, and while the memory of his destruction at Taran's hands brought a brief smile to his face, it didn't cheer him up as he'd hoped.

His hand absently scratched his arm, but it was out of habit, for the sores hadn't returned, and his skin was as clear as the first day the girl had laid a hand on him.

Lexis was next to him whining about the damn girl, their bad luck, the loss of the horses, how far it was to the next garrison town, on and on. Rakan so wanted to plant his fist in his face to shut him up but doubted he would be happy with just the one punch, and he wasn't sure the Rangers would appreciate losing a soldier simply to calm his frustration.

The Rangers had decided to get their bearings from the top of a high hill, and Rakan could only agree with the sense it made as they made it to the top. Going off the kingdom's roads helped keep their presence and mission hidden, but it could also mean them missing the next garrison town and refit.

Despite Lexis' whining, Rakan could only agree that being back on horseback again would be a fine thing. Get this girl off their hands and get back to one of the invasion staging posts sooner rather than later.

War was coming, and Rakan wanted these men ready, and he wanted to have a unit to command. Yes, maybe going to the capital might be a good thing. Surely he could find some of the king's commanders there and use the completion of this mission as an opportunity to find himself a company to take over, or maybe get back to his old comrades in the Nightstalkers.

One of the Rangers came over to pass on orders that their camp would be made on the hill for the night, and Rakan looked back down the track to where Taran was escorting Maya, although, why she was walking ahead, he wasn't sure.

Hmmm, clever lad. Following behind made keeping an eye on her easier. However, if he didn't learn to keep his head down, clever lad or not, he wouldn't last long, especially with these damn Rangers around.

Beyond Taran, the other three soldiers were following even further down the trail. Rakan felt something looked odd but couldn't quite put his finger on it.

Over the next hour, the campsite started to take shape as fires were lit and sleeping areas cleared.

'Lexis, take three men and get some stakes cut to secure our perimeter,' Rakan ordered. Lexis started to complain but fortunately saw the look on Rakan's face and hurried away.

That damn wolf, he thought, best be prepared. Just because they were in kingdom lands didn't mean they were safe, and campfires were easy to see at night, so Rakan approached Darkon, which he hated doing.

'Do you want me to post some of my men on watch later?' he asked.

Darkon turned to him, and even in the twilight, Rakan could see the anger on his face. 'What? Do you think we aren't capable of guarding the camp?' he hissed.

Rakan was tempted to mention the wolf, the lost horses, and wagon, but thought better of it and just shook his head. 'Not at all,' he placated. 'Just seeing if we could share the load.' With that, he turned away, unpacked his bedroll, then pulled a skinning knife to gut the rabbits that two of the Rangers had killed during the day.

He looked around. Lexis and two others were making a mound of sharpened stakes that would be planted around the campsite whether Darkon wanted them or not, and Taran was preparing a space to sleep by putting fern fronds down for comfort. However, instead of putting his bedroll there, he saw Taran gesture to the girl Maya to take the place and then lay his bedroll beside hers on the hard earth.

Rakan shook his head. The fool, if he could see it, without doubt, the Rangers would see it. They would use it to hurt the boy, and there was nothing Rakan would be able to do about it. He'd warned Taran once, and now he was on his own. If Taran lived long enough, he'd make a fine soldier and a friend. Suddenly, Rakan realised the enormity of that thought. *A friend*. Rakan had never made friends, and here he was thinking of Taran becoming one. Or was he one already?

Either way, friend or not, the rules in Rakan's world were to look after yourself first and still look after yourself second. Taran needed to wake up to these rules if he wanted to live.

Rakan sat down on a rock and started gutting the rabbits laid out in front of him, and every time his knife sliced into them, he imagined it was either Darkon or Lexis he was gutting. For the first time that day, his mood lifted. Yes, he thought, as he held another *Darkon*, his knife slicing its belly. This is for you!

Daleth opened his eyes in his bed-chamber after an unusually restless night. It was still dark, the sun yet to fully rise, and for a moment, Daleth thought about going back to sleep but decided against it.

He usually had no trouble sleeping soundly, but the last night he'd received another brief communication from an overseer of a unit heading toward a staging post. The message, 'Kalas is coming,' with an image of slaughtered men, was given to him before the link was broken. The bearer of the news was now likely dead, Daleth surmised.

As it had been the last thing on his mind, this meant his usual dreams of conquest, victory, and the surge of new life that came with it, had instead been ones where a faceless man was always at the periphery of his vision, hunting him, swords dripping with blood. So, he awoke tired and irritable.

Perhaps it was foolish to be worried over one man. He had an army one hundred thousand strong, and here he was worrying over the death of a garrison contingent and now a small unit. In the greater scheme of things, it was nothing, not worthy of his time. But try as he could, he still couldn't shake the fear in the overseers' voices.

Thus he was in a foul mood when just after settling down to break fast, a whisper came to his mind of someone seeking an audience. It was one of the Rangers escorting the girl trying to make contact.

Daleth closed his eyes and listened to the report, then sat deliberating. She was such a special girl, or rather her gift was such a special one, and this wasn't an easy decision to make.

He'd learned that her old village now flourished, and an oasis had been discovered on the valley's rim by the other hunters. To make matters worse, he was unable to draw life from the land she'd healed. Its people, so used to suffering, were now experiencing happiness, and even though they were just one village, he could still feel the tiniest loss of sustenance.

Rangers were already on their way. Their orders were to burn the settlement and everyone in it to ashes, to make everything disappear as if it had never been.

He'd so hoped to use her power, to rejuvenate the land so he could draw on its life again, but her village had shown that this would be unlikely. Then, of course, with a hundred thousand men ready to conquer the Freestates and whatever lay beyond, did he really need the distraction or to take a risk, however small?

Finally, the Ranger prompted him. 'My King?'

'Where are you now?' he asked, and the Ranger shared the view of what he'd seen and reported that they were at least another twenty days of travel to the capital.

Daleth sighed. Alano might be upset that he hadn't been consulted, but that made him smile inside and made the decision so much easier.

'Kill her,' said Daleth, and report back to me immediately when done.'

Taran awoke early from troubled dreams. As he sat up, the sky overhead was full of dark clouds, and there was a fetid, evil wind blowing. It was just before dawn with the hint of light starting to brighten the distant horizon as Taran quietly got to his feet.

As he looked around in the dim light, he saw the silhouette of Rakan gazing into the distance, hand resting on the hilt of his sword.

Taran approached, stepping around the slightly glowing embers of the last night's campfire, and nodded in greeting. 'What's wrong?' he asked, trying to pierce the gloom but not seeing anything untoward.

Rakan nodded down the hill. 'Tell me. What can you see?'

Taran looked, but after a while, shook his head. 'I don't know what I'm supposed to say. There's nothing but the hills, the forest as far as I can see in this light and the way we travelled, but ...' Then he stopped speaking as he realised what he'd just said. 'I can see our trail!' exclaimed Taran. 'How can I see our trail through the trees?'

Rakan shook his head. 'It's not even light yet, and I'm guessing the Rangers have already seen this. Things are going to get interesting very quickly, so stay away from the girl!' As he spoke, he took Taran's shoulders in his firm grasp and looked him in the eye. 'Whatever the Rangers decide to do, stay back, stay quiet, and don't say a word. I will vouch that I was watching you the whole time, and you had nothing to do with anything.'

'But I didn't do anything!' Taran said defensively.

Rakan grimaced. 'That's not the point, lad. These Rangers are quick to anger and just as quick to kill. It could be we'll just move on, but if they feel she's purposely using her gift in this way or there is any kind of risk, there will be serious consequences.'

They stood there together then, watching the light slowly spread across the land. As it did, there it lay, a vivid green trail, the foliage of the trees through which Maya had passed, bright amongst their dying brethren.

As Taran followed it with his eyes, it came straight to the camp. He turned to look at Maya, who was starting to stir, and noticed in the morning light that she now lay on a bed of vibrant green ferns, and the whole of the campsite showed signs of new life, with fresh grass sprouting everywhere. Worryingly, he saw Darkon and two of the other Rangers standing, one pointing to their trail and then gesturing around.

Darkon's black eyes flicked over to where he stood, and the cold smile that slowly spread across the man's mouth chilled Taran, but then the captain turned his attention back to one of his fellow Rangers who was sitting down, eyes closed.

Rakan followed Taran's gaze. 'He's a Spirit talker, that one, and likely seeking orders. The only person they take direct orders from is the Witch-King himself, so whatever directive they're given will be final. Remember what I said,' he reminded Taran, and walked back to where the men were sleeping and started to rouse them, kicking their feet, and the camp came to life.

Men cursed, stretching, yawning, and of course, complaining, but then quiet slowly descended as everyone noticed the change to the campsite; the grass, the leaves on the bushes, and the bright green leaves on the trees rustling in the morning air.

Taran felt touched by the beauty and wondered what the others thought. But then Lexis, and of course It had to be him, broke the silence.

'She's tainted,' he muttered, then started saying it louder, and everyone began to follow suit, casting evil glances and calling curses at Maya as she stirred.

As Maya awoke to the open hostility, her hands went to her mouth. Eyes wide, she looked around, noticing the change her gift had worked upon the land without her bidding, and huddled back against a tree trunk next to where she'd slept.

Taran wanted to go to her, to shield her, but remembered Rakan's advice. The Witch-King wanted her alive, whereas his own life meant little to the Rangers. So he kept his face sullen like the other men and didn't meet her eye. Nonetheless, while stirring the embers of the fire and adding more wood, he stayed close enough so that Maya could feel his presence in case she drew comfort from it.

The men prepared food in the growing flames as water boiled in pans, and it seemed as though the morning might pass without incident.

As Rakan, Lexis, and the others started eating, Taran stood and took some food over to Maya, and nonchalantly tossed some meat into her lap before handing her a small cup of water. But as he did so, everyone stopped talking.

Taran looked around, and there stood the five Rangers on the far side of the fire. Straight away, he realised something was wrong, if only because the five of them were never together. Two were always on watch or out scouting, yet here they all were.

He tried to read their thoughts, but they were dark to his mind, and he cursed his inability to know what was going on. So, trying not to look worried, he moved a few steps away from Maya to a fallen tree trunk and sat down.

The Rangers moved forward without saying anything and made themselves comfortable. It was the first time they'd shared a fire and eaten food together, yet it couldn't have felt less like a friendly start to the day.

As everyone finished eating, Darkon looked around the campfire, a twisted look on his face. 'You might be wondering why are we all sitting together this morning? It wasn't really a question, and no one said anything. Into the silence, Darkon continued. 'Well, it's because this will be our last day travelling together, and whilst this has been a most unenjoyable experience for us all so far, I think we should part on good terms and a high note, don't you think?' He fixed Lexis with his stare as he posed the question.

Lexis nodded. 'Yes, sir!'

'Don't you think, Lexis, that it's unfair that privates in the army like yourself never get rewarded, whilst those above you seem to eat better, have better equipment?' and he looked at Taran's sword at his hip. 'Wouldn't it be proper if sometimes, just sometimes, the lowest-ranked were rewarded as well?'

Lexis looked to Rakan for guidance, but Rakan was staring stonily ahead, and the look in Darkon's eyes didn't allow Lexis to answer in any way other than to agree. 'You're right, sir. It would be proper to be rewarded.'

'Well,' said Darkon. 'Let's get to the point, shall we?'

'It seems that our guest's presence,' and he nodded toward Maya, 'is no longer required at the court of our king!' He looked at Taran as he finished his statement, and Taran tried not to let the shock from the icy fist that gripped his heart show on his face.

'So Lexis, I think the reward for you and your three friends,' and he smiled at the other soldiers, 'should be to have some fun with this girl, and when you've finished, well, how it ends is up to you!'

Taran's head spun, and he heard Maya whimper as what was about to happen suddenly registered. He looked back. Her fists were clenched, knuckles white, her brown eyes were wide, so deep, that he felt he was drowning in the fear that they now held.

He looked over to Rakan, who gave a barely imperceptible shake of his head.

Lexis laughed. 'Well lads,' he said, sneering, 'let's have some fun with Taran's little pet, shall we?' and he started to get to his feet.

Taran knew to try and help her would be to die, but he realised that if she died, a large part of him would die too. When this depth of feeling had grown, he had no idea, but from what he knew of her, she was a gentle soul who had harmed no one, and her only sin, was to have healed. Taran knew in his heart that he wanted to get to know her better, more than anyone he'd ever met.

As Lexis and the other three soldiers stood up, so did Taran. He saw Rakan put his head in his hands, whereas Darkon just smiled maliciously, and Taran knew he'd been manipulated into this situation, but he had no choice.

'Sit down!' Taran commanded Lexis and the other men. 'That's an order. This girl is going to the Witch-King. That is our mission, and we will carry it out!'

Neither Lexis nor the others sat down but instead looked back to Darkon.

'Ahhhhh,' said Darkon. 'A loyal soldier, following our king's orders. Well, put your mind at rest. This girl,' and he jerked his head at Maya, 'well, her life is now forfeit by order of the king himself. But, Lexis having fun, that's my order, and last time I looked, I outrank you. So now you know, I think you should sit back down, don't say another word, and just watch.'

Taran looked back at Maya again. Her eyes were full of tears, yet she blinked them back, a final act of defiance to not give them the satisfaction of seeing her fear. But it wouldn't last long. The horrors she would suffer before she died would see to that.

Taran turned to Rakan. 'Sit down, lad!' Rakan said, a pleading look in his eyes. 'It's an order. The old mission is over. It's time for us to get back to what we do best, soldiering, not looking after some peasant girl.'

Taran sighed. He looked to the sky. The clouds were dark, foreboding, and full of ill promise. Carrion birds circled in the distance, and he breathed the air that smelt of death to come. His instincts told him to stand back, to sit down, to do as Rakan suggested.

Instead, he drew his sword and turned to Maya. 'I'm so sorry it came to this,' and slashed the blade down twice, severing the ropes that held her wrists and feet. He pulled his dagger out and passed it to her. 'At least you can die free, with a friend at your side.'

Darkon bellowed with laughter. 'Oh, I could never have even dreamed of this!' he exclaimed, clapping. 'This shall be even more fun than I anticipated. What do you think, Rakan? He's disobeyed a direct order and drawn his sword to free a prisoner. I do believe your corporal's life is forfeit, don't you agree?'

Rakan nodded. 'That is the law.'

'Lexis, I think it is time for you and your friends to kill this fool so that we can bring an end to his insubordinate behaviour,' said Darkon.

Lexis' face took on a wicked look. 'You know Taran, I do owe you for my crooked nose, and even if I hadn't been ordered, I'd have found a way to kill you someday anyhow.' He drew his sword, and the other three men did the same.

'You don't have to do this!' reasoned Taran. 'Look around you, see what she's done. She's a healer. She doesn't deserve to die!' But even as he said it, he was reading their minds, seeing that they saw her as tainted or worse and him nothing but an obstacle standing in the way of their evil fun, such was the influence of the amulets they wore.

Taran knew this was the end, and as Maya rose to stand behind him, he realised this was where he was meant to be, by her side.

'It might be best if you use that dagger on yourself now,' he said to Maya, lifting his sword to a guard position. But he saw her shake her head swiftly in response.

'Kill him!' commanded Darkon, and Lexis and the others surged forward.

Taran had never fought four men before, having mostly trained solo with Rakan, but negating numbers in a sword fight was much the same as fighting with your hands. He knew Lexis' move even before he made it. He pushed Maya backwards as he moved sideways, putting himself directly in front of Lexis, so he briefly obstructed the others.

Lexis thrust to where Taran had stood a mere moment ago, only to have Taran's sword slash across his throat, and as he went down, blood frothing over his grasping fingers, he saw Taran move on. Angrin, who had been right behind Lexis, tripped over the falling body and never saw the blow that almost severed his neck even as Taran rolled under Aspen's sweep, disembowelling him as he surged to his feet and rammed his sword up into Kazad's groin.

It was over within ten heartbeats, and Taran stood back, blood running from his hands as they gripped the sword.

Darkon clapped again. 'Bravo, bravo. Truly, this day just gets better and better, and yet I do grow tired. Let me see how you fare against one of my men as opposed to four imbeciles! You know Rakan, you really should have trained them all as diligently as your corporal here; they might have done a lot better. Yet, I believe this boy is rather gifted in using his blade … or maybe just gifted. Irrespective, he and whatever gifts he has die here.

'Lazard!' snapped Darkon, and a grim-faced Ranger started to rise.

'Wait,' Rakan interrupted.

Darkon frowned. 'Really, for what exactly?'

'It should be me that kills him!' Rakan suggested.

Darkon looked closely at Rakan, measuring his words, and then laughed. 'Indeed, it should be, and your reward will be reinstatement in your old unit. That is what you said you wanted more than anything?'

Rakan nodded.

'Then go ahead, but take your time and cut him to pieces.'

Taran couldn't believe it. He cast his mind out to read Rakan's, who was starting to stand up. There was no way to beat him without dying. Not once in all their practice bouts had he won cleanly. What he saw made him recoil.

'Please don't,' he pleaded in a whisper.

162

Rakan pushed himself to his feet, his movements slow but nonetheless exuding the violence soon to come. He drew his sword and, bending down, reached out his hand to one of the Rangers and nodded at the man's weapon. The Ranger, after a moment's hesitation, passed it over.

Rakan straightened up and weaved the two blades in a figure of eight, loosening his muscles. He looked at Taran standing defiantly, both hands on his sword, shaking from fear or the rush of blood. The girl Maya was behind him, back against a tree, the dagger in her hand.

As Rakan considered his initial moves, he felt the beginnings of doubt for the first time since joining the army.

It had been so long since he'd felt anything other than anger or hatred until recently.

His mind flashed back to when he'd earned his uniform in the Nightstalkers and gone home to show everyone how much he'd achieved, to make them proud of the small boy they had scorned. Yet as he'd returned, full of positive thoughts, his mind became darker, returning to memories of his unhappiness at their hands, and these had grown and grown out of all proportion.

When his father and mother had seen him, they'd run toward him, arms outstretched in welcome, smiles on their lips and tears on their cheeks, and yet he'd drawn his sword and cut them down before turning on everyone else who'd even looked in his direction with disdain.

Almost thirty years had gone by since then. Rebellions put down mercilessly in the early days, then countless peasants, bandits, and soldiers of the Eyre slaughtered, and not once had he not slept soundly. Soldiers under his command he'd killed if they'd offered him complaint, and he'd harboured grudges throughout his whole life, never once allowing anyone to get close, never once having a friend.

In fact, in this country, this life, this army, there could never be friends. Everyone was a potential enemy, waiting for you to make a mistake so they could climb over your dead body to rise in the ranks.

Yet now, as he looked at Taran, Rakan realised he saw the young lad as a friend, or perhaps even one day the son he would never have. There behind him was the girl, who had with a simple touch removed some of the skin rot that had blighted him his whole life, who healed the land as she passed, soon to be slaughtered by order of the Witch-King. A girl the lad had seemed to grow fond of.

Rakan sighed.

'Sorry,' he said to Taran, stepping forward. 'You know what's coming, don't you?'

Taran nodded his head, and as he did so, Rakan spun, swords flashing as he threw himself into the Rangers who were sitting, waiting for the fight to start. His swords swung left and right, and Taran launched himself forward at the same time, having read his intentions.

The surprise attack looked like it would work, but only for an instant. Rakan managed to kill two of the Rangers in less than a heartbeat, and as the others turned toward him, Taran had run forward to plunge his sword into the back of a third. However, Darkon and Lazard both rolled away from the lashing blades, leaping to their feet unscathed.

Then they attacked.

Rakan had trained Taran well, but nothing had prepared him for this. Within a moment, he had cuts across his chest and arms as he desperately tried to fend off Lazard's strikes. He had no time to make an attack of his own, and then as he tried to block one of his opponent's thrusts, he knew it was too late.

He could almost see in slow motion as the man's sword went past his parry, cut between his lower ribs, and exited his back in a bloody spray. He cried out in agony and shock, collapsing to his knees as Lazard let go of the sword, leaving it protruding from his body.

Taran slowly turned his head, the pain making his vision blurry as he felt his strength ebbing away. Rakan was still fighting, and for a moment, Taran held some small hope as Darkon's left arm hung useless at his side. Yet Rakan was a bloody mess himself, bleeding heavily from numerous deep wounds. Suddenly, Rakan's legs buckled as Darkon attacked, and the Ranger leapt past his weak cut and moved behind him.

He placed his boot on Rakan's back, pushed him face-first to the floor, and then thrust his sword through his body, pinning him to the ground. Rakan screamed in pain and fury, but it was over for him too.

Taran looked around, barely conscious, to see Lazard frantically wrapping a cloth around the wound on Darkon's arm, to stem the blood while all the time keeping an eye on Maya, who stood frozen, seeming unable to move. Taran could hear himself moaning. The pain was agonising, and he couldn't help himself, however hard he tried to stifle the sound.

Rakan was trying to rise but couldn't, and his eyes met Taran's, and he smiled faintly. 'I almost had that bastard. He won't be able to use that hand to pleasure himself again.' Blood gushed from the corner of his mouth. 'Still, he was damn good, I'll give him that, but not as good as I thought he would be! If I'd have been younger, I reckon I might have had him, or maybe just on a better day.'

Taran grimaced back. 'I reckon you could have,' he said, barely able to hear his own words. 'Maybe you could ask him for the best of three?'

'Quiet!' snapped Lazard. 'If you talk so much, you won't be able to hear the screams so well, and we wouldn't want you to miss the fun before you die. Our little gift to you both.'

Taran wanted to shout at Maya to run, to tell these men to stop, but it would be to no avail. He tried to meet her gaze with his own, but her eyes were closed now, not willing to face her fate he imagined, and he couldn't blame her.

Lazard's hand lashed out, knocking the dagger from Maya's grasp, and still she didn't move, and both Rangers laughed.

Darkon struck again with his open palm, and Maya fell back against the tree behind her, and this time she did open her eyes.

'She's awake just in time.' Lazard laughed and pulled his dagger. 'Any last words before we put out your eyes because after that we'll take your tongue. So speak while you still can!'

Maya looked up at them both. She said something, but too softly for Taran to hear above his own moaning, and he saw the two Rangers pause before stepping forward, their daggers raised at the ready.

Chapter X

Kalas stood overlooking the waterfall, which over fifty years ago had seen him bury his armour, bury his memories, bury his shame. Now he stood here, young once again like the day he'd cast it aside, but at least then he'd been free of the daemon's will.

He remembered how it had been when he was first here. The sky bright, the air full of the scent of flowers, the sound of bees, and the rage of the water as it crashed down full of life and force. It had been a beautiful place, but at that time, he'd been unable to truly appreciate anything. Instead, everywhere he looked, he saw his dead friends, their blank eyes accusing him of running away, not fulfilling his vow when everyone else had. Why had he lived when they had died?

The water had laughed at him, and even the birds had seemed to mock him. His mind was lost at that time, yet not so much that he hadn't the presence to hide the armour rather than throw it into the surging waters.

He shook his head and looked again.

The water still crashed, but instead of running clear, it seemed almost oily, the foam yellowish and sweetly unpleasant. The rocks which had once been bright green with moss, with bees busy collecting pollen from the small white flowers dotted all over, were now covered in foul-smelling green slime and bloated flies. Yet reassuringly, the rocks under which he'd put his armour seemed undisturbed.

He dismounted from his horse and hobbled it against a tree, and it dipped its head to graze the grass that was partly edible and carefully made his way over to the mound.

The rocks he'd put in place between the roots of a tree were not small, yet with his new-found youth and strength, he made short work of lifting them away, and there underneath was the oiled cloth that he'd laid over his old equipment.

His hands trembled as he reached down, almost afraid of what he would find, and he paused for a moment. To wear the armour would mean he could no longer hide in the shadows pretending to be part of the Witch-King's army.

He swept the cloth aside, and there it lay. Even though the sky was dark, still the silvered steel shone with a lustre that seemed brighter than the day itself. He'd forgotten how beautiful it was, and he was amazed that the lesser magic that had bound it to him over fifty years ago still kept it free of rust, mildew, or contamination. He looked around, but only the horses kept him company, so he started to pull off the dark armour he'd looted until he stood only in his trousers, linen shirt, and boots.

Reaching down, he lifted the mail shirt first. It chimed softly as he lifted it over his head, slid his arms through, and let it settle on his shoulders. Next the breastplate, then the shoulder guards, the studded kilt, thigh guards, greaves, gauntlets, and weapon belt. Even after all this time, not only did every piece fit him perfectly like a second skin, but his fingers didn't fumble once with the straps and buckles. Lastly, he settled the helm upon his head and reached for the weapons.

The longsword and shortsword he drew from their ornate scabbards. The edges of the blades were still as sharp as a scorned women's gaze. He secured them to his weapon belt along with a long heavy dagger, and finally, the two small throwing knives that fitted into sheaths, one above each shoulder blade.

Finally, he stood ready, and for the first time in a great many years, he felt a sense of purpose other than waiting for death to come and find him with old age. This time he would go and find it, and swiftly.

He turned to his mount, and it snorted, tossing its head.

'Do I look ridiculous then?' asked Kalas of his horse, gently ruffling its mane.

'No!' said the daemon in his head. 'You look like a king returning to claim his throne, and to do so, you and I must swim through a sea of blood together!'

'To kill the Witch-King or die trying,' said Kalas to the daemon. 'We must both die. That is my oath.'

'Let us kill the Witch-King first,' soothed the daemon. 'Let us not think about dying. Then we can consider what happens after in good time. First, we need to eat, and I suggest we do it before crossing the border into the Freestates. It's never a good idea to dine on one's new hosts,' and the daemon giggled manically.

'Good idea,' said Kalas, and wondered briefly why he found it so easy to agree with the daemon.

He swung himself up into the saddle and started humming a dark tune as he rode onward. He couldn't remember where he'd picked it up from, but it brought thoughts and images of bloody battles to be fought and won to his mind, and he felt full of purpose as the day passed.

In the distance, something strange caught his eye. There amongst some thick but dying woodland, in a land full of browns, greys and ill-looking green, was a thin but distinct winding line, like a trail. Yes, definitely a trail, but of a green hue he hadn't seen since the old days.

His curiosity piqued, he turned the head of his horse and dug his heels into its flanks and cantered off, his direction set.

Maya had watched the morning's events unfold with a dread she'd never felt before, ever. Even when her father was killed in front of her, it had happened so quickly that she'd not seen it coming.

Yet when she'd awoken to the men's curses and had seen the unintentional healing her growing gift had wrought upon the land, she knew there would be trouble, but nothing in her imagination had prepared her for something like this.

To hear her death sentence from Darkon's lips and the promise of torture or worse at the hands of Lexis and the other soldiers had shocked her beyond belief.

Maya felt like her mind wouldn't stop spinning as it tried to grasp the reality of what was being said. She had weeks to live surely, weeks before she met the Witch-King, weeks more to get to know Taran a little better, to plan an escape somehow. Why waste all of this trouble to get her this far only to kill her now. Yet it seemed the orders came from the Witch-King himself.

When Taran had stood up to try to stop it, she'd wanted to tell him in that moment how no one had ever done such a thing for her. Instead, she'd just willed him to sit down, not wanting him to throw his life away needlessly.

Then when he'd drawn his sword, cut her bonds and stood willing to die next to her, even amongst such terror, her heart in these last moments of life had beat for the first time with a strange feeling she'd never felt before and sadly realised she never would again.

Then what followed was a nightmare.

In moments everything had turned to blood. It all happened so fast, bodies everywhere, and just when Maya had felt there was a chance, both Rakan and Taran were cut down by the two remaining Rangers.

She'd been overcome with sorrow, wanting to run to Taran to heal him, yet the only thing that ran were the tears falling down her cheeks. Even though Taran had given her a dagger, she couldn't even bring herself to use it, not on herself or against anyone else for that matter, yet she held on to it nonetheless.

Now, after the harsh sounds of battle, the ringing of steel on steel, and the cries of the dying, it seemed so silent and still.

She was vaguely aware of the two Rangers walking toward her, but still she did nothing. She was in shock, and knew it. Inside, she was screaming at herself to run, fight, to do something, but she was frozen. Yet, inside her, something was happening. A feeling of anger, resentment, and fury, was building, rising like a storm, impossible to withstand.

Sharp pain brought her back to her senses, and she found herself with her back against a tree, with the two Rangers, Lazard, and Darkon, standing before her, daggers drawn with murder and worse in their eyes.

'Any last words?' asked Darkon.

Suddenly all was calm. Her panic fled as quickly as it had come, her trembling hands stilled, her heartbeat slowed, and what she needed to do became clear.

'You should run while you still can,' she said, knowing they wouldn't.

Surprise showed in their eyes, for they'd expected her to scream, to beg, to turn into a quivering wreck, but not this. After a moment, they stepped forward again.

Maya grabbed the trunk of the tree, and she let her gift flow like never before, unleashing a huge wave of emotion, directing it through the tree at the two men in front of her.

Her eyes glowed so brightly that for a moment, the two Rangers stepped back a pace and then like lightning, roots and vines shot from the soil around the two men, twisting and writhing, wrapping and binding.

They struggled frantically, hacking in a vain attempt to free themselves, but what would have taken months to grow, happened in mere heartbeats. The two men found themselves enveloped as if in steel chains, completely immobile, unable to move their arms, legs, or body. Only their heads were free as Maya stopped the flow of her gift and stepped forward.

'Say a word,' she said, looking them both in the eyes with a confidence she'd never felt before in her life, 'and it will be your last.'

Now wasn't the time to hesitate if she wanted to save Taran.

She ran to him and his eyes were open in wonder. 'Be ready. This will hurt,' she said.

Before Taran realised what was happening, Maya took the hilt of the sword that ran through his body, and putting her boot on his chest, yanked the blade free. Taran fell backwards, blood spewing from his mouth and the wounds.

She knelt by him, placing her hands on his chest, and again reached for her gift, letting it flow, infusing Taran's body with her power, closing his wounds, strengthening his heart, taking away the trauma and pain. Exhaustion started to take hold of her then, but still her gift flowed.

Colour returned to Taran's face, and his eyes began to close.

She leaned forward, kissing him lightly on the lips.

'Please, please,' said Taran, as consciousness started to slip from him, 'save Rakan too.' Maya looked over at Rakan and started to stand, but Taran's hand briefly grasped hers. 'Just one more thing.' Maya leaned down, her ear close to his lips. 'Maybe when you save him, perhaps don't kiss him as well!' and with those words, Taran closed his eyes.

Maya found herself barely able to stand. Her limbs were so heavy with tiredness, yet she moved over to Rakan and pulled the sword from his body, staggering then falling as she did so.

Rakan made no sound as she crawled to his side, wondering if she was too late but determined to try anyway. She lay her hands upon his blood-spattered face and reached for her gift, hoping she would stay awake long enough to finish the task.

Rakan fell into blackness, the pain excruciating, impossible to resist as it dragged him under. Yet the agony he felt as he was dying was strangely eclipsed by the pain of not being able to save Taran and the girl, the futility of the situation, his defeat at the hands of Darkon.

He was no fool. He'd been a soldier for longer than most in this cruel world, watching hundreds die horrible deaths, and had always known he would never die in his bed; that wasn't his destiny. So as the light from the world started to fade, he'd accepted his fate, wondering whether the next time he opened his eyes, the nine hells would greet him. At least he would have plenty of company. He'd killed so many evil bastards in his life.

Yet, as his mind started to go blank, a light began to fill his head, his mind, his thoughts; not the dark red flickering flames he expected, but a golden glow that seemed to wash away his agony as if he stood in the pouring rain. The light faded, and he started to struggle to open his eyes again. Maybe he could somehow find the strength to push himself from the floor and fight once more with these last gifted moments,

Rakan didn't know how long he'd lain there, but he felt exhausted, yet his efforts were finally rewarded. He opened his eyes and looked up to see dark clouds moving sluggishly across a darkening sky.

This was wrong. He should be face down, mouth full of dirt, blood and bitterness.

He sat up without pain, then jumped to his feet. He knew his time would be short. The kind of wound he'd received should have killed him already, let alone left him able to stand. Then for the first time, he looked around.

The bodies lay where they'd fallen, clouds of flies swarming around gaping wounds. No more than a dozen steps away sat Maya on a log, eyes half-closed as if about to fall asleep, and next to her Taran. They sat there talking, deep in conversation.

There was something strange about Taran, something different he couldn't quite identify, but it was evident that Taran's armour was riven where Lazard had run him through with his sword, and he was covered in blood. Yet, he just sat there, attention firmly on the girl, talking.

Rakan looked down and saw his own broken armour, blood everywhere, yet none was flowing, maybe because there was none left to flow. He really must be dead, this was some parody of his final moments, and soon daemons would appear to continue his torture. Foolishly they had let him keep his sword, so he would make them regret that at least.

Taran stood and walked toward him.

Rakan stepped back, raising his sword. 'Stay back, daemon!' he warned, and the daemon that looked like Taran laughed.

Taran looked back over his shoulder at Maya. 'You might have healed his body, but you seem to have forgotten his brain,' he called, then turned back. Rakan, Maya saved us, she healed us, don't ask me how, but we are alive because of her. I'm no daemon, and we're not in hell.'

'Where are those two bastards, Darkon and Lazard then?' growled Rakan.

Taran's smile faded a bit. 'They're still here, more's the pity,' and he pointed at two strange ivy-clad trees. 'I've been trying to convince Maya ever since we awoke that I should kill them.'

As Rakan approached, he whistled through his teeth, and an evil grin spread across his face. 'Now I know I'm not in hell.' He tilted his head back and roared with laughter at Lazard and Darkon trapped in the vines while they looked back at him fiercely. 'This is definitely paradise if these two are here like this at my mercy!' He bent down and picked up a discarded dagger from the ground and moved toward them. 'Boys, boys, boys, this is going to hurt you so much, I can't even begin to explain.' A shadow of fear crossed the features of the two Rangers.

Maya quickly stepped between Rakan and the trapped men.

'No,' she said softly. 'They're not yours to kill.'

'Sorry, girl,' Rakan growled, bloodlust rising inside him, images of revenge starting to flood his thoughts.

'No!' she said again, this time more firmly.

'Move!' said Rakan, and raised his hand to push her aside then stopped. The hand in front of his face wasn't his hand, couldn't be his hand. Not a single sore blemished his flesh. He raised his other, and it was the same. He sheathed the dagger then rolled up his sleeves to see all the marks gone.

Taran stepped forward. 'She not only saved our lives, but she returned my good looks. See?'

Then Rakan realised why Taran looked different. The wounds on his face from the corporal's marks were gone, healed without a trace.

'Rakan,' Darkon snarled, finding his voice, 'your wounds and sores may be gone, but you're still damned ugly, and when your head is cut from your shoulders, even this girl won't be able to save your pathetic life.'

The rage which had diminished for a moment rose once again in Rakan. 'Well, it won't be you doing the cutting, and that's all that matters.' He lifted the dagger once more, his blood boiling, but again Maya stepped between him and Darkon.

'I've told Taran, and now I'll tell you. I won't allow these men to be killed. We'll leave them here to fare as they will, but we won't be killing them.'

'You don't understand,' growled Rakan. 'If we let them live, they'll escape. Shortly after that, they'll find us again, and he's right; your gift won't save you or me. They'll kill us before we even know they're there. I need to kill them now!'

Maya stood, her head only level with Rakan's chest, half his size but a strength of will radiating from her now that Rakan hadn't perceived before.

Taran stepped forward. 'Rakan, I agree with you,' and he put his arm around Rakan's shoulders, 'but before we push this further, let me ask you this.' Suddenly Taran wrapped his hand around the chain of Rakan's amulet and wrenched hard.

'What the hell, lad!' roared Rakan, spinning fast, his fist lashing out.

Taran ducked, and with a final surge of effort, the chain broke and the amulet fell away as Taran rolled backwards.

Rakan picked up a sword and raised it toward Taran, dagger in the other hand, but then a feeling of terrible pain ripped through his body and mind, and he fell to his knees as a scream tore from his throat.

As he knelt there, the pain gradually faded, and time seemed to slow. It seemed that the angry red mist in his thoughts through which he saw things, and that demanded violence as the answer to any argument, was gone.

So, despite the carnage, he saw for what seemed to be the first time, the green of the new grass beneath him, and the trees' bright colours. Even the breeze felt fresh upon his face. He realised that the lad in front of him was indeed the son he'd never had, and he had a sword ready to do him harm.

'What in the nine hells just happened?' Rakan gasped.

Taran lifted the amulet. 'It's this. When you had me enrolled in the army, Snark put one on me the day before I fought him remember? I felt the bloodlust when I wore it, but something was wrong with the chain, and it broke after the fight. I realised straight away there was some dark magic to the stone that's embedded into it. I've been wearing it since, but I took the stone out.'

Rakan took the amulet from Taran's hand, holding it carefully by the chain, and inspected it.

Maya looked over his shoulder, and there was the stone, strange clouds seeming to boil within it. 'It's incredible that something so small has such a dark power.' said Maya. 'But why?'

Taran thought for a moment before responding. 'Everyone who enters the army is given one of these, and everyone who wears it seems to have their negative emotions heightened. The only reason I can think of is to make the Witch-King's soldiers more formidable, and without question, it enhances the darkest parts of you and diminishes the brighter side.'

'Right,' said Rakan shakily. 'We need to move from here and quickly. Over half the day is gone, and I think the sooner, the better.'

Taran and Maya nodded in agreement, but Maya raised her hand. 'First, I need you to give me your word you won't kill these two.' She looked over at Lazard, who was struggling, striving to loosen the vines, whereas Darkon, with his injured arm, was unable to do much more than scowl.

Rakan nodded. 'I still want to kill them. It's still the right thing to do. But for the life you returned to me, I agree.'

As fast as they could, the three of them scoured the campsite, gathering packs, food, and water. Taran couldn't help but admire

Maya's resolve as she went through all the dead soldier's belongings with a purpose. A little later, they all stood outfitted, ready to leave, each carrying a pack.

Rakan and Taran had recovered their weapons, and Maya had taken a dagger and one of the Ranger's bows, along with a quiver full of arrows.

'Which way do we go?' asked Maya.

Rakan nodded at Darkon and Lazard. 'Let's wait until we're away from camp before we discuss such matters,' he suggested.

'Rakan!' called Darkon, and Rakan stepped closer. 'I'll find you, and when I do, I won't kill you fast. I'll take my time and relish every cut, every slice of skin I pare from your body. I'll be coming for you!'

Rakan stood straight, smiling, aware of his oath to Maya and that she was a step away watching. 'First,' he replied. 'It's hard to take that threat seriously when you look like a tree's stuck up your backside. However, assuming you escape and find me, yes, even with one arm, you're still likely better than me.' Suddenly, Rakan drew his dagger and plunged it into the elbow of Darkon's right arm, twisting it, severing sinew and muscle, before pulling it free, then stepped back as Darkon screamed in agony and shock.

'Now, even if you do find me, I have a feeling I'll win the next fight,' said Rakan winking, as he started to move away.

'Rakan!' exclaimed Maya, shock and hurt in her voice.

Rakan turned to Maya and shrugged his shoulders. 'First,' he said, 'I promised not to kill him, and I haven't. Second, I'm still an evil bastard with or without that amulet, so best not forget it. Now let's go!'

With that, they left the camp and walked into the woods at a fast pace, the piteous cries of Darkon following them into the undergrowth.

Kalas led his horse by its bridle, walking carefully through the woods, following the trail north that showed him the way like a signpost.

He was skilled at tracking, yet even a village boy would have been able to follow the main trail. It was as if someone had painted the trees and bushes along the path the travellers had taken; they were so different from those around them. Yet a village boy wouldn't have known that six soldiers and a captive had passed this way, and Kalas read this from the trail.

He'd learned to track when training as a royal guard and spent months in the forests of the kingdom and the border swamps perfecting his skills, and they came back to him as if yesterday.

Even amongst the random fall of leaves and deadwood, there was still a pattern, a consistency amongst the forest floor. Where animals or people passed, they left marks, imprints, sweeping lines from the fall of feet; however carefully they were placed.

This group had left more obvious signs of broken twigs, bent stalks, and the smell of human waste. They might be on a mission, but being followed didn't seem to overly worry them; only speed toward their destination and discretion seemed to be their prime concerns.

He'd come to the assumption there was a captive because when someone's movement was restricted, however slightly, they naturally compensated by widening their stance. Some of the footprints showed this pattern in uneven areas. He was also sure the captive was a woman, for her prints in the softest ground were smaller and shallow, indicating less weight.

He pushed himself fast, eating and drinking on the move with his concentration frequently broken by the daemon as it whispered of its hunger when, despite the distraction, something caused him to pause. So he stopped and knelt, and there it was. A new set of prints had joined the others!

Kalas tethered the horses and backtracked this new trail, and found that it ran parallel to the main one by some distance. As he followed it, sometimes losing it for a while as the person who had left it was very skilful, he found another and then another.

He returned to his horses an hour later, concerned.

There was the main party of six, and now it was apparent there were some very skilled scouts shadowing the main group. They kept a disciplined perimeter and left almost no mark of their passage, which meant they were highly trained and likely wary of danger.

They didn't know he was following that, he was sure, but forging ahead was no longer an option in case he ran into a hidden rearguard who might ambush him. He was confident he could overcome any foe in hand to hand combat even without the daemon's help. But an arrow through the eye would still kill him, and any serious injury would slow him and eventually mean his death without new life to replenish him.

His armour would do a lot to protect him, but it didn't make him invulnerable, and in fact, made him far easier to spot in a forest, as his shining suit was anything but well camouflaged.

He needed to move quietly and carefully from hereon. The horses had served him well, overcoming their fear of his possession, but were anything but quiet, and in thick woodland, they couldn't be ridden easily anyway. He removed the saddles and gear before releasing the packhorse, slapping its rump so that it trotted off, then turned to the gelding that had served him so well these last few days. He ruffled its mane, and in a rare show of affection, it nuzzled his shoulder, snuffling in pleasure as his fingers scratched its neck.

'I have no friends,' said Kalas, 'and I think you and I have actually become friends.' He scratched harder, and the appreciative horse tossed its head.

His other hand moved to his belt, removing his dagger, and swiftly he drew it across the horse's neck, a deep, swift blow. Kalas held its bridle tightly as eyes wide in shock, it tried to rear, but its legs buckled, and it fell to the floor. Kalas knelt and cradled its head, stroking its mane as its eyes began to close

He removed his helm and leaned forward. He wasn't hungry, but he fed anyway.

The next morning, as light filtered through the trees, Kalas arose.

He looked at his armour. It had been splashed with blood the night before but was again pristine, courtesy of the magic that imbued it. So he grabbed a handful of mulch and tried to get it to stick, but was not surprised when it fell away without a mark. If only the mages had had the foresight and wisdom to recognise that shining armour wasn't always a good thing, he wouldn't be having this problem. He sighed and gave up trying.

He looked over at the corpse of the horse, and for a moment, felt sadness and regret, yet the feeling didn't last long. What was done was done; it was time to focus on more immediate concerns.

Who exactly had made these tracks? It was obviously an important captive to have so many escorting her, but the reason why was a puzzle that intrigued him. So what better way to keep the boredom from his journey than continuing the hunt to find out.

Kalas wasn't hungry, but nonetheless ate some dried meat from his pouch and washed it down with tepid water. Then having covered any signs of his camp, he set out to follow the trail again

As he moved, he divided his attention between the ground at his feet and the surrounding woodland, always alert. Before long, he knelt to examine a deep scuff on a tree root that caught his attention. It was definitely less than two days old, maybe just one. Satisfied with his progress, he left the main trail and followed it a dozen steps to the side, the strange recent growth that marked it easily visible from that distance.

The whole day he tracked cautiously, searching the shadows as he listened for any untoward sound, a break in the rhythm of the forest, yet all seemed as it should. Occasionally he went back to the main trail to gauge how far ahead his prey was before returning to his path.

Kalas was so absorbed in his task that he was surprised to notice that the sky had begun to grow darker. He would need to stop to rest soon, for whilst the daemon could help him see at night and even keep his stamina up, the cost was that his senses would be overshadowed by its growing and insatiable need to feed. Still, he decided to push on just a little while longer to reach the crest of the hill he was currently on. It would be a good vantage point, he told himself.

Then when he finally reached the top, he wondered if his search was over.

He fought the daemon for control then, as the smell of blood filled his nostrils, driving it into a frenzy of excitement. 'Quiet,' he told it. 'You fed last night, remember. Be quiet.'

Kalas circled the campsite that had appeared before him, staying hidden in the undergrowth. As he searched, he found a new trail leading off to the northeast. He was tempted to follow it straight away, yet knew it would be better to wait until first light. In the meantime, he would see what had happened before night closed in. He stepped from the undergrowth, hand resting lightly on the hilt of his longsword, not because he would need it, but more from the comfort it gave, like the feeling of a lover's hand.

'I wondered when you would step from the shadows,' a voice said.

Kalas crouched, sword drawn in an instant, but then cautiously lowered it. He stepped forward, his eyebrows raised in unconscious amazement, for there was the owner of the voice encased in vines and leaves with another man beside him in the same situation.

'I know,' said Darkon weakly, 'I look like a damn tree. Now free us both, and I will see you rewarded by the Witch-King beyond your wildest dreams, whoever you may be!' He looked quizzically at Kalas' armour as he said this. 'But, be warned,' he added, 'if you don't, the Witch-King will see your face and have you hunted down and killed before the next moon rises.'

Kalas looked closely at Lazard then, whose eyes were half open and staring in a trance.

'Your friend is a spirit talker?' enquired Kalas, a smile spreading across his face.

'Yes, dammit. He is communicating with the Witch-King as we speak and what he sees the Witch-King sees. Free me now, or nothing the nine hells has to offer will be as bad as what befalls you.'

Kalas' laughter was deep and loud. 'Oh joy!' he exclaimed and removed his helm. 'It's hard to eat when I wear this,' he added conversationally, then leant forward to bring his face close to Lazard's. Kalas' eyes glowed a fierce red. 'Do you see me, Daleth? I'm coming for you. Kalas is coming for you! Do you hear me, Witch-King? I'm coming!'

With that, he turned back to Darkon. 'You have no idea what horrors the nine hells hold.' Darkon's eyes were wide, and he started to cry for the first time in his life.

'Now,' said Kalas, 'let me show you.'

Daleth opened his eyes in his bed-chamber to find himself covered in a cold sweat.

When he'd first communicated with Lazard, his fury had been incandescent. How could two traitorous soldiers and a girl have bested five of his finest Rangers? The girl, whose every step was now minutely wounding him as she healed the land around her, merely by walking through it.

Through Lazard's eyes, he could see she had found other ways to use her power as both of his Rangers' temporary imprisonment was testament to. Thankfully her weakness in letting them live would soon see them free and on her trail, to kill her and the two wretches in the most horrible of ways. He'd felt better as he imagined the unpleasant things the two Rangers would do, and Lazard had assured him that in two days or three at most, it would be over.

But then he'd watched transfixed through Lazard's eyes as a warrior had entered the clearing, and he could hardly believe what he had seen. A man wearing the armour of the long-dead Ember Kingdom, and not just any armour, but that of the royal guard, shining as if recently forged.

Lazard had wanted to break the communication right then, to try to concentrate on freeing himself, but Daleth had commanded him to watch, to see so that he could learn. Then, for the first time in his adult life, he'd felt a cold hand grip his heart as those eyes had turned red. Kalas was coming for him. Kalas, whom his supposedly loyal general, Alano, knew nothing about.

He'd watched Kalas drain the life and youth from Darkon and then fled Lazard's mind, not wanting to feel the agony of Lazard's imminent death, but he'd still felt the man's fear just before he severed the communication. Death didn't bother him, not when he'd orchestrated the fall of nations, yet still, he'd felt sorry for Lazard. Dying in such a fashion was not how a warrior should meet his end.

He lay on his bed and looked up at the painted ceiling, where frescoes portrayed his reign. Alano had lied to him, betrayed his trust! What should he do about such an act?

There were many reasons he'd kept Alano alive over the years. Initially, it was the awe he'd felt at Alano's display of swordsmanship in that epic battle, then, because he'd enjoyed feeling Alano's despair at being unable to fulfil his ancient oath. But as the years passed, it was for his counsel, his strategic mind, and truth be told, in this world of mortals, it felt reassuring to have Alano around when everyone else grew old and died.

Daleth had never enjoyed true friendship with anyone, but this didn't feel just like treason. The anger he felt was of betrayal by someone he'd grown unknowingly close to and who should never have been able to betray him, even if it was because a daemonic oath bound him.

Did he need Alano anymore as a general of his army? He'd easily conquered this realm when Alano himself had fought against him. Tiredness was taking its toll, he was irritable, and only complete loyalty was ever acceptable. He came to a decision.

But there were other matters to attend to first. He needed to ensure this girl and the two deserters died and quickly. There was nowhere they could hide permanently, not now, not with the girl's gift showing their every move. He closed his eyes and reached out to the senior overseer of the southern staging area, a city called Garnost, where twenty thousand troops were stationed. Less than a month to the start of the campaign, and soon they and others would join him on the march eastward.

Daleth made contact. He shared the location of where Darkon and Lazard had met their grizzly ends and also the image of the girl, the two soldiers, and Kalas that he'd taken from Lazard's mind.

'I want men ready to leave in the morning to hunt these fugitives down,' ordered Daleth, then paused as an idea formed in his mind. What if Kalas could be made to serve him as had Alano?

'The man Kalas is especially dangerous,' he continued, 'but I want him captured alive if possible, he could be very valuable, and the reward for his delivery will reflect that. The other three are traitors, and they should be slaughtered without hesitation. Do you understand?'

'Of course, my king,' affirmed the overseer.

'Report on your troops' status,' Daleth commanded.

'Currently, we have almost twenty thousand men. Fifteen thousand spears, four thousand medium infantry, and as for cavalry, we have four hundred lancers.'

'Send the cavalry out to hunt these fugitives down along with any skilled hunters you have,' ordered Daleth, 'and report back immediately they're dealt with.'

He started to break contact, but the overseer reached out again.

'What?' asked Daleth, with irritation in his thoughts.

The overseer quailed but still voiced his question. 'How many cavalry would my king like to send in pursuit. Would fifty or a hundred suffice?'

Daleth laughed without humour. 'No, send them all!'

Daleth awoke early to a serving girl who brought him food then tended to his other hunger.

They always came with boldness in their eyes; avaricious, sure they could win his heart, yet after so many decades, not one had ever lasted in his favour for long. None of them had managed to bear his child successfully, thus he cast them aside one after another in search of one who could. Many times, a girl would fall pregnant, only to give birth to a stillborn or die midterm. One day perhaps, one day.

He arose from bed, then stretched his tall frame in front of a silvered mirror, the strength of youth in his limbs. He turned to look at his reflection, nodding with satisfaction at his muscled body, then looked closer to discover silvered hair at his temples. Silver hair! The life he received from these lands was diminishing more and more at a time when his needs only seemed to increase. It was a good thing the invasion was on the verge of launching.

He donned fresh clothes of black linen, over which he dropped a light mail shirt, buckled on his weapons belt, and finished the look with soft boots of doeskin inlaid with intricate designs. He strode from his chambers and headed for his throne room, past guards, who snapped to attention as he approached, and serving girls who bowed low even as they tried to catch his eye. When he entered, it was a throng of activity as officers pored over maps while aides and messengers brought in details of troop readiness and supplies. The cascade of sound came to an immediate halt as they waited for him to approach the planning table, but instead, he walked through their midst. The one he was looking for wasn't there.

As Daleth strode from the room, the noise resumed, and he turned toward the stairs that led to the lower halls of the castle.

Every twenty steps or so, his guards saluted, and he nodded to each of them. They were expertly trained and loyal without question. Yet occasionally, he would still have one arrested along with his family, to be tortured to death on the premise of betrayal, so that everyone knew the cost should they ever turn against him.

He felt secure in his castle, or at least he had until last night. Now, however, there was a betrayer in its midst, one without a family to torture. Alano was the only person Daleth knew who could best him in combat, and it was his incredible skill that had seen Daleth spare him those fifty years ago as he admired his last stand, even as his dreams of continuing conquest crumbled.

His steps took him down a wide stairwell lit by flickering torches, and all the while, the sound of combat and the smell of sweat grew on the air. As he reached the bottom, a vast chamber opened before him. Despite being deep below ground, it was almost as bright as day, for sun globes were positioned all around its walls.

The sun globes were a leftover from the Ember Kingdom's mages. The spells that had created them long gone with the magis' passing, and yet here they were fifty years on, still illuminating the training halls. This was the very place that had seen the possession of Alano, Kalas, and their brothers in arms all those years ago; the flagstones permanently stained a reddish-brown from the blood spilt that fateful day. He often made Alano tell him the story, continually fascinated by what had transpired.

On the walls were racks of different weapons; shortswords, longswords, dirks and daggers, maces and clubs, staves and shields.

Approximately one hundred of his finest men were training here to become Rangers. Some worked in pairs, others in groups of four and five. Some wielded heavy wooden weapons, yet here there was also the clash of real steel, for Alano wanted these men to know the taste of its edge and the cacophony of combat. While killing blows were not allowed in sparring, now and again they landed, and were a gruesome encouragement for everyone to train harder. This was the only place in the realm that his men didn't have to come to attention, salute, or anything else, as he spent as much time here as they did, if not more.

He spied Alano on the far side of the hall, a group of about twenty men around him, listening intently to his instruction. They listened, for they knew he was the best; because it was their duty; and because soon they would go to war alongside their king.

Yet they didn't listen to him out of love, comradeship, or loyalty. Despite his importance to their king, Alano was an outsider, a daemon kin who feasted upon the life of others. They had all at times seen him assuage his hunger, a serving girl here or a peasant girl there, and the men despised him even as they respected his skill. However, one day, they too would give up their souls before joining the Rangers in a rite that Alano had never allowed Daleth to witness. Then they would be, as was Alano, takers of life, just in a different way.

Daleth took a greatsword and dirk from a rack on the wall. Most men would have needed both hands to wield the enormous weapon effectively, and yet in his right hand, it felt as light as parchment. He grasped the long dirk in his left, wickedly sharp with curved quillions designed to trap an opponent's blade, thus allowing the other weapon to deliver a killing blow.

He walked amongst his men, fighting in their designated areas, nodding in satisfaction at their form, speed, and power. These men were special, some even gifted, loyal to him and only to him, while a trail of bodies lay behind every one of them as they continued their journey to join the ranks of the elite.

He came to Alano's group and stood behind them, waiting for Alano to finish instructing them on how to deal with multiple opponents, multiple attacks, how to survive as long as possible against unfavourable odds until you prevailed or died in the trying.

The key, Alano was explaining, was not to wait for the enemy to attack as one, but to go on the offensive. It was imperative to dictate the fight, choose your position, put your opponents in each other's way, and to use their bodies as shields or even their spilt blood as a slippery defense.

Daleth waited for a brief pause in the instruction before raising his voice. 'Alano, how many men is it possible for a fully trained Ranger to defend against at once?' he asked.

Alano smiled. 'My lord, any of your Rangers could stand against four or five others not of their ilk, and stand victorious at the end.'

Daleth nodded and took a deep breath. 'My brothers!' he shouted, and the sound of combat was replaced by silence, broken only by the heavy breathing of the men as they listened. 'Arm yourselves with steel and attend me!' Those soldiers who held wooden weapons moved to the walls and placed them on racks to return with edged weapons in hand. They surrounded their king and the training space in which he stood with the twenty men and Alano.

'Today's instruction was a valuable one,' Daleth said, nodding at Alano, who nodded back. 'Soon we go to war, soon we will fight together on a field of battle against our enemies, and soon we will know victory!' He raised his voice at the last and lifted his sword.

The men shouted and cheered in salute; blades held high.

'We must be merciless. Whosoever doesn't stand fully with us, is against us, to be killed without hesitation, without remorse!' Daleth walked amongst them as he spoke to look them in the eye, and their love and loyalty to him shone back.

He slowly made his way to the steps leading up to a dais where a commander could watch his men train, and he turned to them, spreading his arms wide. 'Will you bleed for me?' he asked.

'Yes!' the men roared in return.

'Would you die for me?'

'Yes!' they cried.

'Will you kill for me?' he demanded, and turned to look Alano straight in the eye as he said this.

'Yes, yes, yes,' the men screamed.

Daleth waited, his eyes locked to Alano's, seeing the understanding in them.

'Then my loyal men. I want you to start by killing a betrayer in your midst!' Daleth lifted the greatsword to point toward Alano. 'Bring me this daemon's head!'

'We should have killed those damned Rangers,' muttered Rakan for the hundredth time, as he led Taran and Maya eastward across an open plain toward the sanctuary of the next bit of woodland, and ultimately the eastern boundary of the kingdom.

His mind was conflicted as they moved. Should he split from the other two? If he let Taran and Maya find their own way, his chance of survival would surely be higher, or instead, maybe the lad would see sense and join him on his own. But that thought lasted just a moment. Taran had been willing to lay his life down for the girl. He'd hardly leave her now, even if she were their biggest hindrance in escaping.

He turned and looked back at the valley behind them. In the distance, he could already perceive a subtle change of hue to the long grasses. In an hour, it wouldn't be subtle, and it showed exactly where they were heading. He'd be damned if he could see wherever she placed her feet, but she still left a mark greater than any footprint.

Rakan shook his head. He knew it was the impact of what he'd done that was creating this conflict, not Maya. His whole adult life had been spent serving in the army, it was his family, and he felt safe within it. The lure of splitting from the others was fed by a false hope that he might find a way back to that security because now he felt more lost and alone than he ever had.

Except as he looked back, he realised that he wasn't.

He owed this new life to Maya, a life free of disease and pain; however short it turned out to be. Then there was Taran, who had started to free him from the amulets hold, even before he tore it from his neck. He felt he could trust them to watch his back, not put a knife in it. There was goodness in them both.

Then the choice he'd made to take those damned Rangers down a peg or two had been surprisingly easy to make. So, the question was, if the gods gave him a chance to change his actions, would he do so? Rakan smiled to himself, his mind clearing. No, he'd do it all over again, every time.

The more he considered it, the more obvious it became. He'd gained far more than he'd lost. It was time to repay those debts and keep everyone together.

His mind made up, Rakan called a halt. They gathered close, drinking from water skins as he chose his words carefully.

'Maya, using your gift almost got us killed, and yes, I know it saved us too, but you need to stop using it every step of this journey. It's showing our trail to those who will soon be hunting us, and we will have no chance whatsoever of escape.'

Maya met Rakan's gaze. 'I can't seem to. It used to be that I could hide it, and it only came when bidden, but something's changed that.' She lowered her voice then. 'Or maybe someone.'

'Then there's absolutely no point in trying to hide our direction then,' said Rakan. 'Our trail can't be disguised, so our only hope is to outrun our pursuers, and have no doubt in your minds, those two will be coming for us, and likely any others who are nearby too.'

'We've got one chance in my opinion, and that's to try to make it across the Forelorn mountains to the Freestates, and fast. Staying in this kingdom is not an option. We will be hunted down, and whether it's a day or week, or if the gods smiled on us, a month from now, we'll all be dead. Personally, I'd bet on a week. The Freestates are about a dozen days to the east if we travel at speed and don't get caught or run into trouble. We'll have a chance, a small chance, but a chance nonetheless.'

'So if we make it to the Forelorn mountains, we'll be safe?' asked Maya, a ray of hope in her eyes.

Rakan thought about lying, but he wasn't a subtle man. 'No, our troubles continue because then we have to get across.'

'I've heard of the trade pass through the mountains. Surely we can cross that late at night and find sanctuary in the Freestates.' suggested Taran.

Rakan laughed even if he didn't find it funny. 'Lad. First, there's a damn fortress at either end, and each of those is likely poised for war manned by hundreds of men, if not more. Now, it's not impossible that we could get into the one this side, but before long, we'd be challenged, exposed, then executed on the spot. However, let's say we remained briefly undiscovered. We wouldn't be able to open the heavily barred and guarded gates ourselves, so we'd need to lower ourselves from the walls without being seen. I doubt we'd get that far, but if we did, then we'd get arrows in our back as we crossed the open pass between the two fortresses, or if we somehow made it near the other side, we'd get arrows in our chest instead. This way leads to certain death.'

'So then we make our own way across.' said Maya. 'We get or make equipment, and we find a route over the mountains far from the pass, then we don't need to worry about either side and their arrows.'

Rakan sighed. 'Sorry Maya, you've obviously never been near these mountains. Before we get to the top, assuming we even had the skill, experience, or equipment, it's said you can't even breathe the air for some reason, and that's assuming we don't freeze to death first. But there is maybe one other way to cross, yet that will be fraught with danger too, but it offers us hope nonetheless.'

'Ember town,' continued Rakan. But from the looks on Taran and Maya's faces, he could see they had no idea what he was talking about. 'Realistically, that's the only option we have, and where I suggest we head. It's a town where most are decent folks. They scratch out a living at the base of the mountains, but more importantly, they also happen to sit upon the one other possible route through.'

'I've never heard of the place, even though I've spent several years on the road,' mused Taran, and Maya shook her head as well.

'That's not surprising,' said Rakan. It's not on most maps, nor is its existence common knowledge as it's rather special. The people there are led by an old lord named Laska, the only surviving noble from when the Witch-King invaded the Ember Kingdom all those years ago, hence the name of the town. The man must be way over ninety by now, and it's been years since I've seen him. The Witch-King allows him to carve out a life with his people in return for the usual tithes and occasionally helping agents get over the mountains somehow. I've previously had cause to go there twice, to help escort an agent who had returned from the Freestates.'

'This doesn't sound bad at all,' Taran said enthusiastically, and Maya nodded in agreement. 'How do they get agents across? Is there another pass?'

Rakan shook his head. 'I'm not altogether sure, although there must be. Those who returned were unsurprisingly secretive as agents are not the talkative sharing type. There was some mystery shrouding the route that I could never find out about.'

'It hardly seems dangerous compared to the option of trying to stay alive here in the kingdom or crossing the trade pass,' said Maya hopefully.

Rakan shook his head. 'You'd be forgiven for thinking so. But I've only been there twice because, as far as I'm aware, from the dozens of agents the Witch-King sent, only two actually made it to the Freestates and back again while I was assigned to that sector. Anyway, we will need to convince Laska that it's in his best interests to let us attempt a crossing.'

'Well, if you know the man, can't we just pretend to be on the king's business?' Maya suggested.

Rakan nodded slowly. 'It's plausible he might recognise my authority in this regard,' and a smile spread across his face.

'Are we all in agreement then?' asked Rakan. 'Do we aim to find sanctuary in the Freestates and fool Laska into helping us do so?'

'Agreed,' said Taran, reaching out to grasp Rakan's forearm then Maya's.

'I agree too,' said Maya, gripping Rakan's forearm in turn. 'We are stronger together than apart. Just don't expect me to save your lives all of the time!' she joked, and they all laughed together.

Then Rakan spoke. 'First things first. Taran, you and I need to rid ourselves of armour and shields, for speed is the thing that will help save us now. I hope you both feel up to a bit of exercise?'

'Why's that?' asked Taran.

'Well,' said Rakan. 'Now we run!'

Chapter XI

Kalas knelt and examined the trail in the soil. Three people, one a woman who barely left a trace, and two men were moving with haste as shown by the indent of heal and elongated stride, which indicated a running step.

The captive, it seemed, had escaped and was now with two of the soldiers. Initially, there'd been an attempt to disguise their destination, but now the trail led in almost a straight line through plain and woodland toward the Forelorn mountains. They were going to attempt a crossing to the Freestates.

Damn the daemon and damn his constant hunger and need to kill. He could have gotten information from the two Rangers, yet instead, he'd feasted too swiftly, his hunger clouding his thoughts and ability to make sound decisions.

The captive was important, they'd been taking her to the capital, and as he looked around at the change to the wilderness around and above him, it was now apparent why. This girl, this woman, was somehow healing the land, breathing life back into it with a power that was nothing like he'd ever heard of.

'Imagine what such a powerful life would taste like,' sighed the daemon in his head, and he felt hunger wash over him, insatiable, as if it hadn't eaten in weeks.

'Quiet!' he thundered, pushing back. 'We are going to find the Witch-King and kill him or die in the trying, not pursue some girl just to satiate your hunger.'

The daemon whined and writhed at his sudden strength of mind, filling his head with feelings of gratification should he slay her.

'No,' said Kalas, 'we will not hunt her down.' Yet thoughts came to his mind that the daemon subtly placed without his knowing. 'But, we still need to join the Freestates forces so we can face and kill the Witch-King, so there would be no harm in following their trail a little longer.'

'Then when we slay him,' coaxed the daemon, 'we should perhaps drain *his* life instead, imagine the taste and just imagine if it were possible to gain some of his power; it's so strong.'

Kalas sank to his knees, saliva dripping from the corner of his mouth, blinded by images of glory, of Daleth dead at his feet, his blood on his lips, his life in his veins. He could know a power unsurpassed, and vengeance would be had for his dead friends, for his long-dead king.

'But first,' whispered the daemon. 'Wouldn't it be easier to kill Daleth if we were able to somehow feed off of the girl's power? 'Is that what you're considering?'

'Yes,' mused Kalas. 'Anything that helps us fulfil our oath to kill Daleth. There is no harm in trying to make sure. We should kill the girl first, kill the girl!'

Thunder rumbled. 'A storm is coming,' he told the daemon, 'we should find shelter.' He stood but saw the sky was clear, no storm clouds, yet the thunder was louder, and now the ground shook with its anger. He scanned the hills surrounding his position only to see a line of cavalry crest the ridge no more than an arrow's flight to his north.

He looked back the way he'd come. The cover of the forest was too far away, and he'd been seen. To run would simply lead to him being cut down from behind. He stood for a moment, the daemon quiet for once as he quickly counted the lance tips glinting in the grey light.

There were too many, that was for sure. Daemon kin or no, there were too many. If they all attacked at once, he would fall soon enough, and all his dreams would come to nothing.

He sighed. He'd run once before in his life and had regretted it ever since. The time for running was long behind him.

'Don't worry, my brother,' whispered the daemon in his mind. 'I am with you always. Let us dance together, the dance of death.'

Kalas knelt again, then placed his hands on the ground as the cavalry drew closer.

Captain Kasamda led two centuries of light cavalry as he rode through this dying dustbowl of a land. The evil of the Freestates was growing stronger, sapping everywhere of goodness, and only the power of the Witch-King had stopped the kingdom from being overwhelmed years ago.

He sent a short prayer of thanks to his divine ruler before focussing on the countryside around him. Soon he and his men would join the army to crush any Freestates force guarding the border pass, and then his lancers would be let loose to ravage the countryside beyond and to run down any soldiers who escaped.

First though, there was this demeaning task of hunting down two deserters with a runaway captive and some fugitive or foreign spy that the Witch-King, in his wisdom, wanted to be captured instead of killed.

He and four hundred cavalry had left the staging town of Garnost several days before, and had split into two units of two hundred men. The orders were simple, and Kasamda wanted the reward that went with the capture of the fugitive. Still, he would be happy with just easing his boredom by slaughtering some peasant girl and the two deserters who had supposedly helped her escape. The men laughed as they rode, glad to be away from the confines of the city, and Kasamda could only agree. Riding with the wind in his hair was a feeling that was surpassed only by listening to the screams of those he or his men killed.

The Witch-King had given a general location to the overseer, and they were trying to find it, but also it was said he would use his powers to show them the way. Kasamda knew him to be divine, he was ageless after all, yet he doubted the Witch-King's powers were sufficient to do such so far from the capital. But his doubts had disappeared when they'd come upon the trail earlier in the day.

True to his word, the Witch-King had somehow healed the land and painted a bright line of healthy trees and grass that matched the trail of the fugitives, so he and his men had thrust spurs into the horse's flanks and urged them to speed to hunt their prey down.

As Kasamda crested a long slope slightly ahead of his men, he couldn't believe his luck. I'm truly blessed by the gods, he thought, for there below him in the middle of plain on the trail was the fugitive. It was obviously him, for he matched the description given by the overseer. The armour design was antiquated and certainly not of this realm. It shone brightly in the dim light, and he laughed. This couldn't have been any easier.

Kasamda readied to order his lancers forward to run the warrior down, but to his disappointment, the man who had now seen them sank to his hands and knees in apparent defeat. Dammit, he thought, there goes some of the fun, but more would still be had. Yes, to claim the reward, he just had to bring him back alive, but that didn't mean he couldn't pull a few fingernails on the way.

He raised his hand. A small company of twenty of his men trotted forward in response, urging their horses down the gentle slope to surround the man. Their lances were raised, for he'd made sure they knew to kill this man was not an option unless they wanted their own head on a lance as well.

As he watched, the warrior slowly got to his feet. He wasn't close enough to hear, but he could imagine the pleas for mercy spilling from the man's lips. Kasamda shielded his eyes from the weak sun, which was irritating him more than usual, and wondered why so many of his men were dismounting in such a strange fashion. But then the sound of horses whinnying in terror reached him, accompanied by cries of men in mortal pain.

'Don't kill him!' he shouted. 'Whatever you do, don't kill him!' With that, he raised his hand and signalled for his remaining men to follow him down the slope.

This was going to be even more entertaining if the warrior put up a fight. As he rode nearer, he realised in disbelief that none of his men were in the saddle anymore. In fact, the only man now standing stood in a suit of shining armour that seemed to have shed the blood that must have been splashed upon it.

Kasamda couldn't believe his eyes.

The warrior just stood there surrounded by a pile of dead horses and twisted men, a sword held loosely in each hand by his side. His head was down with the sun casting a strange light on his face, though how that could be when the sun was at his back was not quite right.

Twenty of his men, good men. Damn, he wouldn't have thought it possible. A well-trained man on horseback at one with his mount was worth two or three men on foot, and yet, this warrior had killed twenty, making a mockery of the odds. If he hadn't witnessed it, he would have thought it impossible.

He stopped his horse as a cold hand gripped his insides. 'Sergeant,' he said, turning to the man on his left. 'Take another forty men, capture this warrior, and don't make a mess of it as those other fools did!'

The sergeant nodded, lifted his arm with two fingers raised, then cantered forward. He held his lance lowered but reversed so the haft could be used to knock the man down. The two companies followed suit, taking their sergeant's lead, not wanting to follow their erstwhile comrades to the grave.

Kasamda relaxed a little. He'd known the sergeant for close to ten years, a tough man and an experienced lancer. He would approach slowly to within fifteen paces, then spur his horse forward in surprise. The haft of the lance with the weight of the charging horse behind it would floor this warrior, armoured or no. Then, however skilled, the warrior would be stunned and helpless whilst they bound him.

Having lost twenty comrades to this man, he would make sure he took more than the few fingernails he'd promised himself to appease the hurt pride of his men.

The sun broke through the clouds, and he sighed in relief, its warmth banishing the coldness he'd felt. This would be a good day after all; he was sure of it.

Taran's vision was blurred, and his breath came in short gasps as he tried to keep up with Maya. Rakan had initially led the way, but a new order seemed to have naturally asserted itself shortly into their flight.

Maya had hunted her whole life, so had decisively taken the lead. Her trail craft was unbelievable. It didn't matter where they ran, across a plain, a valley, or through the woods such as they passed through now. She chose without pause a route that followed game trails, natural breaks, or paths without ever deviating from their direction of flight.

Rakan, having been so effectively replaced, gruffly announced he would watch their trail for any signs of pursuit, whilst Taran took the centre.

Taran was rather happy with the change, because he couldn't help but appreciate Maya's agile and fluid movement through the trees, and it made him feel like he chased a creature of the woods itself. However, there was a downside to Maya leading, and that was the unrelenting pace. Taran was strong. He knew he was from all those successive years of smithying and then fighting, but as he called out for Maya to stop, his heart hammered painfully in his chest, and he realised his stamina for running distances was nowhere near hers.

Maya responded to his call and turned with her hands on hips, looking at him from under her tangled hair.

Taran felt his heart beat faster again, but this time not from the exercise. That kiss she'd given him. Had there been anything in it beyond sharing the elation and sheer relief that they had survived a close encounter with death?

She smiled at him, a soft smile that lifted the corners of lips that Taran remembered tasted so sweet, and lifted her hand, unconsciously brushing her hair back behind an ear.

Taran wasn't sure his heart would slow down as he noted for the first time the defined line of her jaw and the pulse in her neck before her ungovernable hair promptly fell back over her face.

'I'm sorry,' Maya said, noting Taran struggling to catch his breath. 'You should have called out sooner. The problem is, when I run, I often lose myself in thought by imagining how beautiful all the land could be.' As she spoke, she reached out toward a small sapling, struggling in the grey half-light. It was weak and twisted, having gained little sustenance from the rotting, dank soil. Maya held its slender trunk, and moments later, the tree started growing taller and stronger, branches thickening. Suddenly blossom erupted all over, and she looked on in delight at her handiwork.

Taran stood watching, mesmerised by this display.

'You see,' she said. 'Imagine if the whole forest looked like this, the whole land, everyone would be so blessed, so gifted.'

Taran nodded mutely. He'd known many women of different shapes and sizes, and was fortunate because most had been beautiful in some way or another, at least to the eye. Maya wouldn't usually have been his type. She was tall, almost as much as he, whereas shorter women were usually his preference. Her looks were ... he couldn't quite put a word to it, but then one came to mind, exotic. Yes, she didn't really look like the kingdom folk. There was an olive colour to what little skin he could see under the filth, her hair the darkest black where it wasn't covered with dust and dirt from the trail.

Taran realised he was staring and looked around. 'Where's our fellow fugitive?' he asked.

They listened and soon heard a crashing getting closer.

'My guess is that's either an angry bear or perhaps a wild boar, or maybe, just maybe, that's Rakan. He's not exactly the stealthiest person I've ever known,' joked Taran, 'nor the subtlest either,' and Maya laughed softly.

Rakan puffed into view. 'What are you two smiling at?' he asked, as he crashed to a halt, breathing heavily.

'I won't bore you with the answer,' Taran replied straight-faced, and Maya's laugh rang out like music, before she covered her mouth with her hand.

'You youngsters should show more respect,' Rakan grumbled, and swung the pack from his back to pull out a water skin. 'Let's take a break. While we need to move fast, if we don't keep our strength up, we'll be useless if we need to fight.' He looked at Maya. 'To be honest, I'm struggling. You may have healed my wounds old and new, but you didn't make me any younger.'

They all sat to catch their breath as they chewed on dried meats and drank sparingly.

'There's no one following us as yet,' said Rakan shortly, 'not that I could see anyhow. Yet while these woods help keep us hidden, it also helps conceal anyone following us as well. We'll come to the eastern plains in a few days, and then we'll be in the open. After that, a couple more days in some heavy woodland before we need to cross the white river. That's when we start getting close to the Forelorn mountains. Crossing the river will be a problem. If there are troops stationed at the bridges when we arrive, we are going to have a fight we might not be able to win on our hands.'

'If that's the case, we could always swim instead.' Taran pointed out.

Rakan shook his head. 'That wouldn't help. The problem is that it's called the White River because it flows so fast from the mountains. It's wide, full of rocks, and I doubt anyone could swim across without being swept away and getting their heads caved in. We have to hope a bridge is clear, and if not, then we'll have no choice but to try and force a crossing if there aren't too many soldiers.'

'Then what are we waiting for?' said Taran. He stood and walked over to Maya, then reached out a hand and pulled her smoothly to her feet when she took it.

Maya leaned in close for a brief moment. 'If this wasn't a race for our lives, I'd enjoy you chasing me,' she said quietly, then turned, put on her pack, and started to run.

'Close your mouth, boy,' laughed Rakan, then patted him on the shoulder before giving a gentle shove to set him in motion. He shook his head and smiled as he saw Taran set off after Maya. Maybe it was him getting old or the fact he no longer wore the amulet, but it pleased him to see the two of them warm to one another. The gods only knew how little time they had left, so if they found some good in this world before their lives were taken, he was happy for them.

He knew they had only the slimmest chance of survival, for the odds were too stacked against them. The forces the Witch-King would send against this girl and the killers of his beloved Rangers were beyond anything they could overcome. Yet, Rakan wasn't used to defeat, and to have stayed alive this long meant all his enemies were dead behind him. So, he wouldn't give up until the last breath left his body, and thanks to the girl, he'd kill a few more of the bastards sent to kill him before he left the land of the living to whatever came next.

He pushed himself into a jog, keeping the others just in sight, then looked back over his shoulder at different times to see if anyone was following, but the trail remained empty. So far, so good. Perhaps he should start thinking of how to live as opposed to how he was going to die.

He moved onward, enjoying the strength in his limbs, all his aches and pains gone thanks to the magic of the girl.

Yes, perhaps when he next met Darkon or, more likely, Lazard with his two good arms, the outcome might be different.

Alano had lived with the agony of being possessed, of having to continually fight the daemon's whim for what seemed years beyond reason. During this time, he'd taken so many lives to sate its hunger, to keep it at bay, and to retain his sanity while he served Daleth.

There were times when he awoke covered in blood to find the cold, shrivelled corpse of a serving girl bloodied in his bed without even the memory of committing the horrific things that had been done, and he would weep in regret and sometimes try to kill himself or kill the king. Yet, each time the daemon would stop him.

Theirs was a strange symbiosis. Alano's iron will held sway for the most during the day, yet the daemon at times took control during the night. It demanded blood for the life it contained, to keep it nourished as well as to keep Alano young, and he would reluctantly or at times unknowingly concede that control.

Yet now, for the first time since that fateful battle fifty years past, he called upon it of his own free will, called it forth to join him.

Alano had anticipated what was coming before the final words left Daleth's lips. The way he'd instructed his men to arm themselves, moved away to the dais, and then looked him in the eye had given away his intentions. He'd started planning before the death sentence was even passed.

The lesson of the day had been how to fight against the odds, two, three, or four against one, and how to emerge victorious at the end with a trail of bodies behind you. Now here he was, one man with a wooden practice sword surrounded by a hundred of the best fighting men in the realm, soon to trial for a place in the Rangers, trained by him.

Still, irrespective of the numbers arrayed against him, the underlying principle of going on the attack before the enemy coordinated, to dictate the fight and not be dictated to, was the same.

Alano called upon the daemon to lend him its strength and speed as his wooden sword swept up between the legs of a soldier in front of him, whose weapon was raised to salute his king. He caught the falling blade before the man even began to yell and cleaved it through the back of his neck a mere heartbeat after Daleth spoke the last word.

As the man fell, blood sprayed over those nearest, and instinctively they moved back, shocked by the sudden violence. Alano dropped the sword, whipped the man's dagger and a dirk from his belt before he hit the ground, then charged into the men in front of him, eyes shining so brightly that they fell back in horror as he bore down upon them.

He plunged the dirk into the belly of the nearest man, having sidestepped his sword and twisted it before cutting to the side, so the man's entrails flopped out like snakes around his ankles. Alano kicked his falling body back into the men behind him.

Alano and the daemon fought as one. He'd never felt so fast, so strong as he pushed deep into the mass of men.

Daleth stood upon the dais, watching as Alano charged right into the midst of the soldiers he'd spent years training, without pause or hesitation, armed only with a dagger and a long dirk.

It was, without doubt, the most stupid move he'd ever seen Alano make. He should have kept the man's sword, fought a defensive action, and taken maybe ten or a dozen down until the weight of the others overwhelmed him. Yet Alano never made foolish moves in combat, and what seemed at first like a suicidal berserk rage without thought, suddenly showed itself as the most brutal strategy Daleth had ever seen.

He'd called the men close, and they were packed side by side. As Alano attacked them, they had little room to lift, let alone swing the long weapons they now held, whereas Alano's choice of weapons were simple extensions of his hands.

The men in front tried to step back to give themselves space to defend themselves, and the men behind tried to surge forward to get to Alano even though most couldn't see him. This chaos of pushing and shoving served only to cramp their ability to fight effectively.

Daleth watched open-mouthed as his men fell like trees in a storm. He could barely see Alano as the man fought with inhuman efficiency, changing direction every strike, using a falling body to shield his back, or the thick pillars that supported the castle above as natural defense to protect his flanks.

There was even more to it than Daleth first realised. Wonder almost overtook the chill he was starting to feel. Alano's blows were not just to kill; they were to maim, to inflict terrible bloody damage. As guts fell to the floor, as blood sprayed from opened arteries, flailing men disrupted their comrade's attacks, had them slipping in the growing pools of blood, and yet Alano always moved on a firm footing.

The noise of the screaming, dying men was deafening. At least fifty of the hundred men who'd been standing now lay upon the floor. Most were already dead, but others tried to stuff entrails back into their bodies or to stem the heavy flow of blood from devastating wounds.

Yet he noticed that Alano was starting to slow. However skilfully he moved, blades had found their mark, and whilst still deadly, Alano was losing strength.

Now, as more men died and the fight lengthened, the remaining soldiers had more space with which to wield their longer weapons.

Alano's winning strategy had now almost defeated itself.

However, Alano was nothing but consummate in his skill and awareness of the changing tide, so as he drove his dagger up through the throat and into the brain of one of the men, he caught the sword from the man's lifeless hands and started to move backwards. The remaining men, now numbering about thirty, made space between themselves and tried to move around to encircle him.

A dozen of the men had taken shields from the walls and behind this additional protection were pushing forward, endeavouring to deflect Alano's blows whilst their comrades tried to strike. Even so, they didn't last long.

Daleth lifted his blade, hefting the greatsword, no longer sure the one hundred would be enough.

There were now only a dozen men left, but they had Alano back against the far wall of the hall. The whole scene shone red like something from the nine hells, and Daleth could only imagine this was a semblance of all those years ago when Alano had first become possessed. Now, as then, the sun globes had been splashed in gore, and the light they shed was red, the red of blood.

The light in Alano's eyes was starting to flicker and fade, and one of his legs gave way.

The surrounding men dashed forward, wanting to be the one to strike the killing blow, but it had been a ruse or at least mostly, for Alano surged to his feet, striking about him. The soldiers fell, while only two managed to move back still alive. Yet now, Alano fell to both knees, and this time there was no doubt as to why.

A shortsword had impaled him just above the right hip, exiting from his back. His left arm hung useless and bloody from his shoulder, and he bore at least a dozen other minor wounds. The blood now pooling around him was his, yet still he grasped a sword in his right hand.

One of the remaining men edged forward, shield raised, weapon extended, only for Alano's sword to sweep out, cutting both feet from under him. As the man fell, Alano thrust the sword into the man's throat. Still, as he did so, the weapon came from his grasp, and he sank back into a kneeling position, his breath rasping from his lungs, bloody froth bubbling from his mouth.

The remaining soldier slowly circled Alano to cut him down from behind.

Daleth raised his voice. 'Hold!' he commanded, then made his way across the floor, every step in the gore of Alano's dance of death. He moved alongside the soldier. 'You survived,' he said, laughing. The man smiled shakily in reply as they turned to look at Alano. His head was down, bloody spittle dripping to the floor.

'What's your name?' asked Daleth. 'I know, it's Ryal,' he said before the man could answer. 'Of course, I know who you are. We will never forget this day you and I, will we, Ryal?'

Ryal shook his head in relief. 'No my king, as long as I live, never!'

'Alano,' said Daleth, and squatted beside his almost dead general. 'Can you hear me, Alano? You are soon to die, you who could have lived forever, seen things men could only dream of, but instead, you are soon to die. Why did you lie to me about not knowing Kalas? Did you hope he would succeed in his quest to kill me and stand by as his blade found my heart? An army of thousands protects me, and I am skilled myself beyond mere mortals. He has no hope of succeeding; surely you know this?'

'Who is he?' demanded Daleth and dropped to his knees. The blood stained his clothes, but he didn't care as he grasped Alano's shoulders and shook him. 'Who was, no, who *is* Kalas? Why lose your life trying to hide your knowledge of someone you haven't seen in fifty years?'

Alano laughed weakly then, blood foaming at his mouth. 'You want to know who he is? He is the one, the only one who could ever beat me. You think I am skilled, yet at my best, I was never his equal. Compared to him, you are nothing, for he will kill you in less than a heartbeat. When he faces you, you will die and your kingdom with you. You should be afraid, Daleth,' he coughed, blood spraying, but Daleth just leaned even closer, listening. 'Do you know why you should be afraid? Because Kalas is coming, coming for you!'

Alano's head dropped, his chin resting on his chest, his voice so soft. 'To kill you or die trying,' he murmured. 'That was my oath fifty years ago,' he coughed weakly. 'I am content to die now, knowing he will seek to accomplish what I wasn't able to do.' Then he fell silent without the strength to say anymore.

Daleth's heart hammered, his hands shaking. He looked around at what Alano had done and knew the truth of it. If somehow he ever faced Kalas on the field of battle, he wouldn't have a chance, not if he was alone.

'Did you know,' Daleth said, looking up at Ryal. 'Alano here is over seventy years old? He fought against me the day I took the throne. I spared him, for I had never seen someone so skilled with a blade. I gave him his life, a life immortal, and all I asked is that he serve me, loyally, honestly.'

Ryal shook his head, wondering whether his king was telling the truth. 'No, I had no idea,' he said. 'It's unbelievable. I have never seen his like; his skill is beyond compare. If this Kalas is as good as he says, we must ensure Kalas dies without ever getting close to you.'

Daleth turned to Alano. 'You've kept me company all these years; you shouldn't have lied to me. Fifty years you kept your oath, and we are about to start the greatest war in two generations, the blood would have flowed, you could have killed thousands, and drunk the life from a thousand more.'

Daleth watched as Alano fell back, the blood flowing from his wounds, saw his face grow paler with every moment, and knew that soon Alano's heart would stop.

An idea formed in his mind.

'Daemon,' he said softly. 'Alano seems keen to die. What about you? Do you want to simply end, to go back to the nine hells yourself, or fade into whatever oblivion awaits you? I understand why Alano wanted to betray me, but not you. If I spare your life once more, would you swear again to serve me, do anything for me, kill your beloved brother Kalas if you had to? Is Alano's eternal desire for revenge worth you dying for?'

Alano's eyes shone a weak red then, and the voice that came from his lips wasn't Alano's, and the sound still made the flesh crawl on Daleth's neck.

'It is true, we indeed withheld the truth, but I was still bound by oath and even now could not have killed you. Spare me again,' rasped the voice, 'and I will stand by your side to fight Kalas and my daemon brother who resides within. But allow me to have dominance, let me take total control of this body and mind. I would serve you unfettered by this mortal's conscience.'

There were but moments left to make a decision Daleth knew. The daemon's oath had lasted fifty years, and it seemed that the lie was due to Alano's love for Kalas and this unholy being's kinship to another daemon. Yet if he still had its loyalty and it was willing to face and kill Kalas if the need arose, then it was a risk worth taking.

Daleth stood and turned to Ryal.

'Do you serve me without question, without doubt, without regret?'

Ryal's eyes opened wide at the question, fanatical fervour shining within. 'Of course, my king.' He knelt in fealty. 'I live to fight and die for you!'

'I'm glad you said that. It makes this so much easier,' muttered Daleth, with a hint of regret. With that, he swiftly plunged his dirk into the side of Ryal's neck, then pushed him down, so the blood from the gaping wound flowed into Alano's mouth.

The light in Alano's eyes shone and grew brighter, and the sucking sounds he made as he drank Ryal's blood made Daleth's stomach churn.

He spun away, and walked through the gore, blood, and entrails that covered the floor, then looked back over his shoulder at the horrific scene and wondered for a moment if this was what the nine hells would look like.

'When you feel able to, come find me!' called Daleth as he mounted the winding stone stairs.

As he reached the landing above, he came across two guards, swords drawn, hands shaking, and Daleth realised they had heard the commotion but had likely been too scared to investigate despite their amulets. His immediate thought was to kill them there and then, but he paused, staying his hand.

'Don't worry, all is well,' he reassured them both with a smile, and he saw their shoulders sag with relief. 'I need you to do something for me.'

They saluted, anxious to please.

'Your general, Alano, is downstairs. Find him and tell him I sent you and that it's time to eat.'

With that, he turned away, a wicked smile on his face, and laughed at his own joke. Cowardice should always be punished, and what better way to punish them than by gifting them to his daemon.

Kalas stood surrounded by the bodies of the horses and men he'd slain. He couldn't believe his luck, for they'd appeared to have been under orders to capture him alive, for not a single one of the men had a blade drawn, or lance lowered as they'd approached, merely expecting him to cower in fear and surrender.

They'd been lulled into thinking him subdued when they had seen him on his knees, his hands in the dust, yet he'd simply been drying the sweat from his hands, the better to grip the handles of his swords in the heat.

He'd cut the first twenty men down, and all the time, they'd been hindered by their orders, not inflicting a single wound upon him.

The daemon in his mind crowed in delight at the blood spilt around him, and he found himself revelling in the bloodshed as well. Wasn't there a time once when he'd felt regret at taking lives? he pondered, but the thought drifted away before it found purchase.

He looked up the hill to see another forty-odd men approaching. This time their lances were lowered but reversed, to knock him from his feet, to stun then subdue him. Again they would pay for this foolishness with their lives. His slaughter of the previous men had not been random, and he stood amongst a circle of dead horses and men, the ground slick and slippery from the amount of blood that had been spilt.

He stood still, arms loosely at his sides, the daemon's voice soothing in his mind, telling him this was what he'd been born to do, had trained to do, to be the perfect killer of men. That this was just another step toward his destiny, and he couldn't fail.

The horses slowly picked their way through the bodies and were skittish at the overwhelming smell of blood. All the while, Kalas waited patiently and identified the sergeant who would soon be the first to charge in an attempt to knock him from his feet. He sheathed his swords and turned his back as encouragement for them to make their move, then nimbly leapt up onto the body of a horse that lay atop another. The daemon enhanced his senses, so he could almost feel the beating of the hearts of the men and beasts upon which they rode.

It was a sensual feeling, and it washed over him instead of doubt or fear. His heartbeat quickened as he anticipated hot blood splashing over his face and the life to be drunk from still twitching bodies.

He heard the horses as the men urged them forward and the men's curses as the animals slipped and foundered. He turned to see the sergeant's horse slither in the mire before going down, pitching the sergeant over its neck. The men on either side frantically pulled their horses away left and right so as not to trample him. Kalas leapt down then and swept up the sergeant's fallen lance. As the man struggled to rise with the wind knocked from him, Kalas drove it through his body and pinned him to the ground. The man screamed in agony, and his fingers dug furrows in the bloody soil.

Kalas' swords seemed to leap into his hands, and he threw his head back and laughed, not realising the sound that came forth wasn't his own but that of the daemon howling, a sound from the pits of hell itself. The surrounding horses whinnied and reared at the unearthly noise, and Kalas' eyes shone red, flickering from the flames deep within. The men's voices rose in fearful shouts, and suddenly into their midst, he charged.

The horses panicked and tried to shy away, twisting and fighting against their rider's frantic attempts to control them. As the soldiers were high on horseback above him, Alano started to butcher the horses. He hammered his swords down upon equine necks, slashed open their throats, or cut their forelegs from under them.

He twisted and spun and used their bodies as shields, so that for most of the men, he couldn't be seen. Horses fell as did their riders and his swords did what they were supposed to do, had been forged to do all those years ago. They ended life after life.

As the men around him fell, orders were forgotten, and lance points thrust toward him. Some soon found their mark, slowing him, hindering him, yet it was too little too late, for the last rider went down even as the man thrust his lance deep into Kalas' thigh.

He knelt, the agony of the lance in his leg taking his breath away, but the daemon helped him deal with the pain. He wrapped his hands around the haft and wrenched it free, his blood spraying into the air. He looked up at the hill through the pain to see way over a hundred men sitting in shocked silence at what they had just witnessed. He needed them to stay there a little longer.

Kalas stood again, moving as steadily as possible to the one man still alive, the sergeant. He pulled the lance from the man's body, then hauled him upright, feeling blood splash over his boots. The sergeant was almost unconscious, but it mattered not. In full view of everyone on the hill, Alano tore the man's helm off, and leaning forward, sank his teeth deep into the man's neck, drinking his blood, feeling wounds heal and his strength return in a rush.

There was no way he could defeat the others, not now. They would have seen what he could do if they tried to subdue him. Next time they would charge from a distance, run him down, spear him through, orders be damned.

The daemon was now urging him to run, seeing past its own bloodlust to the folly of taking this fight even further. 'Run,' it screeched, 'save us.'

Kalas shook his head. He couldn't defeat so many men, not now. Now it was his time to die.

Kasamda sat upon his mount and looked aghast at the scene below him. Sixty of his men butchered by one man. No, not a man, not even close, a daemon ... for what else could he be but daemon spawn?

He remembered his father's tale of when years before he'd helped conquer this land, riding with the Witch-King, and how in the last battle, the Ember King's guard had ridden out to confront their invading army in a final hopeless battle.

He'd scoffed at the story, of how less than a thousand supposedly daemon-possessed warriors had almost routed the Witch-King's army, putting paid to further conquest. Instead, he'd chosen to believe that his father had lost his mind in his dotage. He'd killed him shortly after that, sickened by his apparent weakness.

Yet now, as he looked down the hill at a man he'd seen pierced by lance and sword, stand and rip the throat from his poor sergeant, he realised the truth of his father's words.

He licked his lips nervously.

The men all around him sat in their saddles in deathly silence, not believing what they'd witnessed, awaiting his orders to charge, run this creature down, and avenge their fallen brothers.

He drew breath, about to give the order, when movement below caught his eye. The daemon was running, and for just a breath, he felt relief, but then realised the creature wasn't running away; it was running up the hill, running toward them.

Its swords were in its hands, the fire from its eyes outshone the dying sun in the sky behind it, and the sound that screeched from its mouth was the most hideous noise he'd ever heard. The creature was attacking.

The horses started to rear in panic, and it spread to the men in an instant. Suddenly, one of the lancers nearest Kasamda wheeled his horse around and galloped away. In all his years, Kasamda had never seen someone run; the consequences were just too hideous.

But moments later, shouting with fear, more and more followed the man's lead.

Kasamda turned back to see the daemon closing in, then looked around frantically to find that he was all alone. Not a single one of his men had stayed.

His trembling hand lowered the lance, but as he turned back to face the daemon, he realised it was far too late. The daemon flashed by. For a moment, he thought it had let him be and felt shame that he'd wet himself in panic, but realised as he looked down that it was his blood soaking his trousers instead.

I'm sorry, father, he thought. I'm sorry I didn't believe you. Then everything went dark.

Chapter XII

Taran sat and thought back over the last few days.

They'd covered a lot of distance across all types of terrain, thanks to Maya setting a pace that, while demanding, was also achievable. She would run for fifty strides, then slow to a fast walk for twenty, alternating between the two. Pushing forward, then recovering while still on the move. It had been far better than trying to run all the time.

At times they'd had to circle settlements, giving them a wide berth to ensure their presence remained undetected, and now they were currently camped in dense woodland after Rakan had suggested they break a little earlier than usual for the day. They were exhausted and needed more time to rest and recuperate. There was still no sign of pursuit, but that wasn't to say that Rakan hadn't grumbled and cursed in worry at the need to do so.

Taran had shared his concern, for if Darkon and Lazard had escaped, then they would be following, and yet Darkon had been badly wounded, so maybe, just maybe, they were leaving those two far behind. But Rakan was sure they wouldn't be the only ones who hunted them.

So even as he'd collected firewood earlier in the afternoon, he'd stayed alert for danger, often stopping to listen, and his hand had never strayed far from the hilt of his sword. The task had been surprisingly more difficult than it should have been. Despite being in a forest, much of the wood had been damp and covered with mould, making it unsuitable due to the thick smoke it would have produced, so he'd had to take time to find the driest he could.

After that, Rakan had taken some time to show him how to create traps and alarms. Some were simple, designed to create noise. Small dry sticks slid under leaves so they remained unseen, but that would cause a loud snap to give an audible warning should a foot be placed upon them. Other nastier ones were hunting snares, adapted to spring a sharpened stick into any trespasser's body. Nothing fatal to a human, but enough to cause shock, pain, and alarm, giving warning to the camp.

Maya had left to hunt as soon as they'd chosen the campsite. At the time, he and Rakan had both voiced concerns about her going out alone, but she'd pointed out that she was better off without them if they wanted her to return with any food.

He'd nonetheless worried about her for a while and had wondered if she thought of him as often as he found himself thinking of her. It was strange. Never in his life had a woman kept his attention for more than a few drinks or perhaps a night. Her independent strength was rather attractive, but then he found a lot about her attractive of late.

Now, as the light in the woods started to dim, he started preparing the campsite.

He cleared the ground under the rocky outcrop for sleep and then set to creating a medium-sized fire pit. He dug into the soft ground, lined the resulting pit with stones, and then surrounded it with a half-circle of rocks. Next, he placed a couple of large flat rocks to create a roof to hold the heat and stop the light from being seen as the opening was toward the rock face.

Rakan came back into camp and raised his eyebrow as he picked up some more sticks and started carving the ends to sharp points. 'Damn fine work,' he said. 'Just a shame we can't do anything about the smell once you get the fire going, but at least there's no wind, so the smoke won't carry much tonight anyway.'

Taran warmed under the genuine praise.

It was getting quite dark. As Taran got the fire going, he kept looking around, then to his relief, he saw Maya flitting through the trees, moving amongst the shadows. As she came into camp, Taran could see she carried a half dozen rabbits and a few birds. The pouches at her side seemed stuffed full as well.

Rakan stomped off with a few more sharpened stakes as Maya sat next to Taran in front of the fire. She unslung the game from around her shoulders, then pulled a knife and started to expertly skin the rabbits. She looked at Taran from under unruly hair, her face filthy.

Despite the grime, her eyes shone brightly in the firelight, and Taran noticed that her lips were red, parted, and definitely clean enough to ...

'Hey,' said Maya interrupting his thoughts. 'Great work on making such an amazing fire. I'm sure you'll make a great kitchen lady for a lord one day,' and she smiled mischievously.

'Hmmm,' Taran replied. 'I'm not sure how to take that, but then again, you look like you'd either make a good butcher's wife or a scarecrow. Take your pick.'

Maya laughed as she looked through the veil of knotted hair in front of her face, then frowned. 'You're right. I do look and also feel disgusting. I think I might even smell more than Rakan does.'

'It's strange,' said Taran, leaning forward, wrinkling his nose. 'I think you do smell worse. In fact, I mentioned once that you smelt of bear and never got an answer. So why exactly do you smell that way?'

Maya paused, then in a quiet voice, told the story of the wolf and what had transpired after.

Taran had heard parts of it before when they'd first talked, and yet still he was transfixed, not just by the words, but by her expressions. Maya's hands moved as she spoke, weaving pictures in the air, and Taran was sorry when she finished.

'I think I've been talking way too much,' she said. 'Now make yourself useful and pass me some of those sharpened sticks. Rakan can sacrifice a few of them for the sake of our dinner cooking properly and us having provisions for the next few days.'

With that, she skewered the meat and had it sizzling over the fire before Rakan stomped back in and sat down on the other side of Taran.

'I don't feel safe here,' Rakan complained. 'Those traps I've put out might give us some warning, but we need to keep watch tonight. I'll take the first shift while you two sleep, then it'll be you, Taran, followed by Maya. We sleep with swords unsheathed, and Maya, keep your bow strung and an arrow notched, you hear me?'

Both Taran and Maya nodded. Taran unsheathed his blade and laying it down alongside his blanket as Maya did the same with her bow. Rakan lay his sword across his lap.

'First things first. My stomach thinks my throat has already been cut. I've never been so hungry,' grumbled Rakan.

'Be patient,' cautioned Maya, as Rakan burned his fingers on the flesh of a cooking rabbit as he tried to pull one from a skewer. 'They're almost done, but some we need to overcook because they need to keep for the next day or two without spoiling.' She reached into her pouches and pulled out three large leaves onto which she put the berries and roots she'd discovered during her hunt before adding the hot meat.

'Dinner is served,' she announced, before passing the largest of the portions to Rakan, who nodded in gratitude. He tore into the meat, and the juices ran down over his chin and dripped onto his clothes.

'Hey,' said Taran in mock indignation. 'How come he gets the wolf's share?'

Maya laughed. 'Maybe it's because he has the table manners of a wolf!'

Both Rakan and Taran laughed with her. It was a rare happy moment, and Taran couldn't help but wish there would be many more.

They ate in companionable silence then. Taran continued to feed the flames while Maya apportioned more food amongst them and then made food parcels for the days ahead.

'Best let the fire die now, lad,' said Rakan, 'and you two should get some shut-eye. We'll head off about midday tomorrow, I reckon, give

216

ourselves time to recover fully, and maybe our huntress can find us some water.'

'Oh,' said Maya. 'I've found some already. Tomorrow I'll take Taran, and we'll refill our water skins first thing.'

Maya moved to her blanket and laid down on the ferns Taran had put down to soften the forest floor.

Taran lay down as well, facing Maya, and gazed at her in the dying light of the fire's embers.

Maya smiled sleepily back at him, eyes half-closed as exhaustion started to claim her. 'You know,' she said softly. 'The first time I saw you all in uniform, scars upon your cheeks, I hated you like I hated all the other soldiers. There was nothing good to be seen in any of you. Never did I think for a moment that you were a prince in disguise who would rescue me from my doom.'

Her eyes closed then as she snuggled down, pulling the blanket up to her chin.

Then to Taran's surprise, one of her legs snaked out from underneath, and her foot found and rested gently on his.

'Good night, my prince,' she whispered.

Taran's heart almost flipped in his chest, and he licked lips that were suddenly dry. 'Goodnight, my princess,' he whispered back. But she was already fast asleep.

Rakan's eyes tried to pierce the darkness as he stood silently under the rocky outcrop. His sword was bare, but he kept it behind his back in case it caught and reflected any light, giving away his position.

He breathed slowly and deeply, looked intently for thirty heartbeats in one direction before turning his eyes to another. He tried to memorise the shadows, so he would see if there were any new ones when he turned back again. He never turned his head however, for if he were spotted, then a cunning assassin would only move when his attention was elsewhere. Move the eyes, not the head, yet in the dark, the eyes were one of the least useful senses, for it was his hearing that he relied upon the most.

The rocky outcrop helped conceal them but also gave any unwelcome visitors a veiled approach, so Rakan had placed over half the traps on its far side. He felt confident that if they were discovered, he would hear something, and at least they could face their fate, weapons in hand.

His eyes flickered to the two youngsters, and he felt a strange sense of duty to protect them, especially the lad. Now it was apparent Taran was becoming fond of the girl, and he could see this was reciprocal; he worried for her too.

He relished the fact that for the first time in years, he could move without having to hide the pain from so many old injuries, all thanks to her gift. It was just a shame he likely wouldn't live long enough to enjoy his newfound feeling of youth.

The moon was moving across the sky, and Rakan knew he should wake Taran for his watch, but he let Taran sleep on. Keeping watch was a skill that Rakan had mastered over many years of being in the military, and while he knew the boy wouldn't shirk this duty, neither did he fancy having his throat cut in his sleep because the boy had missed an approaching enemy.

Seven more days, he estimated, would get them to the base of the Forelorn mountains. Then he'd have to convince old Laska that he was there on the Witch-King's bidding, and they were to be shown the passage over the mountains and into the Freestates. Simple.

Simple but likely doomed to failure. Rakan's hopes rested on the unlikely premise that the Witch-King had overlooked this possible avenue of escape and hadn't contacted Laska or sent troops ahead.

But, if they were lucky enough to be believed, the next worry was; why had so few agents made it across and back again over the years? Whatever the mountains held was something that chewed well-trained agents up with ease. So how it was possible that one tough old soldier, one gifted young lad, and a girl with skills in healing and hunting would succeed was beyond his skills at foretelling.

Then he smiled to himself, for the three of them had recently defeated five Rangers and four soldiers, while in his past, dozens of his enemies lay cold in the ground. 'By all the gods, I wouldn't bet against us!' he breathed.

His mind settled, he focussed again on the gloom. Let the youngsters sleep, for he would sleep again when they were safe, or when he was dead.

Kalas reached the top of the hill, the sound of his breath coming in gasps, loud to his ears in the confines of his helm. Tearing it off, he laughed in sheer relief to still be alive when he thought he had charged to meet his doom. Even the daemon's laughter in his mind seemed truly joyful, untainted by darkness.

The blood rush left him, and his hands shook as he took the time to look around. The fleeing cavalry were heading east, and in the distance another group rode toward them. It wouldn't be long before they came back to finish him off. He swore loudly, realising they were between him and his quarry.

Kalas started a gentle run down the west side of the hill, backtracking his earlier path toward the woods. There were so many cavalry, and he couldn't afford to be in open ground, for his luck surely wouldn't hold again.

The daemon whined and cried its displeasure at being so close but now so far from their prey. He soothed it unconsciously within his mind, making promises of blood and life if only it were patient, and it settled down, mewling a little like a kitten demanding milk.

He entered the trees' shadow as around three hundred lancers reached the crest of the hill from whence he came. Some men rode down to investigate the bodies strewn about the grass, and carrion birds protested noisily as they took to the air, having only just started to feast.

Kalas stepped back deeper into the shadows, and then let the daemon light flood from his eyes. The men on the hill all looked in his direction then. He could imagine the chill they would feel as it ran down their spines, as they realised the story the fleeing cavalry had told was true. If they took the risk and followed him into the dense forest, he wanted them scared, jumping at every shadow, not flooding in like an unstoppable tide.

He screamed, letting the daemon take his voice, its howl a promise of horrors beyond imagining, making the distant horses shy away, then laughed in relief as the troop dismounted without approaching further.

The taste of the girl's blood and life would be his to enjoy sooner or later; he just needed to be patient. With that, Kalas hunkered down and thought of the slaughter to come to help pass the time.

Taran awoke with a start, feeling strangely refreshed. Light filtered through the trees, and he sat upright. Rakan sat opposite him, smiling.

'You needed the sleep,' Rakan said gruffly. 'You youngsters have no stamina.'

Taran turned his head to see Maya already up, readying a brief breakfast from the last night's leftovers, and he felt a little disappointed he'd not awoken to find her sleeping next to him. She came over and gave him a large leaf full of meat, fruits, and roots.

'Hey,' said Rakan. 'How comes he gets so much this morning?'

Maya scowled down at Taran. 'I think If he snores like a bear, he should eat like one too.' But the kind smile in her eyes offset the words. She ruffled Taran's hair gently as she walked past to give Rakan his breakfast. 'Don't worry, there's plenty for you too. I feel so very safe protected by two of the wildest animals in the forest; a wolf and a bear,' and she laughed merrily as she sat down to join them.

They ate in silence, although, Taran thought, sitting next to Rakan when he ate was hardly silent. How could someone eat so noisily?

'Right, I'm going to take Taran here as my bodyguard while we get some water,' announced Maya, and she rose, sweeping up the water skins, leaving Taran to get to his feet quickly to catch up with her.

Taran looked briefly at Rakan.

Rakan smiled back at him. 'Go on, lad. I'll break camp. You look after the girl.'

Hmmm, thought Taran, as he hurried after Maya, *bodyguard*, and liked the sound of the title. As Maya led him swiftly up and down small inclines through the trees, what amazed Taran was Maya's unerring sense of direction. She moved through woodland, that to Taran looked the same in every direction, with confidence and purpose as though she'd travelled this way a hundred times before. However, as time passed, Taran briefly considered whether she was lost; but any doubts fled when they crested a small rocky rise.

There, below them, was a spring-fed pool with water trickling down a rock face to gather in the hollow below. It was a large pool that no doubt had once provided life to many of the woodland animals.

'Oh my!' exclaimed Taran, holding his nose. The water was now green with slime, as were the rocks, and the smell of wet wood, the foul water, and rotting vegetation was overwhelming. Taran stood a little shocked, then realised Maya must be testing him. 'We can't drink this. I'm no woodsman, but this will make us sick if not kill us. We'd be better off just eating berries than taking a sip of this. Now, where is the drinking water that you found? Is it nearby?'

Maya laughed, and Taran thought it sounded like sweet music as she turned to him. 'Taran,' she leaned in close, taking his arm, 'do you trust me?'

Taran paused, thinking for a moment, not wanting to give a glib answer, yet realised with surprise that despite hardly knowing Maya, he did trust her. Without even knowing why at the time, he'd opened up, voicing all the painful secrets locked away inside, and then she'd reciprocated. Something was growing between them, and he wanted it to grow more.

'Well, do you?' she prompted, a little frown of impatience at his delay caused a small furrow of grime to appear between her eyes.

Taran nodded, and was relieved to see the furrow, even if not the grime, disappear.

'Well then,' Maya said, smiling again. 'Close your eyes and promise not to open them until I say so.'

'I promise,' agreed Taran, doing as instructed, and reached out a hand to steady himself against a tree.

He barely heard Maya as she moved away and was tempted to peek. Yet a promise was a promise, and Taran knew in his heart that he never wanted to break one with Maya, so he carefully lowered himself to the ground, eyes closed.

Maya was a consummate hunter, and if it weren't for her gentle humming and soft singing, he wouldn't have known she was mere steps away, such was the softness of her tread. Her musical voice lulled him, and the smell of the decay that had seemed sickly sweet now seemed a heady perfume instead, and he found himself drift toward sleep.

'Are you seriously snoring?' asked Maya, a hint of annoyance in her voice.

Taran just caught himself from opening his eyes and shook his head. 'No! Sleeping? Me? Never! Not while I'm guarding your body!'

Maya's voice and breath were suddenly close to his ear, and it tickled softly. 'Well then, as you are not asleep, my prince, open your eyes and see.'

Taran opened his eyes, closed them, and opened them again. 'Truly, you are gifted by the gods to have such a power,' he said, then stood slowly, gazing down at the scene below.

The foul-smelling pool was now pure and clear, no sign of corruption whatsoever. The water trickling down the rocks sparkled like crystal even in the dim light, over vibrant moss, which had white flowers sprinkled throughout. All around the banks of the pool, grass now grew, and healthy bushes with verdant leaves flourished everywhere. Even the tree upon which he'd leaned stood firm, and the scent of freshness filled the air to replace the smell of decay.

'Now, be a good bodyguard and help fill the skins!' As she tossed some to him, Maya laughed, and they both moved down to the water's edge.

Taran knelt next to Maya as they held the skins under the surface. As Taran filled the last one, he held up a hand.

Maya looked at him enquiringly. 'What's wrong?'

'The smell of decay is back.' Taran cupped some water in his hand and brought it to his face, and sniffed. 'Something smells very wrong.'

A worried look crossed Maya's face. 'Really?' she asked, and bent forward to scoop some water in her hand.

As she did, Taran leaned over, placed his hand between her shoulder blades, and pushed her into the pool. She came up spluttering and screeching in indignation.

'Now,' said Taran, sniffing the air. 'That's a little better. But it's going to take more than a small dip to get you clean,' and reaching forward, he put his hand on Maya's head and gently pushed down.

'Don't you dare!' she laughed, reaching up to push his hand away, but suddenly she grabbed his arm instead and pulled him in.

As he came up, coughing out water, Maya sniffed the air. 'Now, that's a lot better!' she said, and they both laughed as they splashed one another.

'Oh my,' said Maya. 'It's been a long time since I was this filthy, and you too, by the looks of it. Let's clean up.' She reached to the bank, pulled two small plants from the soil, and gave Taran one.

'What am I supposed to do with this?' asked Taran, wondering if he should eat it, then started to put it in his mouth.

Maya laughed. 'Don't eat it. Now watch.' With that, she broke the stem and squeezed so that the pulp oozed into the palm of her hand. She put the rest of the plant on a rock, then rubbed her hands together, producing a sweet-smelling lather that she scrubbed onto her face. She splashed water over herself shortly after, then dropped her hands. 'See?'

Taran recoiled in horror. 'What have you done to yourself!'

Maya's hands swept up to her face, questing. 'What do you mean?' she asked, worried.

'You've made a clean spot.' Taran winked. 'Now you're going to have to work on the rest, and maybe you'll freshen up quite nicely given a lot of work.'

Maya wrinkled her nose at him and carried on scrubbing as Taran began to follow suit.

As they washed, she watched Taran out of the corner of her eye and had to admit to herself that she liked him a lot. She'd never been friends with a boy in her village, or anyone at all for that matter, staying far removed in case anyone discovered her gift. Yet here they were, sharing a cleansing, and she felt something was growing between them.

He wasn't the best looking man she'd ever laid eyes on, but his humour, his voice, his kindness, and not forgetting the fact he'd been about to die for her, created feelings she'd never previously experienced.

She watched as Taran pulled his shirt over his head. Now there was another reason to like him, those broad shoulders and muscular arms.

Taran started to wash his shirt, and Maya realised that she would still smell if she just washed herself.

'Time to guard my body while looking in the other direction,' she commanded, then ushered him to do an about-face. She took off her top, enjoying the feel of the cool water lapping against her bare flesh, then hesitated a moment before slipping out of her leggings. She turned her back on Taran as he started doing the same.

They washed quickly then, and Maya sighed as she knew they needed to hurry. After struggling to put her wet clothes back, she turned around to see Taran already clothed with a silly smile on his face. Maya felt her face burn bright red. 'How long were you looking?' she demanded, her eyes flashing.

Taran laughed, 'For about as long as a piece of twine, maybe short, maybe long. What is it about women that they take so long to wash?'

'Yooooou!' hissed Maya, splashing Taran.

Taran reached out with his hands, gently taking her shoulders. 'Do you trust me?' he asked.

Maya laughed, recognising her own words. 'Let me think. Do I trust the man who pushed me headfirst into a pool and who sneaked a look behind my back? I'm not sure!'

She saw the beginnings of hurt in his eyes and decided not to tease him anymore, not just now anyway. 'Yes, I trust you.'

'Well then, turn around and close your eyes,' said Taran. 'Don't open them until I tell you to.'

Maya turned around in the water, and Taran's strong hands encouraged her to lean back against him. She lay her head back on his chest and felt his heart beating powerfully.

Taran's voice was soft and close to her ear as he said. 'You seemed to have washed almost everywhere, and I do mean everywhere because I checked, but you forgot to wash your hair.'

With that, she felt his fingers start to massage the fragrant pulp carefully into her scalp. Had her eyes been open at that stage, they would have closed anyway, for the feeling was so soothing that she wanted to purr like a cat.

As Taran washed her hair, he told her a tale from his youth. The sound of his voice, the rhythm of his hands, the fragrance of the plant all relaxed her so much that she slipped into a light sleep. A short time later, Maya opened her eyes to see Taran's face looking down on her.

'If I snore like a bear,' he said, eyes twinkling, 'then, you snuffle like a piglet.'

'A piglet!' Maya exclaimed in indignation. 'A piglet?'

Taran nodded. 'I don't know if you realise this, but I rather like piglets.'

Maya found herself unable to meet Taran's gaze. 'I rather like bears too,' she whispered.

Maya stood up, turning slowly in Taran's arms. They were so close that their noses almost touched, and she could feel his warm, sweet breath on her face.

His hands moved to the back of her neck as he looked into her eyes, and Maya felt her insides flutter as if suddenly filled with a thousand butterflies. She leaned forward on tiptoes, and her lips found his, her eyes closed, as she wished the moment would last forever.

Rakan had finished breaking camp. He'd gathered the packs together and then spent a moment trying to disguise the fact they'd been there before giving up. It was a lost cause before he even started. The vegetation was all green thanks to the girl's gift and yesterday's trail led right to it, yet it was a habit from many years of soldiering and training.

Taran and Maya were taking too long, but for some reason, Rakan wasn't as worried as he would typically be.

Let them have a little time alone together, he thought, smiling to himself. They seemed well suited, and it would be the last bit of respite before they pushed hard again over the next few days while the provisions lasted.

Rakan picked up the three heavy packs and grunted with the effort. He decided to follow Maya and Taran's trail, to save time by meeting them on their return. There were some simple rules when tracking someone. Not staying directly on the trail itself for a long time was a key one, for it was too easy to walk into an ambush that way. Better to follow from a short distance if the trail was easy to follow, and only return if there was a risk of losing it.

Even though Rakan wasn't likely to get ambushed by Taran or Maya, from habit, he still kept a good five paces to the right of the route they'd taken. The new growth of green, even after such a short time since Maya had passed, gave the trail away, so it wasn't difficult to follow even from a distance.

As he trudged along, he grumbled to himself about how far they'd gone, but at least it was still eastward in the direction they needed to go. The packs were uncomfortable, one slung on each shoulder and one in his hand, so he decided to take a brief break.

He stepped around a large tree and lowered himself to the ground, still appreciating the fact that his knees didn't pop or his back complain anymore. He owed the girl for this, and it was a gift he wouldn't forget. Having lived with pain every day for so many years, its absence was a marvel. He sat for a short while, wondering whether to wait here until the others returned when he heard them moving through the trees not too far away. He was about to call out, but suddenly realised that the sounds were back along the trail toward the camp. Unless they had somehow got past him or taken a different route back, then this might not be Taran and Maya!

Rakan eased himself to his feet quietly, slowly drawing his sword and dagger. The temptation to look around the trunk was hard to resist, but that was a sure way to be spotted. Instead, by waiting until whoever it was passed by, he would remain undetected. It wasn't long before he felt convinced that this wasn't Taran and Maya. That the two unknowns were familiar to woodland was apparent, for they made little noise as they moved, but therein lay the giveaway. Maya made no noise at all, whereas Taran moved like a bear, and Rakan smiled slightly as he remembered Maya likening Taran's snoring to one.

Maybe these were just two people from a local settlement out hunting and weren't any threat? He stood as still as possible in the shadow of the tree as they passed on the far side of Maya and Taran's trail, and then all doubts as to their intentions disappeared.

A woman held a bow, arrow nocked to the string, and next to her, a man carried a long spear. This in itself wasn't unusual, but the fact they brought no foraging pouches or pack and that there was a sword at their hips, which no plain villager would be allowed, meant these were hunters of men.

Luck had favoured Rakan, for if they had decided to follow Taran and Maya's trail on the right side, they would have come upon his and would likely have put an arrow between his shoulder blades before he knew they were even there.

Rakan waited until they were a little further ahead, and as they passed behind a tree, stealthily crossed the trail, staying low, keeping out of their peripheral vision until he was behind them by about thirty steps. He followed stealthily and matched their footfall with his own, so any noise he made was masked. He took long strides to close the distance. So intent were they on looking ahead at the trail as they searched for their prey that they never thought to look behind to see danger getting closer.

The archer was the most dangerous one of the two. Armed with only sword and dagger, Rakan needed to get close to make a killing blow, but with no shield to protect himself, the archer could kill him at a distance. The spearman was less of a concern. A thrown spear could be evaded, and if used as a close combat weapon, Rakan wasn't worried about that either.

He'd closed the gap to twenty paces, knowing to get closer risked being heard, but the problem was the longer he followed, the greater the chance one of them would turn and see him. If they did, he'd be seeing the nine hells far sooner than he wanted.

The problem was how to get close without getting an arrow in his gut. Then suddenly, he saw his chance. The two hunters started to push through a dense thicket of brambles and vines that hung down to the forest floor. They ducked down low, trying to avoid the grasping tendrils and thorns.

Rakan made up his mind in an instant and charged. He didn't roar or shout, just plunged ahead, sprinting along the trail. After just a few strides, the hunters swung around in alarm as they heard him bear down upon them. The archer started to raise her bow while the spearman did the same with his weapon, intending to use it to keep Rakan at bay while his comrade delivered the fatal shot.

Yet Rakan's timing paid off, for as both tried to make ready, the grasping undergrowth fouled their long weapons. The man, realising this first, dropped his spear and frantically grasped for the hilt of the sword at his waist, while the archer desperately tugged at her bow, trying to untangle it, and this proved deadly for them both.

Rakan kept silent, not knowing if there were any other hunters close by, and covered the final steps. His dagger plunged into the spearman's eye just as the man's sword cleared its sheath, and he dropped like a stone, dead in an instant. Rakan's sword then swept down, not aiming for the archer; rather, he slashed it through the vines, smashing the woman's weapon as it passed through to clear his own passage. She threw herself backwards, hands raised placatingly in a gesture of surrender, but Rakan didn't hesitate. He thrust his sword through the woman's right hand, into her throat, and out the back of her neck.

The fight was over in moments, and Rakan swiftly dropped to his knees, looking around, waiting for the gurgling of the dying archer to stop so he could listen for any sound of movement. As far as he could tell, there was no one else. Part of him regretted not keeping one of them alive to question, but he'd had no idea how skilful they might be, or if there were others close by who would have taken the distraction to put him down.

Satisfied there were no others, at least not close enough to be a threat, Rakan thought about hiding the bodies but decided not to. Let anyone else following see what awaited them!

He backtracked swiftly to find the packs and took up the trail again.

Now he was angry. Taran and Maya were off enjoying each other's company, whereas he'd just had to save their skins by killing those hunters, who could have easily killed them had the gods not smiled upon him.

He moved as fast as he dared, looking behind him frequently. He was determined to give the two of them a serious piece of his mind when he found them. This was not the time to mess around; it was the time to run for their lives.

As he crested a small ridge, there they were, and for a moment, his rage was incandescent, yet suddenly it just fell away.

He'd never understood love, never felt the caress of a woman's hand that he hadn't paid for, nor had he ever appreciated the beauty of the world around him. Yet as he looked down at the scene below him, everything changed.

They were oblivious to the world. Taran held Maya is his arms as the two of them kissed tenderly, shoulder deep in a crystal clear pool of water, surrounded by flowers and blooms while blossom fell from the green trees, and a willow's fronds moved slowly in the shallows.

Rakan cleared his throat and saw them reluctantly pull apart; Maya was flushing in embarrassment, and Taran looked a little shy too as they turned toward him.

'Hey, Rakan,' Maya greeted him, looking out from under her wet curly hair. 'We were just about to head back. Is it time to hit the trail already?'

Hot words again came to Rakan's lips as he walked toward them, but then he just sighed and smiled. 'Please tell me you filled the skins before you two decided to cleanse. I'm not sure I want to taste Taran's sweat in my drinking water!'

Both Taran and Maya laughed as they clambered out of the pool.

'Oh no,' said Maya seriously. 'That terrible rotting smell is back!'

'You're right. I think it's coming from the water.' Taran added. 'What do you think, Rakan, is it safe for us to drink?'

Rakan knelt by the pool, leaning forward to cup some water in his hands.

Taran bowed to Maya. 'Be my guest.'

Maya put her hands between Rakan's shoulder blades and pushed as she and Taran roared with laughter.

Chapter XIII

Daleth stood in the stirrups of his saddle and looked back over his shoulder to see nigh on fifteen thousand men stretching to the horizon. Amongst them were wagons full of provisions as well as some of the wealth of this dying realm. Of the fifteen thousand, almost all were fighting men, and yet he was currently more interested in just one riding at his side.

He'd decided to keep Alano close by as the army rode and marched east, leaving behind the city and lands he'd called home for so long, along with every civilian however high their status. They thought themselves lucky that they would escape the horrors of war, not realising that starvation would rob them of their lives just as quickly if not quicker.

Alano, the daemon, now a perfect remorseless killer, sworn to protect and obey him. So why did he now feel some doubt over his decision to allow the daemon full control? Without question, he didn't doubt its loyalty. The daemon may have kept its knowledge of Kalas from him, but it hadn't turned against him. Perhaps it was the absence of Alano's voice, his occasional joke or even half-smile that Daleth regretted, and he wondered if he'd gained anywhere near as much as what had been lost.

True, Alano had always tried to fulfil his vow and kill him. However, he'd also become invaluable, and worked incredibly hard at whatever role he was assigned, immersing himself in strategic matters almost as a way of dealing with his possession and the insanity it would otherwise have brought.

Over the years, Daleth had promoted him to be his closest advisor and general, and his diligence in training the Rangers had been priceless. Had it not been for the daemon, the circumstances of their meeting, and his vow, perhaps he and Alano could have been friends.

Now he was reduced to a bloodthirsty pet. Still, Daleth knew he would be irreplaceable in battle, for that was where he would come into his own, and he was a bodyguard without peer.

His officers rode a little further behind, not wanting to ride too close to the daemon, and Daleth missed the camaraderie that the start of a campaign should have brought out between him and the men. He knew they cursed the daemon. There was no way details of the slaughter in the training halls could be contained, and while Daleth had no need to explain the deaths of anyone, still there was fear, distrust, and anger directed toward the daemon that hadn't been so prevalent before.

Daleth sighed. 'Keep the pace,' he ordered Alano, and the daemon turned its red eyes upon him.

'Yes, my king,' it rasped.

Daleth tugged on the reins and turned back to be with the officers. They cheered as he rode into their midst and his mood lifted. He greeted them by name, making wagers on who would kill the most, who amongst them might die first, and how many women they would enjoy while out on campaign. It was exhilarating, and it almost drowned Daleth's feeling of hunger and growing weakness. He was still stronger than any mortal could dream of, yet this land had given almost everything, and this conquest was coming none too soon.

Only this morning, new grey hairs had shown on his head, and he'd used dye to cover its presence, then daubed his face in war paint so that it wasn't obvious. He couldn't wait to feel the overwhelming rush of life flooding his body as his men conquered the Freestates and enslaved those within, spreading misery and suffering beneath their boots even as the land began to nourish him.

He shook his head, clearing his thoughts and turned his head back to his men. Standing again in his saddle, he drew his sword, lifting it above his head, and waved it in the morning light, roaring his battle cry.

Thousands of throats roared it back as thousands of raised swords saluted in reply. He revelled in their adulation before galloping his horse to the front of the column, then made it rear, loving the theatrics, knowing he made a heroic figure.

As he continued riding, he thought about one of his agents across the border.

While engaged in trade all these years, the two kingdoms hadn't allowed anyone other than a handful of emissaries to enter their lands. All trade and exchange of goods was handled in the pass between the opposing fortresses. Therefore, for his agents to reach the Freestates, they had to attempt the deadly crossing at Ember Town. He'd tried with difficulty to send so many for nigh on forty years, yet few had made it, and even fewer had returned with intelligence.

But he knew of one who remained, utterly dedicated. The attack on the Freestates wouldn't just come from the outside, but from within as well.

Of course, he could have just relied on his military might without the need for subterfuge, yet Daleth believed in perfect preparation, and wars could be won from within as well as from without.

How long till battle was joined, he pondered. Maybe twenty days to unite all his forces, then perhaps a dozen more to bring them into position, at which time a hundred thousand men would hit the pass like a hammer blow. His siege engines would bring the walls down, and then nothing would stop his conquest of the Freestates and the lands that lay beyond.

For a moment, he wondered where Kalas was, and that girl Maya with the two deserters. It was galling that he'd yet to hear anything. He made a mental note to contact the garrison overseer, and spirit travel later to see whether he could find their whereabouts.

The problem was, the weaker he felt, the less his power in the spirit world became. The last couple of times had left him with a splitting headache lasting all day. Tonight though, headache or not, he would travel the paths.

Daleth turned to Alano and saw its red eyes were upon him. 'With the coming of such death,' it offered, 'comes the flow of such life,' and its tongue licked its lips in anticipation.

Daleth could only agree. Perhaps conversation with the beast wouldn't be quite so bad after all.

Kalas had been frustrated at the delay caused by the lancers, but now he was so close to the three fugitives. He continued to push himself hard, but the daemon in his mind still distracted him as it revelled in his recent bloodletting.

A few days before, following his withdrawal into the woods, he'd waited for the lancers to attack or move on, but while he sat concealed within the shadows, they'd done neither. As the sun had set, they'd made camp on the hill overlooking his refuge, settled down to eat, and no doubt drank some bitter campaign wine to banish the chill of the night and the thought of the quarry they hunted.

Kalas wasn't blind to his mortality, even if, at times, the daemon made him feel invincible. If this amount of men made a concerted effort to kill him at once, he would die without question, and thus he needed to either lose them or persuade them he wasn't worth the risk.

He'd chosen the latter.

So, that night he'd waited as the stars slowly climbed into the sky, shining weakly when the clouds didn't cover them. Then he'd waited some more. To help with his plan, he'd stripped from his silver armour down to his dark shirt and trousers, then taken handfuls of rotting mulch from the forest floor and rubbed it into any exposed skin.

Then, in the early hours, once the campfires on the hill above had burned low, he'd crawled from the forest, wary of sentries. As he made his way up the hill, he'd seen two slumped against their lances. Why post more when they were leagues inside kingdom lands, and they were the hunters, not the prey? Foolishly they still wore their helms, which hindered not only vision, but more importantly, their hearing, which in the dead of night, was the most useful sense.

Kalas had snaked his way closer and closer until he was a few steps from the first sentry. He could see him clearly, not just because he was outlined against the lighter sky, but because he felt the man's heart pumping and saw the blood glowing red in his veins.

The man had stamped his feet, turning around more in boredom than for any reason, and Kalas had silently risen from the floor behind him. One hand jerked the man's head back, as the other that held his dirk had drawn its razor-sharp blade across the sentry's throat. Kalas had quietly lowered him to the floor, turning the body onto its side, so it looked like the sentry was sleeping.

He unconsciously licked the blood from his fingers, savouring the taste.

'More,' purred the daemon, and Kalas had crept around the perimeter on his belly, taking his time and dispatching the second sentry in the same way.

Tents were set in neat rows. There were about thirty tents Kalas estimated, so around three hundred men. Each tent had a campfire down to its embers near the entrance. The large tents had helped conceal his presence, for they muffled any sounds from inside or out, creating noise as they rippled in the soft night breeze.

He'd approached the first tent and peered through the crack between the entrance flaps. The soldiers slept with their feet toward the canvas, and as expected, every man was asleep. He'd drawn his thin-bladed dagger before carefully entering. Then, one by one, as he moved between them, he'd driven the blade through the eyes, or the side of the mens' heads into the brain.

Ten men lay butchered in less than thirty heartbeats, and the daemon had screeched in exultation in his head.

Cautiously he'd then moved on to the second tent, and repeated the slaughter, then a third and a fourth. The daemon had crowed, cried out for more, greedy to feast on their life. So as he'd slit the throat of the last man in the fifth tent, he'd drunk his fill, savouring the salty flavour that now tasted divine.

But his luck finally ran out, for as he stepped from the tent, there stood a soldier directly opposite, relieving himself onto a campfire. Despite being half asleep, the sight of Kalas, dagger in hand, face covered in blood made the man cry out in horror.

Kalas had lunged, puncturing the soldier's throat with his blade, and as the man fell, he'd brought the tent down behind him. Men had started shouting and cursing, and Kalas knew his time was up.

He'd hurried back the way he came, but instead of leaving, he turned toward one of the picket lines holding the horses. Men stumbled from their tents to investigate the growing noise, but escape was now the goal, so Kalas avoided them as much as possible and only had to kill two who stepped into his path. Fortunately, some of the mounts were saddled for an early morning scout. So, he'd taken advantage, having secured the girth, and swung up into the saddle of the nearest, least nervous horse.

Kalas swept his blade down, severing the picket lines, and howled, letting the daemon's voice scream into the dark of the night and the hearts of the awakening men. The horses all scattered down the hill as Kalas fought his mount into obedience, then left the camp swiftly behind, seeking the sanctuary of darkness. Behind him, angry voices turned from alarm to panic when the slaughter that had just taken place in their midst became apparent.

As Kalas had ridden down the hill, he'd wondered if he should stay in the sanctuary of the trees or get back on the trail of the three fugitives. The strength of the newly fed daemon had flooded his body, and whilst it was night, he could see as if it were day, a blood-red day. There were several more hours till daylight, but with his mind made up, he swiftly reclaimed his armour, remounted, and recommenced pursuit of his quarry. He doubted the lancers would have the stomach to come after him, and even if so, he was on horseback, whereas most of them would now be on foot.

Now, after a couple of days hard riding, having given the horse its head, he'd entered some thick woodland.

He was so close!

He knelt, studying the trail. Yes, the three fugitives had passed this way only recently, and the new healthy plant growth showed their direction of travel, due east toward the Forelorn mountains and the Freestates border.

He was about to continue again when something else caught his eye, and he moved to the north, pushing through the undergrowth. Night was approaching, yet he could now see a much broader trail running parallel, and the tracks indicated at least a dozen men had recently passed this way.

He had to hurry.

Kalas wasn't sure how the three fugitives planned on getting across the Forelorn mountains if they got there, but he wasn't going to give them a chance, and no one was going to come between him and his quarry.

The daemon in his mind agreed with his every thought. Or was it that they were the daemon's thoughts? Surely it wasn't his idea to hunt down three people he didn't even know just for the taste of the woman's gift? But the daemon inside assured him that it was indeed his idea, and mollified, Kalas pushed on, unaware that his will was barely his own any longer.

Astren sat quietly outside the entrance to Lord Tristan's throne room with his head bowed, fighting to stay awake. He'd been fast asleep in his villa when the summons to attend his king had arrived, and whenever Tristan called, Astren had to answer, and quickly. Having only taken the time to throw on a fresh robe, Astren was now at the Royal Palace within the hour of being called.

The doors opened, and the captain of the Freemantle guards stepped through and beckoned Astren to follow. He rose, moving behind Anthain, whose bulk obscured the view ahead.

Astren looked around, inspired as he always was when he attended the palace. Everything in the Freestates was geared around opulence, so unsurprisingly, the throne room was expansive and reflected the vast wealth enjoyed by the kingdom's rulers. Their footsteps sounded loud as they walked upon polished heart stone, between carved pillars that reached up to the gabled ceiling. Long banners and tapestries hung on the walls, depicting not famous battles or heroic deaths, but rather the god of greed. Gold and jewels dripped from between his fingers, raining down upon the Freestates in approval of their pursuit of wealth, the noblest pursuit of them all.

Even Anthain looked like a walking tribute to greed, thought Astren. His armour, although functional, was inlaid with gold. His sword hilt intricate and fashionable with a large gem on its pommel.

Astren looked down at his sandaled feet and his blood-red robes, plain and simple other than the colour, and knew that Tristan would make his usual comment about him looking like a beggar rather than a courtier in the wealthiest realm to have ever existed. But it was all part of Astren's facade of misdirection, something he'd adopted when he was younger.

As they reached Tristan, who was poring over a giant model of the fortress, Anthain cleared his throat.

Tristan looked up, bright blue eyes flickering over Astren, and a frown settled upon his brow. 'You can bring a man out of peasantry, but not the peasantry out the man,' Tristan declared.

Astren might have felt the sting of an insult from another, but this exchange was long established, and there was a hint of warmth to Tristan's words. Once, years past, Tristan had cast him aside, but now he valued Astren's counsel above many others. Still, he was as fickle as any king.

Astren smiled back. 'True, but what does that say of the king who seeks the advice of a peasant?'

Anthain glowered at Astren, but Tristan laughed loudly and with good humour. 'What indeed would that say about the king?' he mused, but then he became business-like.

'The gods smiled upon us again this day. We've just learned that five hundred spearmen from the desert tribes and as many archers from the people of the Eyre fortuitously came to our city, because of Anthain's hard work, I am sure.'

Astren whistled softly. 'That is good news. Archers are what we need, them and swordsmen. The spearmen won't be so good on the walls of the fortress, but every man counts.'

'What do you know about fighting?' boomed Anthain. 'You are nothing but a seer. A parlour trick merchant who claims he can fly in his dreams. Well, we can all do that. Leave the strategy to the king and I.' As he said this, he leaned over Astren imposingly, glowering in discontent.

'Now, now, Anthain.' soothed Tristan. 'He is right should you care to admit it. Even I know spearmen are best deployed on a field of battle, not fighting on the walls of the fortress, and yet every man we can get will further ensure we repel Daleth.'

Tristan turned to Astren. 'Anthain here advises the repairs to the fortress are near finished, and we now have nigh on six thousand additional men added to the regular garrison there. He assures me we already have enough to withstand Daleth, which is a good thing, for he has left our coffers somewhat empty, but without him organising everything, we would have been lost.'

Astren nodded, waiting. He knew Tristan had summoned him here because he wanted something, not just to share this news, and he didn't wait for more than a few heartbeats to hear what for.

Tristan smiled. 'I need you to travel the Spirit paths, my friend,' he said. 'I would like to know how long we have to finalise our preparations to the full.'

Astren quailed inside. The king had asked as if there was a choice, yet this was not a request, and the warmth and favour Tristan showed to those around him lasted only right up to the second someone crossed or refused him. Anthain wasn't here just to offer counsel to the king, to be his bodyguard or general of the kingdom forces, but to deal out swift punishment at the tip of his sword should the king demand. His presence was a veiled threat and a constant one.

'Of course, my king,' said Astren. 'It has become ever more dangerous; hence I have not tried of late. So many of Daleth's gifted patrol the Spirit Pathways above his lands, and himself as well at times.' Yet even as he spoke the words, he knew they fell on deaf ears.

He walked to a gilded chair on one side of the table and sat down. At his waist were pouches in which he kept some coins, the seal of the royal court and also sleep weed. It was a herb with no taste that, when taken, would induce sleep immediately. However, upon awakening, he would unfortunately have a splitting headache. Still, it was the only way he could fulfil his duty in the here and now, which was the king's expectation.

As he chewed on a leaf, he saw Tristan and Anthain watch him briefly, but then as his eyes began to close, they turned away back to the maps and messages, and then everything went dark ...

He opened his eyes moments later to find himself looking down at his body, seeing the king and Anthain mere steps away. Astren had learned long ago that for him, spirit travelling wasn't as simple as staring through a window and spying on who you wanted, looking over shoulders, hearing everything that was said.

To go somewhere he knew was easy enough, but even though Astren was now a powerful seer, it was hard for him to hear every word unless he projected his form. If you were hidden from others, sometimes their words were hidden from you.

However, he could still hear that Anthain was advising Tristan not to trust the ramblings of a soothsayer charlatan and to have his head removed, and for a moment, he felt a little panic. Fortunately, the king shook his head, placing his hand on Anthain's forearm, and they turned back to the table and its many charts.

Astren let his mind wander briefly back to when his gift had first manifested itself.

As a child, he would fall asleep and regularly dream of floating around the small house he shared with his father and mother. His dreams were often painful, for he would see them and their tears as they fought against debt, as his father's fortunes waned.

They often went without food and were weak with hunger. One morning he'd asked his mother why she put her evening meal back in the pantry for his breakfast instead of eating it, and also why were they behind on paying their taxes. The look of surprise, and the tears that came to her eyes, showed him that he'd seen the truth.

She'd shared that discussion with his father, who that same day put a crude latch on his bedroom door. As darkness had fallen that night and Astren lay under the threadbare blanket, his father had closed the door, the latch falling loudly into place.

The next morning when they'd broke their fast with stale bread, overripe fruit and some porridge, his mother had asked him if he'd slept well, for there were chores to be done. He needed to help repair the roof and find scrap wood for the fire before meeting his father at the market, who would be finishing a deal to put food on the table for a month.

Astren had nodded, but then asked with tears in his eyes, why they were planning to sell him to the slave trader if they still loved him.

There had been a long terrible silence then as his mother swept from the table, tears spilling from her eyes, her body wracked by sobs.

His father's look had pinned him to the chair. Stopped him from running after her, hugging her, and telling her it was ok to sell him, as long as it made her happy.

'Boy, how did you get out of your room last night to hear such things?' his father had demanded. His fist wrapped into the front of Astren's tunic, pulling his face close. 'How did you open and then close the latch from inside of your room?'

His little heart had hammered in his chest, yet he'd gathered his courage and looked his father straight in the eye. 'I didn't leave my bed. I dreamt it!' he'd said defiantly, and as his father had raised a hand to strike him, Astren had held his gaze. 'I swear it; it's the truth. The slave

241

master said he would give you more than I was worth as he owed you a debt, and if you didn't take the deal, you wouldn't have enough money to last the winter!'

His father's eyes had widened as he slowly lowered his hand. 'Tell me everything you've ever heard us say that you can remember!' he'd demanded, and as the sun moved across the sky, Astren had told his father everything.

There had been no fixing the roof, collecting scrap wood, or going to the market that day, as they had sat close, talking, for his father to understand his gift better. The next night with the bedroom door latched and nailed firmly shut, his father had set him a test, to report to him the following day about what he and his mother would discuss.

Astren had found it easy and fun, and his father was happy for the first time he could remember, and even his mother smiled more, so Astren had been willing to do everything they'd asked. His father had encouraged him to see if he could travel beyond their house, so for the next few nights, Astren had passed through the closed door of their small ramshackle home and down the dark streets.

At first he'd been scared, for in the dark doorways loitered thieves and wrongdoers, women selling their bodies and men selling their souls to kill any unfortunate who strayed into their paths. Yet, when it soon became apparent that they couldn't see him, he'd found the courage to move freely and found that he could literally fly around the streets close to his house.

What was strange, however, was a thick fog that stopped him from going places he didn't know or hadn't been, and even though he'd pushed into it a little to see something new, the searing pain it gave him in his mind meant he'd had to stop trying.

The next day his father had questioned him for most of the morning and sent his mother out to buy some fresh bread and honey with money they could hardly afford to spend. They'd all eaten so well that Astren thought he would cry with happiness as they all sat laughing together, licking the sweetness from their fingers.

His father had summarised it well at the end of that morning. 'So you can travel to where you have been before, see people about their business and hear most of what is said, but you are unable to journey to that which is unknown to you.' The young Astren had nodded then, and his father had sat thoughtfully for a while, giving Astren a chance to eagerly eat more fresh bread and honey.

A smile had grown on his father's face, and for the first time that Astren could remember, his father wrapped his arm warmly around his shoulders, pulling him closer, and tears of happiness had welled in Astren's eyes. 'Son,' he'd said, hugging him, 'we are going to be rich!'

The next few weeks had been hard but so exciting. Astren had gone everywhere with his father, met everyone, and would often be ignored as he wandered off to peek into rooms or roamed open-mouthed around large homes as his father bribed an audience with one wealthy merchant owner after another.

Every night Astren would sleep and fly back to the places he'd been, to spy and listen, then report back to his father on deals done or yet to be done the next morning. His father had then used every crumb of information, selling it to competitors, allowing them to undercut bids, or get their goods to market first.

The family's fortunes had changed so dramatically and quickly that within a few cycles of the moon, they'd moved into the wealthy merchant's quarter. People sought his father's advice on everything, paying a considerable premium to put their cases to him. Those were such golden days. His mother happy; his father showing him love and respect and lavishing him with gifts.

But such a meteoric rise couldn't last long.

One night he'd spirit travelled to Glabus, the iron merchant's house. The man was supposedly a friend to his father, and he found eight other merchants sat around a table drinking and laughing. It was hard to hear everything being said, but his father, mother and then his name had been mentioned as one of the men drew a finger across his throat in a definitive gesture.

Astren had listened on a little longer, then flew from the man's house, above the streets toward his home near the top of the hill. As he'd approached, he was startled to see a dozen men running across the lawn dressed in black, short swords drawn. Astren had returned to his body and opened his eyes just in time to hear the front door splinter before the men had poured into the house.

As he ran from his bedroom to the first-floor landing, words of warning about to fly from his lips, he'd looked down only to see his father and mother fall to the floor as they were hacked down by the raiders.

He'd staggered back into his room and pushed the door shut, knowing his death would be moments away. As he had, a ghostly apparition of an old man wearing blood-red robes was standing in the room by his bed, beckoning him. Astren had almost fled back into the hallway, but something about the old man's smile and demeanour held him. 'Out the window, boy,' the man had ordered, 'quickly now, climb down the trellises then jump over the wall by the roses. I'll be in a carriage waiting for you.'

Astren had responded more to the sound of command in the man's voice and pointed finger than the actual words, and had started to drop over the window ledge when half a dozen men had burst into his room, swords drawn, eyes moving from him to the man in red.

The man had turned to meet them and raised his arms as they ran forward, thrusting steel into his body, only for the man to laugh, a deep dark laugh.

Astren had let go in shock and fell to the ground below, yet he'd managed to run, especially as the shouts of the frightened men had chased him from the first-floor window.

His rescuer that fateful night over thirty years ago had been an old seer who had seen him travel the spirit paths and had sought him out to share his knowledge and to seek an apprentice. Fortunately for Astren, his timing couldn't have been better, and it was he who led him into the world of espionage as Astren grew from boy to man and his powers evolved.

Astren brought his mind back to the present. He had a job to do.

Thinking back to such painful memories had no time in the here and now, and yet he couldn't shake the memory as he flew from the palace over the city of Freemantle, heading west. He'd been spying on his father's supposedly closest friend that night because, as his father had said … *only those closest could betray your trust the most*. Those words now echoed in his mind.

He looked down and all around as he flew higher. To survive this night, he needed to keep his wits about him. This land was so familiar to him, and he flew faster and faster, passing over rivers and villages. During his many years in service to Tristan and for various merchants, he'd travelled far and wide, even into the very heart of the Witch-King's lands as an emissary, so that very little west of the Freestates was closed to him.

Over the years, he'd purposefully pushed into the fog, painfully extending the boundaries of where he could go and subsequently awakened to horrific headaches that would last days to gain a few extra leagues of vision over the Witch-King's lands. Now he could travel almost its entire length and breadth, but not without danger, and it was that risk that had stopped him from spying for some time now.

The spirit self reflected the physical being, and thus as Astren travelled, he was in his red robes. In this, he was somewhat fortunate because as travel was only possible at night, against the dark sky, he showed little or nothing of his presence.

However, there were those who could travel, few perhaps but still enough, that were also warriors. Daleth was one, and while he was not as fast or gifted at spirit travelling as Astren was, his astral being also reflected his physical one, and thus he was as armoured and dangerous as in the flesh. Some of his minions were just as deadly should he be unfortunate as to run afoul of them.

It was one such encounter soon after he'd first seen the girl Maya that had scared him so profoundly that he'd not travelled out of the Freestates since.

He'd been doing his almost nightly reconnaissance, monitoring the build-up of troops and supplies, when out of the corner of his eye, he'd seen a darkly armoured man flying toward him. Astren had quickly withdrawn westward, heart hammering, and looked over his shoulder in relief as his pursuer had slowly fallen behind. However, several more had risen skyward and chased him, herding him toward the coastline and the wall of fog beyond. There were a dozen of them, some above to stop him fleeing higher, others below, and he knew there was not enough time to get around them. Soon he found himself facing a dozen evilly grinning men behind dark helms, black eyes glaring balefully as they savoured his imminent death.

The only safe way to leave the spirit paths alive was to return to your body in ethereal form to re-join it, and all avenues of escape were blocked. With his death mere moments away, he moved back further and further, feeling the coldness of the fog add to the chill in his bones, seeing the satisfied smiles of his pursuers.

One spoke, his voice sounding metallic from within his helm. 'There's nowhere left to go. It's time to die.'

Astren's head had spun, yet in those last moments, he'd known what to do. Still facing them, he'd flown backwards into the fog. The pursuing men had instinctively surged forward to chase, yet even as Astren's head felt like it would split in two with pain, his gamble paid off as the men that pursued him screamed in agony, then disappeared one by one.

The pain had caused him to blackout, and he'd awoken a week later, malnourished and on the verge of death, surrounded by servants who'd almost given up hope on him returning to the living.

He was fortunate, for in all his time spirit travelling, he'd never found an enemy this side of the border above the Freestates. In fact, as far as he knew, there were no others with the talent to spirit travel east of Daleth's Kingdom, yet he wouldn't risk taking it for granted simply because he hadn't seen anyone else.

Caution now at the forefront of his mind, he flew high then low, into the clouds then out again at a different place, and often spun around to watch behind. He would have enjoyed himself were it not for the danger, as the ability to truly fly was beyond all men, yet this was as close as one could get. Forget the fact it left you exhausted; it was worth it.

He approached Tristan's Folly that sat astride the pass through the Forelorn mountains. It was a temptation to stop and view the preparations in a bid to delay his journey into danger. As he got closer, he was a little surprised. It was night time, so it was not unusual to see a lack of movement. Still, he would have expected to see men patrolling the walls and more activity, considering around seven thousand men were now garrisoned here. He wanted to stay longer, to look closer at the works and defensive siege engines, but his mission took priority, and he pushed his inquisitive nature to one side.

He continued slowly, passing high over the smaller fortress at the west of the pass, noting something looked wrong. He flew closer, and indeed his instincts were correct, for behind the main curtain wall, everything had been demolished. Once that wall was taken down, the enemy troops could flood into the pass unrestricted. Anthain wouldn't be aware of this, and Astren would enjoy passing this intelligence on to score a small victory.

He flew many leagues westward, astral heart pounding in his chest. It wasn't long before massive siege engines appeared on route to the pass, and the land below became more desolate with every passing moment. It was without question teetering on the edge.

Further and further, Astren travelled, coming across hundreds of camps, fires glittering in the darkness. The soldiers of the Witch-king were gathering and would soon all join forces. They were all at most thirty days from the pass when he'd previously thought they had twice that amount of time. He turned to fly away, yet distant movement caught his eye.

Someone else was spirit travelling this night under the light of the moon!

Whilst it was his duty to report back as soon as possible, curiosity got the better of him, for there ahead flew none other than the Witch-King himself.

Fear filled Astren, but also disappointment that he was no warrior, for had he a sword and the skill to use it, he could have tried to slay Daleth here and now. Instead, he followed at a distance and stayed hidden in the clouds or within the mountains' shadow.

It wasn't long before he saw something else that took him by surprise, for winding across the barren land was a trail of verdant growth, noticeable even in the darkness. Astren couldn't believe his eyes, for while he didn't have the time to follow it back to its source, he knew in his heart that this would lead back toward the girl, Maya's, village. Therefore, the only conclusion that he could arrive at was that she was alive and had been fleeing eastward this whole time, and he smiled.

Daleth had also seen it, for he started to follow the trail to its head. In the distance Astren could perceive the subtlest glow from a dying campfire, and a short time later, the Witch-King floated down into some open ground a few paces to the east of the site, still unaware of his ghostly pursuer.

Against his better judgement, Astren followed, then watched as Daleth walked across the forest floor.

Not a leaf stirred beneath the king's astral feet as he moved toward the camp where two figures lay side by side. A man sat a few paces away, a drawn sword across his lap, eyes alert.

Astren was waiting, holding his breath, standing beneath a gnarled oak tree, when Daleth spoke.

'If I thought I could catch you, little spy, I would fly over and cut your head from your scrawny neck!' As Daleth said this, his cold grey eyes turned toward Astren, fixing him with his gaze.

Astren felt himself turn cold as Daleth continued. 'I recognise you. You came to my lands as an emissary, years past. To think, all that time, you were spying. I could pretend to be affronted, yet I admire any man who risks his life for his king.'

But then Daleth's demeanour darkened. 'Several of my Rangers died on the spirit paths chasing a man in red robes into the fog. Would that be you by any chance? Of course it is,' Daleth answered, before Astren even had a chance to decide whether or not to tell the truth in response.

'Do you know how long it takes to train a Ranger?' he continued. 'Well, we identify those with suitable talents or gifts as young as possible, then they spend the next ten years or so fighting their way over the bodies of their peers for the privilege. All that, so they can be gods amongst men on the field of battle, not to die from the tricks of a spying scholar!' and he spat this last bit, anger mottling his face.

Daleth controlled himself and turned away, then strolled across the dying embers of the campfire. He sat down next to the man on the log, whose eyes scanned the undergrowth, unaware of the unwanted guest who sat at his right shoulder.

'Ahhhh,' said Daleth. 'It's been far too many years since I've enjoyed the warmth of sitting around a good campfire, swapping tales, drinking wine, revelling in the thoughts of a good battle, till now at least, but all that is changing. This man,' he said, turning his head to nod at Rakan, 'used to be in my army and deserted, as did the younger one by all accounts. But it's not either of them we are interested in. It's the girl. Do you know her name?'

Astren found his voice. 'Yes, and I believe you do too. She has a gift that interests me and now scares you if I were to hazard a guess. Although why you're talking to me, I don't know.' As he said this, his eyes scanned the sky, ready to fly off at the hint of trouble, in case Daleth sought to distract him from any pursuers.

Daleth laughed. 'I'm certainly not afraid of this girl or her gift, and I can reassure you that all my Rangers are wide awake. You won't find them abroad this night, spirit travelling to bother you, so you needn't fear them, for most are up to more physical pursuits. I give you my word. Have you realised there's nothing you and your king can do to stop me?'

'Is that why we're just talking?' asked Astren. 'For you to tell me we have already lost?'

'Perhaps,' said Daleth, 'or maybe I'm assessing whether I'm exchanging words with someone who might be a great deal of use to me alive if he could see the benefit of changing sides? This could be a fortuitous meeting for us both!'

Astren shook his head.

Daleth nodded. 'You might be weak of body, but you have a strong sense of duty. I appreciate that.'

'You know, to start with, my interest was to have her brought to me alive,' mused Daleth. 'Imagine if she could heal the land as I drained it. We could have made quite the happy couple!' and he laughed, a deep resounding laugh. 'But our gifts were not compatible, more's the pity. So now she has to die, especially as she's doing her best to escape toward imagined salvation within the Freestates. However, now I expect them to get no further if I'm honest.'

Daleth stood and stretched his arms, then reached down to his waist, slowly drawing his sword. Astren prepared to fly. However, Daleth didn't look at Astren as he moved over to stand above the sleeping Maya. He flexed his muscles and raised his sword high above his head, before plunging it down through her inert body into the ground below.

Astren cried out, but Maya continued her sleep untroubled as Daleth withdrew his astral blade. 'If only I had the power to kill my enemies so easily,' he chuckled. 'However, where this failed, perhaps the real blades of my Rangers might do a better job!' and he started to laugh again.

Astren immediately became aware of movement, but not in the night sky above him. Instead, it was from behind him within the woods, and he realised the conversation had been a distraction this whole time, to stop him from seeing the danger that closed in on the three fugitives, and now it was likely too late.

Daleth suddenly flew at Astren, sword raised, yet Astren quickly projected himself so the man keeping watch could see him. 'FLEE!' he screamed, then followed his own advice and flew into the sky. Daleth didn't bother to follow, but his laughter did, as Astren sped back toward the Freestates and Tristan.

Astren's thoughts were full of sadness. The girl Maya, who had seemed such an innocent soul, would shortly be dead, and the fortress would soon feel the full might of Daleth's army.

Then a small smile tugged at the corners of his mouth, for perhaps next time he'd be the one laughing at Daleth. The might of Tristan's Folly awaited, and Daleth might find that his defeat or death was not far away either.

Chapter XIV

Rakan sat on a log, eyes sweeping the shadows as the pale moon painted everything it looked upon with a silvery hue.

Taran and Maya lay close to one another, on the other side of the fire that they'd put out a while ago, even though with the chill night air, it would have been welcomed.

Rakan was exhausted, and tonight he would hand over the watch to Taran, but not for a little while yet. He looked down at them both and felt a warmth spread through him. For so long, he'd only thought about himself, and yet now he wanted to keep them safe too, for they were … he shook his head and smiled ruefully. They were indeed becoming like family.

It had been several days since Rakan had killed the two hunters, and instead of feeling relaxed, having succeeded in their escape, he felt a sense of foreboding. He knew the safer you believed yourself to be, the more vulnerable you became. He also worried about the danger they were headed toward. Laska wasn't Rakan's friend and still owed his existence to the benevolence of the Witch-King. Would he help or betray them?

Yet, Rakan still had some hope. Laska held no love for Daleth, and his community did have a code as such. Anyone who fortunately stumbled upon his gates, be they villager or deserter, were always given sanctuary for a night while their fate was decided.

A lot could happen during a night.

His musings and the warm feeling inside was dispelled in an instant, for out of nowhere, a ghostly man in red robes barely visible in the darkness appeared, and stumbling backwards by a tree, screamed, 'FLEE!'

Rakan reacted immediately even as the others awoke to the sound of the voice. He grabbed them by the shoulders, hauling them to their feet. There was no point in being quiet now, for he could hear numerous footfalls and crashing from within the forest getting closer by the moment, so he shouted his own warning as he pushed the groggy Taran and Maya. 'RUN!'

Maya swept up her bow and quiver, and Taran already had his sword, but as they started to move toward the packs, Rakan shoved them toward the edge of the camp. 'RUN!' he shouted again, and the urgency of the situation finally got through.

Maya sprinted off, Taran after, with Rakan right behind them.

A strange whistling filled the air as they ran, and Taran wondered what it was until arrows started to hiss by, but the dark, trees, and distance, fouled the archer's aim.

Maya pushed the pace, sprinting, using her keen hunter's eyesight and trail knowledge to lead them safely even in the near darkness. The shouts of their pursuers sounded so loud and harsh that Maya almost sobbed as she ran. For the first time since their escape, she felt vulnerable and certain of their death.

'Slow down,' Rakan called, but Maya still pushed hard, panic driving her on. With a surge of effort, Rakan managed to pass by Taran and grabbed her shoulder, dragging her to a halt.

'What are you doing?' Maya cried, and tried to shake free as Taran demanded the same. The crash of their pursuers which had grown more distant, started to get closer again.

'Listen girl, think! You're normally a hunter, but now you're the hunted. If we carry on at this pace, we'll exhaust ourselves; become easy prey. We need to be able to run for as long as it takes to lose our pursuers. At this rate, we'll soon be done and have no strength for a fight if they bring us to ground.'

Rakan's words reached Maya, for indeed a deer could outrun a pack of wolves in the short term, but the wolves often won in the end, tiring it out, and she knew his words to be true. 'Right,' she said, 'I've got it,' and headed off again.

The exchange had only taken a few moments, yet Taran felt like they'd given away too much of their lead, so as he ran, his shoulders hunched in anticipation of an arrow that fortunately never landed. Taran's face was soon scratched and bleeding as he followed Maya's outline in front of him, and the shouts of the men behind stopped getting any closer as they settled into a controlled run.

If it wasn't for Maya, thought Taran, we'd have been caught by now. Fortunately, Maya's skill at finding a path through the dense forest was amazing, but the pursuers simply had to follow the path she set.

They ran and ran.

Occasionally the hunters got closer, and Maya had to push the pace a little, spurred on by the occasional arrow that hissed by, clattering off a tree trunk or thunking into the ground near their feet.

Taran's breath heaved in his lungs as they continued to run, and he was so glad that Rakan had demanded their supplies be left behind. There was no way they could have kept this up in the darkness with a cumbersome pack getting caught by unseen vines or branches.

Rakan called a brief stop as the voices behind them seemed to drop a little further back.

'We need to get further ahead of these bastards,' growled Rakan. 'If the forest thins, some of these arrows might find their mark. Now's the time for speed. We need to find a way to lose them while it's still dark, or we're history.'

Maya set off faster than before, and as they sprinted, Taran realised it wasn't going to work. They'd been running for too long, every day since their escape, and were at the end of their stamina. He looked over his shoulder to see Rakan puffing along behind him and not much further away their pursuers' dark shapes as they flitted amongst the trees.

They came to a wide clearing, and as they reached the other side, Rakan came to a halt, hands on his knees, bent over gasping for breath.

Taran ran a few more steps, then slowed to a halt before walking back to Rakan. 'How many do you think there are?' he asked, drawing his sword.

Rakan, having regained a bit of composure, stood straight. 'More than enough,' he sighed. 'They'll likely be Rangers. They work in teams of five, so ten or fifteen, maybe more. Even if it were just Darkon and Lazard, I wouldn't fancy our chances too much.'

Maya suddenly came flying back. 'What in the nine hells are you two doing?' she cried, pulling on their arms. 'Come on, we have to run!' she implored.

Taran looked into her eyes. 'Rakan can't go on and nor could I for much longer. They'll catch us as soon as the sun rises when we have no strength left. Go. Try to get away while we hold them for as long as we can.'

'No, I'll not run while you stand!' she said defiantly, unslinging her bow, nocking an arrow.

Now it was Taran's turn to pull her arm. 'Go,' he said again. 'Please don't die here with us.'

Maya looked sad, not meeting his gaze. 'I have a feeling I'd rather die fighting next to you, than live without you. Don't ask me to go again. I won't.'

Taran pulled her to him then, and she buried her head in his chest as he held her tight. He closed his eyes briefly as he nuzzled her hair and breathed in her scent. His heart beat so quickly, and he could feel it matched by Maya's. Fear certainly, but also more, something else making it beat as never before.

As Rakan looked on, he felt his eyes blur as he saw the love that was blossoming between them, and even though he didn't want to take this moment from them, still he reached out to pull Taran to one side.

Maya reluctantly let Taran go, took her arrows from her quiver and pushed them into the soft soil at her feet before taking an archer's stance.

Rakan talked softly but quickly. 'Taran, my boy. The things they'll do to your girl if they take her alive before they kill her ... that can't happen, do you understand? It might be better to kill her now, before it starts.'

Taran stepped back, hot words coming to his lips. But he saw the hurt and anguish in Rakan's eyes even in the darkness, and remembered saying similar words himself when he'd first freed Maya. Before he had a chance to respond, their pursuers entered the other side of the clearing, and seeing their prey waiting in the moonlight, came to a halt.

'Fifteen,' whistled Rakan. 'I almost feel privileged. That's only five each. Do you think you can take five?' he asked Taran with a wry smile.

Before Taran could reply, Maya loosed an arrow. Taran could barely track it in the gloom as it flew towards one of the Rangers, but with unbelievable speed and skill, the Ranger's blade whipped up, splintering it at the last moment.

'Damn, still fifteen,' muttered Rakan.

Maya grimaced. 'Not that it matters much but make that sixteen.'

Taran couldn't help it as he looked at Maya. 'For someone with a beautiful figure,' he said, 'you're not too good with numbers, are you?'

Maya's eyes opened wide at the teasing compliment, and despite the circumstances, she smiled back, saying. 'It's a good thing I'm after your body because for sure I'm not after your brains.'

Rakan looked a little hopeful. 'I don't suppose you could call upon your gift to entangle them all as you did with Darkon and Lazard?' he asked.

'Maybe two or three, if they stand still for long enough,' said Maya doubtfully.

A voice called over, interrupting their final exchange.

'If you three have finished your goodbyes,' said a Ranger, standing slightly ahead of the others, 'I think it's time for you to die.'

As he said this, the Rangers strode across the clearing to kill them.

Anthain stomped down the steps from the Royal Palace, his mood shifting between trepidation and optimism. Tristan had been even more demanding than usual, and Anthain was exhausted, but he couldn't afford the luxury of sleep; there was still so much to do.

Damn him, but Tristan had never taken him seriously, taking any opportunity to mock him, because him being big apparently meant his brain was small. Tristan had not once truly appreciated his abilities.

His father, one of the state's wealthiest merchants who traded in medicinal oils, had shared this opinion, because many years before, instead of engaging Anthain in the family business, he'd enrolled him into the Freemantle officer academy. The intention being that his wayward son would be taught discipline and then, in time, bring a little honour to the family name through his service in the military.

Looking back, Anthain could still feel the humiliation.

The military, even at officer level, would never convey status or wealth, and that meant he'd forever be looked upon with scorn by his peers. He'd begged his father to reconsider, but there had been no changing the old man's mind.

So for the next three years, to keep his father happy and to ensure his allowance continued to flow, Anthain begrudgingly attended the academy.

During that time, with the false belief that being good with a sword would be enough to pass, Anthain tried to enjoy himself as much as possible. He'd taken every opportunity to gamble, get drunk and enjoy the company of women instead. After all, what was the point in learning strategies for attack and defense, troop manoeuvres and supply chains, when the Freestates didn't even have a standing army?

At the end of his three-year tenure, Anthain had returned to the family villa, head bowed in disbelief. He'd been failed.

His father, unable to bear the shame should it become known, invited the academy commander around that very day for a meeting that lasted well into the night. After many hours of negotiation, his father had parted with a small fortune and was set to marry the commander's daughter, whereas Anthain only found himself passed with honours.

Despite this intervention in a land that valued the art of bribery, Anthain had felt cheated.

To make matters even worse, his father, who he'd never felt close to, used the situation as an excuse to cast him out and cut off his allowance. With no other option, Anthain had taken the only route left to him. A position as a guard in the city garrison.

That was over ten years past, and every day since then, Anthain had cursed his father, then later Tristan, and all those others who used him, who didn't see he was meant for greater things.

Fortunately, there was one who had seen see his potential for greatness.

He had over the years, by both force and guile, been promoted, until at last, he'd achieved the rank of captain. This was only one below the king's personal bodyguard and general, Tryown.

The man was his cousin, and yet instead of favouring him, he'd looked upon Anthain with disdain every time he saw him, finding constant amusement in his fall from his father's grace rather than recognising his achievement in rising through the ranks.

One night while drowning his sorrows in a dark corner of one of the city's many taverns, he'd been approached by a woman, Lacyntha.

She introduced herself as a wealthy merchant, and offered to buy him a drink as a protector of their city and great king. Not used to being lauded and admired, Anthain found a good friend that night who saw him for what he was. A man destined for greatness.

The friendship had grown over the weeks and months. During this time, Lacyntha refused to let Anthain pay for anything when they met. The reason for her generosity, she explained, was that someone who would one day be the king's bodyguard should never have to pay for anything, ever.

Anthain had broken down then and confided in his drunken state that while he deserved it, he would never achieve the position because Tryown would see him dead in the ground before that ever happened.

Lacyntha had smiled in sympathy and reassured Anthain that she had foreign, influential friends, who could help him achieve this position if he but asked for it.

Anthain, not wanting to offend his new acquaintance, had scoffed a little but raised his glass in acceptance and advised that whatever opportunity the gods presented, he would take.

Two months later, Tryown was dead, and Anthain never made the connection.

Everything began to change as Anthain was promoted to become the king's bodyguard; a few things were good, but most were bad.

Lacyntha, in recognition of his new status, advised that a monthly payment from his sponsors would be forthcoming. To explain this new income, she suggested he let it be known that his father had grown a little closer and reinstated his allowance.

But other than that recognition, as Anthain grew into his new role of following behind the king all day long, he realised that it was the worst job he could have ever wished for.

Whenever the king was awake, Anthain had to be there, and his time for drinking, gambling and whoring often disappeared. Even worse, Tristan would spend most days bent over a parchment, studying trade deals and counting collected taxes. It was like death from a thousand cuts.

He bemoaned his plight to Lacyntha, who had nodded sagely, advising that in the days of old, kings needed to be warriors like Anthain, not coin counters like Tristan, and how foreign kings could never respect such a physically weak ruler. Anthain, on the other hand, looked like how a warrior king should, tall and strong. A man who shook the earth as he walked.

Over the years that followed, Anthain's dependence on Lacyntha's money grew more and more as she funded his expensive tastes and gambling habits.

Then just under six months ago, Lacyntha had asked if Anthain would like to be king, whether he thought he would make a good ruler? Anthain, after some consideration, had nodded sagely.

Then it's time to make it happen, she'd advised.

To Anthain's initial shock, Lacyntha revealed she was an agent for Daleth the Witch-King, and although he'd suspected this, and ignored it, the confirmation had still made him feel somewhat sick.

Yet Lacyntha had reassured him that Daleth's admiration for him knew no bounds. The Witch-King already saw him as a fellow warrior, and would happily recognise Anthain as a fellow king and ally were he strong enough to seize the crown.

However, what wasn't so reassuring, was that Daleth wanted Anthain to prove himself worthy by killing Tristan himself. Then Anthain, the new ruler of the Freestates, would let Daleth's army pass through Tristan's Folly and the Freestates lands to conquer everything that lay beyond.

Anthain's first achievement as the new king would be to save the Freestates from Tristan's reckless plan to fight, save the people, save himself and avoid a costly war.

Now, all this time later, with less than a month to go till Daleth's army sought passage, Anthain and all those involved in the planned coup were ready.

Anthain looked around him as he quickly made his way to the merchant's quarter. Not that many people were about at this godforsaken hour, except for the eight hundred guards who were waiting for him to lead them.

The sky was clear and bright, the moon a good omen. Anthain smiled. Tomorrow the people of the Freestates would awaken to a new king!

Astren fled as fast as he was able and frequently spun around to see if anyone followed, despite knowing that Daleth had stayed behind to watch the spectacle of the girl's death.

The forces he'd seen would be at the southern pass in around thirty days, and Astren knew the intelligence regarding the siege engines alone had been worth the risk. Time to bring this news to Tristan and Anthain.

He flew back over Tristan's Folly high and fast. He was tempted to take the time to fly down and give the news directly to the fortress commander, but decided he wouldn't incur Anthain's anger by circumventing the chain of command, so would tell him first.

A short while later, he flew over the outskirts of Freemantle. The Royal Palace was immediately visible as it shone brightly in the centre of the city. Even at night, its roof of burnished gold reflected the many torches lit around the grounds. Of course, it wasn't solid gold, just a very thin leaf, and yet from the moment anyone entered the city, it caught the eye. The palace reflected not only the light but the power of wealth that the Freestates and its ruler enjoyed.

Astren drifted down, and was about to enter when he saw Anthain leave through the gates and turn toward the merchant quarter. He followed, and was about to project himself, to give Anthain the news on Daleth's preparedness, when Anthain slipped into an alleyway.

It was such a strange and furtive move that Astren immediately decided to observe rather than be seen. He hovered at Anthain's shoulder, then felt foolish and embarrassed as Anthain turned to a wall to empty his bladder.

Astren started to move away, but just as he did, two of the city guard came cautiously into the alley from the other end, and he instinctively felt that something was amiss.

He floated there, an unseen voyeur, as he waited for the conversation to finish, and then flew directly back to his body and the king.

Daleth floated above the clearing and watched in glee as the three fugitives gave up on trying to escape. To witness their initial blind panic, then the blossoming of hope, only to see it wither when they realised they couldn't outrun the hunters had been exquisite to behold.

Even hearing their last words nourished him, and he wished he could project like that damned seer. He would have loved for them to know he was watching their demise, to know he'd orchestrated it to the end.

The three of them against sixteen of his Rangers. However skilled the two deserters might be, he doubted they'd be able to face just one of his finest, let alone sixteen.

Suddenly something that had been tugging hidden at the back of his mind came clear.

Rangers worked in fives; there should only be fifteen.

His eyes snapped back to the Rangers, casually walking across the darkened clearing, counting. Yes, fifteen. So, why had the girl counted sixteen? Then he saw him, HIM. It couldn't be, it just couldn't be, but it was.

Kalas fell upon the rear left flank of the Rangers as silent as a shadow. His silver armour shone like a beacon, as did his swords, as he clove through the first five men in the blink of an eye.

Daleth screamed in frustration, and it was almost as if his scream was heard, for the remaining ten reacted in that instant.

They were his elite, and they turned to face this fury in their midst, that came from the shadows at their moment of victory. They had never known defeat, and they moved as one. As Kalas charged, they gave way, fell back, flowed away from him like water, trying to avoid his blades. They recognised him for the danger he was, having been forewarned of his presence, and taught by a daemon themselves.

Daleth caught movement out of the corner of his eye and saw Rakan, Taran and Maya flee into the woods, taking advantage of the situation to make their escape again. Daleth screamed every curse he knew but turned his attention back to the spectacle below him.

He cursed his lack of skill in spirit travelling, for his stamina was being tested, and he could feel his body demanding his return. Pain began to course through him as he held determinedly to the spirit paths to watch this battle. He had to know, just had to know how it finished.

Some of the Rangers baited Kalas, then stepped back, while others tried to strike from behind, and yet he somehow always sensed the attacks and was able to face his foes in time. Yet this stalemate couldn't go on forever.

Daleth watched one of his Rangers move back from the group, finding space to draw his bow, and Daleth smiled. He knew all his men, and this one's skill with the bow was extraordinary. His weapon was a gift from Daleth himself, made from the horn of a forest stag. It could put an arrow through a horse. Silian, the archer, drew back on the string, watching Kalas' movements, and Daleth knew the moment he would loose, for he watched Silian exhale before smoothly releasing the arrow.

Daleth's eyes flashed to Kalas, expecting to see him thrown from his feet, the fight soon to end, but instead, he swayed, and Daleth saw one of his Rangers go down, directly opposite Silian, the arrow in his chest!

Again Silian loosed, and this time Kalas' blade deflected the arrow, which swept another Ranger from his feet, screaming in pain.

Kalas didn't wait for a third arrow, and instead charged toward the archer. The other Rangers moved in front of Kalas, trying to keep him from their biggest hope. Yet, Kalas bizarrely tossed one of his blades into the air, and as every eye followed it for a split second, his free hand flashed over his shoulder then down again, and Silian collapsed with a throwing dagger in his throat.

Fifteen down to seven in moments … everything Alano had said was proving to be true.

He watched as his Rangers fell one by one to the dance of Kalas' swords and tricks as if choreographed for months. Several of them even managed to lay a blade on him, drawing blood, yet it didn't seem to give him pause for a moment.

Daleth screamed in pain and frustration, ready to return to his body and the headache of a lifetime. Yet unexpectedly, Kalas' red eyes turned toward him, impossibly fixing him with a baleful gaze.

'I can see you Witch-King, I hope you enjoyed the show, Kalas can see you, and Kalas is coming!'

Daleth's scream now had nothing to do with pain or frustration, as those red eyes and vile laughter stayed with him all the way as he fled back to his body.

The Royal Palace in Freemantle stood higher than all the surrounding buildings. To reach the main doors, a person had to climb fifty steps. Every fifth step was adorned with a statue of rulers past, portraying them bedecked in jewels. It inspired those who worked or lived within its walls, for this was the centre of trade, with wealth beyond measure.

Tristan wondered what the nobles and people would think if they knew that the Freestates treasury was now almost empty. The cessation of trade with the realm of the Witch-King had seen revenue plummet. Now with the vast amount of money spent to repair the fortress and hire thousands of men, funds were running low.

Now, Tristan stood at the top of the steps with no more than a dozen grizzled guards standing nervously behind him, men who'd been in service for decades and were too old to be worth turning against their king. As he waited stoically, looking out into the darkness of the night, he wondered how it had come to this, whether this was really going to happen. Anthain, big, loyal, bumbling Anthain. His bodyguard, general and confidant for so many years, on his way to usurp him, to kill him. Surely not.

Earlier that evening, Astren had told him of Anthain's treachery, and initially, he'd reacted in disbelief, scolding Astren over his petty rivalry. Yet Astren had been so scared, so sure, that it soon convinced Tristan that even if it wasn't true, Astren believed it was. He'd called for the guard, but when no one replied, Astren opened the doors to the throne room to find none at their post, and icy fingers had crawled up his back.

They'd walked cautiously but quickly then, through the many halls and chambers, coming across isolated guards who were just as confused as to their comrades' whereabouts. Every one of them was ordered to join Tristan's growing entourage, which also contained any clerk who'd been working into the night.

It appeared that almost every guard in the capital had turned against him.

Now, as he peered into the gloom of the city, he was surprised to still be alive. However, Anthain needed the nobles' support to legitimise his usurping the throne and was therefore making this a public spectacle. Tristan saw a procession of hundreds of torches approaching from the west, snaking its way slowly through the nobles and senior merchants quarter, and nodded in grudging appreciation.

Anthain maybe wasn't quite the bumbling giant Tristan had felt he was, or perhaps there was someone behind him helping him with his plans, for surely this was a canny move. By waking these key citizens at a time when they would have no chance to protest, they had almost no choice but to join Anthain or instead be slaughtered half-asleep along with their kin.

It would be a while before Anthain arrived, and every moment counted as Tristan waited patiently. The guards at his back shifted nervously, and he turned to them and smiled broadly with a confidence he certainly didn't feel.

Tristan opened his arms wide. 'Fear not, my loyal guards,' he lied. 'I have known for months of Anthain's treachery, but I also wanted to ensnare even the smallest snake that had turned against me. By standing at my side, you have reaffirmed your steadfast loyalty, and such an act will be duly rewarded.'

The men looked at each other, reassured, then back at their king in surprise as he laughed.

Tristan leaned casually against a tall column and wished he felt as confident as his lie had made him sound, because his insides felt like water.

Now, where in the nine hells was Astren, and what was taking him so long?

Death was coming with the dawn.

Chapter XV

Rakan, Taran and Maya surged through the woods, the sound of battle diminishing behind them as they ran.

'We should have stayed to help,' shouted Maya as she led them along a game trail, leaping over fallen trees and ducking under low branches.

Rakan and Taran came behind, far less graceful, but with dogged determination.

'We would have made no difference,' Rakan shouted back in response. 'One extra man against that many Rangers would still see us all dead on the ground.'

Maya didn't need much convincing. Fortunately, the brush with death had given them all a new surge of energy, but it couldn't last forever, so as time went by and with no further sign of the Rangers, she progressively slowed the pace so they could keep running. The moon that had shown them the way began to fade as the beginnings of a new dawn brightened the sky.

A thunderous noise slowly grew louder and could be heard over their footfalls and gasps for breath.

'It's the white river!' called Rakan, answering the unspoken question. 'We might only have delayed the inevitable, but at least we might be able to choose the manner of our death if they catch us.'

They weaved through the trees and undergrowth at an ever-decreasing speed until they finally reached the edge of the forest, where they came to a ragged, breathless halt.

'It must be the Forelorn mountains,' said Maya, pointing to the horizon, where the enormous peaks of the easternmost border rose into the sky, the tops obscured by cloud. 'They seem so close.'

'And there's the White River!' Rakan added.

A frothing torrent of water split the land in two, and the landscape before them as they paused briefly to gaze at it. In the far distance, a decaying forest led to the base of the mountains, but between them lay a wide expanse of rocky ground on this side of the river and a broad grassy plain on the other. Yet luck was with them, for there was a barely visible track bisecting the countryside, leading to an old rope and wood bridge. It hung suspended over the raging waters, offering passage to the plain beyond.

'If we can get to that forest,' said Rakan, raising his voice above the roar of the water, 'it will lead us to the lands where Laska holds sway. Now let's get to that bridge!'

Without further discussion, Maya led the way toward the track, but it wasn't easy going. The soft forest floor now gave way to uneven land, and large rocks thrust upward as if the very ground were trying to eject them as if diseased. They leapt from boulder to boulder and then ran whenever there was open ground.

Suddenly, Maya slipped and thrust her bow into the ground to stop herself falling, but it splintered under the sudden stress, and she fell hard, her foot twisting in a hole, and when she got up and tried to run again, it gave way immediately.

'Quickly heal yourself,' urged Taran, as his eyes scanned the edge of the forest.

But Maya shook her head. 'I can't. My gift doesn't work on me.'

Taran's eyes opened wide. 'That might have been good to know before now,' he said with surprise, then swept her up in his arms. He grunted with the effort and followed Rakan at a reduced pace.

Maya held Taran tightly around his neck, sobbing more in frustration than pain, as he struggled to run with her in his arms. Yet, he barely moved faster than a walk in his exhausted state on the uneven ground.

They finally reached the track, and Taran all but collapsed at its verge.

'Here, let me help!' offered Rakan, taking Maya from an unprotesting Taran, and then set off toward the bridge.

'I'll be right behind you,' replied Taran.

Rakan nodded as he trotted off.

Taran bent over gasping for a short while, his vision blurred, when movement caught his eye. Over where the track reached the brow of the hill to the northwest, crested five armed men. Five men meant they were likely Rangers, and they started sprinting down the hill the moment they spotted him.

Taran broke into a slow run after Rakan, screaming in warning, but the noise of the water drowned his words as he saw them start to cross the rope bridge. Rakan now half-carried Maya, and the two of them held the suspension rope above their head for balance as they walked across the wooden slats that swayed dangerously beneath them.

Taran reached the beginning of the bridge when they were halfway across and turned to find the Rangers almost upon him. He drew his sword, then held the suspension rope with his left hand as he carefully stepped back, his feet finding purchase as he moved cautiously above the raging water.

The Rangers slowed as they approached, and then one by one, jumped up to follow. They were so sure with their movement and didn't even need to hold the suspension rope as a guide.

Taran backed away knowing there was no escape, not for him, and certainly not for the other two if the Rangers got past him.

The lead Ranger, a bearded man with those strange black eyes, stopped a few slats short of Taran and smiled, arms folded, perfectly balanced even as the bridge bounced under the weight of so many people.

'You've led us on a fine chase!' he shouted. 'I have no doubts you are good with that blade, but it won't be enough, I'm sure you know. Best you say your goodbyes,' and he nodded over Taran's shoulder.

'I'll kill you all!' snarled Taran, as he backed further away, sword raised, biding for time.

The Ranger laughed and shook his head. 'You can't beat us, lad. Not me and certainly not the five of us.'

Taran refused to take his eyes off of the man, fearing a ruse, but the man just nodded again. 'Go on, say your goodbyes.'

Taran glanced over his shoulder to see that Rakan and Maya had just reached the other side. As they turned, he met their eyes briefly, then raised his blade in a final salute before turning back to the grinning Rangers in front of him.

'I never said I could beat you,' said Taran grimly. 'I just said I'd kill you all.'

With that, he firmed his grip on the overhead suspension rope and swept his sword down, severing the rope on his right that supported the wooden slats. The bridge suddenly twisted, throwing three of the Rangers into the torrent below. Their screams were swept away with them.

However, the two lead Rangers had read Taran's intent at the last moment and had grabbed for the rope overhead. Now the three of them hung precariously above the water, all the support beneath their feet gone.

Taran hung by one arm, the other grasping his sword. The two Rangers, however, hung by both having yet to draw their blades.

'I don't see you laughing now,' Taran shouted, as the Rangers frantically swung arm over arm toward him, and he put the razor-sharp edge of the sword to the suspension rope and started to cut.

It was old and under so much stress from the weight of the three men that the strands parted almost instantly, and Taran, for a moment felt satisfaction, as he saw the reality hit the Rangers' faces. This was the end.

As the rope gave way, Taran and the remaining two Rangers fell into the freezing water. Taran let go of his sword and held on to the rope with every last bit of strength as the icy flow dragged him under. His end of the rope, which remained secured at the far side of the bank, swung him across the current as he was swept downstream.

Taran hit a rock, and the air was punched from his lungs just as he went under and swallowed a huge amount of freezing water. Blackness replaced his thoughts just as he ploughed into another rock, and he felt his ribs break. It was too much, and Taran finally let go of the rope in agony as he was spun around in the torrent, smashing against one rock after another.

He mercifully lost consciousness a moment later.

Anthain was flanked by his closest friends as he marched. Around him, the city guard, whose loyalty had been bought with the help of his benefactor, cheered him on. Every fourth man held a torch as they worked their way from villa to villa through the nobles' and wealthy merchants' quarter, waking those who remained asleep, demanding support for Anthain, who would save them from the tyranny of Tristan's rule.

Some initially sought to argue, but their screams as they died ensured that those following soon fell into line behind Anthain and his quest for power. So, as he approached the Royal Palace, in addition to his near eight hundred guards resplendent in their ornate armour, there were also now at least five hundred nobles and merchants following behind, chanting his name.

He sat astride a huge black horse, an imposing figure, and waved benignly at those people who opened their doors as he rode past in the morning light, calling them to his just cause. He wondered how enthusiastic his guard and followers would be if they knew the nation would soon be allied to the Witch-King himself. Yet, most likely, as long as they made a profit, they wouldn't care if they served the devils of the nine hells themselves.

As they approached the Royal Palace, he could see figures near the entrance, and his stomach felt a little uneasy to see Tristan standing on the top of the steps with some guards behind him.

True, the man could have treated him better, but to die at the point of Anthain's sword made him want to vomit. Despite having practised with sword and shield for many years, he'd never killed a man, and now he was going to kill his king.

Some of his men laughed as they saw Tristan standing in robes, not even armed, and joked of the wealth they would share, and the positions they would take under Anthain's new rule. He felt a little better as his men formed up behind him, marching forward along the broad avenue that opened up into the grounds surrounding the palace.

The rhythm of the men's boots drummed loudly on the cobblestones as they approached the palace steps, and when Anthain raised his hand to signal the halt, the crash of stamping feet echoed around like thunder. Into the silence that followed, he spoke.

Anthain had been blessed with a loud voice to match his large frame. 'Tristan the generous,' he shouted, using the biggest insult in Freestates language. 'You would bring poverty upon us all, and ruin at the hands of the Witch-King with your extravagant ways. I Anthain, have the support of the Freestates nobility, and they demand your head.'

His men roared, and Anthain felt relieved his voice hadn't cracked as he urged his horse forward a few steps. The nobles and merchants gathered closely behind the guards to watch the bloody spectacle of Tristan's execution unfold.

Credit to the man, thought Anthain, for Tristan didn't move or run, yet perhaps that would soon happen. Tristan leant against one of the giant pillars, and suddenly a shadow of a doubt made Anthain's stomach clench. Why did Tristan look so damned pleased with himself, with that charlatan Astren at his side?

The sound of marching feet answered his unspoken question as from the left and right of the palace marched several hundred armed men. Garbed in long robes that hid their armour, armed with body length shields and long spears, Anthain recognised them as desert spearmen. They came to a crashing unified halt, either side of his column of men, spear butts cracking against the cobblestones, throwing up sparks, as they roared Tristan's name.

Very good, old man, but not good enough, Anthain thought. He looked at his own guard to see uncertainty ripple through their ranks as they hadn't expected a fight. 'They're no more than five hundred to our eight,' called Anthain, and saw his words steady their resolve.

He turned to his sergeant. 'Get ready to give the order. Have two hundred men guard our back as we turn and overwhelm the spearmen on the right first. We'll then finish the others if they have the stomach to fight before we deal with Tristan.'

Anthain felt pleased with his strategy; maybe those years in the military academy hadn't been wasted after all.

Quiet settled over the courtyard, broken only by the crackle of torches and whispering amongst the men. Everyone waited for the reply Tristan would give, that would signal the beginning of what was to come.

Tristan's voice rang out. 'To become wealthy is a laudable pursuit, Anthain.' he shouted.

Anthain swelled at the unexpected praise, yet Tristan continued.

'But it is my belief that you take the gold of the Witch-King himself to achieve such, only to then squander it on buying the loyalty of those who know not the meaning of the word. You will sell this kingdom and have nothing left but dust in your hands, and this is a crime no true Freestates man can ever forgive.'

The insult fell heavily on Anthain, and his face grew red with rage. He needed to decide whether to refute the accusation or to retake the initiative and give the order to attack. Yes, attack, Anthain decided. However, just as he was about to give the command, Tristan raised his hand as if he was about to say something else and everyone hushed for his final words.

There was a moments pause, but then Tristan's hand chopped down to point at Anthain. 'Die!' Tristan shouted.

From the Royal Palace's roof, a rain of arrows fell, as five hundred archers of the Eyre rose to their feet and loosed with deadly accuracy into the packed ranks of Anthain's men below. As scores of Anthain's men fell screaming, the rest raised shields and brought them together in unison to defend against the death that rained from the sky.

Anthain swiftly joined them as his horse fell pierced a dozen times. 'Advance to the front!' he roared.

His guard responded and started to move forward, protected from the archers above as they closed the distance on the palace. Yet as they did so, the spearmen moved in from both sides.

'Shields, high and sides!' cried Anthain, knowing he still had a slight advantage. If they could push to the steps, the spearmen would lose their formation, and the archers wouldn't be able to shoot directly down into their ranks.

Yet even as Anthain's men carried out his orders, the nobles and merchants who were being cut down by the arrows, began to seek shelter amongst his men. As they pushed into the guard's formation in desperation, gaps began to appear between the shields, and without an unbroken barrier, more and more arrows found their mark, and panic started to creep in.

The fighting square they'd formed began to fragment, as the spearmen closed the distance and their spears started to bite home. Cries of pain rose as swords and spears drew blood on both sides as the guard fought skillfully, albeit with growing desperation as the civilians in their midst hindered their efforts at maintaining cohesion.

Despite this, Anthain, alongside his closest friends, carved their way through several spearmen and reached the steps of the palace. Anthain's sword arm was so tired, heavy like stone, yet he felt elated. He'd killed and still stood. Soon his steel would find Tristan's flesh.

'Charge. Kill the king, and this is over!' screamed Anthain, as his sergeant and over fifty of his remaining men accompanied him as they started sprinting up the steps. The screams of the injured behind spurred them on.

Anthain flew up the first ten as if he had wings on his shoulders, the next ten almost as fast. By the time he reached thirty, his legs had started to shake, and then as he got to forty, he barely had the energy to walk.

More archers stepped from behind the pillars ahead, and Anthain raised his shield in time to block several arrows. Surely he was blessed this day. He cut two archers from their feet and revelled in his strength.

As Anthain neared the top, he quickly looked around and realised to his horror that he was now alone. His friends lay dead or dying on the steps behind him, and his gasping breaths turned to desperate sobs as he forced himself up the last few steps to where Tristan waited. He barely had the strength to lift his blade, yet he did so, and none of Tristan's guards moved, perhaps in awe of his prowess. He roared his battle cry and moved toward Tristan and that damned Astren.

An excruciating cramp in his left leg caused it to buckle. He fell heavily and noticed the arrow embedded deep in his thigh. He struggled to rise and had just pushed himself upright when an arrow took him in the other leg. With a crash, Anthain fell to his knees and dropped his sword.

'Oh gods, help me!' he cried, and looked around in desperation for any of his soldiers. Tears ran down his face as he turned to see Tristan walking forward with Astren at his side.

Tristan knelt, lifted Anthain's fallen sword, and grunted with the effort, for he was not a strong man. 'You know,' said Tristan, as he looked down at Anthain. 'Your father paid me a fortune to take you on as my bodyguard, and it was he who paid for this sword to be made. I bestowed this to you as you took office. You swore on your life that this blade would keep me safe from all harm. Do you remember that day, Anthain?'

Anthain looked up, his eyes blurred from the pain and tears, and nodded. 'Forgive me, my king. I had no choice,' he whimpered.

Tristan stood tall. He raised the sword high above his head and brought it crashing down. Yet he was not skilled with the blade, and it deflected from Anthain's skull to slice deep into the shoulder. Anthain screamed in agony as Tristan used his sandaled foot to help yank the blade free.

Again and again, Tristan chopped at Anthain, releasing his pent up fear and anger. After he had brought the blade down a final time, he turned his blood-spattered face to Astren. 'He swore this blade would keep me safe, and he managed to keep that oath in some way after all.'

He raised his eyes to the slaughter that had taken place in the courtyard. All of the traitorous guards were dead, as were nigh on two hundred of the city's wealthiest nobles and merchants.

'You know,' said Tristan, turning to Astren. 'Anthain has in a way done us a huge favour today. We can now confiscate the combined wealth of all those dead nobles and merchants as traitors to the throne. The crown is solvent again.

'But, before we do, make sure you pay the spearmen and archers a hefty bonus and ensure they get thoroughly drunk before they realise this city could be theirs for the taking!'

Rakan had struggled with Maya over the swaying bridge, feeling decidedly unsteady as he saw the water rush by between the slats at his feet. Half carrying the girl with one arm made this challenging feat all the more difficult.

'I'm sorry, lass,' he'd said, when Maya demanded he let her go just before the crossing. 'Even if this hurts your pride, the faster we get to the other side, the better, and it will be too dangerous and slow for you to hop on your own, especially as these wooden slats are swaying and damp with spray.'

He'd moved as fast as possible, knowing Taran was right behind him guarding his back, and again felt warm with the knowledge that he could now trust someone with his life, to protect him when he was vulnerable, something he'd never thought to feel.

So when he finally stepped off of the last swaying slat, his exhausted arms could support Maya no longer, and he lowered her to the ground for Taran to take over.

'Here, lad,' he said, turning, and then Maya cried out as they saw Taran look toward them with five Rangers at his back.

'Rakan, do something!' shouted Maya.

Rakan started to move, not knowing how he could even get to Taran in time, when he saw Taran adjust his grip on the suspension rope.

He'd planned to destroy the bridge once they were all across, so knew immediately what Taran intended. Instead of running on to the bridge, he turned along the river's edge and shouted for Maya to follow him as fast as she was able.

Out the corner of his eye, Rakan saw Taran's sword sever one of the support ropes, and then moments later, the main suspension one, throwing himself and the remaining Rangers into the frothing white waters below.

Rakan leapt from the river bank onto the closest rocks that showed above the frothing water, and made his way out into the river, watching as Taran swung like a pendulum across its width.

Hold on, lad, thought Rakan, as he saw Taran strike a rock then go under the water. Several heartbeats later, Taran rose briefly to the surface only to crash into another rock.

He recognised in an instant that Taran was unconscious, and would pass by out of reach from where he stood. So Rakan drew his sword and dived into the torrent, thrusting it deep into the river bed. As Rakan held on to the hilt, he kept his body low, looking out for Taran despite being barely able to see. Fortunately, the current brought Taran's spinning body straight into him.

Rakan grabbed hold of Taran's shirt, then used all his strength to swing him toward the bank. Just as his breath and grip on the sword hilt were about to give up, Maya's hands came from above and hauled Taran's body behind a rock. Rakan burst to the surface gasping for air, then together they wrestled Taran's body out of the river onto the rock where Maya crouched, and Rakan climbed after.

Despite his exhaustion, Rakan turned Taran on to his back, and Maya gasped.

Taran's head was smashed on one side, his cheek torn, with bone protruding from his face. His shirt was ripped, while shards of his ribs glistened whitely in the fading light.

'Right girl, time to work your magic,' urged Rakan.

Maya leaned forward, placed her hands on Taran's temples, and reached for her gift.

Rakan's eyes widened as he watched a glow surround Taran's broken body, then the terrible wounds began to close.

In moments Taran was healed, yet he still wasn't breathing.

'Oh no, please, no!' moaned Maya. 'Don't leave me, not now, not ever!' She continued to pour all the power of her gift that she could summon into Taran, as she'd done with her father.

Swathes of flowers sprung up all along the riverbank, while the rock they were on became lush with moss, full of life in direct contrast to Taran's inert body.

Rakan was at a loss, but knew Taran would have swallowed lots of water, so he lifted Taran to a kneeling position, got behind him, and pulled his clasped hands, again and again, into Taran's stomach. 'Come on now,' he urged. 'Now's not the time for you to die. Breathe!'

Water flooded from Taran's lungs in response to Rakan's efforts, and all of a sudden, Taran sucked in a huge gasp of air, and colour started returning to his cheeks as his breathing slowly returned to normal.

Rakan lay Taran down and sat back; the moisture in his eyes now matched Maya's.

Maya cradled Taran's head on her lap as she stroked his wet hair. Exhausted now, she closed her eyes and slumped forward as unconscious as Taran.

Rakan felt pain everywhere, but forced himself to his feet, moved to Maya and eased her gently back onto the rock. Next, he lifted Taran in his arms, carrying him to the riverbank and the now lush grass that grew there, before doing the same for Maya, laying her next to Taran.

He stripped off his shirt and Taran's, then threw them on the grass to dry in the weak sun.

Rakan sat down, exhausted. He wanted to fall asleep, but knew he had to keep watch while the other two recovered.

They were now in a dire situation.

Other than a couple of daggers, they had no proper weapons. Their packs and provisions were left behind, and without Maya's bow, there was no quick way for them to hunt for food.

To the east, the Forelorn mountains rose up in the distance, several days' hard travel away, but at least more forest lay between them and their destination, which would help cover their progress a little.

Their fate shortly thereafter would lay in the hands of Laska. Rakan couldn't see how to bluff their way through as if they were on the king's business, especially now that they looked entirely like the fugitives they were.

Also, without any resources, they had nothing with which to barter, bribe or pay. Perhaps joining up with Laska would be a good idea, assuming he would take them in.

Rakan looked back over the river and saw movement in the shadows of the far tree line, so hunkered down in the tall grass, eyes narrowing.

There, moving amongst the foliage in silver armour, was the warrior who had saved them earlier by attacking the Rangers, and somehow he was still alive. Maybe it was a different man? It would be impossible for one man to kill fifteen, yet it was too much of a coincidence.

Rakan was tempted to chance his luck and call for help. Surely if this warrior were an enemy of the Witch-King's men, he might prove an ally. Yet there was something about the way he moved, or that strange glow from inside his helm, that stayed Rakan's hand from rising. Instead, Rakan lowered himself down even further.

The warrior knelt, studying their trail, then rose and walked over to the now-destroyed bridge to look over the river. The silvered helm tilted, as if the man inside listened for something, and then turned toward where Rakan was hiding. For some reason, Rakan held his breath as if it were possible to be heard above the river's roar.

Rakan was glad the water's fury lay between them. How far north or south to the next crossing, he didn't know.

Slowly the warrior turned north, and despite wearing armour, ran along the bank, and jumped from rock to rock, surefooted as a mountain goat.

As he disappeared beyond the crest of the hill to the north, Rakan slowly relaxed. His head pounded as he lay upon the grass, looking up at the clouds.

Please don't rain, he thought, and then without intending to, fell into an exhausted sleep.

Chapter XVI

'Damn that man,' swore Daleth.

He'd awoken to the worst headache imaginable, soaked in sweat. Spirit travel was taxing at best, but to watch the slaughter of his Rangers and for Kalas to then threaten him, had not only put him in the worse mood imaginable, but left him exhausted as well.

Daleth usually rode at the head of his troops, but today he attempted to rest as he lay in the back of a wagon. The inept driver seemed determined to hit every rock imaginable on the way to Tristan's Folly, and the only thing that cheered Daleth up was the thought of the man's head on a spear at the end of this tortuous journey.

The wagon ground to a halt, and Daleth moaned as he pulled himself from the back. It was customary for the troops to pause for a midday rest. A soldier travelled further with short, frequent stops as opposed to a forced march all day over a long period, and Daleth wanted his men fresh for the assault on the fortress.

Daleth looked around in the dull light, feeling satisfied.

There, far ahead in the distance, he could see the wagons that carried the dismantled siege engines. Some of the larger ones were already assembled and pulled by teams of oxen. The hell they would rain down on the defenders would be demoralising, leaving them easy prey for his troops as they stormed any breach.

The fortress on the Freestates side was enormous. The amount of money spent on its construction all those years ago, was by rumour, beyond count. They'd rightly feared for their lives back then as they should now.

He'd bought the plans of the fortress for a man's weight in gold almost forty years ago, and had spent so much time looking at it, that by the time the large parchment had fallen into pieces, he was able to call it to memory with every detail clear in his mind.

The fortress had a curtain wall eighty hands thick, and a hundred and forty hands high, that stretched the full width of the pass with un-scalable sheer mountains on either side. Each wall had four rounded towers that protruded slightly, giving additional range to the defending archers, while also providing cover for the walls should an enemy ever reach the base.

Behind the curtain wall, were three more, successively higher than the one in front, that allowed archers to fire over the heads of their defending brethren, or to sweep the preceding walls clear, should the enemy manage to gain a foothold.

Between each wall was a space of a hundred and twenty paces. This gave a clear killing ground, but had a deep fire trench halfway across, with wooden bridges that would be doused in oil and burned by any withdrawing defenders.

At the base of the second, third, and fourth wall, were stone platforms for defending siege engines. These weapons of destruction could fire huge rocks into the pass, or pitchers of oil that could be set aflame with fire arrows.

The gates which had been open to trade up until six months ago were set deep into the wall. Hot ashes or sand could be dropped down upon any invader through murder holes in the tunnel roof, should the gates come under attack.

Lastly, behind the walls was the massive keep abutting the north wall of the pass. It didn't span the pass itself, and from its heights, defenders could fire arrows down on any enemy that had already breached the walls, and attempted to use the pass without taking it first.

When it was first built, it was a defensive commander's dream. Yet such a colossus needed to be maintained, repaired and manned. Only a year ago, a returning agent who'd infiltrated the fortress garrison, had given a damning report on the state of the fortress itself. It had filled Daleth's heart with confidence.

The walls were crumbling, siege engines had rotted, and even the sturdy gates of iron reinforced wood had warped. The list of failures was long, and whereas it could be manned by upwards of seven thousand men, it had a contingent of barely one thousand men at the time, none of them archers.

Irrespective, Daleth was taking absolutely no chances, for the defender's numbers would likely have swelled in preparation for his assault. His engineers had built siege engines that could throw such heavy rocks, that he doubted the walls could withstand the bombardment for more than a few days.

Normally, transporting any meaningful amount of heavy ammunition for the engines would have been a problem. However, he'd ordered for his fortress to be all but dismantled, and thus the rocks from this demolition were ready and waiting.

He had just over one hundred thousand fighting men for his conquest. Of those, two thousand were specialised assault infantry with armour so heavy that it could deflect most arrows. These soldiers also carried large shields for extra protection, and would lead the attack, taking the brunt of any initial defense.

The rest were various units of engineers, medium or light infantry and spearmen. Then there was the light cavalry - the lancers, ready to overtake any fleeing soldiers and wreak havoc in the countryside beyond.

This vast army would completely enslave the Freestates, then conquer the Eyre to the north and the Horselords to the south, ensuring those peoples were subdued, their lands part of his growing empire. Once these gains were consolidated, he would march his army further eastward then turn south to fight the desert tribes in the lands beyond.

The amount of strength he now received from the lands he left behind had diminished to almost nothing. As its people succumbed, their misery fed him for a while, but once they were dead, he would receive no life or strength from them either.

This invasion would change all of that. When his men carved their way across new lands, the pain and suffering they caused would feed him directly, and then the land itself would nourish him for decades to come.

Daleth couldn't wait.

He cursed as an image of red eyes suddenly distracted him from thoughts of glory. It had been a mistake to consider capturing Kalas. The idea of having another daemon warrior under his control was alluring, but not worth the risk.

He knew he was completely safe amongst this vast host of men, and yet until that man, no, that daemon was killed, he would keep feeling on edge, especially as Kalas had foiled the Rangers' attack on the girl and her companions.

Thanks to these four renegades, he'd lost twenty of the finest fighting men in his kingdom, maybe even the world. A tenth of the Rangers' total ranks, and those were the ones he was aware of.

He calmed himself as he forced emotion to one side. Everything would soon be in hand and would only end one way, with him victorious. He just had to be patient regarding the daemon, because Kalas would come for him. So sooner or later, either the lancers would hunt Kalas down, or Kalas would show himself as they journeyed to Tristan's Folly. Either way, the daemon warrior would be dealt with.

The three fugitives, well, he'd correctly anticipated their destination. It was his meticulous attention to even the tiniest detail that gave him a small measure of personal satisfaction to balance the frustration he also felt. When he'd discovered that one of the fugitives had been in the Nightstalkers, who were sometimes assigned to escort agents, he'd made preparations just in case. Of course, he hadn't expected them to get that far, but his planning for such an eventuality was going to be rewarded.

There was another contingent of the Rangers already on their way to Laska's settlement.

Many of his Rangers had gifts, mostly around speed, strength, or truth-seeking, but there was one leading this contingent that had a skill that would ensure the three fugitives had a very nasty and deadly surprise. He'd almost had the Ranger killed as a young boy when his gift was identified, for it had even been a threat to him. Now he was glad he'd stayed the executioner's hand, for when the fugitives encountered the Ranger and his men, there was no doubt in his mind that this time the outcome would be very different indeed.

He would spirit talk with the Ranger, Brandon, this very night for an update. He was a man full of such contrast, handsome beyond compare, yet with the darkest soul, one to almost match his own. Maybe even the daemon Alano would have felt a kinship.

If only he had the strength to spirit travel again. He could watch the final confrontation and its bloody end, and then afterwards, track down Kalas so he could be found and killed. However, several days of rest would be required before he would be able to do so.

Kalas is coming. The words came unbidden to his mind. Damn that man, he thought, then laughed to the surprise of those around him.

Surely if anyone was damned, it was one who shared his soul with a daemon!

Alano wept inside his mind. He cried out and pushed against the daemon's will, trying to regain control as he'd done ever since the daemon had brushed him aside when he was at his weakest with death approaching.

There had been many times in the last fifty years when Alano had allowed himself to succumb to the daemon's will for a short while, letting it feast so he could gain some respite from its constant demands for blood, for life, that would push him close to the verge of madness.

He'd felt cursed then, but he was at least in control the majority of the time, but now, now he was the prisoner in his body at the whim of the daemon. He looked at the world through a haze of red, saw the blood pump through the veins of all those around, knew constant hunger, and the desire to spill blood just for the primitive joy of ending another's life.

Even worse, the daemon satiated that hunger almost every night, on one unfortunate peasant girl after another, and revelled in their fear and piteous cries for mercy. Whereas in the past, Alano had been able to distance himself from the daemon's feeding, as he allowed it brief control, or was even unaware as he slept, now the daemon controlled his mind and forced him to share in every moment.

No man alive could see the nine hells, yet Alano did, and it had driven his mind to the brink of insanity.

Alano was trapped in a living hell.

To start, he'd resisted the constant killing, tried to regain control of his body, his destiny, and for a while it seemed possible he might even prevail such was his strength. He would be able to stay the daemons killing bite, or thrust, or whatever manner of way he was going to deal death. Shortly thereafter, he could only manage it for a heartbeat, and each time the daemon's dark laughter mocked him, encouraged him to fight on, and took joy from his defeat.

Now, after many days, the daemon had won, his will was not to be denied, and Alano moaned with such sorrow that the daemon responded by laughing in pure joy.

Taran slowly became aware that he could hear a roaring, a noise that seemed quite fitting as he plummeted down to whatever the afterlife had in store for him, likely something hot and very unpleasant.

Yet as his senses started to return, he became aware of something gently tickling his nose. This certainly didn't seem like something from the nine hells, so he tentatively opened his eyes and expected to see fire, smoke and daemons. Instead, he looked up to see Maya as she gazed down on him. Her hair moved softly in the breeze, brushing across his face.

'Welcome back,' she sniffed, then brought her lips down to kiss his, and Taran felt lifted to the sky above in an instant.

'I wish I didn't have to cheat death to wake up to a kiss,' he said sleepily.

'I thought you'd left me!' Maya cried, and suddenly her body was wracked with sobs.

Taran pulled himself to a sitting position and cradled Maya in his arms while his heart beat with concern and happiness all at once. He just wanted to close his eyes and feel her close, but their situation made him look around as he held her shaking body, his strong arms wrapped around her.

The sun was halfway across the sky, and Rakan was fast asleep a few steps away. The roar Taran had heard was the river they'd crossed, and in a rush, everything flooded back to his mind. The flight, then the bridge, and him plunging to what he thought was an icy death.

Taran took note of his shirt on the ground beside him. 'Hey,' he said, trying to calm Maya, 'did you try and take advantage of me when I was asleep?'

Maya looked up, her eyes puffy, but a hint of mischief showed behind the tears.

'I'm sorry to disappoint you, but I think it was Rakan who undressed you, so you'd better ask him that question,' and she laughed softly, as did Taran.

'Oh, look,' she continued. 'He has no shirt on either. I think you boys have a lot of explaining to do.' This time her face lit up with wicked humour, and Taran couldn't help but give her a playful shove. Their tousle ended up with Maya in his arms again, and they lay on their backs and looked up at the brightening sky.

'You know I could happily stare at the clouds all day if you stared at them with me,' murmured Taran. 'But I fear we're not out of danger yet, and if we've been asleep here all night, I think we need to get moving as soon as possible.'

He brushed Maya's hair to one side, noticing some snow-white hair amongst the dark black, and softly kissed her forehead before reluctantly letting go. He stood and moved across to Rakan. 'Wake up before your snoring attracts a wild boar,' he said, shaking him by the shoulder.

Rakan sat bolt upright, looking embarrassed. 'I must have fallen asleep,' he exclaimed.

'Oh, you two look so pretty together,' chuckled Maya, tears running down her face again, but this time with laughter. 'Bare-chested and so strong.'

Rakan looked at Taran questioningly as they pulled their shirts on. 'She's a strange one,' Rakan muttered, 'I think you can do better, lad.'

This time Maya's laughter knew no limits. 'You're so right, Rakan, I can't compete with you at all. You two should live happily ever after,' and she rolled on her back, holding her sides.

'I thought it was Taran who hit his head against the rocks!' laughed Rakan, his own humour starting to rise, but then his face turned serious.

'Right, we need to quieten down. We have no idea how close any pursuers may be,' and with that, he rose to his knees and spent a while scanning all around them. 'Earlier, that warrior in silver armour who attacked the Rangers followed us to the crossing, and I think he's tracking us. There's little doubt he's no friend of the Witch-King, but neither does that make him our ally. We are now probably around four day's journey to where Laska and his men hold sway. Whereas before I thought that we could bluff him into showing us the way across the mountains, considering the state of us, I think we'll have to throw ourselves on his mercy and seek sanctuary amongst him and his folk.'

'You mentioned he survived on the whim of the Witch-King,' said Maya. 'What makes you think he'll risk himself and his people's existence on harbouring us? Maybe it's better we somehow try to make it on our own?'

'Maya,' said Rakan, 'think this through. The reason we're so easily found is the power of your gift, which you no longer have full control over.' As he said this, his hands swept around him. 'Look at what you've done here while saving Taran.' He then pointed across the river to the new growth that led back to the woodland on the other side to emphasise his point. 'Over there is what still happens when you don't consciously use it. Your every breath points the way to those who hunt us, and there is no hiding where you are. We no longer have weapons beyond daggers, and while I know your gift can provide us with berries, fruits, and fresh water, we'll die out here before long. We'll succumb to wild animals, Rangers, or simply starving folk who will be desperate to stave off dying themselves a few days longer.'

'Initially, I thought our best avenue of escape was to cross the mountains whatever the danger, and perhaps Laska will allow us to try if he feels it's in his interest, although without gold or anything else to give him, I doubt it. Instead, I can only hope Laska will offer us shelter. He might see the advantage of having a healer who can help his people and bring prosperity to his land, for without doubt it needs it.'

Taran nodded in agreement. 'It's true. Everywhere we go, the land is rotting and dying, and not only that, but the animals that live off the land will shortly follow suit. Maya, you're the only chance of long term survival his people have.'

Rakan snapped his fingers. 'The other fact to remember is that the Witch-King will soon launch his attack on the Freestates. He might consider that sending more troops to find us and attack Laska an unnecessary distraction if he concludes we're there. He has new lands to conquer and people to enslave.'

'And new life to steal,' added Maya softly.

Taran and Rakan looked quizzically at Maya.

'This might sound a little crazy,' she continued, 'but before I was captured, a man in red robes appeared in my dreams. He believes the Witch-King has a gift that drains the life from the land to sustain his immortality.'

Taran scoffed a little, and Maya shrugged. 'I told you it might sound crazy,' she said defensively.

'Would this man in red robes have a shaved head and be slight of build perhaps?' asked Rakan.

Maya looked surprised. 'Yes. Did you dream of him too?'

'No, but a man like that appeared to warn me of the Rangers approach. Without his warning, we wouldn't be drawing breath right now. So knowing of the gifts you, Taran, the seers, and some of the Rangers have, I feel more inclined to believe you,' Rakan said.

Taran nodded and reached out to hold Maya's forearm gently. 'I am sorry I doubted you,' he apologised, 'and the Witch-King's gift would explain so much about the constant sickening of everything around us.'

'So,' said Rakan, satisfied there was no one close, 'how is that ankle of yours, Maya? Let's see if it's up to walking this morning.'

With that they stood, and as Maya leaned on Taran's shoulder for support, they headed east into the forest, toward the Forelom mountains, toward Laska, and the next step of their journey.

Laska was over ninety years of age, and he felt every one of them. He was a relic in more ways than one, having once been a minor lord in the Ember Kingdom, in those years so distant that they almost seemed like a dream.

Nowadays, when he tried to think back, the good memories of which there were few would fade like mist before the midday sun. But he could still vividly remember the ones containing pain and anguish, especially those regarding the loss of his sons.

He and his forebears had ruled over the southernmost spur of the realm, and had done so for generations. They were not a wealthy family compared to many of their peers, for instead of iron mines, they had lands abutting the coast, and thus they mostly lived off the sea's bounty and the meagre income this generated. Still, even if they had little material wealth, they were well fed, as were the peasantry for whom they were responsible, and there was always a food surplus that was sent encased in blocks of ice to the capital by fast wagon.

The eastern border of their lands flanked the Forelorn mountains. His father and his father's father had spent many years trying to discover the riches they believed might lay within, be it iron, precious metals or gemstones.

He still remembered the day as a young boy, when after almost two generations of unsuccessful exploration, his father's engineers had reported that they'd mined into a series of natural caverns and faults that led through the mountains into a large verdant valley. They were now waiting on their lord before they proceeded any further, so that he might be the first to step foot on this new land, and claim it for his own.

It seemed like the family's fortunes, which for so long had languished, might soon change. An expedition was organised, his father and a retinue of his guard, with Laska, all on horseback. Anticipation filled each and every one of them.

A few days' journey had taken them to the foot of the mountain, and then a day of climbing had taken them to a narrow tunnel entrance, that seemed to be so dark and foreboding, that Laska had cried in fright. He remembered his father had laughed and picked him up, and told him everything would be alright. They'd lit torches and spent almost half of the following day stooping through natural crevices and rough-hewn tunnels, supported by beams. The lead engineer, a swarthy short man with a dark beard, had led the way. Laska had relaxed a little, soothed by his father's voice and the excitement it held.

They'd reached the exit into the valley just as the sun was setting. There before them, barely visible through thick woodland, lay a valley to the north so vast and green that his father and his men had turned and hugged one another, and Laska was swept up in the excitement over this beautiful place.

That night had been spent in the tunnel, warmed by a fire as his father organised how the men would split into three groups of twenty.

The plan was to map and explore the valley then return in seven days to report on whatever riches it might hold.

The next morning, everyone had excitedly bid farewell to one another. The two other groups headed north and northeast as he, his father, along with their guard and an engineer, started to skirt the southern side of the valley toward the east.

The main hope was that these mountains would show signs of mineral wealth. The valley itself was beautiful, the trees huge, yet whilst its beauty was captivating, this would not improve the family fortunes. So for the next two days, they walked at the base of the mountains. The engineer chipped away at the rock and inspected the beds of the many streams, fed by meltwater from the mountain tops.

Frequently, a strange, mournful sound would echo, and the engineer assured a worried Laska that it was the sound of the wind through the mountain passes, and nothing to be afraid of.

On the third day, they came to the far side of the valley, and there in the mountainside was an enormous fissure. They made camp and explored a little, only to find a series of caverns heading further eastward. While no evidence of mineral wealth had been found, his father was excited nonetheless, for if this network of caves and fissures extended far enough, it might open into the very lands of the Freestates themselves. A new trade route, with all the riches that would come with it, was possibly theirs for the taking.

They'd pushed into the caverns early the next morning and spent a whole day exploring, at the end of which they'd found themselves on the other side of the mountains, the lands of the great trading nation to the east at their very feet. Even though there was nothing to celebrate with, the mood of the party was exuberant.

The following morning had seen them return, back into the mountains once more, aware they might be late for their rendezvous with the other groups. But the extra energy brought on by the excitement saw them make up lost time, especially as they no longer stopped to survey. Unexpectedly they'd made it back faster than anticipated, and were the first group to arrive at their initial camp.

So they waited, a day, then another.

Two days beyond the allotted rendezvous, Laska's father, whose good mood had slowly evaporated while waiting for his other men, decided to forge northeast in their tracks to meet them on their return. His demeanour was now such that Laska knew that the other groups would regret keeping their lord waiting.

However, early on into the second day, they had found the first group, or what little was left of them, in a wooded glade.

That there'd been a fight was evident. The ground was churned and bloody, trees splintered, shards of swords and scraps of uniforms scattered around. As they had scouted the area, a body was discovered, impaled on a branch, high in a tree, barely visible through the foliage. What force had thrown a large armoured man there, was beyond imagining.

They'd backed away from the scene of the fight then, swords drawn, eyes alert, and Laska could remember how he could barely breathe, he was so scared. Just as they reached the edge of the small clearing, a giant had stepped from the treeline opposite. Almost as tall as the trees around it, it was at least four times the size of their biggest man, dressed in furs and with a club.

'May the gods have mercy,' his father had breathed, then kept Laska behind him as they continued to move away, back into the undergrowth.

For a moment, it seemed as if the creature would let them go, but it raised its head, and a strange, mournful, warbling, sounded from its throat.

'It's calling for help,' the captain of the guards had shouted, as he took three swift steps forward. He'd thrown his spear across the clearing. It was a throw of consummate skill, a testament to years of practice, for it took the giant in the taut skin of its throat, and stopped its call abruptly.

Fury had lit the creature's eyes as it crossed the clearing in just four enormous bounds, and its club swept down to fling the captain away, broken. The man was lifeless before he hit the ground amongst the trees.

For a moment, everyone had stood transfixed at the behemoth's speed and the ease with which it had dispatched a man who'd spent his life mastering the use of arms. It had then turned toward Laska and his father, but as it stepped toward them, its legs buckled, and it fell to its knees. One huge arm still supported it, prevented it from collapsing completely, as its baleful eyes swept across the remaining men.

His father ran forward and swept his sword across the back of the giant's arm, and as it gave way, the giant fell on to the haft of the spear still protruding from its neck. The spear was driven through its spine, and the creature died instantly.

A sergeant and three men had gotten over their shock and ran forward to form a guard around Laska and his father, as they started to make haste back along their trail toward the tunnel. However, as they did, mournful cries sounded again and again from all around them.

'We need to run. Strip off your armour, quickly now!' his father had commanded.

The rest of the day passed by in a series of horrific events, as giants crashed from the undergrowth. His father's men sacrificed their lives one by one as they baited the giants away from the group, to give their lord more time to escape.

It was almost dark by the time just Laska, in his father's arms, and the engineer reached the base of the slope that led to the tunnel entrance. They were only halfway up, stumbling, exhausted, when a dozen of the beasts had burst from the tree line behind them.

'I love you, my son,' his father gasped. It was the first and last time Laska had ever heard those words from his father's lips. Then his father had thrust Laska into the arms of the engineer who continued up the slope. Laska struggled in the engineer's grasp, and his small arms reached out beseechingly for his father. But his father had already turned away, and having drawn his sword, was charging at the closing giants.

Laska had closed his eyes then, hearing his father's battle cry cut short. Tears rolled down his cheeks, and his sobs were matched by the engineers. His father's sacrifice had allowed them to reach the small tunnel moments before the giants, and they'd found sanctuary beyond their pursuers' reach.

He'd sworn a vow never to return to the mountains after that.

Over the years that followed, King Anders, acting upon Laska's father's discovery, had sent emissaries to try to make contact with the giants. To make peace was the Ember Kingdom's desire, yet every time it was rebuffed with blood, for without being able to communicate, never once was progress made.

Laska, as he grew into his role of Lord of his realm, poured all his energy into the raising of his new-born sons, demanding their loyalty, farming the bounty of the sea, his dreams plagued by nightmares.

How quickly and easily, his vow had been broken.

The arrival of the Witch-King's overwhelming army years later, forced Laska to hastily retreat with his remaining son and people to the very mountain caves that held such painful memories, in an attempt to escape the slaughter.

A year after the fall of the kingdom, Daleth, along with almost three thousand men, surrounded the stockade Laska and his people had erected at the base of the mountain range, and finally, Laska thought the end of days was upon him. Yet, Daleth had not immediately ordered the attack. He'd asked for a temporary truce and sought an audience with Laska. Upon entering the compound with his bodyguard, he'd looked around at the misery and suffering and almost seemed satisfied.

Laska stared death in the face that day, as Daleth told him he would spare his people, but asked if there was any good reason to spare him as a former lord of the Ember Kingdom, or indeed his son. In desperation, he'd told Daleth of the valley of the giants, and its potential value as a dangerous but secret route into the Freestates, and how he was the only one to know of its whereabouts.

Daleth had listened to the tale with amusement. A valley of the giants, surely a desperate falsehood. Yet he'd concluded that there was little point to Laska lying, if but to delay death by a day, so had given him a chance to prove his story.

Laska had shown Daleth and his bodyguard through the mountains to the mouth of the tunnel exit, and looked upon the site of his father's death.

Daleth had gazed in wonder at the verdant valley and ordered several of his men to venture out toward the distant treeline to scout. As they'd run down across the open ground, the strange, mournful cry of the giants rose up, and shortly after, all the men were dead. Daleth had stared open-mouthed as the giants dispatched his skilled warriors with ease, then he turned back into the tunnels without a word.

Later that evening, Laska had been offered his life and that of his son along with his title. In return, he would owe fealty to his new king, assist in the passage of kingdom agents, and keep his people isolated. Laska unsurprisingly accepted.

Daleth had left that night, and over the years, they'd been left alone to eke out their lives in the harsh lands they'd chosen as home.

Yet such was Laska's leadership and strength, that the original few hundred refugees grew to almost a thousand, and Laska offered sanctuary to those who found their way to his land. Despite this success, his remaining son perished to sickness, leaving behind two grandchildren whom he now loved above all else.

Yet now he stared death in the face again.

He didn't worry about himself dying; he'd seen too much pain and misery already, and was the oldest man alive that he knew of other than the Witch-King. But his grandchildren, his people, he wanted them to live. They'd known nothing but hardship, yet they were good.

The crops planted this season had failed, and the land his hunters roamed had sickened to such a state that now the animals were starting to succumb to hunger. Women who gave birth died along with their babies, so to get pregnant was a death sentence, and there were no longer any young children running around.

With only two months of stored provisions before they ran out of food, Laska had risked sending two of his men out far beyond where they were allowed to go. The news they returned with was dire. The land, as far as they had ridden, was at death's door. Whole villages of men, women and children dying from starvation, and Daleth's army was soon to march on the Freestates, who, it was claimed, was behind the cause of this evil.

If they stayed, starvation would kill them. If they took the other choice of trying to enter the valley of the giants, again they would die, although maybe that quick death was preferable to a slow one. The final option was sleep weed. Take too much, and you would pass away in your dreams. Perhaps this would be the best way for his people when they ran out of food.

Then there was the Ranger who stood before him, demanding the heads of the two men and a young woman who now stood outside the hall waiting for an audience, hoping for sanctuary.

It seemed death had never been closer.

Chapter XVII

Rakan, Taran, and Maya, after four long days of travel from the river, had decided not to approach Laska's settlement by stealth, as it might give the impression they were untrustworthy. So, earlier that morning, as the sun was rising, they'd walked openly up to the gates where Rakan asked the guards to present them to Laska, who he knew from times past.

Despite the reservation in the guards' eyes as they looked upon the three hungry and thirsty, bedraggled strangers, they were escorted through the settlement, and after a short wait, were shown into the hall where Laska awaited them.

Rakan had spoken for them all. He'd told of Taran being Maya's husband, and he Taran's father. He wove a story of Maya's incredible gift as a healer, of not only people but the land, and how she could help save the settlement if they were allowed sanctuary. An arrangement that would surely benefit everyone.

It was an impassioned plea, and now as Rakan finished, Taran squeezed Maya's hand, hope in both their eyes as they waited for Laska to speak.

Laska, his face impassive, sat in his favourite chair and studied the three standing below him. He vaguely recognised Rakan and had let the man have his moment, but was under instruction to have them killed irrespective. However, now his interest was piqued, and he needed to bide for time, come up with a way to follow his orders without looking like Daleth's lap dog.

Laska coughed to clear his throat, then nodded at Maya. 'If you have such a power of healing as Rakan claims, then why are you limping like a lame horse?' But before she could answer, he spoke again. 'Show me your gift!'

As Maya started to concentrate, from the shadows, a Ranger stepped forward, nine more behind him, hands on the hilt of their swords. Maya's gasp of dismay was echoed by Rakan and Taran.

They all looked around for an avenue of escape, but the doors to the hall were shut and guarded, and there was an unusual amount of armed men present, considering they were just three unarmed fugitives.

'What should we do?' asked Taran and Maya at the same time.

Rakan shook his head in defeat. 'This is a battle we can't win. We need to see how this plays out, so don't fight until there is no other choice.'

Maya's hand sought Taran's.

He looked at her, and his heart ached as he recognised his failure at keeping her safe. They'd made it so far, but now faced being butchered without a chance.

Laska smiled coldly. 'This is Brandon, a Ranger of the king, and he advises me you are all under sentence of death. I don't know what I find hardest to believe, that you have the power of healing, or that twenty or so Rangers have left this world while trying to hunt down one young woman and her two companions.

'Show me this supposed ability to heal!' he commanded Maya again. 'Give me a reason to offer you sanctuary and not to have your head removed from your shoulders.' Disbelief was on his face as he said this, but he leaned forward expectantly.

Maya looked up at Laska, reaching for her gift, but as she did, she felt Brandon's gaze. All the Rangers she'd seen so far had dead black eyes, but Brandon's were ice blue, and they melted her concentration. However hard she tried to reach for it, her gift wasn't there, and despite trying again, all she could see were those cold blue eyes in her mind.

There was silence for what seemed a lifetime as everyone looked expectantly at Maya until she shook her head in defeat. Tears of frustration were in her eyes as she looked first at Taran, then up at Laska. 'I am sorry. For whatever reason, I can't, but it has something to do with him,' she said, nodding at Brandon.

Brandon's laugh was as cold as his blue eyes. 'What use is a healer who cannot heal. To add to their crimes, they lie to the lord of this hall. Kill them!' he commanded, and the men-at-arms around the hall looked to Laska for his agreement.

Laska hesitated. It was a tradition for all seeking safety to be granted a night's sanctuary while their fate was decided, this was the law that he himself had decreed, and then also as a lord, he wasn't used to being ordered around in front of his men.

Tired of the delay, Brandon put his hand firmly on Laska's shoulder where he sat. Leaning forward, the Ranger whispered in his ear. 'Order your men to kill them, or I will cut your throat where you sit.'

Laska, at that moment, had been about to issue the order, but the Ranger's threat, his demeanour, and his good looks irked him. Then to be commanded in his hall was something he couldn't countenance.

He turned to Brandon, and with his old eyes, looked into the face of one so young and handsome, yet so devoid of compassion. He put his hand slowly on Brandon's and lowered his voice as he mimicked Brandon's whisper. 'Firstly, young man, I have no fear of dying. In fact, it might be a blessing for one so old as me, but I recommend that dying at your age would be something to be avoided.'

Brandon went to pull his hand away, to draw his blade, but Laska held on to it with surprising strength for one so old.

'You and your men without question have skills beyond any of mine,' Laska continued, 'but I think even you'll find it hard to dodge all of the crossbow bolts that are aimed at your heart at this very moment,' and he nodded to the dark galleries set high around the hall.

Brandon looked up, then drew his breath in with a hiss as he saw the bowmen in the shadows. 'You dare threaten the voice of the king!

Death and destruction will be visited not just upon you, but all of yours for defying the king's will once he hears of this!'

Laska shook his head. 'You misunderstand me. I am not defying his will; you can have their lives,' he said softly. But, we have a custom. They enjoy our hospitality for one night before I send them on their way. Tradition dictates it. You can have your killing, but not till the morrow, not until they leave the land of my settlement.'

Brandon's face contorted as he controlled his anger, then he snatched his hand away. 'Enjoy this small moment,' he said, eyes full of contempt, 'for I doubt you will have any such again in the short life that remains to you. But if it pleases my lord,' and his voiced dripped with sarcasm, 'I will keep a close eye on your guests to ensure they do not attempt escape or mischief.'

Laska looked at Brandon. 'If they escape and leave this settlement, you can do with them as you will. Be patient, Brandon, by tomorrow, you will have your fill of blood one way or another.'

Now it was in all the minds of everyone in the hall.

Death had never been closer.

Kalas felt nauseous. He was barely able to stand.

After finding the crossing destroyed, he'd journeyed north, driven to speed by the daemon's demands in his mind, pressing him to hurry so that they could feed.

He'd run north along the river for two days hoping for another bridge. Several times he'd had to hide within the tree line of the adjacent forest as troops of lancers rode by, searching for him, or the other three, which, it didn't matter. The daemon pushed him onward with barely any rest, and his body became exhausted from lack of any real kind of sustenance, save occasional rotten berries.

It was this constant push for haste that had led him to his current predicament.

The forest had given way to a dusty, open plain, yet to his relief, there was also an unguarded bridge across the raging river. Kalas had thought it would be best to wait until dark before moving into the open, yet for some reason, he ignored his own advice and ran across the plain. The daemon had influenced even this decision to seem like it was his own.

Amazingly he'd made it to the bridge and crossed over its rough wooden planks. For a while it looked as if the risky action would pay off as he ran south toward some woodland and the safety of its cover. Yet it wasn't to be. As he'd run across the dusty ground, he heard the clatter of hooves on the bridge behind him and had known he'd never make it to the safety of the trees in time.

Turning to face the enemy, he'd seen twenty lancers spreading out into a long line.

'Attack them,' roared the daemon in his head. 'You've overcome many more than this, and we need to eat.'

So Kalas had charged. The lancers, rather than engage, used their horse's speed to stay out of reach as they tried to lure him further from the safety of the trees to which he'd been heading.

'It's a trap,' Kalas had said to the daemon. 'If they're not fighting, it's because they're delaying, waiting for something or someone.' He started to move back toward the woods, fighting the daemon's desires. It cried piteously at being denied the taste of so much life, but for now, it allowed Kalas' will and experience to make the choice, but it had been too late.

Other horsemen came from the northwest, and while they also carried lances, several carried bows for hunting. They didn't need to put themselves close to Kalas' swords to strike at him, and within moments their arrows hissed through the air. He didn't dare turn his back to them, for his armour only really protected his front, so he kept moving backwards. His swords deflected many of the arrows, while some bounced from his armour, but he was tiring fast.

The lancers then tried to encircle him. As soon as Kalas recognised their intent, he knew if they got into position, he'd be dead. At that moment, he'd turned and sprinted as fast as he could, running left then right, to put the archers off their aim.

Suddenly the arrows stopped. Kalas knew this meant the lancers were closing in as the archers feared to hit them, so he'd turned and rolled under the flashing lance tips, his swords a blur as he cut the legs from two of the horses. The horses and their riders crashed, screaming to the ground as the others wheeled away. Kalas ran again.

The woods were but a few strides away when an arrow had caught him in the left shoulder, and then almost in the same instant, one thwacked into the back of his right leg. He'd rolled to the floor, the hafts of both arrows snapping.

Despite the pain, he'd come up straight away, backing away, keeping the lancers at bay with his red stare and the threat of certain death if they came too close. He'd showed no fear as he retreated into the woods, and let the daemon scream its anger and frustration.

The horses whinnied and shied, and the lancers had watched as he backed out of sight before they returned to their fallen comrades and lifted them onto saddles. They then slaughtered the two injured horses before withdrawing.

The daemon had howled again, for with the horses dead, he couldn't even feed on their meagre life force, and Kalas had sunk to his knees. He'd ripped his trouser leg away to assess the wound, and saw that the arrow had almost punched through the muscle on the outside of his thigh. He'd torn the filthy trouser leg into strips as a makeshift bandage, then reached behind to grasp what was left of the shaft of the arrow in his leg. It was slippery with blood, and he'd gripped it hard, before, with a sudden push, the head came out the front of his thigh.

The pain had been excruciating, and his vision had misted, but the daemon lent what little strength it had left as he drew the arrow out. Blood flowed freely before he plugged the wound front and back with dirty cloth, and secured it with more strips of the same.

Unfortunately, the broken shaft of the arrow behind his left shoulder had been unreachable and was still there.

Now here he was a further two days later, slowly moving southward, hoping against hope to come across an injured animal that could give the daemon a small amount of life to help heal him. His vision was blurring, and he felt hot with fever. Nausea threatened to overwhelm him.

'Come on,' urged the daemon, yet Kalas could feel it was scared. It was scared of him dying and itself with him. Then, just like those fifty years ago, it started to withdraw, not willing to face death, hiding away once more in the back of his mind, allowing him to see clearly for the first time in weeks.

Tears further misted his eyes, not out of self-pity, but at what he'd planned to do; kill the girl and her companions. For what? To satisfy the daemon's curiosity as to whether her life force would further strengthen the daemon's own. But the cost, the lives of those who had done him no harm!

He'd lost sight of who he was, the values he'd once held dear, and felt ashamed.

Better to die than become this monster again when there was no real hope of controlling it. Time to find a good place to end his days. He hobbled a little further until midday when he came across a small glade that let the meagre sunlight shine through.

Kalas sat down with his back to the tree and closed his eyes.

Regret consumed him. He wouldn't complete his first oath, to kill the Witch-King, but at least now he would keep his second one, to die himself having failed.

He found a little relief recalling memories of old, casting his thoughts back to a time when he didn't know better. The future had seemed so bright when he was young.

His fondest recollection was the ceremony to mark his promotion when he'd become weapon master of the royal guard. He could still remember the feeling of pride as he'd received his swords from King Anders all those years ago. He'd never been so happy or so drunk.

He smiled, albeit in pain, as he recalled Alano making a speech during the celebrations afterwards. He'd started with a tale of how he'd found Kalas in bed with a serving wench, and quoted Kalas' favourite saying as the punchline, 'Kalas is coming.'

They'd been such good times.

'I can't think of a way out of this mess,' said Rakan quietly, as he, Taran, and Maya, wandered around the settlement, shadowed constantly by Brandon and his Rangers along with several of Laska's men.

They'd been given free rein to wander as long as they didn't attempt to leave the settlement, on pain of death, and now looked for anything that might help them. Everywhere around them seemed busy as they walked. Preparations were in full swing for a celebratory feast that night, for it was midsummer's eve and tradition dictated that dancing and wine would flow despite the shortage of provisions.

'I haven't seen any horses or unattended weapons or anything that might help us so far,' Maya added, then looked to Taran.

Taran used his gift to delve into the minds of all around him, but again learned nothing of value. People's thoughts were full of worry, hunger, desperation on the one hand, or eagerness to eat well that night for the first time in many moons on the other. Some looked upon them with pity, others with distrust or resentment, thinking it unfair that they'd be eating some of their precious food later that night.

Taran shook his head. 'All that I've learned doesn't help us at all. This town's small armoury is guarded within the cellar of Laska's hall, and so far, I've only seen guards carry weapons larger than a dagger. The only way we will be able to arm ourselves is by taking them from their dead bodies.

'We shouldn't take these people's lives to extend our own,' Maya stated. 'These people have done us no ill. It's the Witch-King and his Rangers who seek our deaths. If any die, it must only be them.'

Rakan slowly shook his head. 'I never thought I'd agree with that sentiment,' he said, 'but after all these years, I must have gone soft.

The problem is there's no way we can get the weapons from just the Rangers without dying in the attempt.'

'Maybe Laska will grant us sanctuary on the morrow?' asked Maya innocently, but the look in Taran and Rakan's eyes told her the truth of the matter, and deep down, she'd known the answer even before she'd spoken.

'Tomorrow, he will cast us out, and as soon as we are beyond the walls of the settlement, the Rangers will finish what they've been sent to do. Laska has seen nothing to gain by keeping us alive and everything to lose. We have this day, my friends, and unless a saviour appears in the shape of that warrior in silver armour … well, this could be the end of our journey together,' Rakan said with sadness.

'I just can't get that man's eyes out of my head,' said Maya, and looked back at Brandon. 'He is using some kind of gift against me, I'm sure. If only I could show Laska how I could help heal his land, maybe he would reconsider.'

One of Laska's men approached and stood before them.

'Just in case you want to sleep during your last night with us,' he laughed, affirming what they already knew, 'there are two cabins you can use. Follow me.'

He took them through the muddy ground of the settlement to the two cabins which backed onto the rocky mountainside. 'One for the husband and wife, and one for the old man.' He laughed again, walking away.

'Please thank whosoever let us use their lodgings!' called Maya.

The guard paused and looked over his shoulder. 'You can thank them soon yourselves. They died last month.'

'Why am I not surprised,' muttered Rakan. 'I doubt I'll sleep much anyway if there's drinking and dancing. Who knows, maybe the guards will get drunk or distracted, and we can try to make our escape.'

Yet his words sounded hollow, and neither Maya nor Taran felt any better as they started to scout the huge settlement again, the shadows of the Rangers close behind them.

Astren sat astride a horse and wondered if his back was going to break.

Having discovered Anthain's betrayal and come up with the plan to defeat him, he was now officially Tristan's closest advisor. Thus he found himself jarred mercilessly as they headed to where he never dreamed he would go … toward a battle. Four days in the saddle had already passed, with twice as many to come before they arrived at Tristan's folly.

The guardsmen who remained loyal were back at the capital. They'd been tasked to train a peasant levy as guards to ensure civil unrest didn't break out. That they'd been promised many of the newly vacated merchant houses as a reward upon Tristan's return, only increased their allegiance to him further.

Astren had always planned to disappear quietly should word of the fortress falling reach the capital. If such an event should occur, he'd already used a considerable amount of money to secure a carriage and guards to see him to the desert tribes, with enough left over to buy himself a retirement far from the war. At least until it caught up with him, as he was sure it would someday. Now, all that money and all those plans might well be going to waste if he couldn't find a way to get back home again.

Tristan, who rode alongside looking far more comfortable in the saddle, smiled.

'Astren, my friend, here we are, riding to war. Isn't this preferable to running away to those stinking desert tribesmen?' and he said the last bit quietly, for they rode at the head of the spearmen who had helped put down the insurrection.

Astren's insides turned to ice, and Tristan laughed so loud and full of humour that Astren almost cried with relief.

'Oh, Astren. However deep your pockets are, mine are deeper. You should know that whoever you pay, I pay them more to tell me about all that you do. If I were worried about your loyalty, your head would be the only thing accompanying me on this trip. Still, as you had arranged to escape, only should the fortress fall, I thought it better if we had you invest some of your talents in ensuring that it didn't fall at all. That way, I can enjoy your company that much longer.'

Tristan became serious again. 'If only my sources were as good as I thought, then Anthain wouldn't have gotten as close to usurping me as he did.'

Then he laughed as Astren almost slid off of his saddle. 'I swear watching you ride a horse is the funniest thing I have ever seen ... by the gods, I swear it!'

Astren shook his head. 'Us low born were given two good feet to walk with. Only the noble class have pokers inserted up their backsides at birth that enable them to ride as if attached to the saddle.'

'Ah, but it's a solid gold poker, solid gold!' retorted Tristan. 'It won't be long, Astren, before we see where my gold has been going these last six months. I want to inspire the men at the fortress, and let's not forget, they're less likely to betray me if I'm there overseeing them.

Tristan stood in his saddle and turned to the men who marched behind; the desert spearmen and the Eyre archers. He drew his sword, then raised it above his head, and while he looked somewhat diminutive, he still had a good voice.

'For honour and for glory. We march to save the Freestates!' Tristan shouted.

'To hell with the honour, to hell with the glory, we do it for money!' roared the troops at his back. Tristan fell back in his saddle and laughed so hard he almost fell off.

'The honesty of the peasant is priceless,' he cried, 'priceless.'

'I think they'll be quite happy to see us dead,' Maya said sadly to Taran and Rakan, as she looked across one of the many roaring fires that were scattered throughout the settlement. Many looks of distrust were turned their way as they were given platters of meats and goblets of wine to join in with the midsummer celebrations. They sat upon a log that had been hauled from the forest. It was covered in thick moss, and with the heat of the fire warming the bones, felt somewhat comfortable.

Some of the settlement's people were oblivious to the tension, blissfully unaware of the fate that would soon befall the visitors in their midst, or perhaps it was that the wine was more plentiful than the food, but dancing started to break out. Laughter, so rarely heard these days, rang clearly. The beat of drums and the sound of various instruments filled the air.

Maya had such a terrible headache. She kept trying to use her gift, even in the smallest of ways, yet every time she tried, Brandon's eyes would fill her thoughts, and it seemed as if her gift had never been further from her reach.

Taran looked around surreptitiously. More of Laska's guards stood in the shadows, and across the fire, Brandon and the Rangers sat. The Rangers all sipped sparingly from their drinks, and never took their eyes off their prize that lay so close.

As Taran's gaze continued to rove, they were met by a woman's whose own eyes stared back almost in a challenge. She smiled broadly as his attention lingered a moment, and he hastily looked away, slightly embarrassed, and unconsciously his hand sought Maya's next to him.

A few moments later, as he listened to the music, gazing down at the fire deep in thought, a pair of sandaled feet stopped before him. He looked up, and his heart sank, for there stood the woman. She was quite a beauty, of that there was no doubt, and in days past, Taran would have enjoyed finding out what lay behind that bold smile, but now he wished she would find someone else to bother.

She smiled enticingly, but Taran didn't respond, and he felt Maya stiffen ever so slightly beside him.

The woman curtseyed very low, showing a full cleavage. 'Would our guest do me the honour of a dance?' she asked.

Taran smiled politely but shook his head. 'No. I'm sorry, but my wife and I have yet to share our first dance.'

The woman frowned. 'You probably don't appreciate that I am Yana, granddaughter of your host Laska, and it is rude to the point of an insult to refuse a lord's blood kin a simple dance. So, I suggest you entertain me at least for a little while, or you might find yourself cast out earlier than you would appreciate!'

Her eyes were full of fire as she said this, and Taran knew it wasn't an idle threat. So with an apologetic look at Maya, he stood. Yana grabbed his hand and, within moments, pulled him around the fire with the other people in a slow close dance.

Her perfume was heady, her smile bright, and she was obviously used to getting her way, yet Taran could only wish his first dance was with Maya, who he occasionally glimpsed through the fire looking very sad on the other side.

'You do realise,' said Yana, 'that you should be doing your very best to impress me. You might find I could persuade my grandfather to seek to have you spared, but only if you please me enough.' She moved her body closer, arms firmly around his neck, as her mouth sought his.

Taran pulled back. 'No,' he said, and started to turn away.

'Now, now, you can't blame a girl for trying, can you,' Yana pouted, and she was all sweetness as she pulled him around in a whirl of colour. 'You seem different from the others,' she continued.

Taran wondered for a moment if Yana had somehow recognised his gift, but as he started to read her mind, he noticed from the corner of his eye Brandon staring at him in interest, and now just like Maya, he couldn't call upon it. Taran stared his hatred, but the Ranger just raised his goblet and sipped cautiously from the wine, a mocking smile on his face, then turned back to Maya and Rakan once more.

Yana saw Taran's look and laughed. 'He is ever so handsome,' she said. 'Yet, there is something special about you.' Her hands moved over his shoulders. 'So wide, so strong, a woman could easily lose herself in your arms and know happiness.'

Taran started to pull away again, but Yana held on. 'Listen first to my proposal. I had hoped to enjoy you for a full night, but I can see now that will never happen. You are a rare one, and I'm more than just a little envious. So, one kiss, just one kiss from those full lips of yours, and I will grant you a small favour. Nothing dangerous. I can't help you escape, I can't give you weapons, and I certainly can't kill those Rangers for you, but perhaps I can ease your passing. I could arrange for a little sleep weed to find its way to your cabin. Take that, and you might be too drowsy tomorrow to even feel the executioner's blade. No fear, no panic, just one breath here, the next gone. What do you think?'

Taran thought for a moment, then leaned forward to whisper in Yana's ear. She looked thoughtful for a moment before her broad smile returned, and she nodded.

Her hands went to the back of Taran's neck again, and this time he didn't pull away.

Maya sat next to Rakan feeling despondent.

Not only was the sentence of death hanging over their heads, but Rakan seemed on a mission to get blind drunk. He drank goblet after goblet of wine as if he had hollow legs, and now Taran had been pulled away by this woman, who Maya had to admit was breathtaking by anyone's standards.

She understood why Taran had said yes, but it still hurt a lot. Despite their situation, she'd wanted to dance with Taran and had been waiting for him to ask her. The music was slow, then just when she felt he would, this Yana had come up and pulled him away in a swirl of bright colours and lots of exposed flesh.

In her heart, she knew Taran liked her a lot, but slow dances such as these on midsummer's night were supposed to be for those you felt an attraction to, or even more. You just didn't dance slowly with someone unless something was there. Fast dances were different, but slow ones, no. Without a doubt, it seemed that this Yana was very interested in Taran, and it would be hard for Taran not to see the numerous qualities of this brazen woman either.

Thankfully, they had moved to the other side of the fire, where they were almost out of sight, for she didn't want Taran to see the pain in her eyes.

After what seemed an eternity, Taran reappeared, looking very sheepish and sat down beside her.

'I'm sorry, truly I am,' he said softly.

Maya found herself angry with Taran, and yet she didn't want to feel this way on their last night together. So why had he kissed Yana? What possible reason could there be beyond the obvious?

'Was it worth it?' Maya demanded. 'The dance, the kiss?'

Taran shook his head. 'Likely not. She offered to try and have my life spared if I lay with her, but I refused.'

'But you kissed her anyway,' hissed Maya, feeling like her heart would burst. 'The dance was bad enough, but why the kiss if you refused? Do you know of the hurt you've caused me?'

'The kiss was because I asked her to add a little sleep weed into Brandon's cup, and that was her price,' Taran explained. 'It seems Laska and her have no love for them, but they have no choice but to do the Witch-King's bidding. I had hoped it might cloud that damned power of Brandon's because now, every time I try and use mine, all I can see are his eyes as well. So no, it was not worth it, and I regret having done it. I would take it back if I could.'

'You do realise I've been waiting to dance with you,' Maya said, slightly mollified, but her head and voice were downcast. Taran's hand gently lifted her chin, and she looked into his blue eyes and saw the sorrow and genuine regret there over having hurt her and knew his pain matched hers in some way.

'I so wanted to dance with you too,' Taran said sincerely, and he took Maya's hand in his and bowed a little from the waist. 'If my lady wife, as Rakan earlier declared us, would care to honour me with this dance, then my happiness would know no limits.'

'Lady wife? Aren't we a little too presumptuous?' Maya smiled a little. 'I feel I need to get to know you better before I'm ready to take that step!'

With some reluctance because of the hurt inside, Maya allowed Taran to hold her in his arms. They moved together to the rhythm of the music, and Maya laughed nervously, for this was her first-ever dance with a man having been kept from every village gathering since she was a child. Despite looking down, Maya found herself treading on Taran's feet, however she tried to avoid them.

'I'm terrible,' she muttered, and tried to pull away in embarrassment, but Taran firmly refused to let her go.

'Look into my eyes,' insisted Taran. 'Let me lead you.'

Maya felt his arms and body guide her as she stared into his eyes, and then laughed in relief as they smoothly circled the fire twice more, before coming back to where they'd started.

As they sat, Maya frowned and rubbed her head. 'For a moment there, those damned eyes of Brandon's almost faded away!' she said, and they looked across the fire to see the Ranger looking back at them. Yana was serving him and the other Rangers drinks, but as ever, they only sipped lightly, taking their duty too seriously to indulge.

Taran glanced at Rakan and shook his head as he saw him finish another goblet.

'Would you walk with me?' asked Taran. 'Somehow, if this is our last night, I don't want to have to share it with so many people.'

Maya's hand slipped into his, and they stood up. 'I do believe we have a cabin of our own,' she said. 'Do you think we could stay up all night and talk, just the two of us, make the most of this time? I want to know more about you before ... well, before it's too late.'

Taran noted two of the Rangers and Laska's guard start to follow them as they slowly walked away from the fire. Yet, he was pleased to notice Brandon stifle a yawn even as those cold blue eyes burned into his. Taran cursed as he turned away, for their image stayed with him.

The walk to the cabin lasted only a short while, but Maya leaned into Taran as they walked, and his arm wrapped her waist. On any normal night, it would have been the perfect stroll.

As they entered, Taran turned to close the door and saw their four escorts station themselves a little distant to overlook the lodgings.

Someone, likely one of Laska's retinue, had lit several candles, and the inside was infused with a homely glow. A small fire burned in the hearth, two chairs in front of it, with a clay pitcher of water and two goblets placed on a table.

Taran went to sit, but Maya shook her head, reaching out her hand.

'I'm tired. Can we lay down?' and led Taran to the bed in the corner of the room, which had a thick fur draped across it.

Taran lay down on his back, and Maya crawled up right next to him, her arm draping over his chest and her head nestled into the crook of his neck. Taran wrapped his arms around her, and she held him tightly in return.

'I can't get his damned eyes out of my mind,' Maya complained. 'They've faded a little, but still, all I can see is them. When we danced, they almost went away, but now they're back. I want our last night to be just you and I. Help me, help me get him out of my head!'

Taran was desperate for an answer; he had to do something. 'Look at me, I have an idea,' he whispered, and slowly moved his face closer as Maya's dark eyes stared back into his. Taran gently brushed his lips against hers, then kissed her softly, his mouth lingering.

Maya moaned and closed her eyes. After a while she opened them again. 'That helped, but now you've stopped, his eyes are back.' Her lips found Taran's, and their kiss lasted longer, much longer.

'Better again,' she gasped, 'but not enough!' and quickly, she grabbed Taran's shirt, then pulled it over his head. They hesitated for several heartbeats, searching for something in the other's eyes. Taran tugged at Maya's shirt, and within moments they were beneath the fur, warm bodies pressed against each other.

'If this is to be my last night, I want to feel alive like never before. I want you now!' Maya demanded.

Taran paused for a moment, and then Maya was underneath him, and the time for words was over.

Later, much later, Taran held Maya in his arms. She breathed softly and snuffled as she drifted off to sleep. Her legs entangled with his, and Taran's heart was so full of happiness that he could hardly believe it.

The sound of the revelry was soft in the background, and the hypnotic beat of the drums combined with Maya's warm body made his eyes close even as he fought to keep them open. He needed to tell her something, but she seemed so peaceful, and however much Taran wanted to, he wouldn't wake her; wake her to the reality that death would soon find them.

So instead, he closed his eyes and surrendered to exhaustion, but as he did so, he thought the words he wanted to say.

'I love you, my princess,' and as he did so, he fell asleep.

A few moments passed, and Maya sleepily opened her eyes, a smile upon her lips as she kissed Taran's bare chest.

'I love you too, my prince,' she said, and sleep found her again.

Laska was not well known for being at his best in the mornings.

He was known to be a fair man, but if you got on the wrong side of him in the early hours, then you might find yourself digging and filling the latrine pits all week.

Thus, when the banging on his door woke him, despite the fact it was still only just brightening outside, he knew something had to be wrong, very wrong, for one of his guards to so awaken him.

He sat bolt upright in bed, pushing a young woman to one side as he did so. He was far too old to fulfil her physically, but he enjoyed the company nonetheless. Sighing, he rose and opened the door, one hand behind his back, dagger ready just in case.

A guard stood there looking petrified.

'What is it, man?' asked Laska, with a growl.

The guard managed to find his voice. 'I can't explain it, my lord. You need to see it for yourself, please come.'

The guard's tone and demeanour conveyed the urgency, so Laska quickly threw on his clothes from the night before, and was out the door before his side of the bed cooled. He walked down the long hallway, across creaking floorboards, designed so that anyone approaching his rooms would give themselves away, then walked down the circular steps to the hall below. It was full of detritus from the last night's festivities, and several of his men still slept where they had fallen asleep, goblets in hand.

'Attend your lord!' he called.

The men roused themselves from sleep and were soon swaying unsteadily at Laska's side as he strode out of the hall, following the young guard who guided them to the east of the settlement where it abutted the mountains.

Laska's heart sank with every step, for now he knew where the trouble lay.

Had those damned Rangers slaughtered the fugitives in their sleep? It was unlikely they'd escaped in the night from under the noses of the guards. Laska, too impatient to wait any longer, grabbed the soldier leading him. 'Just tell me, man, what is it?' he demanded.

'Here, my lord, just a few steps further,' was the response, and then they turned a corner.

'By the gods above,' cried Laska, eyes open wide.

The guards that followed, alarmed at his distress, pushed forward swords unsheathed. As they surrounded him, first one, then another exclaimed in disbelief.

Laska stood there, mind racing, eyes flicking back and forth. This was going to be a day bathed in blood, of that there was no doubt.

'Fetch the bowmen and men-at-arms!' he ordered the man standing next to him. 'Fetch them now, and fetch them all.'

Chapter XVIII

Taran had awoken early to find Maya still in his arms, and her warm body pressed close.

For a moment, with his eyes closed and still feeling sleepy, he felt nothing but overwhelming joy, and the desire that this moment would last forever. The memories of the night before, of giving themselves so willingly to one another, whirred around in his mind. Now, for the first time in his life, Taran realised what love was all about.

He felt something tickle his nose, but as he didn't want to wake Maya, he just wriggled it, but still the tickling persisted. So he opened his eyes slowly, hoping that it would still be dark and that dawn was some way off, to see the most beautiful butterfly sat on his nose looking back at him. Then he saw the room beyond the butterfly, and he couldn't believe his eyes.

It was as if he'd woken up in paradise. The simple wooden cabin with its bare walls, sparse furniture and packed earthen floor was now anything but. The cabin walls were now covered in vines, and these had blossomed, so that as Taran looked up, there was a canopy of green leaves and white flowers over the bed amongst which other butterflies flew.

The earthen floor was now covered by a bed of grass so long and lush that it reached up to the side of the bed itself, and Taran reached out an arm to run his hands through it, before carefully shooing the butterfly from his nose.

Even the bed's wooden posts had grown once again, having rooted themselves and turned into saplings. They spread slender branches above, covered in pink flowers to mix with the white.

Maya's gift had not only returned, but it had returned far stronger than before.

'Oh, my princess,' he thought, 'never have I been in love before until now.'

Maya opened her eyes and smiled sleepily into Taran's face. 'I have never been in love before either,' she said, 'and I want to hear you say it for the rest of our lives.'

Taran sat up quickly.

'Hey,' said Maya, 'that's not quite the response I expected. What's wrong?'

She sat up too then, her eyes opening wide. 'My gift, it's back!' Maya laughed and turned to Taran, throwing her arms around his neck before kissing him softly on the mouth. 'There is truly magic between us, for you brought my gift back.'

'And you mine as well,' said Taran, 'but much more than before.'

'What do you mean?' asked Maya.

'Kiss me,' thought Taran.

Maya smiled, and was about to do as Taran bade when her hand went to her mouth. 'You didn't say anything. You didn't speak the words, yet I heard them!' and her eyes opened wide as she said this.

Taran held Maya's face gently between his hands and looked into her eyes. 'Even though this is our last day, I will fight for who I love. I can't let them take what we have away from us without trying. We have to fight.'

Maya's eyes shone. 'We fight,' she said.

'We will have to kill,' Taran cautioned.

Maya nodded. 'We will have to kill,' she said, repeating the words back to him, and looked him firmly in the eye as she did so.

'Now we need to get Rakan before the sun rises much more. We need to fight together to be at our strongest,' Taran said, and at that moment, the latch to the door lifted, and the door swung open.

317

Maya pulled the fur blanket up over her as Taran leapt out of bed.

Rakan walked in and pushed the door closed behind him before turning to look at Taran.

'I'm not sure I want to go to my grave, with that, the last image on my mind,' said Rakan with a roll of his eyes. 'Quickly get some clothes on!' and as he said this, he turned his back to them both, hands moving over the grass and blossom, looking at the butterflies, and shook his head in wonder.

'This could change everything. If Laska now sees what you're capable of, he might try and stand against the Rangers. He can see the land is dying, and after that, his people will follow, but this,' and Rakan gestured around the room. 'No one can deny Maya's power to heal the land and her value now.'

'Could his men win?' Taran asked, as he and Maya finished getting dressed, and they moved to stand before Rakan.

Rakan grimaced. 'On their own, I doubt it. But if we somehow manage to coordinate, fight together, we might have a chance. But how can we convince him and agree on a plan when there are two Rangers outside looking as unhappy as I've ever seen them? I doubt they will let us have an audience.'

'Perhaps this could help?' thought Taran, projecting his question toward Rakan.

'I swear I just heard you say ...' started Rakan.

'Perhaps this could help,' Taran finished for him.

Rakan's mouth fell open. 'So, not only has Maya's gift returned, but you can make people hear your thoughts. This will give us a chance, but we don't have much time, so let's plan as much as we are able, for our very lives depend on it!'

With that, they huddled close, ideas flowing between them, as they sought a way to avoid death.

Brandon awoke with a headache like none he'd ever experienced before and cursed loudly.

He opened his eyes and swallowed back the bile in his throat. Why was it so light outside? He should have been called for watch duty in the early hours, and here he was, waking up past dawn. He sat up fast, then fought against being sick as he looked around the room to see seven of his men still fast asleep.

None of them had drunk much last night, just a few sips of heavily watered wine until the three fugitives had gone to their cabins. He'd then set two Rangers to guard them, and they should have been replaced twice since then, including once by him.

His heart was racing as he jumped from his bunk to rouse his men. He had to shake them to even get them to stir. We must have been given sleep weed, he thought, and the only people serving food or wine were Laska's men or his granddaughter, who seemed to have set her eyes on Taran.

Looking out the window, he was relieved to see the sun had only just cleared the horizon, so even if Laska had been stupid enough to let them go early, they wouldn't have gone far, and their blood would wet his blade before midday. He smiled grimly. Once they had spilt the blood of the three fugitives, he would brighten his day by slaughtering that old fool Laska and his granddaughter too for good measure. It wasn't part of his orders, but he'd justification enough, and Daleth would be sure to accept his decision under the circumstances.

His men had all readied themselves, so he opened the door to their room, and they all followed Brandon, quiet as death, as they crossed the upper floor of the great hall toward Laska's chambers.

A guard spied them coming and saved his own life without knowing it by bowing low. 'Lord Laska, if you're looking for him, left a short while ago on some urgent duty and has yet to return,' he volunteered.

Brandon looked across to one of his men, Dantal, who nodded in response. Dantal had a gift as a truth-seer and had confirmed the man's word as such.

They turned and descended into the hall, noting the absence of the majority of Laska's retinue, as only servants were present, clearing up from the revelry of the night before.

Anger rose within Brandon, but he quashed it. Anger clouded judgement, and he couldn't afford the luxury. He needed to find out what had happened to his other men, find Laska, find the fugitives, then spill a lot of blood.

They strode out of the hall, their pace quickening. He didn't need to say anything to his men now; they'd trained together for most of their lives. They spread out as they moved into the settlement, heading east toward the cabins. People who saw them coming slunk into doorways or moved out of their way, for the menace surrounding the Rangers was almost tangible. Brandon relished the power he felt as he noted the fear in the eyes of all who looked his way.

It wasn't long before the clearing that led to the fugitives' cabins came in sight. The cabins had been chosen at his insistence because the dead ground surrounding these two buildings would offer no cover for concealment or escape.

Brandon stopped, unable to believe what lay before him.

Somehow the girl's gift had returned, but not only that, she must have used it throughout the night, for what was once a muddy clearing, was now a field of grass waving in the wind. The two cabins looked as if they were woven from living trees, and the mountainside against which they sat was covered in purple ferns. A small stand of withered saplings had been nearby, but now they stood tall and strong, branches laden with leaves, no sign of decay or rot.

Amongst the trees, Laska stood with his granddaughter Yana, his men-at-arms, and a half dozen crossbowmen.

Brandon was also relieved to see his own two men standing watch over the cabin. He waved them over, and as they approached him, they dropped their heads in shame.

'The fugitives are still in their cabins,' a Ranger called Sabeth reported. 'But,' and he paused, 'we fell asleep last night.' They knelt, fully expecting their lives to be forfeit.

Brandon motioned for them to rise. 'I believe we were all given sleep weed. You did not fail in your duty. This day we not only rid our king of these fugitives, but it's time to rid this world of Laska and his granddaughter as well.' As he looked at Laska, considering whether to kill the old fool and Yana first, the door to one of the cabins opened, and Maya, Taran, and Rakan came out.

His eyes narrowed, and he called upon his gift, realising now that the drug must have broken his hold over the two youngsters. He saw Maya's hand go to her temple and Taran's brow furrow. This was going to be a good day.

He would have preferred to pull them kicking and screaming from their beds, and had dreamed of killing the girl slowly, opening her throat, so Taran could watch as her life drained in front of his eyes. His other thought had been to set light to the cabins, just to hear them burn to death inside. But maybe just butchering everyone here quickly, then getting back in the saddle and riding from this wretched place as soon as possible, would be as pleasurable a way to start the day as any.

The girl leaned on a wooden staff as Brandon moved toward them, and he was surprised when Taran and Rakan stopped while Maya walked several steps further ahead. She pointed the staff at Brandon, and he was surprised and even slightly impressed when her gaze met his without flinching.

'I challenge you to single combat,' she called out, her voice loud and unwavering. 'The Witch-King is weak, his soldiers are weak, and the Rangers the weakest of them all!'

Brandon stopped, but only because he suddenly found himself laughing, a sound that was echoed by his men behind him. 'Oh, girl,' he said, 'I applaud your bravery, I truly do. I might have half expected it from the old man or even the young one, but you seem to be the one with the stones, not them. I have to thank you. You've no idea how bad a mood I was in, but this day is quickly getting a lot better. I accept! I've no idea how so many of my brothers came to fall in this hunt, but this game ends here, and it ends now.'

Brandon put a hand to the hilt of his sword and beckoned Maya toward him. 'Do you know that there are no more than two men that I know of, that can beat me in combat, only two. One of them is the Witch-King himself, and the other a devil he keeps alongside him.' He moved confidently closer, sliding his feet through the grass.

'Good thing I'm a woman then,' hissed Maya, as she stepped two paces forward, swinging her wooden staff at Brandon's head.

He laughed dismissively, caught the clumsy blow with ease, and then pulled the staff and Maya toward him while he reached for his dagger, intending to gut her. This had been too easy, he thought. Hopefully the other two would put up a better fight.

Then he heard a piercing scream.

The last thought that crossed Brandon's mind was that if the girl's eyes were glowing so bright, why was it getting so dark?

A little earlier, Taran had managed to communicate with Laska right under the noses of the two Rangers. The shock on the old man's face as Taran had projected his thoughts was readable even from a distance, and Laska's men had looked on in consternation as he'd steadied himself against a tree as Taran put across their plan.

Laska listened but had specific ideas of his own. He insisted that Maya prove not only her gift once again, but more importantly, that she would put herself at the same risk she was asking of Laska and his men before he made any move against the Rangers.

After discussing it with Rakan and Maya, and realising there was no other way despite the danger to Maya, Taran had agreed on their behalf.

Now Taran, along with everyone else, looked on in shocked silence for several heartbeats, before violence erupted all around.

Maya had just proved herself.

The staff that Brandon caught so easily, had, in the blink of an eye, sent roots burrowing into his hand, along his arm, then throughout his body before finding purchase in the soil at his feet. His body was torn apart from the inside. As his scream died away, there were a few moments when everyone just watched in disbelief, but then everything happened at once.

Maya, as Rakan and Taran feared might happen, stood there in numb shock at what she'd just done. Taran ran forward, as did Rakan. Rakan grabbed Brandon's sword and then tossed Taran a dagger as they took up guard position between Maya and the now remaining Rangers.

The remaining nine Rangers surged toward Maya, Taran, and Rakan, intent on avenging their commander as well as meting out their king's justice.

'Now,' screamed Laska, whereupon his six bowmen raised their weapons and shot at the unsuspecting Rangers.

Two Rangers were flung from their feet as the heavy bolts hit them, but once fired, the crossbows took a long time to reload, so the dozen men-at-arms closed to engage. Six Rangers, over the initial shock of this surprise betrayal, turned toward the threat of Laska's men at their flank, while one sprinted toward Rakan, Taran and Maya.

'Come on then, you whoreson!' screamed Rakan, moving to meet the Ranger as Taran circled to the side, but Rakan felt confident, for they knew what to do. When he'd heard of Taran's new skill, he came up with an idea for Taran to share his thoughts and intentions, so that when they fought alongside the other, they fought as if with but one mind.

Taran stepped forward and lunged, and Rakan knew before the movement even started. The Ranger turned to parry even as Rakan's blade scored his side in the same instant.

The Ranger was individually far more talented than the both of them, yet their coordination was near perfect. They exchanged a dozen blows, maybe more, and while Taran received numerous cuts, none were serious, and the Ranger died quickly, Rakan's blade deep in his heart.

There had been a dozen men-at-arms, and while skilful, they were now down to just four men, and Rakan could see they were not going to be able to stop the Rangers for much longer. The vulnerable crossbowmen who were still reloading would then be slaughtered, and all hope would die with them. Laska was backing away from the bloodshed in front of him, his sword held weakly out in front as he pushed Yana behind him.

Two of the Rangers spun away now that the outcome with the men-at-arms was no longer in doubt and headed toward Rakan and Taran.

Rakan turned to Maya and shouted above the din of clashing blades and the screams of Laska's men as the Rangers' blades found their way into flesh. 'We need you, Maya. You need to slow the Rangers. Do you hear me?' But there was no response.

'Make her listen, lad,' Rakan implored of Taran. 'Those bowmen need just a little more time, and if they don't get it, we're dead, all of us. You and I can't fight two Rangers and live.'

Taran looked into Maya's eyes, but she was shaking like a leaf and unresponsive. So instead of shouting at her, he reached out quickly with his gift. He tried to soothe her with his thoughts and projected his desperate and immediate need for her to protect him.

Where Rakan's shouting had failed, the moment Maya felt Taran was in danger, her eyes focused. She sank to the ground, her eyes glowing fiercely as she looked at the two Rangers, who slowed, approaching cautiously. Beyond them, the other Rangers had killed all but two of the men-at-arms, who were frantically doing all they could to stay alive a few moments longer.

Her hands pushed into the soil, and suddenly, as had happened with Darkon and Lazard, vines erupted from the ground at the unsuspecting Rangers' feet, grasping and entangling. Swords at the point of delivering a death blow started to frantically hack at the tendrils that held feet and legs as firmly as encased in steel, as the two last men-at-arms backed away, their lives spared.

'Bowmen!' shouted Laska, and as they finished reloading, they ran forward, one to each Ranger, crossbows raised. The Rangers screamed with desperation as without the ability to dodge, to move, every bolt found its deadly mark.

The grass a few moments ago, so green and so lush, was now splashed with vast swathes of red around the twisted bodies of the dead. What had recently looked like a paradise was now mixed with glimpses of hell.

Maya approached Laska's two remaining men-at-arms, who still stood despite suffering a multitude of wounds. 'Kneel,' she commanded, and they sank exhausted to the ground. These men had risked their lives, so regardless of the price she would pay, she laid a hand on each of their foreheads, and the blood running from their numerous wounds ceased to flow.

Gratitude shone from their eyes in direct contrast to Taran's, which were filled with worry over the use of her gift and the effect it would have, even if it had been the right thing to do.

'Girl, over here,' pleaded Laska, as he knelt close by, cradling a dead man-at-arms. Tears flowed freely down the old man's cheeks as he looked beseechingly at Maya. Yana also wept at his side. 'Save my grandson!' he cried.

Maya could see a gaping wound in the dead man's neck that would have killed him near instantly. He was already gone, and she shook her head tiredly, barely able to stand. 'I cannot.'

'Save him,' growled Laska, rising determinedly to his feet, fury in his eyes. He raised his sword, and Rakan tensed, as did Taran at this unexpected twist.

Maya nodded. 'I will try,' she agreed, then dropped to her knees with Taran next to her.

Taran looked at her, and she at him. 'I can only try,' Maya whispered. Her hands went to the young man's head, and she reached for her gift, letting it flow as it had with her father. It healed the wounds, closing them in moments, and Taran could only look on in concerned wonder.

The grass all around them grew higher, flowers bloomed, and the scent of heady perfume from the blossom on the trees began to mask the smell of death. Still she continued, and the earth around them erupted, more trees shooting into the sky, covering them all with a canopy of green. Suddenly Maya shone so brightly that even Taran fell away, and when he looked again, Maya was on her side, eyes closed.

Laska's grandson was still dead, and yet the anger was gone from the old man's eyes even if the sorrow remained, for there was no doubt that Maya had given her all.

Taran swept Maya into his arms. 'Maya,' he cried, but she just lay there. He called for her with his mind, yet again there was no response.

Townsfolk gathered now the fighting was over, and they looked in horror at the death all around, yet their eyes were wide in amazement as they gazed at the miracle before them.

As Laska ordered men to help carry the dead, he led the way to the Great Hall, insisting Taran bring Maya to be cared for under his protection. As the procession slowly moved amongst the people, they bowed, not to Laska, but to this young woman in Taran's arms, who had healed a part of their world.

Chapter XIX

The girl flew through the air lost. She had no idea where or who she was, but it was more than just her name or sense of direction that was missing, and her heart ached.

She was so high, and the stars in the night sky above the clouds were so bright that for a moment, she considered if it were possible to fly to them, but for some reason, knew now was not the time.

Willing herself lower, she passed through the clouds above a large desolate island, devoid of all life. Everywhere there were bleached bones and ruined buildings, yet nature was not reclaiming this place, for nature had been defeated.

Other lands were nearby, so she flew to investigate, to find large cities, part of a once-thriving civilisation. She called out as she passed, hoping someone might hear, but only the lonely howl of the wind blowing through empty streets answered her cries, and she shivered at the absolute absence of life these places held.

She headed eastward, hoping to meet the rising sun, feeling in desperate need of its warmth. As she passed above the coastline, all manner of creatures floated dead near the shore, yet further away from land, the sea began to teem with life once more, and her heart lightened somewhat.

Then on the horizon, another landmass loomed, and she hastened to its shores, hoping to find something that would remind her of her identity and purpose. To her horror, this land was also in its final throes, and death seemed to be everywhere.

In the distance, a vaguely familiar fortress was visible. She approached, only to find the streets of the city surrounding it strangely quiet. However, at least here, there were some signs of life. Sadly, what men or women there were to be seen, whether adorned with rags or riches, scavenged side by side amongst refuse, desperately trying to find food.

She flew into the fortress itself only to find much the same; largely deserted halls, the recent dead and dying the only residents.

Rising from the confines of this tomb, she headed eastward once more, the blinking of a thousand fires in the distance quickening her heart. Drawing closer, it became apparent this was an army, and it seemed the very life of the land from all around was being sucked toward its centre.

Frightened by the darkness it exuded, she skirted the camp, continuing her journey eastward before coming to, then crossing over, snow-capped mountain peaks that spoke of both beauty and death.

The sight beyond lifted her spirits, for there was a land as yet untouched by sickness. The twinkling of lights caught her attention, so she went to investigate. More soldiers, but this time without the malaise that had overshadowed the army to the west.

She flew down to the camp where soldiers stood on guard at the perimeter, looking out into the darkness, and walked up to one.

'Excuse me,' she said. 'I am lost.' Yet the soldier carried on staring into the distance.

She wondered if he hadn't heard, so reached to tug at his arm, but her hand passed right through him, and she fell backwards in horror. She ran into the camp, between some tents, amongst men talking and drinking by firelight, trying to get their attention, but again no one heard her cries or felt her touch.

She wandered to the centre of the camp, unseen, unheard, then collapsed by a large fire, unaffected by its heat, crying her heart out, lost and lonely in a world of the dead.

'My child,' said a soft voice.

She looked up to see a man in red robes standing there, and no one else was close by. 'You can see me?' she asked.

The man smiled. 'But of course my child, just as you can see me. What pains you this night, and why do you cry so when you have this wonderful gift?'

'I think I must be dead,' she replied. 'Or, everyone else is dead because everyone is a ghost. Or am I the ghost?' Then she started crying again, frightened.

The man knelt beside her and laughed kindly. 'Fear not, little one. No one here is dead, least of all you or I. You have an amazing gift, and this must be the first time you've experienced it. You are spirit travelling, which means your mind has left your body asleep while your spirit flies free to soar into the sky, to visit places you know. You can do things others only dream of.'

The girl looked up at him. 'But I don't know this place or any of the others I've visited. I've flown all night, and I'm lost,' and she told him of her journey and that she'd forgotten her name and where she was from.

A frown slowly appeared on the man's face, and when he spoke, his demeanour became more serious. 'My child. Spirit travelling doesn't normally allow you to roam places you have yet to go or see, not without excruciating pain. So I need to understand if this is true. I have only ever met one other who could do this, and she is dead.'

He knelt and looked closely at the girl. 'My name is Astren, does this sound familiar to you?'

The girl nodded. 'It's a strange name, yet I feel I've heard it before.'

Astren reached out his hand and placed his fingertips on the girl's forehead. He whispered one word.

'Maya.'

Suddenly, the girl was a little girl no longer. Instead, a young woman now sat in front of Astren, and he smiled. 'Welcome back, Maya. You were lost, but now you are found, and I cannot tell you how surprised I am that you still live.'

'Astren!' exclaimed Maya, looking around. 'Where am I, and how did I get here?'

'As to the where,' Astren replied. 'Your spirit form has found its way to the Freestates. I am currently journeying to Tristan's Folly that guards the pass through the Forelorn mountains. As to how. It may be that your spirit was drawn to mine, but I've never met anyone other than you, who could travel unhindered to places they'd yet to visit in the physical world. I never got to question you about it when we first met as our time was so short, but it seems you are unique in more ways than one. To travel where you will is unheard of, and the possibilities of your gift are unbelievable. So, tell me what happened, where you are, and whether your companions still protect you.'

Maya spent a while talking to Astren about her journey but then stopped, for there seemed to be a strange emptiness where some recent memories should have been. She remembered saving Taran when he'd nearly drowned, and then heading toward Laska's settlement, but beyond that, while she knew other events had happened, she couldn't recall them.

'I don't understand.' said Maya, into the silence that followed the abrupt ending of her tale. I simply can't remember anything more.'

Astren nodded, concern written across his feature. 'Maya,' he said, 'I think we had best return you to your body. The fact you've lost memories and even wandered here in spirit form as your child-self would indicate you've suffered great trauma in the physical world. Your body might well be fighting to stay alive, and your mind seeks to protect itself by escaping here to a calmer place. Without your spirit, your body will eventually die. Even if pain awaits you, you should return to face it, or here you will remain until your body dies, then you will simply fade away.

'I could help awaken you with a touch, but I think we should find what awaits you and thus be prepared for any eventuality. Let me escort you, for I know the whereabouts of the settlement you would go, despite not having heard of this Laska, and I can at least accompany you there. But, we must move carefully, for Daleth or his agents might well be abroad this night, and if we come across them, we flee, for surely we cannot fight.'

They flew together, Astren leading Maya back toward the Forelorn mountains, over Tristan's Folly, then along the border of the Witch-King's lands, following the mountain range south.

What would have taken weeks by foot took little time at the speed with which they travelled, and there in the distance twinkled the many soft lights of a large settlement.

'If there's danger flying over these lands, why didn't we pass over the mountains?' asked Maya, nodding to their left.

Astren shook his head. 'I am jealous,' he stated, 'and that is not a feeling I am used to. You forget, I cannot easily travel where I have yet to go. In time I could push into the fog that I see and travel that way, but it would take months.'

'You see, many moons ago as a young man, I managed to travel this land quite extensively. There were still many areas I hadn't visited. So, over the following years, I set out to reach them on my spirit travels instead, only to suffer terrible headaches for weeks as the price. But because of this, I am now the eyes and ears of the Freestates over these lands. I rarely come now as the perils are too great. We already know of Daleth's plans, so there is little reward to the risk, or at least I thought so until now.'

He didn't elaborate any further, and they flew closer toward Laska's settlement, skirting the mountains.

Maya felt herself irresistibly pulled downward and mentioned it to Astren.

'That's good,' he said. 'You are still connected to your body and it seeks your return. Let it take us to where you are, and then you can prepare yourself to awaken once again.'

However, as they came closer, Astren called a halt. 'There is a fog over much of this settlement,' said Astren. 'I cannot go any further. This place must have changed dramatically from when I first discovered it.

Maya thought for a moment, then, somehow knowing it was the right thing to do, reached out to hold Astren's hand. He looked at her questioningly then his eyes widened as the fog started to lift before him.

'Your gift is stronger than I could ever dream of!' breathed Astren in awe, then whistled as he saw the transformation Maya's gift had worked upon the eastern part of the settlement, an oasis amongst a desert and the more beautiful for it.

Maya felt herself drawn toward a large building which she now recognised as Laska's Great Hall. They drifted down and passed through the roof, whereupon Maya felt forcefully pulled toward a room outside which a guard stood.

They entered to find Taran upon a bed, cradling Maya's body in his arms. Tears ran down his face, glistening in the light of a bedside candle, and Maya's heart ached. Then suddenly, everything came rushing back in an instant. The night she gave herself to Taran, the fight, and trying to save Laska's grandson.

She started to move toward her body, but Astren reached out, holding her arm.

'Wait a moment,' he cautioned. 'First, look at yourself. You bear no obvious injury for which I am grateful, but neither are you the same.'

Maya looked closer, and her hand went to her mouth in surprise. 'It is of no matter,' she said, but her eyes betrayed the lie.

'Secondly, you need to ask yourself what happens next,' advised Astren. 'Daleth will soon find out that you live, and he is unlikely to stop hunting you until you're dead. Wherever you live, you cannot hope to hide. Your gift will always give you away until one day they put an arrow in your back and that of anyone else with you. There's no safety for you within his kingdom. So, I believe you should try and find your way to me. The Freestates is currently all that stands between Daleth and the rest of the world we know. If he conquers us, everything he visited upon your lands will happen there, as men, women, and children will die in the hundreds of thousands. Then the land itself will follow, and from what you've told me of your journey, it might never recover unless by your touch.

'I'm not sure if there is anything you can do to help stop this, but we can offer you sanctuary while we can and help you escape should we fall. Try to reach us, get to us before Daleth does.'

Maya nodded. 'I need to go,' she said, her heart torn by Taran's misery, and she couldn't wait another moment to ease his pain.

'A final thing,' said Astren. 'It would be ideal if we could maintain contact. Try to reach me by taking your spirit to the fortress, I should be there soon, or better still, use it to simply talk to me. It takes some practice as both minds must recognise the other, but concentrate on me, and in time I will hear your call. That will likely be safer than flying the spirit paths in case you meet one of Daleth's agents or the man himself.'

She turned to him then. 'Thank you, Astren.'

The pull toward her body was irresistible, and she merged with it becoming one, body and soul. She opened her eyes, to see Taran's closed, and reached out to gently caress his face. His eyes opened, and in an instant, their lips met and didn't part until they both gasped for breath.

'It's ok,' she said, as Taran shook with emotion. 'I am here, and I will never leave you again.'

Taran held her close, eyes shining with love as he brushed back the unruly hair that always fell over her face. Hair that was now streaked with purest white.

Maya leaned over to blow out the candle.

'We are fated to be together,' Taran whispered in the darkness, 'in this world and the next.' And this time, when their lips met, their bodies followed, and everything else was forgotten.

Rakan sat opposite Laska and Yana, deep in conversation, the early morning light shining feebly through the windows, when he saw Yana's eyes narrow.

Following her gaze, he turned to see Taran walk down the stairs holding Maya's hand tightly in his, almost as if he let her go, she would suddenly disappear.

He leapt from his seat mid-sentence to run across the hall and embrace them both, lifting them from the floor in his happiness, and his eyes were wet as he finally let them go. He stood back to look at them. They were both dressed in new clothing provided by Laska, and the two of them were as handsome a couple as he could ever imagine.

'It's so good to see you on your feet girl, it's been a worrying two days for us all, and none was more worried than Taran here.' Rakan smiled at Taran. 'I'm so happy for you, son.'

Taran's eyes widened in surprise, and Rakan looked sheepish at having used such an affectionate term, before gruffly clearing his throat.

'Laska,' Rakan said, looking over his shoulder, 'is not in the finest of moods. He regrets not just the risk he took in helping us defeat the Rangers but also the loss of his grandson.

Rakan led them across the hall, and Laska's old, hooded eyes, followed them every step of the way. Whereas Laska's brow was furrowed and his visage dark, Yana's was less foreboding, and she flashed a bright, welcoming smile at Taran as he approached.

Laska nodded for them to sit, and as servants brought food to the table, both Maya and Taran realised just how hungry they were and set to eating with enthusiasm. The others ate at a more measured pace.

An uncomfortable silence grew after everyone finished their meal, but then Yana broke it. With a somewhat malicious smile, she nodded at Maya. 'You seem to be ageing a little prematurely,' she said. 'White hair seems to suit you as it goes with those new lines around your eyes.'

Maya's hand went up to brush the white shock of hair back from her face, and she felt Taran's hand squeeze her leg under the table in support.

Taran scowled. 'Do you realise that was the price she paid to try and save your brother,' he said, voice shaking in restrained anger, having now fully understood the cost to Maya whenever she used her gift to heal someone.

Laska's fist slammed into the table. 'A brother who died to save your lives,' he roared, 'best you never forget it. A few white hairs don't go near far enough to make up for our loss, and the loss endured by the families of the men who died saving you!'

Rakan raised his hands placatingly. 'Let us not dwell on what has happened; instead, let us look forward to what happens next. We sought sanctuary in this, your home, and would reiterate our pledge to serve you - if you grant us refuge. We ask that you honour our agreement and advise us how best we can work under your command.'

Laska cut in. 'I've heard all this before, and these last days I've given it a lot of thought. How you can pay me back, how you can work off the debt you owe me.' He looked at Maya. 'You are the only one who can repay it. For the next week, under the protection of my men, you will travel my lands working that gift of yours. Heal the land, heal the crops, cleanse the waters, whatever it costs you.' He saw Taran about to interject and raised his hand. 'Whatever the cost!

'Then, once you have done this thing for me, and my land and people's future is secure, you will all leave this place never to return, for without question, wherever you are, the Witch-King or his men will likely go.'

Rakan's face went white. 'This was not the bargain we struck,' he said, eyes narrowing dangerously. 'You guaranteed our safety, a place to live, and you will need our swords and help in defending what you will gain.'

Yana piped up. 'How about we just give Taran sanctuary as a compromise,' she said, licking her lips enticingly, enjoying the look of hurt on Maya's face.

Suddenly, Maya spoke. 'I agree,' she said, and such was the shock at hearing this statement, that Rakan and Taran stopped and stared as did Laska. 'I agree because Laska is right. The Witch-King will come for me, come for us, wherever we are. There is nowhere in this kingdom I can hide that he won't find me should he try. We repay the debt we owe them, and then we leave.'

Maya then told them of her meeting with Astren and his suggestion that they seek refuge in the Freestates while it still stood firm.

'So, how do we get across?' asked Rakan, looking at Laska. 'This was the first reason we thought to come here, for I know there's a passage of some kind that might help us escape these lands.'

Laska smiled grimly. 'Oh, there's a passage, but as you might know, very few ever make it across. It leads to the valley of the giants, and if you can make it past them, and I can assure you in the last fifty years very few have done so, then the Freestates is on the other side.'

'Giants,' scoffed Taran incredulously. 'You cannot be serious.'

Laska looked at Taran. 'Boy,' he said, 'you can disbelieve all you like, all the way up to when they tear your arms and legs off when they catch you.

'You have a week,' he said. 'For seven days, you do as I request, and I will outfit you for your journey and show you on your way to whatever fate awaits you.'

Maya stood. 'Time is short,' she said. 'The Witch-King and his army are only a month away from attacking the fortress. We need to reach Astren before the attack. For whatever reason, he says he can help us, and I believe him.'

'The enemy of our enemy, is our friend,' said Rakan, quoting an old saying, and Taran nodded.

Laska called over a guard. 'You start now,' he commanded, and turned away, pulling Yana with him.

'She's too old for you, Taran,' Yana called over her shoulder. 'You should find yourself someone closer to your own age. Just let me know if you change your mind,' and she walked after Laska, hips swaying.

As the guard led them outside, men, women, and children turned as Maya passed by, bowing their heads.

'Now,' said Maya looking at Taran. 'Let us make a garden the like of which has never been seen before.' She took his hand, and followed by Rakan and their escorts, they walked toward the settlement gates and the land beyond.

Kalas lay upon his back, vision almost gone, his whole being an agony.

He'd thought he would slip away quietly in his sleep and not feel the approach of death, but these last few days had seen him suffer horribly as his body was wracked by thirst, hunger, and the wound in his back that had turned foul, the stench of which pervaded every breath.

In his lucid moments, he tried to control the involuntary cries of pain, knowing that if anyone deserved this, it was him. This was his punishment for the lives he'd taken, the life he'd drunk, even if it was the influence of the daemon that had made him do so.

Then again, maybe the daemon simply encouraged the darkness that already existed inside of him, to do what he'd done. He hadn't risen to become the weapon master in the king's guard because he was a kind man, but because inside of him, there was a desire to attain power, influence and status. He'd trained so hard for the ecstasy of standing over men who lay beaten at his feet, anguish in their eyes. His shining armour was a parody of the darkness inside his soul, even before the daemon had made its home there. How far would his ambition have taken him if not for the invasion of the Witch-King and his legions?

He chuckled to himself, choking up blood as he felt his life finally slipping away from him.

'Time to go home, daemon,' he said. 'We are going back to the nine hells from whence you came, or maybe just me, for I have a feeling you will end your days here.'

He felt the daemon sob distantly in the back of his mind, having hidden itself away just like those many years ago, and Kalas felt some satisfaction at its imminent demise.

Darkness was falling. He felt his heart slow, the distance between beats growing longer and longer, and the pain started to recede.

He thought of his wife Syan and her boy Jay. He hoped at least that part of his life had been selfless. He just wished he could have saved them, or at least have died alongside them.

As he moved toward the darkness, he felt sure he could feel the heat of the fires of the nine hells that awaited him growing hotter. Distant voices whispered, and then a bright light grew and grew, and then ... nothing.

Chapter XX

Taran, Maya, and Rakan walked from the settlement gates accompanied by several of Laska's retainers, and surprisingly, Yana accompanied them, with the two surviving men-at-arms as her bodyguards.

Everyone was armed; Maya with a longbow and quiver full of arrows, Taran a shield on his back and a longsword at his side. Rakan had two shortswords and a throwing dagger.

There was little doubt that once Daleth knew of this latest failure, he would likely try to hunt them down, and there was no telling how close other troops of his might be.

Nonetheless, as they left the settlement behind, Maya took Taran's hand in hers. As she walked, she sang softly under her breath, and her heart skipped a beat as she looked at Taran, to find his gaze already upon her. If the eyes were the windows to the soul, then surely his was shining so brightly, and her own responded as she felt his arm slip around her waist.

Taran leaned in close, softly kissing her cheek, and then as she turned her head toward him, a further one on her parted lips. As the kiss lingered, she felt his love for her in her mind, as Taran unconsciously projected his feelings, and she took his hand and pressed it to her heart.

They held each other close then for a moment until Taran murmured. 'Have you noticed how your stride matches mine,' and she smiled, for it was true. As they walked, every step they made unconsciously matched the others.

'It would seem we fit together rather well in every way,' she said mischievously, enjoying his look of surprise and the sound of his laughter as it rang out.

The men-at-arms looked around at this sound of merriment, and Maya noticed even they smiled, for despite not having heard her joke, no one could overlook how happy they were together, and it warmed the hearts of all who saw them, except one. Yana's smile wasn't so kind.

'How will you go about doing what Laska has commanded?' enquired Taran.

'If you didn't just have eyes for me, you would have noticed already,' Maya responded.

At this, Taran looked behind them to see the grass looking healthier, and that the trees already stood stronger.

'Now,' she said, 'tell me more about your hopes and dreams as we walk, so we forget those around us and enjoy these moments. We've been running and hiding almost every day since we first met, and while I fear we shall be running again soon, for today at least I feel safe, especially in your company,' and she rested her head on Taran's shoulder.

Around the settlement they walked. The land as they approached was dank and dark, but what they left behind was transformed. Back and forth, they walked, forever pushing further away from the settlement, and occasionally Maya would stop and sink to her knees, close her eyes and focus a little more, turning those places into areas of breath-taking beauty. Every time she did, she would stop and smell the blooms, as did Taran, and then their lips would meet. Even if the guards kept an eye on them at a distance, they still felt alone and far away.

They were moving further north than before, with Taran pulling Maya by her hand, occasionally spinning her into his arms, when there was a shout of warning from one of the retainers up ahead. Everyone readied themselves as the two men-at-arms dashed off into the undergrowth.

Taran turned to look at Maya as he readied his sword and shield, and despite the impending danger, felt his breath taken away. She stood there; arrow nocked and drawn, perfectly poised, a picture of effortless grace. Even the ageing whiteness of her hair somehow enhanced the youthfulness she also exuded. If he could remember her like this forever, his heart would know eternal happiness ...

Taran's thoughts were interrupted as Rakan ran to him and Maya, a shortsword bare in his hand.

One of the men-at-arms returned and came over to report. He bowed to Maya. 'Quickly, my lady,' he said. 'We have found someone who needs your help if he's not already beyond it.'

They followed the departing man swiftly, and shortly thereafter came to a clearing. On the far side, the other man-at-arms beckoned them over, and as they approached, they noticed a warrior in silver armour, lying back against a tree, his face deathly pale, tinged with grey and bluish lines.

Rakan lifted his hand to his nose. 'This doesn't smell good,' he said, looking around warily.

'He has an arrow in his back which has caused an infection, and a wound in his leg. He is barely breathing and is soon to slip away,' the man-at-arms offered.

'Is this the man who saved us?' Maya asked of Taran and Rakan.

'I can't be sure,' said Rakan, 'but I've never seen the like of that armour before, so I can only assume it is.'

Maya went to kneel, but Taran restrained her gently. 'Remember what healing others does to you. Are you willing to pay the price for healing a stranger such as this, who is so close to death's door? We don't even know who he is.'

Rakan chimed in as well. 'Maya, there's something not quite right about this man. I can't put my finger on it. But to survive against so many Rangers, the way he moved. I am sure he was following us, he is not entirely human, he is ...'

'Perhaps gifted like Taran and I,' finished Maya. 'He saved us,' she continued, 'and if he is that accomplished a warrior, then what better than to heal him. Then hopefully, he will join Laska to defend what we have saved.'

'Take the arrow out of his back,' Maya instructed Taran, and he leaned the warrior forward, almost gagging as he gripped hold of the broken shaft of the arrow and wrenched it clear. The man didn't make a sound, and Taran wondered if he'd already moved on to the afterworld.

Maya sank to her knees and felt for a pulse, nodding as she found one, even though it was so faint. Then she placed her hands upon his head and reached for her gift, releasing its power into the fallen warrior.

As Taran watched, the colour returned to the warrior's face, the man's chest started to rise and fall regularly, as his breathing became even and deep. Simultaneously, the smell of putrescence was replaced by that of blooming flowers as everywhere around them responded to Maya's power.

Maya sagged back into Taran's arms, her head resting on his chest. 'I'll be alright,' she whispered, 'it tires me so much.'

Taran kissed her forehead and looked at the new white hair that adorned her brow, then kissed the lines that had appeared around her eyes as well.

'Rest easy,' he said, and with that, his hands went to her head, and he slowly stroked her hair.

Maya fell asleep in an instant.

The guards moved away, leaving Rakan and Taran watching over Maya and the fallen warrior.

Rakan took the man's swords away and several daggers. 'I'd rather he isn't armed when he wakes up,' he said, 'just in case he isn't too grateful.' Taran nodded.

342

'Look at these weapons,' continued Rakan, turning them over in his hands in wonder. 'The sword I gave you for defeating Snark was something, but these, they're unlikely anything I've ever known, and nor is that man's armour. It looks as bright as the day it was made, I warrant. He isn't from the kingdom, nor the Eyre, and from what little I know, the men from further east have darker skin and have no craft to create something like this.'

They sat for a while, Rakan keeping a sharp watch over the fallen warrior while Taran turned his attentions back to Maya. Her head was in Taran's lap now, and he traced her features with his fingers, running them softly over her eyebrows, her cheekbones, her lips. Featherlite touches, which were as much for him as they were for her.

It was in the afternoon when Maya finally awoke and smiled sleepily up at Taran. 'I could get used to waking in your arms,' she said.

Taran smiled back, then bent to kiss her softly before they rose so that Maya could test her strength.

Yana came over, a look of impatience on her face, with her guards just behind. 'If I were in your arms, I wouldn't be sleeping so much, I can assure you,' she said jealously. 'Let's find a few more strays for her to heal, and perhaps you won't be so dismissive of me then.'

Taran's reply was to pull Maya closer to him, and Yana, annoyed at her jibe not having much effect, turned to the silver warrior who lay still, eyes closed.

'What the hell is wrong with this fool,' she said, kicking him hard in the side. 'He's healed now, isn't he?'

She swung her foot back to kick him again, but as she did, the warrior moved with astonishing speed. He twisted, so his legs hooked under hers, spinning her to the ground where she hit her head hard, then rolled to his feet in an instant. As Yana's guards started to draw their weapons, he jabbed one in the throat, and as the man's hands went to his neck gasping, he spun and elbowed the other in the face, knocking him unconscious.

Rakan was on his feet now, raising the warrior's own swords against him, but as Rakan moved forward, the man turned, his eyes glowing red, and he moved like quicksilver to the side of Rakan's thrust. It was as though Rakan was a novice, for the warrior reached forward with both hands to somehow twist the blade from Rakan's grasp, before shoulder charging him to the ground.

Taran stood between Maya and the warrior. Maya knelt, and was trying to summon her gift but seemed too exhausted to draw upon it. Having seen the man's speed, Taran knew he had no chance. He reached out to the man's mind to try and read his thoughts, but the images that flooded his mind stunned him, and the next moment Taran was on the ground as well, head spinning so wildly that he wondered if he'd been mortally wounded.

The warrior stared down at Maya, the tip of his sword under her chin.

'I've waited for this moment for a long time,' he said, eyes shining so bright that Maya could feel the heat radiating from them. Then his eyes flickered, becoming normal for an instant, and he staggered back, dropping the sword, then fell to his knees. 'Kill me quickly,' he beseeched, 'before he retakes control,' and his eyes flashed from red to green as he first grasped and then cast down the sword.

Having recovered, Rakan rose and drew his other sword before bringing the flat of the blade down, knocking the warrior unconscious once again. 'Quick, help me bind him,' he said.

Despite the nausea, Taran pushed himself to his feet, and together with Rakan, bound the warrior as the other retainers came running to the sound of the disturbance.

A voice was raised in concern, and Maya saw the two men-at-arms kneeling by Yana, who was making a terrible noise as she rolled on the grass. 'We need help,' called one, and Maya rushed over.

There was Yana, face deathly pale twitching with blood running from her nose and ears, eyes wide open. She looked up at Maya, hand raised like a claw, and Maya didn't hesitate.

She knelt and reached for her gift. It came slowly and with great effort. She'd never had to use her gift this frequently to save lives and could feel hers being drawn from her.

'Enough!' she heard, but still she continued, knowing that to stop too soon would be to lose Yana. 'My princess, enough,' she heard again, and then she felt Taran's arms enfold her in his strong arms as the world around her went black once more.

Daleth sat on a camp bed inside his tent, listening to the sounds of the men outside settling down for the night.

He felt invigorated as he contemplated recent events, a benefit of moving toward the borders of his kingdom where the land still had some life left to give, and also because he now shared a twisted feeding ritual with the daemon, Alano.

Daleth now organised for a victim to be brought to Alano every night on the understanding that their death would be slow. He would then watch, feeding on the pain, fear and anguish, before Alano finally drained the victim's life.

The aged husk Alano left behind was gruesome to behold, and was wrapped in a burlap sack before being cast onto one of the many campfires that burned every night. Their unholy alliance seemed unbreakable because of this, and Daleth felt his trust in the daemon's oath as strong as it had ever been.

But now, other matters filled his thoughts. Progress had been slow the last couple of days as unseasonably heavy rain had fallen. The wagons carrying the heavy equipment bogged down, churned the roads to mud, and made keeping a reasonable pace impossible. It mattered little in the greater scheme of things, but every extra day of delay taxed his patience.

The other concern was Brandon. He'd been unable to reach the Ranger's mind to hear the detail of Maya and her companions' deaths. Still, now having recovered sufficiently from his previous spirit journey, he'd be able to go and see for himself.

Daleth lay on his camp bed waiting impatiently for sleep to take him, the noise of the camp frustrating his attempt, so he took a small amount of sleep weed and chewed it while wondering how much better he'd feel if he got his army to take it instead. That way, they could suffer the resulting headache. However, as he pondered, he fell asleep, and willed his spirit to free itself.

As he floated upward through his tent, he looked around, noting his guards alert outside, and he nodded in satisfaction. He flew across the vast sprawling camp, pleased with the discipline he saw, with tents pitched in neat rows and sentries set throughout.

Some of his commanders had asked if this were strictly necessary while they were in friendly territory. Daleth then suggested that he would let Alano drain the life from any one of them if they were found to be unguarded in the camp. There'd been no need to discuss the point further.

Alano was proving useful in a multitude of ways, and that was even before they got to the battlefield.

He headed east, surveying the land and checked on his scout's reports. Fortunately for them, the estimates they gave were accurate. If they resumed a good pace once the ground firmed, then they were around fourteen days or so from the pass.

His fortress had been wholly dismantled now. The enormous blocks of stone stacked in readiness for his siege engines. Beyond this point was a grey fog, and Daleth cursed the limitations of his skill. He was neither fast in travelling nor had the strength of will to push the boundaries. He so wanted to see the Freestates fortress with his own eyes and berated himself for not having previously taken the time to visit personally.

He turned south over a land blighted by his years of rule, and as he looked down, he saw something ugly to be left behind. Daleth could still appreciate beauty, but differently from most. A lithe maiden or a verdant landscape were both vibrant and full of life. But he saw it as life and strength that would one day transfer to him.

The mountain range to the east was covered in fog, so he didn't fly too close; the headache he would get from even touching its fringe just wasn't worth it.

Excitement mounted as he flew. It was unlike Brandon not to contact him through spirit talk after a mission was completed. Yet, Daleth had been exhausted, so likely the issue was with him, as opposed to Brandon overlooking his responsibility to make contact.

Flying as fast as his gift allowed, he crossed withered forests and dying grassland, then followed the white river, which he knew would bring him close to Laska's settlement. He had a feeling Brandon might have gone beyond the boundaries of his mission and taken it upon himself to cause mischief with Laska and his people. Daleth would usually be furious if someone went beyond the instructions they'd been given, but Laska and his ilk would have died along with the land in time anyway.

He slowed now, floating down toward where he knew Laska's settlement and lands lay, and then stopped, eyes open wide in dismay. For there in front of him lay a bank of fog over not just Laska's settlement, but much of the lands surrounding it.

How could this be? This was his land. He'd been here, he should be able to see it, and not only that, to fly down and look upon Laska's old decrepit face as he lay sleeping or dead. Then realisation hit him. It could only be that damned girl! She must have healed and changed the land so much that it was no longer recognisable.

So what had happened to Brandon and his men? Surely not more casualties in the hunt to bring this girl and her companions to justice. Yet that would explain why he hadn't heard from him and this debacle below him.

Daleth was furious, yet he didn't allow his anger to cloud his thoughts. There was no point wasting more time here now. He couldn't change the past. He had to focus on the present and the future.

He turned back toward his encampment, studying the land below him as he flew, and wondered whether he would see a pair of red eyes looking up at him. Perhaps fortunately, the only movement was from the night animals, and there weren't many of them as this land was soon to perish and everything with it. Laska's settlement would seem to be the exception, as that was now likely to flourish.

He returned to his body, merged, and awoke with a groggy head. He sat up in his camp bed and reached for a pitcher of water. As he turned to pick it up, there were a pair of red eyes in the darkness, staring right at him.

Kalas was here!

Daleth threw himself backwards and rolled across the floor to rise with a blade in his hand, heart hammering, as he prepared to face his killer. He was about to shout for his guards, if only so he would die in good company, when Alano stepped forward into the dim candlelight and bowed mockingly to him.

'What in the nine hells are you doing in my tent?' growled Daleth. He hoped his heart wouldn't burst out of his chest as he walked back to the bed, then picked up the dropped pitcher to rescue the last few drops of water to assuage his thirst.

Alano spoke, and shivers ran down Daleth's spine. The voice was always dripping with evil, and he never got used to it.

'My king,' Alano said. 'I was simply watching over you when at your most vulnerable, and I wondered if you had news from Brandon on the execution of the fugitives, or whether by any chance he'd seen any signs of my brother, Kalas?'

Daleth sat down and reached for a flask of wine, deciding he needed something stronger, and told Alano of what he'd seen, and that he believed Brandon and his men were now feeding the worms.

'What action do you think we should take?' he asked Alano.

Alano's smile was sickening. 'We should hunt them down and drink their blood immediately,' he said, his tongue lolling out to lick his lips.

Daleth shook his head. 'That's a daemon's advice. I want the advice of my old general Alano, sage advice, not one driven by the need to drink the lifeblood of everyone you come across!' He looked at Alano some more, but then shook his head as the daemon just stared back. At times like these, he wished he could have the man and not the daemon.

Daleth slammed his fist into a table. 'Damn them, but I need to focus on the campaign, not get continually distracted by these renegades, not yet at least. If they try and cross the valley, they'll be pulled limb from limb by the giants. If they stay with Laksa as is likely, then once the Freestates lies bleeding at my feet, I can personally put an end to all of their lives. Imagine their despair when they allow their hopes to rise, thinking that I have turned my back on them, only to find us camped on their doorstep one morning a few moons from now.

'Leave me,' said Daleth, 'I need to rest,' and he rolled into his camp bed, the image of red hungry eyes in his mind, as he tried to fall asleep.

Tristan and Astren rode through the fortress's eastern gateway, looking up at the massive stone blocks as they passed under its arch.

The men that marched at their backs, feet stomping in unison, cheered loudly now that their long journey was over.

Tristan called their commanders forward to him.

One, a savage-looking man with skin burned dark by the desert sun and a thick forked beard, was called Sancen. The other, the Eyre commander Dritz, was a small man as were all his kind, with a skin tinged green from generations of his forebears living in the swampland.

'It seems no one is here to greet us, my lords,' said Tristan, offering them a genteel title.

Sancen looked around with disdain on his futures. 'You westerners with your high walls. Where is the honour in hiding behind such? There is no hiding in the desert, you face your enemy in the shield wall, and the only thing between them and you are your spear and shield! You fight and die with honour.'

Dritz nodded slowly. 'I don't much like this place either, too much stone, no trees. But I, for one, am happy there are walls between the enemy and us. I would be happier to live and spend my pay than die honourably on the battlefield.'

Sancen laughed. 'But if half my men die, then the rest all take home twice as much. My way is better!'

'Please order your men to make themselves comfortable outside of the walls until we meet the commander,' interrupted Tristan. 'It might not do his nerves any good to have nearly a thousand armed men march in through his gates without being forewarned.'

Drizt and Sancen jogged off to pass on the instructions.

Tristan waited for the return of the two men.

'This truly is awe-inspiring,' commented Astren, looking all around. 'I've flown over it, and it looked impressive from above, but from down here, it truly is a feat of tremendous engineering.'

Tristan nodded as he swung himself down from his saddle, and Astren followed suit, thinking he would never be able to walk properly again as the insides of his thighs ached so terribly.

Drizt and Sancen came back, and Astren wondered if maybe marching with them might have been a better idea than riding with Tristan.

They headed past the keep which had been constructed against the northern side of the pass, having tethered their horses against a picket line that looked like it wouldn't hold if their mounts decided to test it.

'It's a good thing we aren't the enemy,' muttered Astren, as they wandered around unchallenged. 'But I guess if we were and inside the fortress, we'd have lost the war already.'

Here and there, men sat laughing and talking, while a few others seemed to be repairing weapons at a smithy that belched out smoke, and yet there was no sense of urgency.

'Remind me, how many men are supposed to be stationed here now?' asked Tristan, noting how quiet it seemed.

Astren looked around, then shook his head. 'Around seven to eight thousand and growing daily.'

'If there are eight thousand troops here, then they're either all out fighting or very good at hiding,' suggested Drizt. 'That or maybe they're sleeping off hangovers.'

Tristan had worn a long robe to cover his gaudy armour on the journey. Astren wondered why he didn't remove it, then concluded that Tristan wanted to see what was going on before they were challenged - if they were ever challenged.

Astren felt the best place to start would have been the keep, which was no doubt where the fortress commander was in office, and of course, where the soldiers would be housed, yet Tristan headed along the pass toward the fourth and highest curtain wall to their west.

It was so tall and imposing that for a moment, Astren felt reassured. Its towers stood higher than the wall itself, yet as they came closer, he saw that many of the enormous blocks of stone were crumbling or even askew. Astren walked up to the wall and probed with his fingers between the blocks, pushing them into the mortar to find it crumbling and dusty. 'My king,' he said, to catch Tristan's attention.

Tristan drew a small dagger and stepped forward, then scraped it between two blocks. A torrent of mortar dust blew away in the gentle afternoon breeze. 'We better hope the core of the wall is stronger,' he commented, and everyone could only nod in agreement.

Soldiers from the garrison strolled past in their dusty uniforms, and while some cast a curious glance in their direction, not one challenged them.

How could the king of the land, with nearly a thousand troops, turn up, and no one raises even an eyebrow at his arrival? Astren thought it was ridiculous.

They entered the base of one of the towers then climbed the circular steps, stopping on occasion to look through arrow slits, noting the same state of disrepair everywhere. Higher and higher, they climbed, and as they reached the top, Astren held tightly to one of the battlements to steady himself as a wave of dizziness washed over him.

He saw Sancen doing the same and felt a little better that a fearsome warrior could also suffer from a fear of something. Drizt, on the other hand, leapt nimbly on to the very battlements themselves, then hopped from one merlon to the next, sure-footed despite the breeze.

'Amazing,' he cried, sheer joy upon his face, 'I could fire an arrow to the very moon itself from up here,' and he leapt around laughing at the looks on everyone's faces.

From this vantage point, they gazed westward, and there in the distance at the other end of the pass was a wall; all that remained of the fortress that once stood denoting the border with Daleth's lands.

'Ours is bigger than his,' said Drizt, laughing.

Astren couldn't help but smile at his constant levity. 'If it were just about how big one's fortress is, then yes, we'd win hands down. However, I fear what will pass through its gates is more what we should be concerned about,' he replied.

'Come,' motioned Tristan, and they turned, heading back down the stairs, cautious of the loose rocking steps as they walked upon them.

They stopped their descent partway and stepped out on to the wall. As they walked along studying its condition, Drizt constantly fooled around until Sancen threatened to push him over the edge if he jumped up one last time.

'To push me over the edge means you're going to have to get close to it, and at the moment, from the look on your face, I think I'm pretty safe,' challenged Drizt. 'You sand eaters have no idea of fun.' Yet he didn't jump up again either, noting perhaps the serious look in Sancen's eye.

After inspecting the crumbling wall, they descended another set of steps by the wall's gatehouse into the courtyard, and Sancen knelt briefly to place his forehead against the rocky ground.

Astren hoped they would now go to find the commander and wash the dust from their throats with a good wine. However, Tristan seemed on a mission to inspect the whole fortress, even though the sun was past halfway across the sky.

They continued their inspection, passing through a large open gate, and were hit by a wave of sounds and smells. The area between the walls was full of small pens, with chickens, goats, and pigs kept as fresh meat for the garrison. While up against the wall, wooden lean-tos had been built so the animals could be slaughtered and butchered.

Drizt laughed. 'Look there!' he said pointing, and they followed his arm toward a catapult at the base of the wall. What had made him laugh however, was that the goats were using it as a climbing frame. 'I wonder if they're the ammunition?' he quipped, before turning to Sancen. 'Would it be honourable to be killed by a flying goat on the field of battle, as long as you were in a shield wall?' he asked.

Sancen's arm swung out to cuff Drizt, but the small man was too agile, and Astren sighed with relief when Sancen's deep laughter matched Drizt's.

'Beware we don't fire you over the wall at the enemy, little man!' he boomed, smiling. 'They'd all run away rather than listen to your chatter all day long.'

This exchange lightened the mood, and Astren felt his spirits lifted further.

Occasionally they made way for garrison soldiers as they walked around, but not once did they come across any of the substantial numbers of troops that were supposed to be based here.

Between the third and second wall were a few piles of rubbish, but it was mostly empty. The barren ground was split with a wide trench that bisected the pass, over which three wooden bridges spanned the gap. Finally, they passed through the gateway of the second wall into the shadow of the main curtain wall, the first line of defense against the Witch-King and his army.

Here, at last, were the signs of activity that Astren had perceived in his spirit travels. Wooden scaffold towers were up against some parts of the wall, and several dozen men seemed to be slowly working along its length.

Tristan led the way, across a wooden bridge, toward the middle of the wall and the main gatehouse, which housed the pulleys that helped open and close the gates.

As they got closer, Drizt whistled, his keen archer's eyes seeing into the gloomy tunnel ahead. 'Let me riddle you this,' he said to everyone. 'When is a gatehouse just a house?'

Sancen, rising to the bait, shook his head. 'I don't know,' he replied.

'When there are no gates!' announced Drizt, and everyone except Sancen laughed until they realised it wasn't a joke at all.

For sure enough, as they walked closer, the main gates to the fortress were nowhere to be seen.

'We should kill him,' advised Laska, 'for he is too dangerous, and he carries a name of ill omen.' He'd decided to put Kalas' fate to a vote, at his granddaughter's insistence, assuming it would be easily won, and now he leaned back in his chair, eyes challenging anyone to disagree with him.

Laska wanted Kalas dead for the harm he'd initially brought upon Yana. Rakan nodded as he also wanted him dead for the unstoppable danger he represented, whereas Maya shook her head in disagreement, reiterating her earlier stance.

Yana added her voice. 'No, grandfather,' she said, causing Laska's eyes to open wide in surprise. 'Maya has asked that he be spared, and in this, I would have you grant her wish. There is also something familiar about him even though I've never met him before.'

Rakan shook his head, both at her decision and because he was unable to believe the turn of events. He looked across at Taran, who was also somewhat bemused at the bridges Yana was trying to build with Maya. She now seemed to be doing everything possible to make amends for her earlier behaviour, even if it meant opposing her grandfather's wishes.

Several days ago, upon awakening from Maya's healing, Yana had seen her sleeping in Taran's arm's, recovering from the drain it put upon her body. She'd walked across and knelt next to Taran, eyes lowered, looking down at Maya, at the new lock of white hair that shone in the dying light, and the fine lines around her mouth.

'I am sorry,' she'd said, looking at Taran with moist eyes. 'Truly I am,' and her guards had brought water and food for when Maya awoke.

Over the following days, as Maya had finished her healing of the surrounding lands, Yana had frequently spent time at Maya and Taran's side. While Maya had been reticent at first to accept Yana's change of attitude as genuine, she couldn't help but recognise her continued efforts. Taran and Rakan had welcomed the shift as well.

Kalas was currently bound in chains in one of the cellars beneath the great hall, and he was watched over by crossbowmen with orders to kill if he showed any signs of trying to break his bonds. It was unlikely the possessed warrior could escape, but Laska wouldn't take any chances, and no one disagreed with him in this regard.

Laska, Rakan, Maya, and Yana turned to Taran. 'It's down to you, boy,' Laska muttered, 'to determine this man daemon's fate. However, if he lives by your choice, know this, he cannot stay with us when you leave and will be cast out into the wilderness. So, consider your choice carefully.'

Taran thought back to the moment he'd glimpsed Kalas' mind when Kalas first attacked them, and even now, it brought bile to his throat. In an instant, he'd seen such shocking images that had plagued his sleep ever since. He'd also sensed the unquenchable thirst for torture, killing, and the draining of life that the daemon directed toward everyone, but specifically Maya.

So while this was sufficient cause to support both Rakan and Laska's decision to have Kalas killed immediately, he still paused to deliberate before voicing his thoughts.

'When I looked into Kalas' mind for the second time as he lay subdued and unconscious, I got to see many things, and it's the man's mind I will judge him on, not the actions of the daemon who possesses him. It is hard to believe, but I saw his thoughts and the truth of them. He is,' and Taran shook his head in disbelief, 'a former guard to King Anders, who ruled this land many, many years ago.'

Rakan snorted, but Laska leaned forward, eyes wide. 'I haven't heard that name in over forty years!' he said incredulously, and his eyes softened imperceptibly.

Taran continued. 'I believe Kalas to be a good man and a warrior of unsurpassable skill. He's under oath to kill Daleth, and his possession was a means to accomplish that over fifty years ago. It seems he failed then, but now seeks to complete this mission or die in the trying. However, the daemon is powerful and constantly struggles for control. It desires not just to kill, but to drink from its victims' life force to feed an insatiable hunger.

'Maya has now healed his body, but that is not what matters if he is to live. It's his mind. If he can't control the daemon fully, irrespective of his worth as a man, he has to die.'

Maya looked up in dismay, and Rakan nodded vehemently. Laska strangely didn't voice his support anymore; instead, Taran thought he might have seen him brush away a quick tear.

'So, if Maya can only heal his body, then we have no other course of action but to kill him.' interjected Rakan, starting to rise.

Taran shook his head and squeezed Maya's hand reassuringly under the table. 'No, we don't kill him yet, for where Maya failed, I believe I can succeed. If I don't, then, and only then, should the executioner's blade fall.'

Laska's face was red, and his voice shook with suppressed emotion when he spoke. 'One more day and you leave my lands, and I truly hope Kalas the man travels with you, for if not, we bury Kalas the daemon behind you. You have one day.' With that, he stood up, knocking his chair over and stormed off, his eyes red and puffy.

Yana followed, looking somewhat perplexed as she hurried to soothe him.

Maya spoke softly to Taran in the silence that remained. 'I don't like this idea at all. You've cried out in your sleep ever since you read his mind. If trying to heal him hurts you even more, I would rather ...' and she stopped for a moment before continuing, 'I would rather he die.'

Taran looked into Maya's eyes, seeing the love and concern there and felt his heart swell within his chest. 'My princess, this world needs your compassion, your tenderness, your healing. You show the way of forgiveness and redemption, whereas the rest of us only add to the darkness by turning to anger and killing as a way to solve our problems. I want to choose your way whenever and wherever possible. So tonight I will try, for to take a life is so easy, but to give one, therein lies a true power that few in this world possess.'

Rakan cleared his throat, and they both looked across. 'If this fails, it will be my way instead,' and he spun his dagger on the table while looking at them meaningfully.

Taran grimaced as he said. 'If I can't solve our problem, you can end it,' and Maya slowly nodded in agreement.

Shortly after realising that the gates within the first wall were missing, along with over seven thousand men, Tristan, Astren, Dritz, and Sancen had turned back toward the keep to find the garrison commander.

Tristan was incredulous as they marched briskly back through the fortress, muttering under his breath. 'Where the hells are my gates, my men and my money?'

Sancen was muttering too. 'When is a gatehouse not a gatehouse,' when suddenly he stopped and roared with laughter. 'I get it,' he said, holding his sides. 'When there are no gates. It's a joke!' and laughed uncontrollably, whereafter Dritz told him some more.

Astren wondered to himself how many days it would take the slow-witted Sancen to work them out.

The laughter wasn't doing Tristan's mood any good. 'Can't you stop laughing?' he growled, as they neared the keep. 'And you,' he said pointedly at Dritz, 'perhaps keep your repertoire of jokes and riddles to yourself. This is no laughing situation.'

'King Tristan,' Dritz responded, bowing low in an exaggerated fashion. 'You have paid good coin for my men and I to fight and perhaps even die in your employ at the point of a sword, but I have no recollection of said contract saying I would ever face dying of boredom.'

Astren held his breath, waiting for Tristan to explode, but before Tristan could react, Sancen began to laugh, that deep booming laugh.

'Die of boredom, die of boredom. Does anyone else get it? Drizt, you are the funniest green skin I have ever known. In fact, you are the only green skin I have ever known!' and then he started laughing at his own joke.

Tristan couldn't help but smile a little. 'Astren, let's leave these two simpletons to look after their men, while us educated individuals find out what in the hells is going on.'

As they approached the keep, they were finally challenged by two guards who sat at the bottom of the steps.

'Who are you?' asked one, and pushed back his helm to scratch his forehead, nodding at Tristan and Astren. 'You look a little familiar,' he said to Tristan, 'I think I might know you from somewhere. But you,' he frowned at Astren, 'I've not seen you before. What are you doing here?'

Astren looked over at Tristan to see his face growing that dangerous shade of red, and yet Tristan controlled his anger just enough. But when he spoke, it was with menace.

'You do know me,' replied Tristan, 'for you swore an oath of allegiance to me when you put on that uniform. You do know me, because it's me who pays you coin every month, and you do know me, because this is MY BLOODY FORTRESS!'

Into the silence that followed this declaration, Tristan threw off his dusty robe to stand resplendent in the armour of the King of the Freestates.

Even though he was diminutive and slightly balding, still he had a commanding presence about him, and the guards, now appreciating who stood before them, sprung to attention. Other soldiers were wandering or sitting around, and Tristan's shout drew them, and they hastily pulled armour straight or put on helms as they understood who was in their midst.

'Now you know who I am, show me to the commander of my fortress.' Tristan glanced across at Astren.

'Elender,' Astren helpfully prompted.

'Yes, Elender,' Tristan confirmed. 'Take me to him now!'

The two guards looked at one another, and there was a subtle shrug of the shoulders that neither Tristan or Astren missed as they started walking up the steps to the keep's entrance.

Tristan saw Dritz, standing with Sancen, pretending they hadn't listened to the exchange.

'Oh, come on, you two,' said Tristan, beckoning them over. 'You are my official bodyguards as of now.'

Drizt pumped his fist in the air. 'Yes!' he said, and jogged over with Sancen lumbering behind. 'You hear that, Sancen, we are getting an enormous pay rise!' The four of them followed the guards up the steep steps. Drizt whistled. 'Sancen, my slow friend. When is a doorway just a way?'

'When there's no door,' boomed Sancen, and Drizt slapped him on the back as they approached the archway, which should have held the heavy reinforced doors to the keep, but instead, was just an empty, stone arch.

'Guards,' Tristan called, and the two of them stopped and turned to face him. 'Perhaps you can tell me why in the first line of defense, the curtain wall has no gate, and the keep, the last line of defense, also has no door? I'm at a loss, and whereas my two friends,' and he raised his eyebrows at Drizt and Sancen who were still laughing, 'find this somewhat amusing, I am more of a mind to be, worried, concerned, or maybe bloody furious would explain it better.' As he said the last words, his voice rose to a shout again.

The guards exchanged horrified looks while they tried to think of something to say.

Tristan sighed. 'Forget it. I'm sure Elender will have a good answer, because if not, Sancen here is going to throw him off the top of this keep.'

They walked through the dark entranceway, past numerous gloomy passageways lit with flickering torches, and then started ascending the circular stone stairwell, following the guards who advised that Elender's quarters were at the top, the fifth and final floor.

It was cold inside the keep, backed against the very mountains from which it was hewn. Astren shivered, even as he laboured up the steps. Sancen was muttering about the cold too, and Astren knew he would feel it even more, having come from the hot desert far to the southeast.

Drizt, on the other hand, as ever, was enjoying himself. He was so light and agile, and the many steps bothered him not at all, and every time they went past an arrow slit, he would peer out and nod in approval - especially as they got higher.

'Personally,' Drizt said, 'I prefer to live in my swamp, amongst the trees. Yet to fight from up here, my arrows will fly so far as to be given wings.'

Finally, they reached the top floor and stopped and stared. Opulence was a given in the Freestates, but the one place it was not to be expected was the western frontier in this fortress, and yet as they came to the top of the cold stone stairwell, finery was everywhere. A thick red carpet lined the floors, mirrors abounded, and tapestries hung from several wall spaces. There were also several imposing carved stone busts.

Astren peered at one. 'I don't recognise who this is,' he said to Tristan. 'It's good workmanship for sure, but which old king is it a likeness of?'

Tristan shook his head, so Astren looked at one of the guards enquiringly.

'That is Elender,' the guard offered.

'You pay your garrison commander a lot of money,' observed Sancen. 'Do you pay bodyguards a lot as well?'

'No,' said Tristan. 'I certainly don't think the coin I pay could ever extend to this opulence.'

'Something certainly doesn't smell right here,' stated Drizt with a more serious demeanour. No gates, no men, now all this. Something is amiss.'

The guards were taking off their boots.

'What are you doing?' asked Tristan in wonder.

'Lord Elender doesn't allow us to wear them in his chambers,' shrugged one.

'Keep your boots on, men,' said Tristan, and when the guard hesitated, he asked. 'Whose authority is higher, the commander of this garrison, or the king to which the commander owes allegiance?'

So with boots on, the six of them made dusty footprints on the red carpet as they walked down the long hallway, past open doors, leading to rooms all equally well-appointed.

'These are his work chambers,' said one, and bowed, standing back to one side of a large door.

Voices could be heard faintly from within.

'They do have some good doors then,' commented Sancen.

Drizt chuckled and slapped the big man on the back, yet there was a seriousness in his eye when he said. 'Not all good doors open onto good things,' and his hand went to the hilt of his dirk.

Tristan picked up on Drizt's veiled warned and turned to the two guards. 'You are dismissed,' he said, and after a brief hesitation, they walked back through the hallway and disappeared down the stairs.

Sancen put his hand on the iron door ring and looked at Tristan, who nodded. Sancen pushed the door open, and they stepped quietly through, one by one, into a large chamber.

It was, like the hallway before it, furnished beautifully. Heavy carved wooden chairs surrounded a large table upon which were numerous parchments and charts. Polished and ornate cupboards were placed around the room, and heavy rugs covered the cold floor. To their left was a series of stone archways that led out onto the battlements overlooking the pass.

Outside stood a man and woman deep in conversation. The man, from the likeness to the busts in the hallway, was Elender, and he wore the embellished armour of a commander. The woman looked vaguely familiar to Astren, and although without armour, was armed with a sword and dagger.

As they walked quietly across the chamber, both Elender and the woman caught sight of them and turned. Elender's face twisted in anger. 'How dare you!' he started to rage, then caught sight of Tristan, bedecked in his finery behind the bulk of Sancen.

'My, my, King,' he stammered. He looked at the woman with panic in his eyes, then as his face flushed red, he started to kneel.

'I've seen that woman before with Anthain,' said Astren, recognising her.

The woman said nothing but inclined her head slightly to Astren in acknowledgement, then drew her weapons and attacked.

Taran entered the cellars below the hall alone.

Rakan and Maya had argued that they should accompany him, yet he knew he would be distracted if they were there.

'How is it you think you can help Kalas?' Maya had asked.

'In all honesty, I don't know and won't until I try,' Taran had responded. 'But, since our night together, both of our gifts have come back stronger. So who knows what is now possible?'

So now Rakan and Maya waited at the top of the stone steps as Taran looked through the bars of a door at the shackled figure and then motioned for the guards to unbar it.

'My Lord,' said one, bowing to him. 'The prisoner seems to change all the time. One moment himself, begging to be killed, the next silent. Then when his eyes turn red,' and the man shuddered, 'the voice is something I will always hear in my nightmares.'

The guards retreated quickly as Taran walked into the room. He sat on a wooden bench several long steps from Kalas, who wore simple homespun trousers and shirt. Taran wondered if he was asleep, which might make things easier, but even as the thought crossed his mind, Kalas looked up.

'Why are you here, lad?' asked Kalas, his voice sounding tired. 'You don't look like an executioner to me, although in my saner moments, I doubt I look like a daemon-possessed warrior either!' and he laughed mirthlessly. 'Seriously though, I am lost. I thought to control him, but since he has come back, I have done nothing but kill, and I would have killed you and your friends too.

'He's coming!' Kalas gasped, and his face twisted in pain, eyes glazing, and then the next moment, he was straining at the chains, the screams coming from his mouth from another plane of existence.

The flickering torches on the walls, those shining red eyes, and the unearthly screams, almost made Taran flee, yet he steadied his resolve. He took a deep breath as the daemon screeched at him, called upon his gift, and reached out. This time he was slow and careful, trying to find a way past the terrible rage and darkness that boiled in the front of Kalas' mind, instead of charging right in.

Amongst this storm of violent, torturous, and degrading thoughts, were flashes of a woman and child, laughter and comradeship, love and duty, loyalty and friendship. Yet this time, Taran turned his mind's eye away from all of these flashing images, and searched, not knowing for what until he eventually found it.

In front of him, there was a bubble of sorts that changed colour from dark to light. He pushed his way through, escaping from the kaleidoscope of memories to the relative tranquillity within. He now stood on a dark hill with storm clouds boiling above, and there stood two identical men locked in mortal combat, weapons of all kinds strewn around. As Taran drew closer, he could see, as he knew it would be, that both were Kalas, clad in silver armour, wielding two swords as they fought for what ... control of his soul?

'Help me!' cried one. 'I cannot stand against him much longer.'

Taran reached down and picked up a discarded sword then stepped forward, yet even as he did so, the flow of battle changed, and the other one also cried for his assistance.

Taran looked at their green eyes as they fought. There was no giveaway there, so how could he tell them apart?

Blades clashed together, and each of them lost a sword as they shattered into shards. Taran could see that they were identically matched in skill, neither able to gain a lasting advantage. He stepped in close, yet knew he was safe, for if the daemon Kalas tried to kill him, then the good one would have an opening to slay the other, and the battle would be won in that instant.

Back and forward, they thrust and parried, spun and leapt, neither gaining the upper hand, and Taran sought for something, anything, to identify the good from the evil.

Suddenly, the flurry of blows came to a halt, as each Kalas grasped the wrist of the others' sword hand, locked together, as muscles strained and veins bulged with effort.

'Kill him, and save us,' groaned one, and his arms shook as he took a small step back, 'I can't hold him!'

Taran knew what to do. In the blink of an eye, he thrust his sword into the one who'd cried for help.

'You fool, it's not me. It's him!' his victim cried, but Taran twisted the blade, driving it deeper, and the man's knees buckled, and he fell to the floor.

Taran stepped back, pulling the sword free as the remaining Kalas turned to face him, a smile spreading across his face. Suddenly, Kalas' sword whipped out fast, and Taran's blade parried first one, two, then three strokes, that were so quick he surprised even himself, and yet the fourth parry saw the sword spun from his hand.

The tip of Kalas' weapon lifted to Taran's throat. 'Very impressive,' Kalas said, 'but not good enough, although with training, you could be deadly.' Kalas lowered his sword and let it fall from his fingers. He stepped forward and embraced Taran briefly before grasping his wrist as one warrior would to another. 'How did you know?' Kalas asked, 'Was it a guess?'

Taran nodded down at the floor. 'It was in the footwork.'

Kalas shook his head. 'No, we were identical,' he argued, 'there was no way we were different.'

'Your skill and movement were the same,' admitted Taran, 'but you see, I believed you and he were fighting for your respective souls, and his being a daemon's, is far darker and heavier than yours. Everywhere he stepped, he left an imprint, whereas you never left a mark.'

Above them, the clouds dissipated. Light began to flood across the hilltop, and the body on the floor faded away.

'Is he truly gone?' asked Taran.

Kalas nodded. 'I think so, but let us see for ourselves.'

Taran opened his eyes in the cell. The torches still flickered, and he shivered, soaked in a cold sweat.

Kalas sat looking at him, hope shining from his green eyes. 'Keep alert,' he said. 'We need to make sure. Now, cut me,' he instructed.

Taran stood and drew his dagger. 'How much?'

'If the daemon is gone, then I'd rather it as little as possible!'

Taran leant forward cautiously and lightly drew the dagger across Kalas' bound forearm, then stood watching as beads of blood formed and slowly dripped to the floor. 'What are we waiting for?' he asked.

Kalas looked up. 'The daemon could heal minor wounds instantly,' he replied, 'but, as you can see, the blood flow is slowing on its own. We need to try one more thing. The daemon was dormant for almost fifty years before it was awoken by the taste of blood from another. Cut yourself and place your bloodied blade upon my tongue. If the daemon remains, I'm sure it won't be able to resist!'

Taran winced as he made a small cut, and presented the dagger to Kalas, who licked some of the blood from the flat of the blade.

Moments later, Kalas spat on the floor, and when he looked up, his eyes were moist. 'I truly no longer feel his presence,' he smiled. 'I will never forget the debt I owe you for this.'

Taran called for the guards, then sent them to tell Laska of their success. Maya and Rakan came running at the sound of his voice.

Maya flung herself into Taran's arms, relieved beyond belief that he was unharmed, and they sat down.

Rakan spoke. 'Taran here has told us a wild tale of whom he believes you to be. Even if it is half true, then you have a story unlike any other to tell, so best you talk.'

'Where would you like me to start?' asked Kalas.

Maya smiled. 'Where all stories should start, at the beginning.'

As the woman moved forward, both Tristan and Astren backed away.

Astren wasn't armed, and even if he were, he had no skill with weapons whatsoever. Tristan drew his sword, but he gave ground, knowing his skill was limited.

However, Drizt and Sancen moved forward, noting the confidence with which the woman held herself and the steady look in her eyes.

Drizt had two heavy dirks, one in each hand as he sidestepped nimbly forward, and Sancen drew a short sword and a dagger and circled a table to attack the woman from behind.

However, the woman didn't wait. She leapt onto the table and jumped over Sancen's sweeping sword, her own flashing out in a blistering response, cutting a deep furrow in the desert man's brow, causing him to leap back, shouting in pain, blood flowing freely into his eyes.

The woman moved forward to deliver the killing blow, but Drizt jumped on to the table behind her, and she turned to face the new threat knowing Sancen was out of the fight.

Astren ran to help Sancen, who had dropped his blade and fallen to the floor, and Astren realised the wound was worse than he thought.

Tristan ran forward, shouting to distract the swordswoman, but she kicked out and caught him on the jaw, spilling him to the ground. Now just the woman and Drizt faced one another.

Drizt attacked, and Astren was amazed to see his speed and skill, considering he was an archer, and yet the swordswoman was unfazed by the man's shorter weapons and reach. She blocked every blow with ease while her own flicked out in response, making a dozen small cuts all over Drizt's body and arms. Drizt was fast enough to escape several killing blows, but he couldn't evade them entirely.

Suddenly, the woman's sword came up, meeting one of Drizt's dirks in a ringing blow and knocked it out of his hand, and then, as her dagger caught Drizt's other blade, her sword slashed out toward Drizt's throat.

In an amazing feat of agility, Drizt somersaulted backwards while flinging a small throwing knife at the swordswoman with such incredible speed that she only just managed to parry it, the blade scoring a cut on her shoulder as Drizt landed on the floor.

The woman paused and raised her sword in a mocking salute. 'That's the first time in over fifteen years that I've seen my blood,' she said, 'but it's not enough.' She jumped down, and Astren knew all was lost as Drizt moved back … yet Drizt didn't look concerned.

'You're better with a sword than I could ever hope to be, but that's more than enough. You lose!' said Drizt grimly, as the woman staggered to her knees, her weapons falling to the floor.

She looked up in confusion as Drizt moved forward.

'Salamander poison,' Drizt answered the unspoken question in the woman's eyes. 'Us swamp dwellers never fight fair.' As he walked past, he drove his remaining dirk through the woman's eye into her brain.

Drizt ran over to where Astren was trying to help Sancen, and knelt, looking into the desert man's eyes. 'May you rest in the oasis of your fathers, and forever drink from its cool waters,' he said, pushing the handle of his dirk into the man's trembling hand. Sancen's bloodied eyes held Drizt's for a moment, and there was an almost imperceptible nod, and then they rolled back in his head, and he slowly slid sideways to the floor.

Astren felt tears come to his eyes as he looked down at the warrior, blood pooling on the floor around him.

There was quiet for a moment before Elender began to sob by the battlements.

'I'm sorry,' he cried, 'I had no idea, I thought our nations were going to make peace,' and he raised his hands as if praying.

Astren went across to Tristan and felt for the king's pulse. 'He's just unconscious,' Astren confirmed.

Drizt moved toward Elender, his face as foreboding as thunder. Elender was a big man, gone to fat, yet still half again the size of Drizt, but he cowered away from the smaller man and the darkness in his eyes.

'Us men of the Eyre, we don't make friends outside of our own kind very often,' Drizt said, almost no emotion in his voice, 'but when we do, we would die for the other or kill to avenge them.' He cocked his head to one side, thinking. 'Where are the gates to the fortress wall?' he asked.

Elender, caught out by the question, just shook his head. 'They're g-g-gone,' he stammered.

'Then what use are you,' said Drizt, and quick as a flash, he bent and grabbed Elender's legs, then heaved him up and over the battlements. He looked over the edge and nodded in satisfaction when the man's screams stopped abruptly moments later.

Tristan was moaning as he came around, and Astren helped him to sit up. He looked around at Sancen and then the swordswoman's body, then looked around some more as he gathered his senses. 'Where's Elender?' he asked.

Drizt turned from the battlements. 'Oh,' he said. 'He's down in the courtyard.'

'What the hells is he doing down there?' Tristan demanded, returning quickly to his usual self as he rose unsteadily to his feet.

'He didn't say where the gates were, and I recall you saying Sancen would throw him over the battlements if that were the case. So now he's in the nine hells where he deserves to be.'

Drizt turned away, and Tristan, having seen the pain in his eyes, decided not to push the issue. Instead, he turned to Astren. 'So, not only do we not have any gates, or an army, we now have no fortress commander. How could this get any worse?'

He turned to Drizt, who was standing by the body of Sancen, looking sorrowful. 'Drizt, I need you to get your archers and Sancen's men into the fortress. I want Sancen's men to look after his body and to dispose of that filth,' and he nodded to the woman's body on the floor, 'and the one who tried to fly. Then I want both yours and Sancen's men to take up guard duty throughout this keep.

'Tell the desert soldiers to pick a new commander and have him report to me soonest. If Elender couldn't be trusted, it could be that the rot carries on down through the ranks. I have no idea how we will find out who has turned and who hasn't, but let us hope it stopped with him.

'We have to get this place ready for war. We have maybe three weeks, according to Astren, before the enemy is at our gate. Ye gods,' he sighed, 'where are my damn gates? Now, come on Astren,' he beckoned, moving to one of tables laden with charts and letters and some ornate cabinets. 'Let us see what insight any of this gives us.'

Tristan opened the door to a dark wooden cabinet, ornately carved with falling coins and inside were row upon row of wine bottles.

'Hold on, Drizt!' Tristan called, as the archer moved toward the doorway. He reached down and pulled a bottle out that was already open, then poured some into three goblets that were inside as well, before passing one to Drizt and Astren.

'To Sancen. May you rest in the oasis of your fathers and forever drink from its cool waters,' he said, quoting the ode to the dead of the desert people, as Drizt had done earlier.

They raised their goblets, and when they had finished, Tristan and Astren sat while Drizt walked out of the door, casting a final glance at his dead friend as he went to do Tristan's bidding.

Chapter XXI

Maya, Rakan, Kalas, and Taran sat looking out of the narrow tunnel exit over a beautiful valley, that was now starting to suffer the effects of Daleth's gift. The devastation wasn't as bad as the kingdom lands, being on the fringes, but even so many trees and plants close by showed the signs of withering and decay that would only get worse in time.

The far side of the valley, barely visible, seemed unaffected, but in time, that too would suffer the same fate as the rest.

Maya, Taran, and Rakan were fully outfitted with weapons and supplies, notwithstanding Laska's doubts that they'd stay alive long enough to use them. Kalas sat with them as well, yet despite his escaping the curse of the daemon, Laska had insisted Kalas remain bound until such time as they were all ready to leave. Kalas' armour had been returned, yet his weapons were packed away in a roll of animal skins carried by Rakan.

Laska and his men were further back in the cave with Yana, and there was a heated discussion ongoing, but Taran was too worried about what lay ahead to worry about what lay behind.

Rakan shook his head slowly. 'I find it hard to fathom there is such danger here,' he said. 'We've been sitting here for the best part of the morning, and there's been no movement, no disturbed birds or other wildlife. I don't think that anyone or anything is watching this cave. I don't doubt Laska, and it would be foolish to do so, especially as Taran confirmed he was telling the truth. Yet maybe the giants have died out over the years or have simply given up watching this cave.'

Maya nodded thoughtfully. 'I might agree with you, except you believed that of all the agents who crossed over, only two ever made it back. So I'd suggest that there's danger in these lands whether we can see it or not!'

Rakan shook his head, but not in disagreement. 'You are right,' he said, 'but we can't stay here. Our supplies will only last a week, and nothing will change in that time, especially not Laska's mind. I think our best bet is to wait until sunset, then try to make our crossing under cover of darkness.'

Maya turned to Taran. 'What do you think, my prince?' she asked, loving the way he smiled when she called him that. 'You've been planning something, I can tell.'

Taran looked at Laska. 'Rakan's right. Laska will never change his mind. I know I shouldn't have, but I touched upon his thoughts. He cannot wait to see the back of us, and especially our new friend here.'

Taran turned to Kalas. 'Any observations?' he asked, but Kalas shook his head. Despite his initial happiness at being released from the daemon's control, he'd been quiet ever since, his eyes rarely leaving Yana or Laska, perhaps reflecting on his recent deeds. Taran was tempted to read his thoughts further but had decided against it. Kalas was one of them now, having sworn to join them in their quest; to repay the debt he owed Maya and Taran whilst at the same time seeking to fulfil his oath. Taran would respect his privacy as he would Rakan, Maya, or any other friend.

Taran sighed. 'There's only one way to do this,' he said. 'One of us needs to go and take a closer look inside the treeline to see whether any giants are hiding there. My initial thought was to send Maya, as being our gifted hunter, she can move amongst the trees like a woodland nymph. I'm sure she could spy anything untoward.'

Maya glowed at his compliment.

Taran carried on while looking at her. 'However, if they saw you when you saw them, I fear however graceful or fast, they would kill you without pause. Laska told us all of their terrible speed.

'Then I thought of sending Kalas. His skill with weapons is beyond compare. Yet, even if Kalas prevailed against any he encountered, surely we would not survive as a group against a host of their angry brethren seeking revenge. Lastly, I considered Rakan, for he is the ugliest of us all, and they might sense a kinship and let us through due to an undeniable family bond.'

Rakan spluttered indignantly at this, while Maya's laughter rang out until she covered her mouth with her hand, and even Kalas couldn't help but smile.

'Yet, it has to be me,' finished Taran.

'No! You can't,' Maya exclaimed, grabbing his hand tightly.

Taran smiled reassuringly. 'It makes sense,' he continued. 'Laska advised that the giants communicate using strange sounds. If they're out there, and we have to assume they are, then the only chance for us to make it to the Freestates without leaving a trail of blood, ours and theirs, is to see if I can use my gift to convince them we mean no harm and hope they let us pass. If this doesn't work, then we'll have to carve our way through and likely die in the trying. I told you, Maya, you lead the way with your approach of healing and compassion, and I want to follow that path whenever I can. So, let me go out there alone, let me find and talk to them, and if my head is crushed, it will be all your fault!' Taran stood as he said this, and the others followed suit.

'Let me walk by your side,' argued Maya, a look of fierce determination on her face. 'Let me share the danger as we share the love,' and she clasped Taran's hand firmly in hers, pulling him close.

'You know,' he said quietly, 'I would happily walk through this life with you at my side every step of the way. However, there are times you need to trust in me to go first, for my gift might keep me safe, but it can't always keep us both from harm.'

Taran turned to Rakan and Kalas. Kalas just nodded, but Rakan came over.

'Are you sure?' Rakan asked. 'We can wait until nightfall and try our luck then?' However, he saw that Taran had made up his mind even without receiving an answer, so Rakan smiled and embraced Taran briefly.

'I'll not venture far.' Taran reassured them, 'I will stay clear of the trees and give myself plenty of time to escape should any giants appear.'

Taran's heart beat fast, and with the course of action set, he stepped into the open. The sun high above shone upon him like a beacon.

He couldn't quite believe Laska, and even while the old man's mind showed the truth of the stories, Taran felt sure that Laska's memories were warped by fear and time. There couldn't be actual giants, yet the trees had been cleared away from the cave entrance as if ripped from the ground. It was a good two hundred paces from the cave to the treeline, and Taran took his time ensuring his movements were slow and calm.

He was two-thirds of the way, and there was no sign of any creature, giant or otherwise. The treeline was close enough now to look inside. Surely he would be able to perceive a creature of the size Laska described? Not seeing any danger helped Taran relax, and he breathed a huge sigh of relief.

He looked back over his shoulder and waved to his distant friends, only to see their demeanour change from happiness to shock in the same instant as the ground began to shake beneath his feet.

As he turned around, there, charging from the trees, was a giant, club raised. Taran thought of running, but it moved too fast, and he knew there was no escape.

The giant opened its mouth, letting out a warbling sound as it moved toward Taran like an avalanche. It seemed unstoppable, an incredible force of nature.

He heard Maya and the others shout in the distance but stood his ground, and signalled over his shoulder for the others to stay where they were, hoping they would understand his gesture. He studied the giant as it moved, seeing its rage, and he spread his arms wide away from his weapons. Then, rather than running away, Taran started to walk toward it.

Reaching out with his gift, he tried to read the giant's thoughts and found them to be as clear as any humans. Yet they were so full of hate, and Taran realised even as he tried to communicate, that it wouldn't work, not now, not yet. The giant needed to be in a state where it could listen to more than just its desire for blood.

He knew even as the giant did, of its decision to swing its weapon, a club so large that it would break every bone in his body if it connected. It swung downward, and Taran deftly rolled to the side and back to his feet as the club sank into the stony soil. Dirt flew in all directions from where he'd just been standing.

The giant cried out again, readying its strike, and just as it attacked, Taran rolled between its legs. It tried to adjust its swing but lost balance and spun to the ground so hard that a dust cloud rose into the air. Taran kept his arms outstretched and just walked around as the giant cautiously got to its feet, picking up its club once more.

The giant kicked rocks at him, threw its club at him, grabbed at him, and once even tried to bite him, but each time Taran read not only the giant's mind, but also the move of its body, the drop of its shoulders, or the turn of its feet to avoid harm. After a while the giant was gasping for breath, and while Taran felt like doing the same, he kept his poise.

The giant played its final hand.

It ran forward, arms out wide, and dived, hoping its abnormal reach would stop Taran's escape. Instead, Taran ran forward too, and in the last instant, as it flung itself to the ground, expecting him to dodge left or right or get squashed underneath it, he leapt high onto its shaggy head, and ran down its back, before circling to stand before it.

The giant's uncontrollable gasps for air pulled blades of grass toward its mouth, and Taran could easily have drawn his sword at that moment and driven it through the creature's eye into its brain. Instead, he thought of the approach that Maya would take, and he sat down on the grass just within its reach.

'My name is Taran,' he projected into the creature's mind. 'I have no wish to fight you. This valley is too beautiful to be marred by unneeded death.'

The giant's eyes narrowed as it heard Taran's message. 'It is your kind that brings death!' it thought instinctively in response, and memories of another time flashed through its mind, of soldiers killing one of their young so far back, as to be decades ago.

'That was not me nor my friends,' Taran thought. 'Do you judge everyone not of your kind as an enemy?'

The giant's eyes fixed on Taran's sword. 'Everyone who carries such a thing who tries to pass through our lands also tries to kill us as well. You bring tools of death, and you wonder why you are met with the same?'

Taran's head whirred, but he realised the giant must be referring to Laska's foray all those years past, and then of the agents who had tried to pass this way over the years; fighting to the last in mostly futile gestures against these massive creatures. He sighed in his mind, then unbuckled his sword belt. He rose and slowly walked toward the giant, which raised itself to a sitting position. Taran looked the giant in the eye then lay his sword at its feet before taking a step backwards.

'I would not bring death to your lands,' Taran stated sincerely. 'Instead, I would bring friendship, and yet more importantly, as I look at your valley and the disease that is starting to affect it, I would rather bring life as well. Let me have my ...' and Taran searched for the word he should use, '... my wife, join us.'

'Only her,' the giant responded, before adding. 'Can she jump around like you?'

Taran nodded. 'She can do that, but she can do so much more if only you'll allow it. May I go to her?' he asked, and the giant pondered. Taran could read its thoughts as it mulled over letting him go. The giant decided it wouldn't be able to catch him one way or another, so it nodded.

Taran stood and moved away from the giant, and as he drew closer to the cave mouth, Maya ran from it to throw herself into his arms then covered his face with kisses.

Rakan stood back, grinning from ear to ear. 'Well done, lad,' he said. 'I don't mind telling you my heart was in my mouth.'

Taran walked into the cave and briefly explained to everyone that he would take Maya to prove their peaceful intent since memories of man's incursions had left behind a hatred that had to be overcome.

So, Taran took Maya's hand and led her into the sun, walking slowly down the hill.

As they approached the giant, Taran could feel that its distrust had returned full force, and it was contemplating whether to attack again.

Taran knew he could easily dodge any assault, but he also knew Maya would have no such chance. He turned and kissed her gently on the lips. 'Stay here and work your magic but don't come any closer. Let everyone see the power of your gift.'

With that, he continued walking down the hill, arms open as he projected his thoughts to the giant. 'Behold, my big friend. See the truth with your own eyes and know that whereas those who came before had neither good intent nor heart, we are as different to them as fire is to water.'

He turned a little but kept the giant in the periphery of his vision. He could feel it wavering between attacking, while he seemed distracted, or seeing if there was some truth to his claim, when its thoughts turned to disbelief.

Taran looked back fully at Maya. She walked back and forth across the hillside, and all the while, her hands softly brushed the withered grass. Occasionally she would pause and bend down to smell a dying flower, only to rise and resume her meandering path. Taran felt enchanted by her movement. She had an animal grace and light as a fawn, she trod softly, carefully, and behind her, the land blossomed. Taran had seen it so many times before now, and yet every time was like the first. He felt a thrill pass through his veins as she shone lightly, not just from the sun, but from an inner light. He'd wanted her to stay further away, but Maya made her way down the hill until she stood beside him, then her hand slipped into his as they turned to face the giant together.

The giant's thoughts were so confused that it was hard to discern its intent, but then it lifted its head, and that strange noise emanated from its throat. Suddenly, from the trees strode a dozen other giants all bearing clubs or staffs. Remarkably they must have been there the whole time, and within moments they were surrounded.

Taran felt Maya's hand grip his tightly in worry, but he turned to her and smiled.

'Fear not,' he said, and knelt, only to take her hand and kiss it. As he did so, the giants also knelt and touched their foreheads to the green grass in homage.

'It is not just me who worships you,' Taran said with a smile as he stood. 'Now we need to get our friends, for they want us to meet the Elder of their clan, the oldest giant of them all. Wait here a while,' he continued, 'they mean you no harm at all, and that will extend to all who travel with you. So let me get the others,' and then Taran made his way up the hill for the final time.

As he entered the cave, he saw that Rakan was ready to go, while Kalas, who'd been freed, was now gathering his equipment. Yana was also there and had a pack on her back.

Taran raised an eyebrow in a silent question.

'I'm coming with you, Taran heart-stealer,' she said. 'It's decided, so don't even think to argue,' and she brushed past him to head outside.

Rakan followed while Kalas made himself busy. 'I'll be with you in just a moment,' Kalas said.

Taran turned back into the sunlight, his pack over his shoulder and Maya's pack in his hand, then headed down the hill to catch up with Rakan and Yana.

In the cave, Kalas walked further into the gloom and stood before Laska.

Laska waved his guards away and met Kalas' gaze.

'Will you please forgive me, father, after all these years?' Kalas asked, shaking with suppressed emotion.

Laska looked unsteadily back at him, torment in his eyes. Then, after a short silence, he slowly shook his head as the expression on his face hardened. 'My sons died years ago, both of them!' he choked, and turned along with his guards, walking back into the tunnels.

Kalas strode out of the cave toward his destiny, heart broken afresh.

Astren shook his head, and Tristan looked up at the movement and raised an eyebrow, not bothering to speak. They were both in the erstwhile commander's quarters, poring over papers, maps, and charts.

'It seems Anthain almost won Daleth's war for him before it even started,' Astren sighed. 'This letter to Elender introduces the holder as a peace and trade emissary from Daleth. That one advises that new gates will soon arrive, and to remove the old ones in readiness. Another instructs that half the garrison be disbanded and for Elender to keep the excess payroll as a token of appreciation. It goes on and on.

'Anthain's betrayal has been long forged,' Astren continued. 'We can now be sure he never sought to raise men to defend this fortress, and who knows where the gold went. I think in light of this, we should immediately seek help from our neighbour states, for he will have misled them just like Elender. We should also send riders to the Eyre and the desert tribes. We can request military aid, but even if they don't send it, they will be forewarned, for Daleth's conquest won't stop with us.'

Astren looked thoughtful. 'Is it worth sending riders to the Horselords as well? Next to the Eyre, they're our nearest neighbours and have a fearsome reputation,' he asked.

Tristan shook his head. 'There's a reason we've paid them a tithe for time immemorial to leave us alone. Imagine if they took advantage of the situation. No, one enemy horde is enough to consider facing for now. Not forgetting they'll simply kill any outsiders on sight, emissaries or not.'

Tristan turned to an Eyre guard who stood at the door opposite his desert spearman counterpart. 'Send for Drizt,' he ordered, and the man hurried off.

Tristan started putting quill to parchment, and Astren leaned over to see him write requests for help from the other Freestates leaders, offering gold, tax exemptions, and more, in return for men to help with the defense of the fortress.

Tristan looked at Astren, answering his unspoken question. 'I know you can spirit travel to them, but they will give no credence to you unless a written order from me first sits in their hands.'

Drizt walked in shortly after that and looked over the letters.

Tristan took them back, rolled them up and sealed them with wax before imprinting them with the royal ring. 'I need you to select trustworthy men to take these messages. With good fortune, we might get a little help from our neighbour states in time,' ordered Tristan.

'Why have you offered to reward them for helping defend their own lands?' asked Drizt quizzically. 'If we fail here, they lose everything. Surely they will send what troops they have anyway because of the impending invasion?'

Tristan sighed. 'You might think so. But our strength, in this case, is our weakness. No Freestates leader will act in haste unless he sees a profit, and in fairness, each state only has a small city garrison to keep public order.'

'Is everything about money with you people?' asked Drizt. 'What about loyalty to king and country, a sense of duty or honour?'

Astren chuckled. 'All those things mean little to the citizens of the Freestates. Our god is money, and everything else is secondary. The other lords might well refuse our king, but they are less likely to refuse their god.'

Drizt called in one of his men and gave him the written orders, instructed him on what to do, then sent him on his way. 'Riders will leave before the midday sun,' he said, turning to Tristan, who nodded in acknowledgement.

Astren cleared his throat, and Drizt turned toward him. 'We need your help in taking stock of our stores here. Can you assign some of your men to do so?'

Drizt nodded. 'They're bored, so giving them things to do will ease that. By the way, the desert tribesmen have almost finished nominating their new commander. As soon as they're done with the ritual, I'll have him sent up.'

'What ritual is that?' asked Astren in interest. 'How do they choose?'

Drizt shook his head before replying. 'Those who wish to take command have to face the sting of the scorpion. The one who takes the most stings and lives will be the new commander. The ones who fail will not need to apply for the role.'

A soldier from the garrison was shown in, and he bowed to Tristan.

'My king,' he said, 'I hear you're interested in the whereabouts of the gates to the fortress wall and the keep itself.'

'What's your name, and tell me what you know,' demanded Tristan, getting up to look the man in the eye. 'Speak freely and fear not the nature of your answer.'

The man shifted his feet nervously. 'My king, I am Galain, sergeant of this garrison and second in command to Lord Elender before his,' and he paused, searching for the right words.

Drizt chimed in. 'Before his fall from grace.'

Astren sighed but also smiled ruefully. Even the death of Sanœn couldn't keep Drizt's good humour entirely subdued.

'Yes, yes, before his fall from grace,' Galain continued. 'I also lead the engineers and carpenters here.' He coughed before continuing. 'Lord Elender ordered my men and I to take the gates down about two months ago, saying we'd get replacements shortly after. We were to take down the gates in walls two and three as well, but we hadn't got around to it yet.'

'Thank the gods you didn't,' said Tristan.

'But, why my king, if you don't mind me asking? Lord Elender said trade was soon to resume!'

'Galain,' said Astren interjecting. 'Does every soldier in this garrison believe we are at peace, and war has been averted?'

Galain nodded. 'Yes, sir. Lord Elender told us himself just before he sent five hundred of our lads home a few months back, saying they wouldn't be needed in a time of peace. But that's right, isn't it, sir?' he asked, his voice rising as he asked the question.

'Galain, I have a task for you,' said Tristan.

Galain stood tall. 'But of course, my king. What is your wish?'

Tristan looked through the window at the sun in the sky before saying, 'I would like to address the garrison troops. Organise this for tomorrow morning, first light. Have them ready in the courtyard.'

Galain saluted and started to turn away.

'Wait,' said Tristan, 'I almost forgot, what happened to the gates? Where are they, and can we get them put back up?'

'Excuse me, my king,' Galain replied, 'but they're right in front of you and all around you.'

'I don't want riddles!' snapped Tristan.

Galain hurriedly carried on. 'The table you're sitting at, the wooden panelling on all the walls, in the corridors. The furniture throughout these rooms. The boys and I did a great job, didn't we; we are craftsmen.'

'Oh my,' said Astren, and pushed away the piles of paper on the huge table that they sat around. He followed Tristan's gaze as he looked around the walls, gloriously polished and buffed to a sheen, then finally to the exquisitely carved cupboards that housed the wine and more.

Tristan sighed. 'A craftsman you are, Galain, a craftsman you indeed are. I don't suppose you could undo this amazing work and turn tables, chairs, and panelling, back into gates by any chance?'

Galain laughed, then pulled himself together and stood to attention as he remembered who he addressed. 'My king, I'm a craftsman, not a mage. I think we will need to wait until the new gates arrive, then we'll put them up, especially as you're burning some of the pieces in your fire yonder.'

Tristan sighed. 'I'm now burning my gates, wonderful. You're dismissed. Get the men ready for me. I'll be down shortly.'

Drizt wandered over to the fire. 'Sancen wouldn't have been able to stop laughing over this,' he said with a half-smile, warming his hands over the burning gates. But as he spoke, his voice broke slightly, and Astren saw the sheen in his eyes.

'Right,' said Tristan softly. 'Let's find out who the new commander of the sand dwellers is. We have maybe fourteen days to get new gates, get more men, get the men we have ready, ensure we have enough stores, have our catapults ready for action, create a field hospital, and so much more. Then we have to face an army of a hundred thousand bloodthirsty men, and a Witch-King intent on killing us all, enslaving the Freestates and likely everything beyond.'

'Thankfully, when you put it like that,' said Drizt, 'it sounds so easy!' But even this attempt at levity didn't lift the mood, as they each contemplated the daunting tasks before them.

'This feels like a strange dream,' muttered Rakan, to Kalas and Yana. They passed the time talking amongst themselves, while Taran and Maya communicated with the Elder giant.

'This must be how ants feel when they see us walking by,' added Yana, as she looked around feeling dwarfed by everything, and the other two nodded.

It had taken them a day to reach the Elder giant who awaited them at the centre of the valley, and along the way, they'd seen many giants who'd called out in their strange haunting tongue, to be answered by their escorts in similar kind.

It transpired the giants didn't have a village or a town, as they lived apart from one another for the most as shepherds, and only came to

382

this meeting place to choose a mate, to celebrate the birth of a new giantlet, or for other matters that required serious discussion.

Now, as they all sat waiting, Rakan looked up. The giants had woven the trees here into a canopy that provided shelter, and it was as if they sat under a living roof of twisted beams covered in leaves and alive with animals. Yet, there were signs of disease here, with some flora turning a sickly green, and leaves fell slowly like gentle rain. Even here, far from Daleth, the land succumbed to his life-draining force.

The Elder giant sat cross-legged some distance away, and before him sat Maya and Taran. It was strange to watch, not only because of the difference in size, for it all looked out of perspective, but because whilst they were deep in conversation, no words were being spoken.

Yana turned to Rakan. 'Don't you feel uncomfortable knowing that Taran can read your mind at any time?'

Rakan smiled at her. 'No, girl. Taran reassured me long ago that those he views as friends or companions can feel safe in the knowledge that he will never look unbidden into their thoughts. He's an honest lad. Imagine the advantage he could have taken with his gift throughout his lifetime, the riches he might have accrued, the power. Yet instead, he chose a life far less glamorous.'

'He is rather special,' sighed Yana, her eyes taking on a faraway look. 'Imagine being in the arms of someone who knew exactly what you wanted and was able to give it to you without being asked. Maybe I should invite him to look into my mind.'

Rakan looked hard at her then. 'Listen. Taran is like a son to me, and he loves Maya with a rare passion that anyone can see, and that love is reciprocated. I like you well enough, Yana, but make no mistake, if you do something, anything to interfere with what they have, you will have me to answer to!' As he said this, his hand went to the hilt of his dagger, eyes narrowing.

Yana flinched away, shock in her eyes at the ferocity of Rakan's words.

'I would like to add,' said Kalas, and both Yana and Rakan looked to him, 'that I couldn't agree more with Rakan's words. Interfering with true love is not something that should ever be condoned, so on that, we agree, and I ask you to heed his warning.'

Rakan nodded his gratitude at Kalas, yet the eyes that looked back at him were unexpectedly cold.

'However, let me give you fair warning, Rakan. If Yana suffers by your hand or any others, then it shall be answered with death.'

Both Yana and Rakan looked at him in surprise then.

Kalas lowered his eyes for a moment then looked directly at Yana. 'I wondered why I didn't kill you all back in the glade when you kicked me. Then when I found out who you were, it all made sense. You see, Laska is my father, even though to this day he refuses to forgive me for what he sees as a betrayal, leaving my ancestral home when I was young to join the king's guard, and that, of course, makes you my niece, blood of my blood. Somehow deep inside, I recognised this, and it stayed my hand.'

Rakan's eyes opened wide in shock, but this was nothing compared to Yana's as she looked closely at Kalas' face.

'How did I not see it?' she said in a whisper. 'My father died when I was young, yet you are so similar, and there was something about you when I first saw you too.' Yana threw her arms around Kalas' neck, and surprised, he slowly held her too. Yana sighed. 'We have a lot of catching up to do. I have so many questions to ask about my father, your brother. My grandfather didn't talk of him much as it brought him too much pain, and he never once talked of you, I'm sorry to say, yet I knew there was a sad secret that constantly ailed him.'

Yana smiled. 'Will you forgive me for kicking you so hard?' she laughed.

Kalas nodded. 'But only on one condition.'

'What's that?' she asked.

Kalas' demeanour turned serious. 'Don't interfere with what they have,' he said, indicating Taran and Maya. 'For if that happens, I'll let Rakan kill you. The problem is I'd then have to kill Rakan, and I'm pretty sure killing the father of the man who gave me back control of my soul, will condemn it back to the nine hells that he might have saved it from.'

Yana looked over at Taran and Maya, and back to Rakan and Kalas, then nodded.

Kalas and Rakan seemed satisfied, for the mood lifted, and they started talking together again as if the matter had been resolved.

But even as they relaxed, Yana smiled inside. Men could sometimes be so gullible, and they hadn't even asked her to make an oath. There would be plenty of time to make Taran hers; she just had to be subtler from hereon. Satisfied with her train of thought, she excused herself from the conversation, lay back, closed her eyes and let her thoughts run wild.

'Men, I stand before you as your king,' said Tristan, raising his voice so that the assembled soldiers could hear.

He knew he wasn't an imposing figure, being neither tall, nor broad, or even handsome, but he was a relatively confident speaker, and the words flowed from his lips without pause.

'Today, I am here to tell you the truth that was withheld from you by the treachery of Elender and the machinations of Daleth the Witch-King. War is coming! We few, are all that stand between the Freestates and the invading horde of the Witch-King. We number a mere fifteen hundred men, and they, one hundred thousand. Yet what does that matter, when the glory we earn will be remembered forever! They will be upon us within a month, and in that time, we shall make ready; sharpen our swords, burnish our shields and straighten our spears!'

He raised his voice loudly at the end as well as his sword, then brandished it in the air expecting cheers from the men before him, but they shifted nervously, murmuring amongst themselves.

Drizt, who was standing with Astren several steps behind Tristan, murmured under his breath. 'A short speech and to the point, but I don't think he hit the right chord. Mentioning one hundred thousand enemy soldiers wasn't perhaps the best piece of intelligence to divulge.'

'It would have been intelligent not to use this intelligence,' offered Astren.

Drizt chuckled. 'Indeed, my friend, indeed. But now the damage is done, I fear.'

Tristan paused, wondering what to do. He slowly lowered his sword, and one of the men stepped forward, shuffling his feet.

'My king,' he said. 'Of course we're all ready to fight for you, but we're more used to keeping the traders in line and levying taxes than fighting ... how did you put it, an invading horde?'

Tristan's face grew red, but he tried again. 'You men are the finest soldiers of the Freestates first and foremost. You have trained for this; you have been waiting for this moment your whole lives to give it true meaning, to sacrifice yourself, to give your lives for the greater good.'

'Oh by all the gods,' muttered Drizt, 'if he says any more like this, there won't be a garrison soldier left by dawn.'

He strode forward.

'My king,' he called, as Tristan was just about to say something else, and Tristan spluttered to a halt as Drizt continued walking past him.

'My friends, my brothers,' he said, opening his arms as if embracing the men before him, and the muttering stopped for a moment. 'I stand before you small, green, and perhaps rather ugly,' and the men before him laughed at his self-depreciation. 'I don't stand before you as a king, but rather as a soldier like yourselves, and I stand steady. We've just heard the king tell us of a little bit of trouble on the horizon, and I am here to tell you that it will take more than a few thousand unwashed westerners to take a fortress like this one.'

'A few thousand!' shouted one of the soldiers. 'There's a hundred thousand of 'em, and unwashed or not, that's too many, I tell you!' and around him, men started to nod.

Drizt put his hand on his hips and laughed, trying to think quickly of a way to mitigate Tristan's mistake in divulging the enemy numbers. The only way, he decided, was to bluff.

'You,' he said, pointing at the spokesman of the group. 'You look like a fine soldier with a strong sword arm and mind. Tell me, how many men can a fortress like this defend against. Cast your mind back to your training days. What did they tell you?'

The man puffed his chest out at this compliment and turned to whisper amongst a few of his friends. 'We can defend up to ten times our number,' he called out, 'ten times!'

Drizt clapped his hands and threw a salute at the man. 'There you have it, from the very mouth of experience standing amongst you all. We have nearly fifteen hundred men and the Witch-King just a hundred thousand. Even a thick green skin like me knows that's not ten times as many as we have. We will not only hold them … we will destroy them!'

The soldier counted on his fingers, looking perplexed, but not wanting to appear stupid, he shouted. 'By the gods, he's right!'

'But at what cost?' cried another. 'What do we stand to lose? It's all well and good defeating them, but I don't want to be one of the dead at the end of it!'

'At what cost?' shouted Drizt, calling the men's attention back to him. 'I, for one, am glad you mentioned that. You're right, men will die, but …' and with this, he turned and swept his arm toward Tristan, 'your king has put forward a war bounty of ten thousand gold coins for those who survive this fight. You asked at what cost, but I ask you what do you stand to gain? When you stand victorious, the riches you will have will mean you can retire as rich as the king himself, and if some die, then there's more left for the rest!

'Forget honour, forget glory, forget your country, but whatever you do, don't forget the gold! For gold!' he shouted, raising his bow above his head.

'For gold!' the men shouted back, lifting their swords, cheering. Drizt turned away and walked past Tristan.

'What have you just done?' Tristan muttered out the corner of his mouth. 'I can't afford to pay that!'

Drizt stopped for a moment. 'You can't afford not to. If I hadn't done that, every one of them would have deserted by tomorrow daybreak. Now, I bet they'll all stay. You are the one who educated me that the people of the Freestates worship gold, so now you are their god from whom the riches fall.'

Tristan raised his sword again. 'For gold!' he shouted, and the men raised theirs back in salute.

Taran had sat with Maya for most of the day. They were both tired, and they leaned toward one another. Taran had his arm around Maya as he rested his head lightly on hers.

The discussion that had begun at dawn with the Elder giant had given Taran a pounding headache, for he'd never used his gift for such an extended period, nor in such a way. He'd opened his thoughts to both Maya and the Elder at the same time, because it was the only way to communicate efficiently and without hidden intent.

The conversation had paused now, and the Elder warbled away with the other giants in attendance. It was a strange sound, mournful almost, and fitted these giant creatures perfectly.

Taran moaned slightly in discomfort. In response, Maya's hand rose to knead the knotted muscles of his shoulders, and he relaxed as she used her touch to ease his pain. He could quickly have fallen asleep but resisted the temptation. Instead, he closed his eyes and thought back to the morning's conversation, and wondered how the others would react to the decision that he and Maya had reached.

When they'd first sat down, the giant had wanted to know who they were, what was happening in the outside world of men, and how they came to be seeking passage across the valley. Taran, and Maya through him, had told the Elder everything they knew, as it sat there unmoving, considering their words.

Afterwards, Taran had asked the Elder his name and how they came to be here, hidden from the eyes of normal men.

It transpired that the giants referred to each other as treekin, and it was the intonation of the greeting that identified them as individuals. As to the story of the giants' origins, it was incredible. If Taran hadn't experienced recent events that had challenged his view of the world and what was possible, he would have dismissed it as utter fantasy.

The Elder had explained that many hundreds of years ago, when humankind first came to the western shores of this land, there were those who'd started to change, altered by the capricious gods.

Some became faster or stronger, some could talk with their minds, and some like him and his kin grew far larger. Most of those with gifts could walk amongst others and go unnoticed, but not those who showed signs of becoming a giant. They were feared and cast out, and over the years, those giants who lived long enough came together and decided to find a new home.

The land of men would not have them, and while the Forelom mountains proved impossible to ascend for a normal man, the giants searched for and found in the high mountains a means to escape persecution. They had come across this beautiful valley hundreds of years ago, cut-off from the outside world, and had worked to make it their own.

Taran had looked at the giant before him and those around him somewhat differently then, recognising that despite their difference in size, they were gifted, had also fled for their lives, and were in many ways just like him.

However, the power of normal speech was denied them, and the giant explained that those who were gifted were also cursed. The giants were given prodigious size and strength, and their lifespan was many hundreds of years, yet their curse was losing the power of normal speech as they grew and also infertility. For a mated pair to conceive was so incredibly rare that their population had hardly grown from when this valley first became home.

Sadly, the last giantlet to be born had been slaughtered many years before by the soldiers of man, and they were still in shock half a century later: thus, all subsequent incursions had been met with death to protect their way of life.

Taran had questioned the Elder giant then, about those who were gifted being cursed, and the giant looked at him for a long time before answering.

'Everyone who is gifted, young Taran, is also cursed. Mark my words. Look to your chosen beside you. When she uses her gift to heal others, she ages herself. This Daleth, the Witch-King, as you call him, lives for hundreds of years, yet has no heirs and likely suffers from being unable to sire children. Kalas, your new comrade, would seem to have been gifted with extraordinary speed and skill, but was then possessed by a daemon.'

Taran had smiled at the giant before him. 'But I am the counterpoint to your argument,' he'd said, 'for I am gifted,' and he'd held Maya close, 'and gifted more than once, and I do not feel cursed in the least.'

The giant looked solemn then. 'Taran, so it has always been, thus it will always be. Just because you don't feel cursed doesn't mean that you aren't. In time you will come to know the price you will pay for the gift you have been bestowed.'

The conversation had moved on then, for the Elder, having understood that the malaise of the land and people were down to Daleth, wanted to know what Taran and Maya could do to help.

Maya had spoken through Taran in answer to this. She'd offered to spend time healing the valley, restoring its life, before they sought refuge beyond in the Freestates.

The Elder looked thoughtful as he replied. 'We will gladly accept your offer and then assist in the safe passage of you and your friends across the valley. You will have our eternal friendship as well, for it has been too long since we've had cause to welcome others to our lands who bring life and love,' and he'd smiled at the two of them sitting before him.

'Yet my concern is more what happens to the world outside or even in this valley when you die Maya, for die you will, one day, even as we do. Will the magic of healing you've wrought upon our valley and other lands unravel? Will the Witch-King live until the day the whole world has given him it's last breath for him to perish last of all?

'You say you are escaping from Daleth's clutches to a kingdom which may fall against the power of this man and his armies. If that transpires, it seems likely he will continue hunting you; thus, you will spend the rest of whatever days you have left running. Don't you wish to have the chance to live your lives together, to feel the blessing of true love every single day, to have children, and to know complete fulfilment in peace and tranquillity?'

Maya had looked at Taran then, her eyes shining. 'I would love all of that,' she'd said, and her eyes dropped as she'd sighed then repeated the words, 'children together.'

Taran's heart had never been happier, and he'd held Maya close. Everyone had looked over then as their love made her shine, and all around them, small flowers had grown and bloomed.

'To this end,' the Elder had said, 'I believe that to have any degree of certainty in your future, you will need to fight to make your dreams a reality. For the sake of this world, for everyone, this Daleth must be opposed, and he must be stopped. If he is not defeated, then the alternative is death to everyone and everything!'

Maya and Taran had considered the words.

'I'd hoped we could put the fighting behind us now we had escaped. But the Elder is right, nowhere is safe until Daleth is defeated,' Taran had agreed reluctantly.

Maya had nodded. 'We must do what we can to aid the Freestates, and we must meet with Astren and offer our help, and hopefully, that of our friends as well if they agree with us. But I'm frightened, my love, for you, for me, for our friends, but I fear even more what will happen if we don't do anything.'

At this stage, the conversation had ended while the Elder had started to communicate with his treekin.

Taran's musing was interrupted as he realised that the Elder was now calling to him, and his eyes snapped open, bringing him back to the present.

'We have agreed, young Taran, that your party can rest here for two days while Maya works her healing upon our lands. Thereafter we will show you to the passage leading to the lands you know as the Freestates, and to your destiny.'

'My kin are so insular, yet I had hoped some might be willing to assist you. Sadly, I've been unable to persuade any, and I feel lessened by this, for if you are willing to risk yourselves in this endeavour, then we should be offering our help as well. Thus, in the absence of others, on my people's behalf, I will travel shortly hereafter to join you in your fight.

'The land of men will once again see a giant amongst them!'

Chapter XXII

Astren looked around him and not for the first time wished he were far away in Freemantle or indeed further still. It had been a week since their arrival, and time was against them. The Witch-King's army was only two weeks or less away, and despite Drizt's rallying speech, morale was low.

The lack of gates in the first wall was proving to be their biggest worry.

Trom, the new commander of the desert spearmen, had come up with a simple solution to take the gates from the third wall to fit them to the first. Unfortunately, it transpired that they were too small and it would be weeks before suitable timbers arrived to make a replacement. Astren had suggested using the trees in the forest beyond the pass entrance, and everyone's hopes had risen at this simple solution. These hopes were dashed when Galain explained that only Sandalwood and Mornal trees grew in the shallow rocky soil close to the mountains. Sadly, these beautiful trees were useless, for they warped when cut and were extremely flammable.

So, now they had a team of unskilled soldiers trying to carve blocks of stone from the mountainside to fill the gate tunnel, yet this was also proving ineffective. The opening was so high and wide and the rock of the mountains so hard that tools were breaking faster than they could be repaired. They also lacked the necessary tackle and pulleys to try and remove blocks of stone from other walls, and this major weakness in their first line of defense was a cause of consternation.

As Astren walked around, surrounded by activity, he moved down to the gatehouse. Outside of the walls, a hundred spearmen stood guard and took shifts with their fellows to ensure a ready defense until the breach was closed. Likewise, above on the wall, a hundred Eyre archers were now stationed, but they seemed few and far between along its length.

As Trom had explained, even if Daleth's main army was weeks away, he still had forces in his garrison who might seek to strike early to take advantage.

The other concern was that out of the six defensive siege engines; not one was in working order. Galain's engineers swarmed over them, trying to make repairs, but the timbers had split after being exposed to the elements for so long. They had already taken several apart and were soaking the timbers in leaf oil, hoping that some flexibility might return to the wood, which would otherwise splinter if put under immense stress.

Overall, suitable timber was the main problem in this area dominated by the mountains, and everything had historically been brought in from far afield.

Drizt, on investigating the storerooms below the keep, had found tens of thousands of arrows and had whooped with joy until he realised every single one of them was warped and beyond use. Thus the only current usable arrows were those he and his men carried in their quivers - twenty per man.

Therefore, when off the walls, his men whittled new shafts from any useable timber they could find, from storeroom doors to wagons, attaching the heads and flights of the old arrows to create new ones. Worryingly, as Drizt put it, his men were making about fifty arrows each a day, yet could loose that amount in the time it took to draw twice as many breaths. He needed more, or his men would be throwing stones over the walls after the first few days.

So little hope, Astren thought. Fifty years ago, when it had first been built, fully manned and stocked, there had been some doubt as to whether it could stop the Witch-King before it transpired his army had suffered catastrophic losses. Now, here they were with a fraction of the men and everything in disrepair. They needed divine intervention, or things would go from bad to worse very quickly.

Yet despite all of this, he still felt excited, for he would soon meet Maya and her friends. The previous night had seen her successfully communicate with him for the first time, and he'd been astounded to hear that she was not only in the Freestates, but would be with them on the morrow. She'd told a tale of having found passage through a valley of giants, creatures long gone from the land of men and into folklore. He still found it hard to believe and couldn't fathom why she would embellish an already incredible tale.

The sun was setting, and shadows hastened across the valley as he turned toward the keep and a meeting with Tristan, Drizt and Trom.

When he'd arisen in the morning and tried to explain this exciting news to Tristan, he'd been waved away over such an inconsequential piece of information. But now, at the end of every day, they came together to report on the fortress's progress toward readiness, and he would raise it again.

Astren climbed the many stairs to the top floor of the keep, now taken over by Tristan, and had to admit to himself; he was a little unhappy. The chambers there were many, richly appointed but empty save for the treasures Elender had collected, so Tristan could easily have let Astren, Drizt, or Trom take a room and still had privacy. Yet, the only people to share the floor at night were the guards at the top of the stairs.

Astren and the others slept in the cold halls and rooms below, along with the garrison soldiers, archers and spearmen. Sometimes Astren saw goodness in Tristan, yet abject greed and the promotion of oneself was the Freestates way of life. It was hypocritical to judge Tristan harshly while he followed the same tenets, but still, he questioned his choice of someone he might call a friend.

No, he thought, Tristan is a friend only when he needs me, and my king when he doesn't. Even Tristan's presence here near harm's way wasn't for the sake of the people; it was to protect his position and wealth.

Astren nodded to the guards and was walking down the plush carpet hallway when he realised something was different. He paused, and then his eyes opened in surprise, for the statues that had depicted Elender had been meticulously reworked to look like Tristan by an artist's hand.

Astren shook his head as he continued down the hall. To have Galain waste time on this instead of putting more work into the siege engines or other defensive measures was the height of vanity.

He opened the door to the large chamber where they had first come across Elender, and where Drizt, Trom and Tristan all sat drinking wine from the seemingly inexhaustible supply they had inherited. Astren sat down and poured himself a goblet of wine, then listened to the reports and resulting discussion, waiting for his time.

'So,' said Tristan, to Astren. 'Did you spirit walk last night, and can you tell us how long before Daleth arrives at our gates?'

Astren nodded. 'It seems he's been delayed. Even though we've enjoyed good weather here, the same cannot be said for his army. The last few days have seen them struggling through mud which has slowed his advance. Fourteen days at the outside, maybe less if he pushes his men to make up the time, yet I think he is too canny a commander to unnecessarily tire his troops.

'I've also organised a field hospital for the casualties we will inevitably suffer, yet there are only two men trained as basic healers. I'll send for physicians and apothecaries as well, but I suggest we have another dozen men trained to help in this regard.'

Tristan sighed. 'Fine. The men need to know they will be cared for if badly injured. Yet none of them will have time to recover if we don't hold the walls, for I fear they'll be killed in their beds.'

'We need men assigned as stretcher-bearers,' said Drizt, snapping his fingers. 'There is so much we don't know, and every day something new comes up. We can't have people trip over the corpses of their friends or be distracted by the screams of the injured ones. We need to assign maybe fifty of our soldiers to this role.'

'So, let me get this straight,' interrupted Tristan. 'We have around fifteen hundred men, and from what we've discussed this night, we need fifty as stretcher-bearers and a dozen assigned as healers. We also need soldiers to carry water, cook food, and stand watch at night. Why do I also get the feeling we've still missed a lot out, and things are only going to get more demanding!'

Trom shook his head. 'In the desert, it's easier. We march, we fight. If we win, we come home and eat, and then make more children to replace those who die.'

'In the swamps, we make more children before we go to battle, just in case we die and miss out on all the fun,' said Drizt, winking.

Trom looked across at Drizt, a smile slowly forming on his face. 'Your way is much better,' he said, 'much, much better.'

Tristan sighed. 'Anything else, or can we finish here? I'm tired and hungry, and hearing about your mating rituals isn't what I had in mind.'

Astren cleared his throat. 'I have some good news,' he said, drawing everyone's attention. 'At noon tomorrow, we will be joined by five ...' and he sought for the best way to describe them, '... five new recruits.'

'Are these recruits the fugitives you tried to tell me about earlier?' Tristan asked. Astren nodded. 'Fine, tell us quickly why we should be bothered and let me get some food in my stomach.'

Astren spent the next glass of wine telling them all he knew and had garnered. By the end of it, the others were leaning forward intently.

Drizt spoke first. 'So much of what you say sounds beyond belief, yet this woman's gift is incredibly valuable if what you say is even half true, and I have no reason to doubt you. However, the part about the giants is laughable and almost undermines her story's credibility, even if it makes an entertaining addition. But what worries me is those who travel with her.'

Astren looked across. 'I don't see a problem,' he stated.

'She's travelling with a knight who claims to be from a kingdom long dead who should be in his seventies by now, so that doesn't sound right. Then there are the two deserters from Daleth's army, and the kin of a lord from within his kingdom,' Drizt explained.

Tristan nodded slowly. 'This does warrant further discussion. However, first things first. When they arrive, we will meet them and see if this Maya's gift is everything Astren and she claim it to be. Now, Astren, you are dismissed, and you two,' he said, turning to Drizt and Trom, 'should stay for one more drink.'

With that, Astren rose and bowed before heading out into the hallway again. His stomach rumbled. Time for some of the gruel they served in the barrack's kitchens, he thought, and as he walked down the carpeted hallway, all of Tristan's statues stared mockingly back at him.

The last week had been the happiest Maya could remember for a long time, and it had everything to do with Taran, who walked at her side.

No, she corrected herself, it wasn't just these last days of safety, first in the giant's valley, and then as they entered the Freestates, it had been every moment from when she'd first started to know Taran better, first as his captive all that time ago, and every moment after as they ran for their lives.

While during that time, Maya had never been more frightened, she'd also felt more alive than ever before. It was as if her every sense became heightened, and as Taran ran with her, the excitement she'd felt as her blood rushed through her veins had eclipsed everything else.

Then as they'd grown closer, Taran had found a way of touching her heart and soul, let alone her body, that made her shine. By return, Maya found a desire she'd never known before; to prioritise someone else, to make them happy, and this had grown to a point whereby she realised that she was no longer the centre of her life, Taran was.

Having seen her parents together, she knew what love looked like, and yet this seemed to be beyond and above what she'd ever witnessed, and the way he helped bring out her gift with his love was beyond words.

After their meeting with the Elder, Taran had accompanied her as the giants bore them around the valley on their massive shoulders. Maya had been terrified at first, yet hearing Taran's infectious laughter, and him sharing the merriment of the giants' thoughts, had allowed her to relax in the safe company of these enormous creatures. After that, she'd savoured every moment, every breath, as though it were her first and last.

The valley was mostly in good health, and simply passing by was all that was required for her gift to start reversing the signs of decay. Yet here and there, Maya asked to be put down, to wander across a field of crops or through an orchard hand in hand with Taran, but not because they needed more attention. Rather it was because she wanted him by her side, matching every step with his own, pulling her close and demanding of her affection.

On their return to the centre of the valley, they'd met with the others, and as a group, talked again of their decision to fight and the reasons behind doing so. Everyone felt the same way, and they'd vowed to stay together for the fight to come.

Now, here they were, on their approach to Tristan's folly, having followed the Forelorn mountain range northward after they'd left the tunnels shown to them by the Elder.

As they drew nearer the fortress, there were roads amongst the plains and woodland, leading to the pass entrance, and occasionally a wagon could be seen rumbling along them.

Rakan nodded in approval. 'It looks like they're preparing. I just hope whatever they have is enough.'

'We'll soon find out,' Maya replied, 'but whatever they have, we will only strengthen them. For who can stand against a blacksmith's boy, his old mentor, a warrior of over seventy years old. And not forgetting the two helpless women by their side!'

'One old and one young,' added Yana laughing.

Surprised, Maya looked at Yana but found no malice in her smiling face, so laughed along. Yet the words stung a little, for she knew her hair was streaked with white, and she had enough crow's feet around her eyes, that someone might be forgiven for thinking her far older than she was.

She looked across at Taran, who, with Rakan and Kalas now moved away, swords drawn. She wasn't concerned, even though bared steel would normally have caused that reaction. With Rakan's encouragement, Taran had started to refine his gift and its use in helping them fight as a team. So sword training had been resumed, and often it happened while on the move.

To see the three of them twist and whirl, swords glittering in the sunlight, was as graceful a thing Maya had ever seen, and yet she also felt a slight chill as she recognised its deadly purpose.

They were going to join a war.

Until now, whoever they'd killed had hunted them down, and that had been the only option to survive. Yet despite having finally escaped, they'd now chosen to seek the fight head-on.

Taran, smiling Taran, whose eyes she could drown in, whose smile shone brighter than the sun, would soon be a killer of men through choice. Would he change, would he become darker, empty of compassion, as every killing stripped away his humanity?

Then what about her, she thought. If Taran fought, nothing would stop her from fighting by his side. What price would she pay to keep him safe? Her skill with a bow could be just as deadly, but learning other skills to help her protect Taran wouldn't go amiss, and there was no time like the present. Laska had outfitted them all thoroughly for this journey and at her side was a long, narrow sword.

She turned to Yana next to her, who was also studying the practice. 'Who says the men should have all the fun.' Maya smiled as she drew her blade. 'Let's see if we can surprise them.'

Yana smiled back, drawing her two swords. 'Yes, let's do that.' Then as they ran at the three men, she thought, but I'd prefer to surprise one in particular.

A while later, they sat to eat and drink. The entrance to the pass lay a little distance away, and shortly beyond that, the rear wall of the fortress, the foreboding keep rising high above it. Through the open gateway, a hive of activity could be seen.

The weapons practice had left them all happily tired, and they'd eaten mostly in silence, but it was approaching noon, and it was time to move on.

'Right,' said Kalas, 'I think Maya should lead our group in. It makes sense as she is the only one who knows Astren, whom she has told us much about.'

Maya nodded. 'He'll be waiting for us and will introduce us to the king and his commanders. We will have to find our place, see where we can best help, but the main thing is that we stay together, for we are family!'

'Well said,' Taran agreed. 'I've never known what that word really meant until now, but even as we turn to face Daleth and his armies, I've never felt happier or more secure than I am now, surrounded by those I trust.'

He stood, and everyone stood with him, and they all embraced. 'Family,' they echoed as they enjoyed the companionship of the moment.

They gathered their gear and set off together, Maya leading them toward the gates, toward their new home, to hope, to the dawn of a new beginning.

Many leagues to the west, the dark mass of the Witch-King's army crawled across the land to leave it trampled and dead in its wake.

Daleth breathed in deeply and tasted moisture in the air. The sky was dark overhead, for clouds had gathered, and it would soon rain. He called for his horn bearers to sound an early stop to the day's march, so the men could make camp in time to ensure they stayed dry before nightfall. More rain … so unusual for this time of year, but it would refresh the troops and replenish their water stocks.

He smiled as he dismounted. Another day was now over, with another soon to begin, and every day they drew closer to Tristan's Folly, where the very gates to the Freestates waited to crash asunder before his might. Beyond that were lands that would feed him with the essence of life for decades to come. This was what he'd waited for, prepared for … for fifty years.

It was a new beginning.

THE END OF BOOK ONE

If you enjoyed this book, be sure to read the sequels;

Tristan's Folly
and
The End of Dreams

out now

Please also take the time to leave a rating/review on Amazon or Goodreads. It might only take a little time, but it would mean a lot.

Thank you
Marcus Lee

M&M

Marcus Lee

Kings and Daemons

Marcus Lee

Printed in Great Britain
by Amazon